CRAZY TIME

A Bizarre Battle with Darkness
and the Divine

L. Andrew Cooper

Horrific Scribblings, LLC, North Hollywood, CA, USA

CONTENTS

FOREWORD

I was fucked up when I first drafted *Crazy Time* in 2016. The fucked up I mean isn't the kind you attribute to drugs and alcohol, so I don't want anyone writing off the strangeness of this book to such influences. No, having survived some of the worst years of my life, years in which
(1) I was paranoid, and
(2) People really were out to get me, and
(3) Really bad people really got me, and thus
(4) I ended up with either a new form of PTSD or an aggravated form of the PTSD I already had.

Crazy Time is about many things, but PTSD (post-traumatic stress disorder) may be its core. It begins with a major trauma and continues in that trauma's aftermath as more and more traumas pile on. The feeling that trauma is inevitable, repetitive, and inescapable is central to many people's experiences of PTSD, as is the feeling of being cursed, as is the desire to fight back somehow while lacking a target or facing impossible odds. *Crazy Time* takes these feelings to Biblical extremes (without endorsing Biblical thought) and becomes rather far out, but I built its spine from very real emotional experiences that millions of people share.

Do we all conclude, like Lily in this novel, that we're cursed like Job, dealing with divine and/or Satanic forces? No. But most of us, also unlike Lily, don't get to explore a supernatural world where we might be able to fight against the forces aligned against us. I spent years thinking I do way too many horrible things to Lily in this book. I now realize I also allow her to live a fantasy of empowerment out of reach for almost everyone.

Although I tried to share it with a rather obnoxious group on Facebook who fancied themselves philosophers--they were regurgitating the same old shit about final girls in horror, shit settled about twenty years earlier, and said I was spamming them when I asked if anyone would like to discuss phenomenology in relation to my current project (which plays a lot with being in time)--I didn't really try to get the book exposure until I felt ready, in 2022. Then I self-published it because I figured it was too controversial and too intellectual to do otherwise. It found a small audience, but I have always regretted the many mistakes I made with my first attempt at direct involvement with publishing.

Many people have helped with my recent work and therefore made a new, better edition of *Crazy Time* possible. Early readers, such as Nancy Brandel and Tim Riley, gave me faith that I'd created a solid hero in Lily and that I managed to break up the bleakness with humor every now and then. Thanks to Sean Taylor for assuring me that some of the locust bits are as messed up as I hoped they would be. Thanks to *The Authors' Show* and *The Graveyard Show* for having me as a guest to talk about the book; thanks to all the reviewers who wrote responses, even the ones whose responses mostly consisted of "WTF!" Thanks to Ruth Anna Evans for the amazing new cover, and thanks to all my new friends and colleagues who have been supporting my work lately, including David-Jack Fletcher, Jonathan Butcher, Ryan Harding, Chandra Claypool, Megan Stockton, Jason Nickey, JG Faherty, and Lisa Lee Tone. Last but farthest from least, thank you to my husband, first reader, and partner in editing as well as, well, everything, James Chakan.

L. Andrew Cooper
North Hollywood, CA, USA
August 2025

WARNING

This novel contains graphic violence, explicit sexuality, sexual violence, extensive suicidal ideation, suicide, controversial representations of religion, critical thinking, and other material readers might find unsuitable. It is recommended only for mature readers who are not sensitive to or offended by such material.

PART ONE: DOING THE JOB

"the terrors of God do set themselves in array against me"

-    Job 6:4

"The unheard of sufferings this luckless creature has experienced... have something about them which is too extraordinary for me not to open my eyes upon my own self."

-    The Marquis de Sade, *Justine, or, Good Conduct Well-Chastised*

1

Plenipotentiary, Lily Henshaw, Ambassador to the Night. "Pleni" meant *full*, and "potenti" meant *power*, or potential, and "ary" didn't mean much of anything, but Lily liked to think it meant "airy," as if she had the *air* of reaching her full potential tonight, after three martinis with Eric and Kris and Mia. The December air felt cold rushing through the open car windows against her exposed arms, but not too cold, not this year. Now that the bars had closed, they rode in Kris's swanky BMW through mostly empty city streets. Kris had probably had too many glasses of wine to maintain her role as designated driver, but she was the best off of all of them, and no one cared. Two days after Christmas, on Eric's birthday, the cops were home celebrating, the lights still hung in everybody's windows, and everyone still shone with miraculous possibilities. Plenipotentiary. The night welcomed them.

Kris signaled to get onto the highway, and a car honked as she swerved onto the entrance ramp. The city streets were *mostly* empty. They would never be entirely empty. A few other headlights always appeared in the rear views, which Lily could see by tilting her head left or right from the passenger seat. She could also see Eric and Mia in the back, Mia with her head on Eric's shoulder, Eric hunkered down and humming. While Lily had consumed three of the bar's special pear-infused martini concoctions, Eric had done it up like a straight guy, downing untold amounts of straight Irish whisky while sermonizing about the pleasures of age, which, having just turned thirty-two, he knew least well of all of them. Lily, at thirty-four, was second youngest. She and Eric were the only ones who had never been married. All four of them were single now.

Going home with a gay man and two other women meant her *potenti* would do her a fat lot of good, as she would likely say goodbye, let herself into her apartment, and *maybe* pop some popcorn to soak up some of the alcohol before passing out on her sofa or possibly, *possibly* get all the way to her queen-sized bed to sleep alone. She'd had dates but not brought a man home in over a year. Well, other than Eric, who more than once had slept over drunk on the sofa or even in her bed. Was that normal? She didn't know. Or care much, really, except Mia said they needed to have just-girls nights sometimes, but Kris and Lily had known Eric since college, and Kris said she wished she had married him instead of Peter, as a husband who sucked dick would be better than a husband who was one.

Mia said they didn't understand the difference having a night of just girls would make, and Lily said they understood just fine, and now Mia had her head on Eric's shoulder. *Plenipotentiary. Potenti* did not require other men. The four of them, here in Kris's fine automobile, were *pleni* on their own.

Lily might stay single forever, as long as she could have nights like tonight. People were still off work and crowding the bars, so they'd had to wait for a table at the pub they'd chosen for after dinner, but once they'd gotten in, they'd settled down and received a lot of attention from the server, who provided eye candy and conversation during each of his frequent visits to check on their drinks. Kris insisted that he... Brett... was flirting with all four of them, a very twenty-first century approach to getting a big tip, which worked. Brett had pretty hair and eyes and said he was from Hawaii. Lily had brown hair and blue-grey eyes and was from Kentucky, white like Eric, Mia, and Kris but like them, too, in being open-minded. Brett looked fit, and when Eric asked, he said he played soccer, whereas Lily mostly sat at her office and in front of the television and was beginning to worry that her favorite skirt was getting too small. During the first drink, Brett's flirting did nothing for her, but after the second, she realized she was, in fact, *in on it*, and the fantasy that made her friends giggle made her giggle, too.

The cold air from the windows lifted her hair and made her voice disappear as she hummed softly along with Eric. *Pleni.*

Another car honked, this one speeding up from behind and passing them. Lily tilted her head away from the open window, toward Kris: "What was that about?"

"I must've cut them off. Screw 'em." Kris's grin looked a little maniacal.

"Hey," Mia said from the back. Her head had left Eric's shoulder. "Drive safe."

"Yeah," Eric touted. "Dwive slafe." He laughed. Mia slapped him and laughed.

Kris gave an exaggerated sigh. "And the annoying jerk award goes to?"

"Someone whose birthday it *isn't*?" Eric offered.

"Must be it," Lily said, balancing the divide.

"Technically," Kris said, pointing at the car's console clock, "your birthday was yesterday."

"Birthdays extend into the a.m. of the next day. It's the law," Eric said.

"He's right." Lily wagged a finger at the clock.

"Can you believe this jerk behind me with his brights on?" Kris asked.

"What jerk?" Mia turned her whole body in the back seat as Lily twisted her neck. "Uh! I'm blind!"

"No kidding! I'm tempted to check the brakes." Kris sounded serious.

"That's my cue." Eric buckled his seatbelt.

Mia righted herself in her seat and pleaded, "Don't."

"She wasn't serious," Lily said.

Adjusting the central rearview, Kris agreed. "I wasn't serious." She changed lanes to the right and slowed down.

"Don't flash your brights, either," Mia said.

Lily felt a chill in her spine. The feeling of *pleni* started to leak from her tailbone, draining as she felt high color leave her face. She thought of putting up the car window.

"What?" Kris asked. "Is there some guy with an axe there in the backseat with you two?"

"Yeah, didn't I tell you? I took Brett home in my pocket, and he's got a really big... axe." Eric laughed alone.

Potential. "Mia is talking about the other one," Lily said.

Kris asked, "The other what?"

Mia responded, "The other... what do you call it, urban legend. About cars with their brights on."

Not the one you were thinking of, Miss Kristy. Not the one where the woman is in the car ALONE, and she's terrified because the car behind her keeps flashing its high beams at her, and when she changes lanes, it changes lanes—

The car with the high beams on had not changed lanes, but it hadn't passed.

—and when she slows down, it slows down, and it flashes its brights again. How did that story end? The car behind wasn't the bad guy, of course, because the bad guy was an axe murderer hiding in the back seat, and every time he would try to get up to attack, the other car would flash its brights to scare him back down. But did the murderer finally attack anyway, maybe when

the stupid driver finally drove away from the high beam flashing car that was trying to protect her? Or did the driver pull over to confront the people in the other car and thereby discover the danger in time? Or thereby unleash the murderer to kill them all? How the hell did the story end?

"What urban legend?" Kris asked.

"I know what you gals are thinking," Eric said. "The high beam initiation."

Everybody dies in that one. That's how it ends. Everybody dies. An axe murderer? Who knows. But a gang initiation? Everybody dies in the end.

"It's a true story, too," Eric said. "These gangs—"

"*Shit*, Eric, all of these stories start out, 'It's a true story, too.'" Mia scoffed.

Kris looked preoccupied with driving.

"It might not have *been* true when it started," Eric said, "but it's true now. Because people act out the story. Gang leaders make their new recruits drive around with their high beams on, and when somebody flashes them, the gang runs them off the road—"

"But that's not how it goes," Kris said. The car was behind them again, but its brights weren't on. It looked like a pickup truck. Hard to tell what color.

"Come to think of it, you're right," Mia said.

"I'm confused," Lily said. She looked at the truck in her side mirror. It was following pretty closely but not doing anything else.

"The gang car doesn't start with its high beams on," Kris said. "It drives around with the lights off. Then, when someone flashes it to let the driver know his lights are off, its brights come on, and it runs the Good Samaritan off the road. Moral: don't try to help people."

"That's kind of the moral of the other one, too, when you think about it," Eric said. "The people flashing their lights are just trying to help the dumb bitch with the axe murderer in the back seat, and she thanks them by thinking they're the psychos."

Mia slapped him again. "That's sexist, you dumb bitch."

Eric giggled.

The pickup truck signaled right and started inching up alongside Kris's BMW. On Lily's side. Lily put up her window and said, "If we flashed our lights, we wouldn't be doing it to be helpful. We'd be making a point. *Turn off your brights, asshole,* or *you forgot to turn on your headlights, asshole.* Either way—"

"Either way, we're calling the other guy an asshole, is what you're saying," Eric said.

"I didn't do anything," Kris said. "What's this 'we' crap?"

The truck was beside them now, some shade of red or orange, visible in the highway lights, but the windows were too dark—tinted?—to see inside. "We're all in this together," Lily said.

"What's *this*?" Mia asked.

"Oh sister, our Lady Lily is getting *freaked out,*" Eric said.

Was she? Maybe she was. Lily had gone from thinking about fullness and power to axe murderers and gangs, and it wasn't a pleasant trip, not at all. Maybe they could take her back to where she'd been, and that would be fine, but the nice little buzz in her brain had sunk to a different pitch, and now she couldn't stop glancing over her shoulder at that truck, which was going a little faster than they were, pulling ahead. Kris had both hands on the steering wheel. She wasn't talking as much, didn't have the same light tone as Mia and Eric. Did she feel the truck, too, bearing down on them? For Kris, was the truck something other than a light subject of conversation, a casual, laughable launch-pad to the oh-so-funny matters of axe-murder and gang initiation?

The truck was almost all the way in front of them now. It looked like one of those heavy-duty, four-wheel-drive deals, maybe with a back seat in the cab and an extra-wide bed. The rear window was opaque, too. No sign of a gun rack.

"Look at that," Kris said. "He's signaling left now, getting in front of us." The truck pulled in front of them, close. Lily noted, cutting off an inhale, that the truck lacked a license plate. The bareness reflected the BMW's headlights.

"Hey," Eric said. "How do you know he's a he?"

"The pickup truck kind of screams penis to me," Mia said.

"Good point," Eric said.

"You guys," Kris said, "he is *right* in front of us, and I think he's matching our speed on purpose. We are the only ones on the road right now. This is ridiculous." She changed lanes to the left and sped up.

"Kris, be careful," Lily said. The truck would appear at her shoulder again soon.

"You know that's my exit up ahead," Mia said.

"I know," Kris said, watching the speedometer. "I'm just going to pass this fucker."

"The lane to the left is clear," Lily said, not sure whether anyone heard. The truck, with its uninviting windows and many speeds, all calculated to thwart what started out as such a triumphantly pleasant ride home, needed to be *far*, far from the world of Lily and of Kris's BMW, which mocked the workmanlike sincerity of the truck's wide bed and sticker that said 4-WHEEL DRIVE. It was not a beat-up old pickup truck. It sparkled in the light with newness, extra cleanness. Someone cared about that vehicle. If it had hands and feet, it might not line up for a mani-pedi, but it would maintain even, square-cut nails that left tiny marks when it bundled up fists for mighty blows. The truck was serious, calculated, and Lily wanted it *away*.

"There," Kris said, and she changed lanes, putting the truck back in the rearview. It signaled left and started pulling up closer to the driver's side. "This is ridiculous!" Kris yelled. She sped up.

"Kris," Lily said.

"Drive safe," Eric said, no irony.

Mia: "My exit—"

The truck matched speed, pulled ahead, signaled. "I'll be damned," Kris said, "if I let this fucker pass me again." She sped up. Lily looked at the speedometer. Close to one hundred. Over one hundred.

"That was my exit!!"

"Let him go!" Eric yelled.

"Kris," Lily said, but Kris wasn't listening. Kris must have been thinking, *I'll be damned if some pickup truck thinks it can outrace ME. You think you know fast? BMW is pleni-fucking-potentiary.* One-ten. One-twenty. The truck fell back a bit but did not fall behind.

The BMW's passengers took turns yelling, "Kris!" Engines were audible through windows still down, with wind ripping through, but the wind's mad flag-rippling noises underscored a greater silence, no blaring music or car horns, nothing but intentness from the two vehicles, going faster, faster. One-thirty.

"We're going to die tonight," Lily said. The words left her lips without the aid of thought or volition. The wind was so loud, her voice so soft, that she thought maybe others didn't hear her. But the words fell with a solemn weight of truth, and they must have hit Kris, because another sound, a foot leaving the accelerator, reached them all, and the pickup truck to their left lurched ahead before it, too, began to slow.

"Thank God." Mia's voice, from the backseat, sounded tame. Then the voice screamed, and Eric's voice joined it, and Lily heard herself screaming as well. Confusion. Panic. Kris was too busy wrestling the steering wheel to scream. The jolt they all felt had them flailing in their seats, and the motion of the truck, which seemed to bounce from becoming one with them on their left to being two lanes over to being in front of them to being off to their right, mimicked the rocking of their emotions as they tried to find inner moorings. Kris tapped the brakes, causing a partial spin, but she had the sense to let the car right itself while straddling two lanes, then, with momentum, skip from lane to lane until she managed to slow and find sense in the chaos of lines and dashes that defined highway order. Another car with the misfortune of sharing the road with the pickup and the BMW blared its horn as it dodged and sped by the two vehicles that were hogging the road. When the new vehicle's noise had passed, and the BMW again carried forward in a more-or-less straight manner, Lily understood, and she felt her friends understand, what had happened.

The pickup had tried to get back in front of Kris, and it had sideswiped them in the process, sending both vehicles wild across the many lanes of the highway. Now, they both moved forward at sensible speeds, regaining bearings.

Kris slammed her horn. "Goddamned idiots! Goddamned idiots!" She slowed and signaled right.

Panic still in her voice, Mia said, "Kris, what are you doing?"

"Pulling over is what I'm doing! And those fuckers are coming with me!" The BMW pulled dangerously close to the righted tail of the pickup, blared its horn, flashed its lights, and signaled demonstratively before pulling right. The truck seemed to hesitate before it pulled right, too.

"They're coming," Lily said.

Eric said, "We don't know who these guys are."

"Yeah, we do," Kris said. "They're the people who just scraped the shit out of my car, and I'm at least getting their insurance. Somebody, get out your cell and call the police."

Lily got out her phone. Do you call 911 for traffic problems, even if they're not emergencies? A sideswipe was a little more than a fender-bender, but not much. A sideswipe plus an urban legend was scary, sure, but the police in a city like this one were unlikely to be appreciative. She had better call the operator and ask. On cell phones, do you still press 0 to get an operator? She felt sober now, but her brain wasn't working right. She pressed 0 and the call button. Maybe she should call 411. She knew that would work.

Both vehicles came to a stop in the breakdown lane. Kris unbuckled her seatbelt and got out before anybody could object. Lily had trouble connecting, so she hung up. Eric and Mia talked about whether they should get out. Doors on both sides of the pickup truck opened. They'd parked between two bright streetlights, which revealed the truck to be as fire-engine red as the BMW was midnight blue. One of the streetlights had a fast flicker.

Two men got out of the pickup truck. Lily dialed 411 and asked for the police listing. Eric opened the door on his side, Lily's side. Kris was moving toward the two men. One of them wore a soft, brown leather bomber jacket and collared shirt, a polo, with grey slacks, and the other wore jeans and an army-green coat with many pockets and the kind of shirt people called a "wife-beater," a sleeveless undershirt. Both men were white, which contradicted Lily's idea of a gang, middle-aged, too, the collared guy mostly bald and the wife-beater with a few days of scruffy beard growth, both a little paunchy and jowly. Their regular-white-guy appearances set her more at ease, which made her feel guilty, guilty yet more at ease, even as 411 told her to call 911 to report the accident.

"WHAT THE HELL DO YOU THINK YOU'RE DOING?" Kris yelled.

"Oh shit," Eric said, and he got out of the car. Mia followed. Lily stayed seated, the phone her excuse. The streetlight, the one a little closer to them, flickered. A few lanes over, a car sped by.

"Evening," Mr. Collar said. Mr. Wife-Beater agreed.

"Evening?" Kris said. "Are you two so stoned out of your gourds that you don't even know how late... how early... it is? What time it is? And why the hell were you driving like that? Huh?" She did a half turn and gestured toward what must have been long scrapes on the driver's side of the BMW. "Do you see what you did to my car?"

"We know what time it is, sure," Mr. Collar said.

Standing back by her door, Mia said, "Kris," and Lily thought, *dwive slafe.*

"You just thought it would be *fun* to drive in *circles* around somebody? Well look what happens!" Kris was indignant. Lily imagined the wide-eyed, expectant look on Kris's face. 911 had her on hold.

Eric moved forward, stood near Lily's window, then got closer to Mr. Wife-Beater. Eric and the green-coated man exchanged nods.

Mr. Collar took a step toward Kris, who took a step back. "Ma'am, do *you* know what time it is?"

"It's after three in the morning," Lily said by accident, out loud, and the phone made a click.

"911, what is the nature of your emergency?"

Eric backed past Lily's window again, and Mia gave an aborted yelp. Lily looked at neither of them for more than a glance. Instead, she looked at Mr. Collar, who said, *"It's crazy time!"*

And Lily said, "Oh my God he's got a gun."

And the gunman said, "Rob, get that bitch with the phone out of the car."

Rob, Mr. Wife-Beater, smashed Lily's closed window with a tire iron, and Lily screamed into the phone. The voice on the other end asked questions about who had the gun, where was she, and so on, but Lily called out no answers as Rob snatched the phone from her fingers, threw it down on asphalt, and smashed it with the iron. When Eric bent as if to stop him, Rob swung the iron and almost sunk the claw into Eric's head.

Stunned, Lily felt her door open as she watched Mr. Collar approach Kris, gun pointing out of the bomber jacket like a surprise twist from a noir movie. Kris backed into Mia, who had been standing behind her, deer in headlights. "Ladies, please go to the other side of this fine automobile," Mr. Collar said.

Fine automobile, the words plucked from Lily's brain.

As the gunman ushered them around, the streetlight above flickered like a bug zapper in a swarm and went out. In the car, Lily whimpered, and Rob told her to get out, and she did, standing beside Eric, soon joined in the newly shadowy space by Kris and Mia. The car now separated them from what little traffic drove the clear, fast, dark patch of highway through the city.

Crazy time.

Kris would hate herself for it, but she was already crying. "What do you want?"

Mr. Collar and Rob stood on either side of their four-person cluster, forming two walls while the car and the highway's concrete embankment formed two others, penning

13

them. From the working streetlight, nearest the truck, to the broken one, behind the BMW, they stood Rob, Lily, Eric, Mia, Kris, and Mr. Collar. "What do we want," Mr. Collar said, pointing the gun at Kris's face. "What do we want? Rob? Tell them?"

"Sure thing, Earl. Ladies and gentleman, please put your phones on the ground. Do it gentle, though. You break it, you bought it. Except you." Rob touched Lily's hair, and Lily wanted to throw up. The other three prisoners took out their phones, all smart flat rectangles, and set them on asphalt.

"Good," Earl, Mr. Collar, said. "Now tell me, which one takes the best video?"

A pause. Earl pressed the gun against Kris's lips and repeated the question.

Eric said, "Mine. I think."

"Eric!" Mia said.

"Thanks, Eric." Keeping the gun on Kris, Earl walked around, picked up Eric's phone, and gestured for Rob to join him in examining it. "Now Eric, I want you to open this up and show me how to start the video." Eric complied. "Good boy. Now smile everybody." Phone pointing from one hand, gun from the other, Earl used the phone's camera to capture the four of them standing in a line, Lily shaking and dazed, Eric slack-jawed and staring at his phone as if it had betrayed him, Mia with a flat look of disbelief, Kris intent on the gun. "Come on now, Rob, trade with me, would you?"

Rob took the gun, and Earl took the tire iron. The gun, Lily noticed, was a revolver of some kind, but she didn't think that information was helpful, as six bullets would be more than enough. Rob's hands shook when he took the gun. That was something. He didn't have Earl's confidence. At this range, though, confidence seemed optional. The barrel pointed at Eric. Earl walked back toward Kris with the tire iron and the camera.

"W-w-w," Lily said. The look on Rob's face terrified her. It was pity.

"Shhhh!" Mia said. Eric stared into the gun like he had stared at his phone.

All eyes turned to Earl as Kris said, "I don't know what you hope to accomplish. We don't have much money, and we don't—"

The movement was swift. The tire iron bent back like a baseball bat and swung forward, cracking against Kris's skull. The spray upon contact hit Mia and the BMW and disappeared in the direction of the darkened streetlight. In her periphery, Lily might have seen a swatch of skin and hair torn away by the blow, the blow slowed down immeasurably by the shock of perceiving it as her own knees gave way, but as her mind replayed it a thousand times, adding brain and bone and more, she would never know what was real. She just knew that the collision of iron with head made a cracking noise that synced with the passing of a car, and she went down at the same time as Kris, only Kris went down further, spinning so her back hit asphalt, and her spattered face pointed up at the night with wide eyes.

Mia and Eric screamed, which made the gun go crazy, pointing from one of them to another, but Lily only felt the pain in her knees from where they'd slammed into asphalt. Earl was laughing and panning across the four of them—three of them and Kris's body—with the phone camera. Rob was saying, "Here we go, here we go, here we go, here we go!"

W-w-what is—

"*CRAZY TIME!*" Earl matched Kris's dead eyeline and shouted at heaven. Mia bawled as Earl recited, on camera,

"Nothing in heaven was e'er so sublime

As the three blind mice during crazy time.

They ate the kitchen and then through the den;

They ate the rooster and gobbled the hen.

They chomped and they chomped until they got fat,

They ate up the house, even the old cat.

Watch out for those mice, before they are through,

They'll eat all your goodies—even eat you!"

Earl giggled and giggled and stepped in the growing puddle near Kris's head, smearing it with his foot. He videoed the smear.

Mia and Eric weren't screaming anymore. They stood hypnotized by the gun that oscillated between them. Lily watched and tried not to think about the pain in her knees, which seemed trivial compared to everything else, but it insisted on attention, because she had fallen so fast and so hard, but not as fast and hard as Kris, who might have broken her head open with the fall, if it hadn't already been... already been....

"So Earl, what's next?" Rob asked. He looked to his leader.

Eric acted. He dove at Rob, whose gun lowered when he turned to Earl. Rob turned at the moment of impact, and the gun went off. Stumbling, Rob kept his footing, and Eric flew back with the force of the shot, striking and shaking the car before he crumbled. Lily couldn't see where he was hit. Without standing, she pivoted to him, searching his prone body for signs of a wound she quickly found in a gush from his midsection, near the right hip, some of which seemed to be missing. Lily's fluttering hands gathered up shreds of surrounding clothes and applied pressure.

Earl laughed as Rob returned and aimed the gun down at Eric, who shouted, "Fireflies!"

Mia seemed about to join Lily in helping Eric, but Earl said, "No way. One of you needs to stand up here and enjoy the night sky with me, right? Come here, beautiful." He gestured for Mia to come closer.

"No!" Mia said.

Earl used the tire iron like a hook. "Come *closer*," he said, pulling at Mia's shoulder.

"Earl!" Rob pulled the gun in close again, noir style. "Lower the iron!" Rob gestured, and Lily turned to look. A police car was driving by, slowing. Lily realized Kris had left the BMW's lights on—good for her—and though three of them were down, the other three—Rob, Mia, and Earl— were standing and visible from the road, despite the broken streetlight. The scene looked like some kind of accident. The police car was stopping for them.

It passed but pulled over beyond the pickup truck. "Keep it cool, Rob. Trade." They switched gun and tire iron.

Maybe the police car was stopping because of Lily's phone call. They could have traced it, could have used the GPS in Lily's phone before Rob smashed it. If so, then the cop would at least be on his guard when he got out of his car, expecting some sort of funny business with the two men and the woman he could see from the road. Eric had almost gotten the better of one of them, and he'd never been in a fight in his life. A cop with a gun could do much more, get much further, maybe even take the two men (assailants) down, maybe even shoot them (the murderers) before they could make up their minds to strike first, so Lily had to hope Rob and Earl would try to cover up what was going on, the fact that Kris was (dead) lying on the ground in a pool of blood, and so was Eric (Lily had to stop the bleeding).

Lily was applying pressure, but all Mia had to do was scream. Earl started walking toward the cop car. Rob kept the tire iron low but ready, his eyes shifting from Kris to Mia, threatening. All Mia had to do was scream. Lily had to apply pressure.

Eric moaned.

"Evening, Officer," Lily heard Earl say.

"More like good morning."

"It's that crazy time when neither night nor morning seems quite right, does it?"

"Stay back with your vehicle, please sir."

Good. That was suspicion. Lily couldn't see the cop, but she imagined his—the voice was a man's—hand on his holster when he gave the order. She'd never wanted to see a cop so much before in her life. Crazy, stupid thought. She imagined a cute guy, maybe around her age, catching a glimpse of what was going on, not letting on until he was sure he'd be the quicker draw, then BLAM! Down goes Earl. With Earl down, Rob would be sure to surrender. On first appearance, Rob was the badass, with his wife-beater shirt and military-looking coat, but that was all appearances. He was the backup; Earl was the brains. Without Earl, Rob would fold in a second. And a second would be all Officer Hero needed to turn this situation over and set it right. Maybe Kris was just unconscious. If the cop acted fast, an ambulance might save her and Eric both.

They'd all be okay, and then maybe the cop would ask her out on a date or something. *Potenti.*

"Hey Officer, you know something funny?" Earl said. "That light up there, that streetlight, went out right as we pulled over. You see? The one up there."

DON'T LOOK!

"Hey Officer? Smile for the camera!" The gunshot cracked the night.

Quiet. Officer Hero must have looked up, then down too late. Or maybe…?

"Earl? You get him?" Rob didn't take his eyes off Mia, the tire iron poised. Lily kept trying to stop Eric's bleeding, but she listened and watched as she could.

Earl stepped back into Lily's range of vision and handed Rob a pistol. "Should have seen his face," Earl said, "while he had one." He laughed. Rob laughed, too, but he was faking. Mia made a sound like she was trying to scream, but it sounded like a retch instead.

Eric said, "Please God."

"No," Earl said to Eric, "I don't think so. But I need *you* to do something for me." He tucked the gun into his belt, behind him. "Your stupid phone cut out when I was with that cop, which means my movie got cut. I need you to tell me your PIN number."

Lily thought of Eric always saying "PIN number is redundant" and hoped he wouldn't say it now. She thought of him saying "fireflies" a moment ago and realized he wasn't likely to say much of anything at all. The bleeding was slowing.

From somewhere, Earl produced a pocketknife, a big one. He opened it and said to Lily, "Hold up his head and make sure he can see me." She kept one hand on the bleeding wound and used the other to hold up Eric's head as well as she could. His eyes were open at slits. Whether he saw anything she couldn't say. "It's Eric, right?" Earl asked.

Eric said nothing.

"Bitch," Earl said, "make him nod." Lily froze. "Bitch, nod his fucking head!" Lily moved Eric's head to make it look like he was nodding. "Good. I want us on the same page. We've got to be *on the same page*, don't we, Ron?"

"It's Rob tonight, Earl."

"Oh. Yeah. Rob. Same page, right?"

"Same page."

Earl took the pocketknife and jabbed it into Mia's stomach three times. She gasped and doubled over, holding herself, but she did not fall. Instead, she leaned back, supporting herself against the BMW. "Now Eric," Earl said, "I realize you probably feel like you're dying and shit, and hell, you might very well be, but I need a four digit number from you, and you'll either give it to me, or I'm going to find more non-essential places where I can stick this knife in your girlfriend. Or maybe—" and he took a step toward Lily and grabbed a wad of her long brown hair—"your other girlfriend." He giggled as he cut off first one, then another huge lock of hair and threw it down in Eric's blood.

Eric's mouth started moving, but the initial sounds lacked shape. Rob said, "He's trying to talk."

"Well shit," Earl said. "He'll have to try harder." He paced back and forth. Mia slid down the side of the car, not quite curling down to a sitting position, her hands cupping her bleeding stomach.

Lily glanced over her shoulder as a car, merely a car, drove by on the highway. The driver couldn't *not* see them, but at any significant speed, under the dim streetlight, they would look like a parked car and a parked truck, little more. But Officer Hero had to have radioed in his position before he stopped to investigate, right? And when he didn't radio again, dispatch would send another car, maybe two or three... any moment now, help would come. They just had to survive. Lily could see no rising and falling in Kris's body, no sign of life at all, but Eric was still making noises, and Mia wasn't even sitting. And Lily wasn't a doctor. They could all make it out of this alive. They only had to survive a little longer. Had to—

"Give me the tire iron," Earl said. Rob complied. Earl bounced the iron in his hand, gaining momentum. "I said you'd better try," he bounced, "a little," he bounced higher, "HARDER!" Earl brought the iron down on one of Eric's legs.

At the resultant snap, Eric didn't scream, but his body contracted like a spider on its back. His head tipped to one side, and heavy drool leaked from his mouth. Lily kept pressure on the wound, where bleeding gained force with the rising of Eric's damaged legs.

"A NUMBER!" Earl yelled, and he hit the same leg again, forcing it back down to asphalt. No snap. A limp thud.

Barely able to breathe, Lily said, "Seventeen seventy-six."

Earl readjusted so he held only the phone, and he punched in the number. "Well I'll be," he said. "You knew all along. Could have saved your boyfriend some hurt, couldn't you?" Earl pressed some buttons and lined up the camera. "And we're go! Rob, if you would finish this bastard, please."

With no apparent shyness about how badly his hand shook, Rob aimed the cop's pistol at Eric. Lily thought she should protest, cover Eric's body with hers, but she knelt silently by her friend, watching. She saw Rob's finger move on the trigger.

Nothing.

"Safety's on," Earl said.

"How's it work?" Rob held the gun so loosely he might have dropped it.

"It's that little switch...." The two men almost huddled, and for a moment, neither one of them had eyes on any of Lily's friends. Mia couldn't run because she'd been stabbed, and though her backside hadn't ever reached asphalt, she was dazed in her position by the car, and her hands had fallen limp at her sides, no longer cradling her bleeding stomach. Eric hadn't been fully conscious for a long time. The only thing stopping Lily from charging out onto the highway, where a car passed at least every minute or so, was the pain in her knees, and that, compared to the bullet in Eric and the knife wounds in Mia, was nothing, nothing at all, but it throbbed, tightened, told her she could do *nothing*.

Another crack in the night. Earl stood away from Rob, who had, at last, pulled the trigger on a ready weapon. Eric died.

"Great shot," Earl said, referring to the camera, which he held close to the chest wound. Lily felt blood on her. On her face, soaking through her clothes. She didn't know how much. Earl pointed the camera at her, then at Eric again, then at Mia, whose jaw hung open. He brought the phone right up to her gaping mouth, and she didn't move. "Weird," he said. "I didn't think I hurt this one too much." He grabbed her and pulled her forward, away from the car, and she splayed out on asphalt.

Without thinking, Lily fell backward. Enormous relief flooded her calves as the pressure in her knees released. She was sitting on the asphalt now, and it felt good. Rob stood close to her. Earl was walking around to the other side of the car. "Damned bitch took the keys out of the ignition." Lily watched him come back around and search Kris's body. Definitely a body. She wasn't breathing any more than Eric was. Mia was still breathing but not much. Wouldn't be for long. You could only bleed for so long on the side of the road where nobody noticed.

Earl took the keys and started Kris's car. "Now that's an engine that *purrs*," he said. "Hey, uh, Rob, finish the last one after I go, will you, and then meet me at the ron-day-voo?"

Earl drove off, and Lily looked in Rob's eyes. He returned that same pitying look before he shot her.

2

After two surgeries on her abdomen and three months, one of which she spent in bed, Lily was not okay.

"You do a lot of things," Vince said. Vince worked with her at Professional Performance Printing, "P-Cubed," as all the signs and business cards said. Vince did design and layout consulting and preparation for the bigger print jobs. He had a web design business on the side but gave P-Cubed his all for forty hours per week. Vince was white, a little older than Lily, married, two kids, and a churchgoer. "You do a lot of things," he insisted, "but you don't hate God."

For the third time this week, Lily wanted a cigarette. She and Eric had quit when Eric had graduated college, but Eric was dead now, and Lily wanted a cigarette. "You have to believe in him to hate him, right?" She tried to ask politely.

"I don't know, but you sound like a hater to me. Does that make you a believer?" Vince sat back in his desk chair and played with his patchy yellow beard. He and Lily were the only ones in the office, which meant Lily had reception, if anyone decided to drop in. They got most of their new customers on the phone and the web. Almost nobody dropped in through the front door, and it was almost closing time anyway.

You'd sound like a hater, too. She didn't want to argue. How could he understand? How could anyone, unless? Everybody had advice to give. Everybody. Like they understood getting shot. Even the ones who had been shot, in Afghanistan or somewhere else—nobody had been shot like she had been.

She ought to be dead. Cops showed up after the BMW and the pickup truck with no license plate drove off. Cleaned up the bodies, cleaned up Lily, who was *almost* dead. Ought to be dead. Cops showed up. The city-wide manhunt, the search for the cop-killing duo who "also" murdered two women and a homosexual man, turned up nothing. The sketches based on Lily's descriptions could have been a lot of different people. They didn't help much. *She* didn't help much. She ought to be dead.

How did it happen? Why did Lily and her friends pull over? *They got sideswiped.* Did they call the police? *Yes.* A lot of fucking good it did. They were in the middle of EVERYWHERE. In the middle of the city. Under one broken streetlight, but the other one was working. Cars were driving by every minute. Someone should have seen. Someone should have helped. If there was a God—

You sound like a hater to me.

No, but if there was a God, he was sleeping on the job. The bars' closing time must have been God's beddy-bye, because he was nowhere to be found when that pickup truck started toying with them on the open, visible highway where nobody saw anything. Nowhere to be found when the tire iron, knife, and gun started chewing their ways through Lily's friends. God? No. Not a hint.

It was worse than that. "Life itself," she said to Vince, and she stopped. *Life itself has no principles.* Or it works from negative principles. No justice, no peace, no hope, no absolution. Absolution? Why? Survivor's guilt, they called it. Why did Lily get to live? Eric tried to fight back. Kris talked back. Even Mia, maybe, in her way. But Lily just sat there, or knelt there, and she got to live. And none of her friends could forgive her now. She told her story, told other people about trying to stop Eric's bleeding, and they said, inevitably, *You did what you could.* Some even said, *You did ALL you could*, but that word of difference, ALL, was a rare treat. Usually, somewhere in the mincing of words, a hint crept in that she might have done more. And even in "could," wasn't there a suggestion of a limitation of ability, a *could not*, an *im-potence* that had caught her that night and made her somehow into the death of her friends?

If God was supposed to be omnipotence and omniscience, God's opposite was not Satan. God sat across from a weak irrelevance that required no belief because it simply *was*. It was a reservoir of passivity, a being acted upon in which one found oneself immersed. Instead of infinite strength and wisdom, it was closely bound weakness and absurdity. Satan and God's opposite were a lot like two visions of the government, Lily supposed, the conspiracist's and the actual. The conspiracist sees the government as monolithic, so organized that it can accomplish magnificent, decades-spanning secret plots coordinated at points all over the globe, whereas in actuality, the government is fragmented, so disorganized that it can barely function from hour to hour, much less year to year, and its programs are incoherent from town to town, state to state. The conspiracist sees the Devil in the details—the realist sees God's opposite, the sad truth of crumbling chaos.

Lily said to Vince, "Life is the opposite of God."

Vince said, "Am I supposed to have any idea what that means?"

"No."

"Good." Vince leaned forward. "You say you don't believe in God. I accept that. But whether or not you believe in God, I believe that everything happens for a—"

"I swear to God, if you say everything happens for a reason, I'll—" She wanted to say *blow your fucking brains out*, or *blow my fucking brains out*, but she couldn't manage either. Every time she heard a politician comment about gun control or the Second Amendment, she wanted to spew the greenest of pea soups. A shake of her head cut off the threat.

"I can't help it," Vince said. "It does."

So, there was a reason for the tire iron smashing Kris's head? For the knife wounds and the gunshots? She had never known Vince to be so wondrously stupid.

"It's time for us to close up," Vince said, getting out of his chair. "Let me take you to this place I know. Show you something."

Lily flashed to a hundred bad joking retorts, but she thought of Vince's wife, a kind woman who baked things for their small company gatherings, and she held her tongue. Instead of astringency, she offered a smile. "I don't think I'm very good company." *If I were a lion, I'd eat your Christian heart.* Not fair—if Lily was anything, she was Christian. She'd been raised that way. Now, though, if forced to choose, she'd say she wasn't anything. An office manager with a gnarly scar from a bullet. If she'd had a fish on her bumper, she'd have taken it off. She remembered the nakedness of the pickup truck's backside, no license plate, no identifying marks. Her car, just a little Toyota, had a license plate but no stickers or other ornaments. Lily couldn't remember whether Kris had put anything on the back of her BMW. She thought stickers might have endorsed some political candidate or other. Did the police know that? Should they? They'd never found the car.

"Oh, I think you're good enough company. And I promise not to keep you very long. I'll drive. Just leave your car here. I'll bring you right back. Promise. It won't take..." he looked at his watch, "an hour."

Vince drove her to a dog park. Close to the office but still not a park she'd heard of, it had fences high enough for a batting range, but the wire meshes did little to disrupt a remarkable view of the city's main skyline, fronted by nearby Spring Street, where towers had ceased development during recent market troubles but were now rebounding with new investments that slathered the street with cranes, scaffolds, and other signs of cautiously expanding industry. Above it all, the sun dipped orange and low, and that was what Vince had brought her for: the sunset.

Not dogshit, a sunset, but as they stepped through the gate and were nearly knocked over by a black Labrador off its leash, Lily became aware of her shoes, her only pair of comfortable flats that were appropriate for work, and the shit they might get into if she took a wrong step on the soft, treacherous ground. The setting of the sun also brought a dimness of light, and the park's illumination was just regular streetlights, on poles surrounding the fenced rectangle at regular intervals. Little turds might easily hide from casual observation on the dark ground, within blades of mashed, dead, and dying grass, and ruin her shoes as she stepped unwitting to follow Vince to whatever vantage he had chosen for whatever presentation of God's lightshow he intended to make.

"Would you look at that?" Vince said, directing her gaze away from the ground and toward the sky. She looked down again, and he touched her chin. She looked up. They stepped forward. She had to trust that the softness beneath her soles was mud. "Don't the edges of the buildings seem to glow?"

Many of the towers, especially the newer ones, had shiny reflective exteriors, like silver-tinted mirrors, so they picked up a sheen of orange on the edges closest to the sunset. Technically, then, Lily had to grant that they seemed to glow. "Yes."

Vince looked at her and chuckled. "Of course they do," he said. "It's all reflections, right?"

Right.

"But think about it," Vince said. He took a deep breath. Dogs nearby barked, ran past, but didn't intrude. "Where do

27

you stand in… in time? Look at the city. The newest building takes in all the rest as part of its design. The designer *knows* he is completing a picture, might have stood in this very spot to contemplate that picture. But look at the older buildings. They're a part of today's complete picture, too. And if you stood at their moments in time, you know, at the moments when they were built, they were just as calculated as part of that complete skyline, *but the calculations also worked with the future that hadn't happened yet.* Because the skyline happens all at once. On the one hand, the skyline is a timeline. It's the history of the city's construction. On the other hand, it's a single moment, *this* moment, Lily, set on fire by all this glorious orange light, all moments, the entire history. And both ways, it works as a whole, in harmony. It's designed to be beautiful, from any point in time, wherever *we* stand. I think the skyline is, well, the city, really, is—"

Don't say it!

"—a miracle."

A dog barked. Lily thought about barking, too, because she didn't have much else to say. She didn't know whether what Vince said was bullshit, *transcendental* bullshit, or just gobbledegook, but she was fairly certain it qualified as one of the three. She'd been an English and Philosophy double major in college, useful shit, and she'd liked the Romantics then, and something about what Vince said about time reminded her of Wordsworth, maybe, but she'd always hated Wordsworth. Wordsworth ought to have been shot in the gut and then wandered lonely as a fucking cloud.

"And that's why…" Vince was saying.

Why the hell was Lily thinking about poetry she didn't like that she hadn't read in more than ten years? She was an office manager at a small printing company, an office manager whose three best friends were killed in this very city, on a highway that cut through it not too far from this spot, not *too* far from any spot, really, close enough to be *seen* and *protected*, but it wasn't.

"...I think..."

He's going to say it again! *'I don't know what you hope to accomplish,' Kris said, and then the tire iron smashed into her skull, spraying them all with blood and brain. She stayed on her feet, a portion of her head missing, and looked at Lily through one good eye.*

"... everything happens for a reason."

"Vince," Lily said in a soft voice.

One of the streetlights surrounding the dog park began to flicker. Lily looked up at it and looked back at the skyline, still burnished orange. "You think," she said, and the words came out on a wisp of air, as she was breathless, struggling for a solid breath.

"I do," Vince said. He looked not at her but up and out at the city, gesturing. "I know you've seen evil the likes of which I can hardly imagine, but remember the good, Lily! Remember it! Don't let the word 'God' slow you down."

"G... g..." Lily gulped. A second light started flickering. Her chest tightened, and her vision narrowed. Her purse was in Vince's car.

"Having faith is in some ways more important than what you believe *in*, Lily. I haven't been through what you've been through, but my life hasn't exactly been perfect, let me tell you. I think you can either let the worst things—and you've been through one of the worst things I've ever heard of—"

Please stop. Please stop. You mean well. Please stop. A third light was flickering. Her chest felt tight. Her arms had icicles inside of them, piercing.

"—you can let the worst things make you give up on life, give up on God or whatever you want to call it, or you can come back and look at something like *this*," and he gestured toward the sunset, the sun already hiding behind buildings, "and realize there's still purpose left. Not just for you, but for everything."

Her legs felt weak. Her insides felt like she might need to make like a dog at any moment and squat. Her eyes confirmed that her hands were shaking. Vince was too busy gazing off into the sunset to notice. "V-Vince?" she whispered.

"Why are you shouting?" he answered, looking at her, finally. "Oh my God, Lily, are you—"

One of the lights went out, and she fell backward, into the mud, and said, "Oh!" Her left hand landed in a pile of dog shit.

"—okay?" Vince finished.

A second light went out, and all of them seemed to flicker. She whispered, might have shouted, "Vince Vince Vince it's happening Vince it's happening again Vince help me I don't know if they're coming Vince he hit her in the head and tore her open tore her head open knocked her skull open the bleeding I can't stop it Vince I can't stop it so much on my hands…." Her left hand rubbed the shit on her pants.

She was drawing a crowd, people and dogs both. She must have been shouting.

Vince crouched next to her. "Oh God, Lily, what do I do?"

"Somebody call 911!" a woman's voice said.

"NO!" Lily said. She had to think. She had to think clearly. She had to think about something other than blood on asphalt. Had to think about where she was now, what she was doing, and where she was, what she was doing was: "Panic. Attack. Pills. Need my. Pill!" She sat up. She knew she was shouting every word, but she couldn't stop. Five or six people had gathered around, but everyone but Vince stayed at a safe distance.

The shit stain on her pants would not be too difficult to remove. Good.

A third streetlight went out above them all, and while everyone else looked up, Lily screamed.

"Where?" Vince asked.

"Your car. My purse. Go!" He went. The others gawked. *You will be quiet.* She told herself. She closed her eyes, but when she did, she saw Earl, his leather jacket, his collared shirt, and Rob, reluctant gunman, taking aim. She opened her eyes, felt another scream at her lips and bit them from the inside, forcing air in sharply up her nose, down her narrow windpipes, inflating her viselike chest. The sound when she exhaled might have made the dogs howl, but they only stared.

Vince rushed back, handed her the purse. Shaking hands fumbled with the zipper, got it open, searched for the brown prescription bottle, couldn't get the safety cap open. She handed it to Vince, who opened it. "How many?" he asked.

She wanted to say, *All of them,* but instead she said, "Just one." Klonopin. Not usually for immediate relief, but if she put it under her tongue, it would dissolve and help. It was all she had for the panic attacks. It would have to work. A hand, more in seizures than shakes, took a pill from Vince and forced it under her tongue. The psychological reaction preceded the physical: the crowd around her would not shoot or maim her. The darkened lights were just darkened lights. All she had suffered was a shit-on-her-pants humiliation.

And can you tell me the *reason* that happened, Vince?

He drove her back to the office without saying much, and she resisted the urge to say things that might crush his tender idealism. Instead, she thanked him for the "lovely idea." He said she was "welcome." Her stained pants made his car smell bad. Back at the office, he offered to walk her to her car, a gesture of gallantry she didn't mind, considering, but she

31

refused, saying she was going inside to try to wash off some of the stains before they set in anymore. She really didn't want the smell of the early evening to follow her all the way home.

After scrubbing at the stains with hand soap and warm water and achieving some success, she emerged from the bathroom and was merely startled, not panicked, by the human form lurking in the office. Burt Wells, P-Cubed's owner, stood at one of the tables trimming what looked like a poster.

From behind him, Lily said, "Evening, Burt."

He yelped, turning in a jump. Lily didn't know his exact age—early to mid-forties, she'd guess—but his fit, narrow body contained tremendous energy, which almost crackled with the surprise that turned him toward her. His lips smiled, and the lines around his brown eyes looked gentle as all of him softened in recognition. "Lily," he said. "I knew somebody was here. This order is making me jumpy, I guess." Despite his dark complexion, Lily could tell that Burt was blushing. "Come to think of it," he said, "I saw your car parked outside. Should have known it was you."

"Yeah," Lily said, walking closer, curious about the sort of print order that could make Burt jumpy. "I just got back from an excursion with Vince."

"Uh-oh. I should have seen that coming." Burt stepped away from the table and, intentionally or not, blocked Lily from seeing what was on it. "Let me guess. Coffee and Jesus?"

Lily laughed and tucked a lock of hair behind her ear. "No coffee." She wanted to say *Just dog shit*, but she thought that would be too mean. "The dog park. Jesus was implied."

"Hmm. And how was the experience? I mean, I know how I'd react if I were in your...."

She looked at him and found him searching her face, her shoulders, her torso for something ineffable, a return of feeling she couldn't emote in the way his hopeful gaze desired.

In the years Lily had worked for P-Cubed, Burt had never said or done anything inappropriate. A quick pat on the shoulder, one of the Zones of Appropriate Touching according to most sexual harassment training guides, was all he had given her. He had declared no feeling for her beyond his admiration for her work ethic, which others agreed was top-notch. But he couldn't make his searching looks lie, even now, when he was forming solidarity with her over Vince's tread on improper territory.

"To be honest," Lily said, "it was kind of awful. But Vince meant well. I don't hold it against him."

Burt smiled. "No, you wouldn't. But I don't imagine hearing that God includes making you the victim of random, heinous violence in some kind of Master Plan is likely to win you over to His side of things."

"It's like you were there," Lily said.

"I haven't been through what you've been through," Burt said. "But I've been around, and I know people. I know Vince, God love him." He laughed. Lily laughed, too. "What I don't know is what kind of people would order *this*." Burt pointed to the table and stood aside for Lily to look.

As she approached, she asked, "Which order is this?"

"Mansworth Futures and Securities," Burt said. "1500 Spring Street, the tower with the new expansion."

Lily knew the place. She'd just been looking at it from the dog park. She reached the table and gasped.

À propos of their conversation, the image was Biblical, four men—if you could call them that—on horseback. The first horse was white, and on it rode a man with a bow and arrows, wearing a crown. The white horse trod over men and women whose flesh erupted with ooze where arrows had stricken them, and the same ooze poured from the crown. The second horse was red, and the horseman carried a sword, and bundles of heads tied at the hair hung tethered to the horse's red saddle while dismembered corpses lay littered around its hooves. While the first two riders looked like robust conquerors, the second two looked skeletal, wraiths. The third rode a black horse and carried a scale: he had skin, but it was wasted to the point of hugging bone, and the people gathered around the horse looked mostly alive, supplicating, straining to reach the death only provided at the horseman's very front. The final figure, naturally, rode a pale horse, and was Death. Nothing but bone, it did not look wicked, or anything, simply factual upon its horse, and the bodies it trod had already gone into decay.

"Well," Lily said. "That's the most... vivid... depiction of the Four Horsemen of the Apocalypse I've ever seen. What does a business want with it?"

"Look at the caption," Burt said.

It read, "Test Drive Your Potential!"

Lily did a double-take. "Di... w... huh?"

"Kind of makes you wonder what kind of future Mansworth is securing, doesn't it?" Burt joked.

"No kidding. Except that—they've got to be kidding, right?"

"That's what I thought when I saw the first one," Burt said, "but there are six more. Take a look at this one."

Burt pulled another poster from the adjacent table. It was a detailed image of a great flying thing. If Lily had to guess, she'd say the thing's body was that of a locust, but it had a long, curved tail with a point at the end, a scorpion's tail, and it had a human face with flowing, feminine hair, parted by what looked like a golden tiara. Its body was armor. The caption? "Sting the Competition!"

"This is a wee bit sick," Lily said.

"A suitable tonic for your Jesus overdose?" Burt said.

Neither of them laughed.

The third poster he showed her depicted an enormous, dragon-like creature in the sky, with a red wingspan that covered half the poster and scaly body that looked cold and metallic. Its head had giant ram's horns, and its face was, again, human. Its arms reached down to a mass of people, some of whom seemed to rejoice at it, some of whom fled, but none of whom—men, women, old, young—seemed out of reach, for its arms that stretched from the sky burst into thousands of red strings, tendrils that reached out to every figure. When a tendril touched a figure it fastened onto its head, and when it let go, it left behind a mark: 666.

The caption: "Protect Your Brand!"

The next caption Lily saw was "Jazz Up Your Work," and it showed seven angels with seven trumpets, and each trumpet rained some horror from its horn, hail, fire, blood, lots of blood. A similar poster showed seven vials pouring out horrors: an earthquake-inducing concoction, lightning, floods (more blood), etc., with the caption, "Weather *Any* Climate Change!"

Returning to the monster motif, an image of a red dragon—cousin to the other dragon-creature, except with seven heads and ten horns—showed one of its heads wounded but healed, with the caption, "Get Over Yourself!"

Finally, Burt showed Lily the best one. A woman rode upon the back of a flying dragon that might have been the same as the one that had been wounded, seven heads, ten horns. The woman's purple and red robes draped around her body without hiding much, revealing her bulging breasts as a focal point, and featuring jewels of every sort imaginable. On her forehead, part of a head that was four or five times as large as it should have been, appeared the words "Mystery, Babylon the Great," and the caption read, "Come Soar with the Whore!"

"Now *that's* classy," Lily said.

"The strangest thing of all," Burt said, "is that they put these posters on a rush order. Best possible quality, order came in this afternoon, want it tomorrow morning, top dollar for the rush."

"Pretty expensive joke," Lily said.

"The guy called up on the phone and then emailed me the files to print. He sounded dead serious." Burt looked her in the eyes again. Lily felt a chill. "What do you think it means?"

"Easy," Lily said. "God and Satan are real, and they're going to duke it out on Spring Street, where, thanks to Vince's doggie God squad, we'll have front row tickets."

Burt forced a snicker. "No, really."

"*Really*." Lily crossed from the table they used for custom in-house jobs to her desk, where she leaned on the edge. "Really, I don't care a whole heck of a lot about all this God and Satan stuff right now. They can have one another, for all I care. Locust-scorpion-people? Dragons? These images look like somebody got really, really high and then went to work. At least Vince's brand of miracles is something I can see. His whole point today was to show me a sunset."

"Hey," Burt said with another forced laugh, moving closer to Lily's desk, "Mansworth Futures and Securities paid us so that people can see their point, too."

"And what is their point, do you think?"

"Well, the images are from the Book of Revelations—"

"And? The captions?"

"Motivational."

"So now the end of the world has replaced a kitten dangling from a branch saying 'Hang in there!' What the heck are we supposed to take away from *that*?" Lily couldn't stop a small smile.

Smiling, too, Burt said: "The end of the world *is* a good

motivator."

"It's like those T-shirts. 'Christ is coming. Look busy.' The End is a scam." Lily looked at her fingernails. They were dirty.

"To what end is the end, then? I mean, what's the point?" Burt asked with an air of whimsy.

Lily didn't feel whimsical, but she liked Burt's attitude, so she tried to replicate it. "It's like Santa Claus. 'He sees you when you're sleeping. He knows when you're awake. He knows when you've been bad or good, so be good for goodness' sake.' The promise of an endpoint when scores are settled makes us behave. It makes us believe in a justice that doesn't exist."

Burt said, "I don't get the feeling these posters are, like, rah-rah for justice."

"That's what Vince was trying to argue today," Lily said. "That you can't believe in evil without believing in good. You can't hate God without believing in him. So... believing in The End is... believing."

Burt looked down and up again. "Does that mean the Left-Hand Path is still righteous?"

"Say what? What's the Left-Hand Path?" Lily had a guess. Something sinister.

"If we're soaring *with* the whore, I suppose we're not against her, are we? But if being with her means we believe in God, I guess that's better than the alternative, so being with her is better than not being with her...." Burt smiled.

Lily felt fatigued but smiled anyway. "So, a negative is closer to a positive than a double negative, in this case. My head hurts." She had a daring thought: "Hey. Take me somewhere and buy me a drink."

And he, a little too eager, said, "Okay."

She looked back at the posters and said to them, silently, *So putting my faith in celestial monsters would be better than not believing in anything at all.* Burt started leading her out the front door, and to the posters, she finished, *Good luck with that.*

3

"Nothing in heaven was e'er so sublime

As the three blind mice during crazy time."

Lily didn't think about it until *after*, when she thought of it almost every day. Mom used to call the kids—Doris, David, and Lily—the three blind mice. Mom mostly used the appellation when the kids were running around the kitchen or the living room, chasing one another or the dog, generally being rapscallion-y. Mice running around with their tails cut off seemed less violent than chickens running around with their heads cut off, which is what she said they truly reminded her of. Did Mom ever mention crazy time? Lily couldn't remember for certain, but the rhyme seemed more deeply familiar, childhood-familiar, the more she thought about it. She wrote it down, tried to recall the exact wording. The only lines she could be sure of were the first two, especially "e'er so sublime." It sounded e'er so silly when she said it out loud, by herself, to herself. In Earl's voice, in her head, it sounded terrifying. Especially now. Knives were out. Mice were on the chopping block. The call came the day after Lily's visit to the dog park with Vince.

"Lily." The voice belonged to Rose. "How quickly can you get to the hospital?" *It's your brother.*

David?

When Doris, David, and Lily saw each other, as they

had two days before Eric's fatal birthday, on Christmas, they sometimes hummed the proper tune for "Three Blind Mice" in recognition of the shenanigans that might ensue from their reunion. Shenanigans inevitably did not ensue, not for the adult mice. Doris would get to the second "See how they run!" of the "Three Blind Mice" song, and one of the kids, likely Daisy, would run into the room, howling, "Mommy, Donnie won't stop looking at me!" and Doris would have to be Mommy instead of Sister. Donnie was Daisy's older brother, a quiet boy with the power to turn little girls to stone with a glare. Lily preferred her nephew's company to her niece's, mostly for the quiet, but he preferred hand-held gaming of some kind to the company of adults, except, of course, when adults were out of the room, at which point he would commence tormenting his sister with jibes and silent, stultifying looks. Or so claimed the little girl. If the boy could be roused enough to protest, he denied all.

Holiday camaraderie among siblings also halted with regularity due to David's telephone, which he kept on the arm of his chair at all times so that he could see when its signal light changed colors or started blinking to signify that someone in the world outside their mother's home had tried to contact him. Rose, Mom's sister and, for lack of a better term, life partner since Dad died, tried stealing the phone once, which sent David into fits. He commandeered everyone in the house, kids included, to go searching, and the phone's hiding place, the toaster oven, was eventually discovered. Rose never confessed, but Lily knew. Lily didn't disapprove of the phone addiction as much as Rose did, or for that matter as much as Doris did, but she did find competing with the device for her brother's attention rather tiring, as she knew, in her heart, she would never win.

David was six years older than Lily, and Doris was ten. Lily had been a surprise. Dad had died two years later. Rose came to visit to help out and never left. Lily thought of Rose as a second mother, but not in that lesbian way, even though she got teased about it when she was a kid. She'd had to learn about incest when she was quite young because people talked about it. Ethel and Rose in a "Boston marriage." Ethel and Rose as an affront to God. Ethel and Rose. Ethel and Rose. Rose had been married, too. She had the scars to prove it, but she didn't talk about them. Like Donnie, she didn't talk a lot, but she knitted instead of playing handheld video games. Knitting, games, and phone; Rose, Donnie, and David.

Who was it who kept sending David little messages, most of which he swiped away in an instant? Lily caught glimpses of Friendbook and other social media. Not a lot of it seemed personal. On the way to the hospital, she imagined her own phone, all the crap she swiped away without reading, and wondered whether David kept his phone out merely to monitor crap, as if somehow in the midst of it something magical might appear, source unknown.

The Christmas tree that year had all-white lights, with a white-gowned, oversized angel at the top who appeared to be showering icicles—along with peace, joy, and good will toward men—down upon the lower branches. Daisy was still young enough to want to get up first thing in the morning, before sunrise, and open presents, so by midday everyone was tired and cranky. By David's insistence and Mom's acquiescence, the nog came out with heavy doses of dark rum, which made Rose drift in and out of sleep with her knitting still on her lap. Donnie disappeared with a new game, and Daisy busied herself in a corner, drawing with a new set of glittery pens, a surprise hit that Lily had picked up at a department store at the last minute. After setting out some deviled eggs, Mom disappeared into the kitchen to prepare infinite side dishes to accompany the afternoon's ham. Doris, relieved of Mommy responsibility, handed the TV remote to David with the injunction, "No sports." With the non-phone hand switching between remote and nog, David searched until he found a station with what looked like news.

"It's news, and it's a problem we need to discuss, but people say that talking about the problem can make it worse as well as better, so we have to be careful about it, Andrew," a woman on the television was saying.

"That's why," the white-haired man onscreen said, "we again advise that younger and more vulnerable members of the audience may want to skip this segment. Again, we are reporting on a series of deaths in Downslake County, the fourth of which just came in on this holiday morning."

The woman, half his age, blonde, wearing a vibrant blue suit that contrasted with Andrew's dull grey, responded, "And before we continue with the connection among the deaths, does the holiday itself play any apparent role?"

"Well, Megan, national studies indicate that while most people underestimate the degree to which suicide is a common occurrence and a real national health problem, the popular belief that suicides are common around Christmas is actually false. According to Dr. Randolph Case, the presence of family and other support systems around the winter holidays may actually decrease the numbers of crises that lead to suicides, whereas we see a spike in those crises in the spring, when people might feel that their own hopelessness contrasts too sharply with the rebirth going on around them."

"So that's the general situation, Andrew, but what about this case today?"

"Who is Andrew?" Mom called from the kitchen. "And what is he doing in my house at Christmas?"

"It's the news, Ethel," Rose snapped to attention and answered. "David put it on."

"Put on the dog show. Isn't there a dog show?" Mom called back.

Doris and David looked at each other, and Doris smiled.

David did not. Lily shrugged. "It's a compromise, Mom," Doris shouted. "At least it's not sports."

"Well it sounds morbid," Mom pronounced. The screech of metal on metal, a tray sliding into the oven, punctuated the pronouncement.

Andrew was continuing, "All we know is that it was a shock to the family, and our thoughts and prayers are with them."

"Of course, Andrew. And now on to our focus, the relationship between this shocking tragedy and the three others that have so recently rocked Downslake County."

"Do we have to watch this?" Rose asked. "It *is* morbid."

"So what?" David said. "The kids aren't listening. I'm interested."

Lily said nothing. Doris looked over at Daisy, who paid the television no attention, and shrugged. Rose adjusted her knitting and closed her eyes.

"Because we've had four deaths ruled as suicides in Downslake, people are starting to talk about what they call a *point cluster*, Megan," Andrew said. His TV voice had the same volume as others in the room.

"Referring to a suicide cluster," Megan said.

"That's right. Now the term 'suicide cluster' refers to any time when a group of suicidal behaviors or successful suicides happens together in an accelerated time and sometimes, as in this case, but not always, in a defined geographic space. When they occur close together, especially in space, they're called a point cluster. Clusters are part of what some people call *suicidal contagion*."

"Wait a minute," Megan said. "Does that mean suicide is actually contagious? Like you can catch it from somebody?"

Andrew shook his head. "Not exactly."

Clicking and clacking—Rose hadn't fallen asleep. She knitted and watched the television beside Doris on the sofa. Doris watched with a grimace. Daisy was still making art in the corner, seeming not to pay attention. Mom was still in the kitchen. David's phone was blinking beside him on the reclining chair but received no attention.

"People have worried about the phenomenon of suicidal contagion," Andrew said, "at least since the 1700s, when Goethe's novel *The Sorrows of Young Werther* supposedly inspired young readers to imitate the main character, who takes his own life. The fear is that when people, vulnerable people, especially young people, encounter the idea of a successful suicide, they might be more inclined to try it themselves. The same type of phenomenon motivates copycats with other tragedies, like school shootings."

"So contagion is most common among young people. However, although we're withholding the name out of respect for the family, isn't it true that the case today is of a middle-aged father of two, rather than of a vulnerable young person?" Megan prompted.

"We know the man's age and that he had children," Andrew said, "as you say, Megan, but we don't know what his mental state was, and we don't know what he knew, if anything, about the three earlier deaths. If he was already in a depressed mental state, and he became interested in the other deaths, then he might fit the profile of suicidal contagion, even though he wasn't necessarily a young man."

"I see."

Doris nodded along with Megan. David started humming something. Lily didn't know what it was, but it wasn't "Three Blind Mice." Something more up-tempo, more rhythmic, rock, funk... familiar. "David that's awful," Doris said.

Lily got it: "Another One Bites the Dust," by Queen. She

sighed.

"Hey—I'm gonna get you, too!" David sang with glee. Daisy looked up from her drawing.

Doris stood up from the sofa, Lily and Rose looking up after her. "That's it. I'm changing the channel. This is *not* Christmas—"

"Over my dead body!" David said. "I want to hear this." He guarded the remote, close to his chest.

"So instead of banning novels," Megan was replying to Andrew, "today people try to ban newscasts about suicide because of their supposed relation to the cluster effect."

"That's right. In addition to the guidelines I mentioned, some medical authorities have gone further than Dr. Case in recommending a ban on virtually all coverage of such deaths, as coverage constitutes, allegedly, a threat to public health. These recommendations have very little support, and such a ban would clearly violate the First Amendment, and especially with four deaths in so short a time in Downslake—"

Doris wrested the remote from David's hands and turned off the TV.

Clicking and clacking stopped. "They were trying to dodge the fingers pointed at them," Rose said. "I don't think they care if they're making it worse. How they talk about their own blame—that would be the good part."

"Sure," David said. "Blame the media."

"There wasn't going to *be* a good part, Rose," Doris said. Keeping the remote, she settled back down with Lily and Rose on the sofa, glaring at David, who hummed a few more bars. "There's nothing good about sensationalistic, morbid reporting on Christmas."

Nothing in heaven

"So you'd ban it, too," David said.

Doris looked over her shoulder at Daisy, who had been looking at them a moment before but now busied herself with the sparkle markers. Lily imagined her drawing a big lake for Downslake and a pile of dead bodies with X's on their eyes and showing her masterpiece to them as evidence of television's bad influence. It could happen.

was e'er so sublime

"I'd ban anything that killed people, if those doctors turned out to be right," Doris said.

"So you'd not only get rid of the First Amendment," David said, with a sound suggesting he was about to win the argument, "but the Second, too."

As the three blind mice

Doris's sigh was so deep that Donnie might have heard it wherever he had secured himself to play video games uninterrupted. "What are you talking about, little brother?" Doris always called them "little" when she felt impatient with their opinions.

"So, these doctors are saying that showing a vulnerable person a newscast increases the likelihood of their committing suicide, so we've got to ban the newscasts. What do you think the doctors would say to handing vulnerable people guns? Would that raise or lower the likelihood, do you think? Should we ban guns, then? If the logic applies in one case…."

Lily thought her brother's point was pretty solid.

"I'm not saying we ban *all* newscasts, just newscasts that treat suicides in harmful ways. If people are making guns for the purpose of suicide, I guess we *should* ban those guns, but who's making those guns, huh?" Doris's retort was fast and, in Lily's mind, difficult. Lily hadn't heard of a suicide gun.

"*Any* gun is a suicide gun," David said.

"*Any* gun is a suicide gun," Daisy repeated. She had come

over from the corner to show them all her drawing. It was a very sparkly Christmas tree, far more colorful than the drab white that Mom and Rose had topped with the oversized angel that was watching over their battle of amendments.

"And any careless statement," Doris said, "can be mimicked."

during crazy time!

Three months later, her mind mimicked Earl's sing-song-y rhyme, in a childlike register, throughout the brief phone conversation with her sister.

"Hello?"

"Hello, Lily?"

"Yes, Doris, it's me."

"Lily, I—I didn't know if I should call."

"Doris, what's wrong?"

"With all you've been through."

"What's wrong?"

Doris paused. "I can't," Lily's sister said, and with a gulp, she fought and failed to hide the sound of tears.

A new voice appeared on the phone. "Lily." The voice belonged to Rose.

"I'm here."

"How quickly can you get to the hospital?" Rose sounded composed, forcefully composed.

Lily felt the composure like a rod shoved through the center of her spine. "Mom? What's wrong with Mom?" She thought of her mother's extra cheesy macaroni casserole and imagined clogged arteries.

"It's… it's your brother," Rose said.

"David? What about him?" Lily imagined David with a

bullet in his forehead, dead at Earl's feet. IT'S CRAZY TIME!

"He's… in the hospital." Context clues, Rose! That much was clear. Why did they need two of them to make this call? What was so bad about being in the hospital? How hurt could he be?

David was single, always had been. He had a small one-story house, two bedrooms, one-car garage, nice patio, and a maid named Viv who came by once a week to combat the dust and cobwebs that collected while David was workaholicking as a Senior Manager in a tech support consulting firm.

Mom would've been happy if David had married Viv. Rose was happy with David single but thought if he was going to get married, it should be to someone "serious." Viv seemed plenty serious—had come over from Ireland, worked for citizenship, established her own little service company—but not white collar enough for one of Rose's quasi-kids, her sole nephew. David insisted nothing existed between Viv and him. Mom hinted he was hiding something. Doris hinted David was a late-blooming gay. Eric had said no way. Now, driving her little Toyota over side streets because the highway would risk another panic attack, Lily considered that after more than thirty years of knowing him, she knew very little about her middle-child big brother. Perhaps none of them knew much about him. Perhaps he liked it that way.

On the phone, Rose would not say what was wrong with him, not exactly, "His lungs," she said. Some sort of chemical? A gas? Rose was hard to understand, but in the background, Doris was blubbering, so Lily knew she had the best available source of information. The bottom line was that Lily needed to be at the hospital. Doris's husband Joe was keeping the kids, an occasion rare enough to underscore severity even more profoundly than Doris's blubbering, so Lily drove fast. She hated driving. Every light in her rearview mirror was from a red pickup truck. High beams. Low beams. Initiation. A path to a new world, another time, opening.

Crazy time.

Because Lily knew. As she signaled to pass another car going only ten miles per hour above the speed limit, she knew what was wrong with David because the memory of Christmas replayed in her head with such clarity. Suicide clusters. Sometimes the suicidal contagion, the seed or germ, lies dormant beneath the culture and then pops up in a nearby place, at a not-too-distant time, to start another cycle. The word was RHIZOME. Suicide was a rhizome, like certain mushrooms and plants, popping up in bunches here, bunches there, connected deep, deep within the soil by traveling particles. The soil—

The land was rotten. The whole country was rotten with clusters of crazy-time mushrooms. Taking the side streets instead of the highway to the hospital meant driving through some neighborhoods where a middle-class white woman alone in her car, even if it was just a Toyota and not an invitation-to-psychos BMW, was not supposed to go. Here the rot stood out visibly, as if "economic recovery" had never occurred, because people lived on the streets and in houses so broken down that they were exposed *to* the streets. She would like to see an Earl and a Rob, middle-aged white guys out joyriding and marauding, try their shit here and be wiped out, not even a memory; the street would devour them as well as her, indiscriminate. She tried to find comfort in the idea of them being eaten as she would be and found none. The streets had bumps from cracked, uneven pavement, and broken windows of once-fine buildings framed by trash stuffed into gutters cried out a need for vengeance against every human being alive.

Lily stopped at a traffic light and wondered whether, like they said in movies, she should drive straight through. No. The skittering movements in all corners could come for her if they wanted. The streets had bloomed with the mushrooms of crazy time. They could come, and she wouldn't find out what was happening to her brother, even though she knew.

She didn't know *how* she knew, not with this degree of certainty. It wasn't a psychic phenomenon, a brother-sister link, or woman's intuition, or Sherlock-Holmesian deduction. When you eliminate the impossible, whatever remains, however improbable, must be the truth. Mushrooms. She knew what David had done just as surely as she knew she could get out of the car and parade the impoverished streets in a skirt of hundred-dollar bills and still arrive at the hospital unscathed by the fungal bloom. Eric was dead. Kris was dead. Mia was dead. Gun, tire iron, knife—and Lily remembered Christmas, with knitting, games, and phone—and the three blind mice being Doris, David, and herself—different clusters of meaning, different clusters, coming together.

Three, three, three. *Protect your brand!*

Mushrooms. Clusters. Crazy time.

The scene, in Lily's head: David got home from work, tossed his keys on a small table he kept by the door. She'd only seen the table, and the house beyond it, a couple of times; he never had anyone over, least of all his sisters. Tossing his briefcase on the sofa, which had a tear in the upholstery, he crossed to the kitchen, where he opened the refrigerator. Examining leftovers, he lingered over pizza but selected the carton of Chinese, which he withdrew and dumped into a bowl from the nearby cupboard. The bowl fit neatly into the nearby microwave. For two and a half minutes, David watched the bowl rotate inside the microwave. His gaze did not waver. The bowl spun.

When the microwave finished spinning the bowl for him, he got some reusable plastic chopsticks from a drawer and sat at his small breakfast table, where a few newspapers and other odd ends lay stacked. Looking at nothing, he sat and ate. Whatever he ate might have had baby corn and bamboo shoots but would not have had mushrooms; David hated mushrooms.

Finished, David took the bowl to the sink and washed it. He was fastidious. With the clean bowl and the chopsticks in the drying rack, he left the kitchen and went back to the living room, to the sofa where he'd left his briefcase and the table where he'd left his keys. He retrieved the keys, thought for a moment, and held onto them while he sat on the sofa and turned on the television. There, he sought news.

What did he see? Local: at least an armed robbery, assault, or rape, probably a homicide. National: some politician blaming a minority for the country's problems, and groups rioting in reaction. International: someone bombing someone else, with the United States getting ready to bomb everyone in response. The mushrooms were fucking everywhere, and David had a headache. He clenched his keys.

And he stood from the sofa, using the remote to silence the television, which left the house hollow and quiet, making his heartbeat pound like a kettle drum along his nerves.

The small house's living room opened onto the dining area, and where the rooms joined, a narrow door led to the garage. Lily's imagination had trouble at this point. Had David stopped to think about a lot of different things, or had he gone on, automatically? The latter would be easier to fathom. David had made up his mind about the thing and then gone into a mode. In that mode, he got home from work, carried out at least a partial routine, went out into the garage, started the car, and did his best to take a nap. What else could Rose have meant by lung damage from breathing in the car gases? Not much she had said made sense, but the phrase "did it to himself" had been clear and so had the bits about lungs and gaseous chemicals.

Harder to imagine was David going through some

motions, stopping to reflect, and then going on. Maybe his daily life sucked. Lily barely understood his job. It sounded kind of neat to her, since all she did was manage a small office, fill out a lot of forms related to print orders, make more copies than God, and the like—but what did she know? He might have been miserable. They hadn't been close in a long time. But so what? Who *isn't* miserable a fundamental part of each day? David was probably lonely, too. Lily was single. Kris was single and said it felt a lot less lonely than a bad marriage. Lily supposed she'd be a lot lonelier now that her closest friends were all dead. Misery and loneliness offered very little, least of all explanations.

His reflections, if he reflected, likely didn't carry him in those directions. Not just that he wouldn't compare himself to Lily—of course he wouldn't—but he would have to eschew all comparisons, or rather, any comparisons he considered he would have to dismiss as irrelevant. Whatever the suffering of another person might be, his was such that it needed to end by means of his death. And if his death caused suffering? If he reflected, surely he reflected on that. What about Mom and Rose? Or Doris and Daisy and Donnie? They might not have been close-knit, but they weren't strangers. Did David think he had no one? They were all gathering at the hospital for him right now! Well, Doris, Mom, and Rose would be there, and everyone was a mess. Blubbering, borderline-incoherent, and Mom—who even *knew* about Mom. If he had reflected, taken a roll call, his count might have included one or more of the people devastated by what he had tried, yet he had tried it anyway.

David went through the narrow door into the garage. Without opening the exterior garage door, he closed the door to the house. The light switch connected to a burnt-out bulb, so he found his way to the car in the dark. A light in the car came on when the door opened, so the rest was easy. Turn the key, pump the gas a little, and open the window enough to let the car fill up. He thought about looking for a hose to run from the exhaust pipe to the car window—quicker—but decided against, since the garage was small. Nervous, he checked to make sure he could detect exhaust coming from the tailpipe and thickening. Even though the prize, carbon monoxide, was supposed to be odorless and colorless—check!

David had trouble sleeping in the best of circumstances, so he was unlikely to sleep with the car running beneath him and death pouring in all around him. Did it start with adjusting to the foul smell and taste of car pollutants? Which overwhelmed him first, the nausea or the drowsiness? They must have combined as consciousness ebbed, and the field of vision became like heat rising from asphalt in the desert. Reflection might have continued then, but no second thoughts, no doubts, because up until nearly the last minute, when consciousness trickled beyond retention, all he needed to do was open a door, turn off the car, either, both. Any limit on his exposure might have made the difference between a conscious David and David in the condition of the other word Rose had repeated:

COMA.

Sleeping in a field of mushrooms, where his lungs fought damage from gaseous chemicals.

Lily obeyed traffic signals but went on again, quickly, when they allowed. She reached the hospital less than an hour after Doris and Rose's call. Mom met her in the waiting area of the ICU. Her eyes had the crusted look of recent long weeping, and they had sunk within her head. Her hair had unnatural frizz. A strange man stood at her side. "Lilith," Mom said. Mom only used her given name at the gravest of times.

"Yeah Mom, I'm here."

"I want you to meet Scott Whelan, my lawyer." Mr. Whelan extended a hand, which Lily shook uneasily. "I guess he's *our* lawyer."

"Nice to meet—Mom," Lily said, "why do we need a lawyer?"

"It's about your brother," Mom said. She was too calm. Mom was not supposed to be calm. She was supposed to be a broken mess for the rest of them to rally around. Rose being strong on the phone made sense. Mom in a lawyered package of serenity made no sense.

"Of course, David is why we're here, but is he in trouble? Did he wake up? I want to see him!" Lily said.

"You'll go in, in a minute," Mom said. Tears began to re-form in the corners of crusted eyes. "Doris is in there, talking to him now."

"So he *is* awake!" Lily felt excitement pushing away disbelief.

"No," Mom said. "We just hope he can hear us. His lungs are… I think the word was… 'scorched.' Other organs have shut down. Machines are keeping him alive. For now."

"So… what are they going to do? Is there an operation? A transplant list? Something?"

Rose entered the waiting room carrying two cups of coffee. Both of her hands shook, dripping brown fluid over the sides of the Styrofoam cups. She gave one cup to Mom and the other to Mr. Whelan, following each with a napkin. "Sorry for the drips," she said.

Mom said thank you. Mr. Whelan gave a canned smile of consolation.

"Lily, darling, your brother is dying. The damage is too extensive for anything but the machines to keep him alive now," Rose said.

"How long does he have?" Lily asked.

Mom was crying again. Mr. Whelan offered a handkerchief and, when Mom took it, looked at his watch.

Why was he here?

"Not as long as we'd want," Rose said. "Mr. Whelan, you're sure...."

"I've reviewed it." He straightened his straight tie. "Everything looks unimpugnable. Although I've never seen a hospital move this fast, they're to the point where action is called for."

"Aunt Rose, what are you talking about?"

Mom was working up to a bawl, becoming more of what Lily had expected. Rose lowered her head. The lawyer looked from one woman to the next, waiting for one of them to take charge. Finally, Mom swallowed, hard, and wiped at her eyes with a clenched fist. "David has an ad... advance directive."

Lily looked from Mom to Rose. "And? And what does that mean?"

Mr. Whelan spoke up: "An advance directive is also part of what's known as a living will, and it tells us what to do in cases like—"

Lily gave the lawyer the sharpest glare she could manage. "I don't want to know about cases *like*," she said. "What does it mean in THIS case?"

"David wants us to pull the plug," Mom said. She laughed. "He killed himself before he tried to kill himself. Simple as that. He's making us, or the hospital, finish the job." She laughed again, short, pointed.

Rose said, "I'm sure he didn't plan it that way."

Mom shot her the same look that Lily had tried to give the lawyer. Rose shrunk away. Mom bawled.

Lily looked at the lawyer. "When?"

"I managed," the lawyer said without self-congratulation, "to make them wait until you arrived."

Doris appeared. "Maybe you want to say something to him? They only want one of us... one of us in at a time until we all go in for the last...." *For the last goodbye.*

Lily looked at Rose, Mom, Mr. Whelan, and Doris, and she felt herself shrinking. Again, a mushroom, or maybe the circumstance of being surrounded by older family and an authority figure during a crazy time, but she felt like a little girl, knowing what everyone expected of her but feeling in every nerve ending that she wanted, *needed* to do the opposite. Why would she go see her comatose, dying brother? Not even dying—DEAD? For he would be dead as soon as Lily had whatever her say would be. He awaited her words, then some ceremonial circle, then a figurative pulling of a plug, more likely the pressing of a button. Her visit was all that stood between him and death, and she didn't want it. Skip me, she wanted to say. Take me home. She had already watched too many people die.

Lily stepped into David's alcove of the ICU. She almost didn't recognize him, skin ash-blue, like putty, face obscured by the mask attached to the main tube, other wires going into and out of his arms, beeping machines with more lines than she could attach meaning to. The pump beside the bed was the main thing, though, the thing forcing air in and out of damaged lungs that would not inflate or deflate on their own, would not function because they'd been "scorched" by the hands that they'd fed with oxygen for four decades.

"David," Lily said. "You ass. This isn't supposed to be you. It could be me. *I* have a reason, you know. You? Fuck you. Not you." She was crying. "What do I know? We all have reasons." She felt sick, nauseated. She looked around the room and saw a tiny trash can. If she needed to, she could use it to puke. Instead, she hummed a few notes of "The Three Blind Mice." Then she said, "Nothing in heaven was e'er so sublime, David. Doris was too old. You were the one who looked out for me. You were the one I looked up to. God damn it, David. Damn it." She considered.

"I'm not going to ask why." She considered again.

"I'm going to ask—who? You're not the first, are you? This is one of those… clusters… we heard about on Christmas? It's not a coincidence? It happened in Downslake, and now it's happening here. I'll watch the news, and I'll find out you were the second in the area, and then there'll be another. Because there have to be three. Right David? But there were more than that on the other news report… so that's not right. I'm not going to ask why. I'll ask how. How does this work, David? I wish you could talk to me. Because this is crazy time, David, and you're part of it now. You and me, and maybe Doris, too, but I hope not."

She studied his ashen face. "I have to say goodbye to you. But I won't, like I won't ask why. Because I think I won't be far behind. Someone's coming for me, David. I can feel it." She hadn't thought the thought to herself, but saying it, she knew it was true.

Within the hour, David was dead.

4

Lily awoke to a tickling in her left ear and, brushing it away, sat up in bed. The sun was up. Her eyes adjusted to what seemed like a normal day before the events of two weeks ago, the events that culminated in the shutdown of machines that ended David's life, occurred to her. On those events' tails came the events of three months earlier, Kris and Mia and Eric—and her hand massaged the sudden ache between her breasts, and she took in a long, halting breath. The sunlight streaming from her windows dimmed, either from cloud cover or from a darkening of her own perception, she couldn't tell. Every morning during the two weeks Burt had insisted she take off, with pay, for "bereavement," waking had followed this pattern: seconds of forgetting allowed her a taste of normalcy to be snatched away by vicious memory. Every morning, for a moment, she got to be no one, and she treasured that moment, in retrospect, as she became herself, got out of bed, and figured out how to face the day.

As she stood, she felt the tickling sensation again, this time near but not on her ear, tucked into the hair between her ear and the upper part of her left cheek. Semi-absently, her fingers went to brush away what she sensed as an errant lock of hair, but her fingertips detected something more solid and separate. Turning fingers into pincers, she grabbed at whatever the solid thing was and felt a little crunch. She brought the object around to her field of vision and grimaced. A bug. A *big* bug. Harmless, though: a grasshopper. Those things never came inside. How odd to find one like this.

The one between her fingers was dead in a squish of tiny legs, bug-innards, and fluids that felt more like greasy pus. She left the bedroom for the bathroom, where she threw the tiny corpse in the toilet and washed its splatter from her fingers. She shivered. Having *any* kind of bug crawling around on her while she was in bed was bad, but at least it hadn't been a spider, or an ant, or worse, some kind of many-legged slimy thing like a caterpillar or centipede. *Yuck.* Grasshoppers were kind of cute, and she couldn't think of anything menacing about them. They were supposed to be green, of course, and this one had been more yellow brown, with spots. But who cares about color, when it could have been something not only grosser but *dangerous*, like a bee or a wasp? Some kinds of flies bite. Ants. Mosquitoes. Scorpions. And what about locusts?

Sting the Competition!

Lily stumbled away from the bathroom. Her morning thoughts weren't clear yet. She remembered now that grasshoppers *were* locusts, at least some of them, and if she imagined the thing she'd just killed with a scorpion's tail, a human face, and a woman's hair, it would look like that poster from Mansworth Futures and Securities—

She hustled back to her bedroom. On her pillow, where her head had been, two more locusts crawled. Rushing back to the kitchen, she didn't know what she was going for until she opened the pantry and withdrew the broom. The sweeping end might have done the job, but when she returned to the bed, she wielded the handle like a bludgeon and smashed the pillow, aiming for the two locusts and missing again and again, eventually hitting them more from probability than aim. Her pillowcase smeared.

Her chest heaved, and she considered whether she needed a washing machine or a fire for the soiled linen. *Three locusts.* Hardly a swarm, but they had been near her head, one of them on the precipice of her ear. Did it want to crawl inside her, take up residence near her brain? What sorts of things might it whisper to her there?

During the last two weeks, most of which, since David's funeral, she had spent alone, Lily had come to realize she was paranoid. She understood that, as the saying goes, being paranoid doesn't mean they're not out to get you, and recognizing her paranoia as such did nothing to dissuade her conviction that someone, or something, was after her. But watching for *it* made her paranoid, suspicious of every little thing, bug-size or otherwise. She couldn't rationally expect Earl or Rob to come for her again, but she saw them, one of them, both of them, lurking around street corners, browsing at newsstands, driving by in all manners of vehicles, watching. CNN, Fox, MSNBC, and the other news channels played constantly on her television; once one of them told her that yes, a suicide cluster that could count David was active in her city, she couldn't stop watching. The number of deaths, counting David's, was greater than three, but Lily, never much of a churchgoer, knew her Bible well enough to watch for multiples of three, six, and seven. Would Vince be pleased that her newfound belief went far enough to make her fear Biblical numbers? Granted, these numbers formed a significant portion of available single-digit integers....

Suicides. Highway accidents with unusual injuries, high body counts. Auto thefts with serious injuries or killings involved. She watched for them all, plotted them on a map in relation to her apartment, examined them for other patterns, but the only pattern she could follow was the clustering of suicides around David's vicinity. A woman had thrust her arm into a garbage disposal and aligned the blades with her wrist. The blades hadn't really been sharp enough: waiting for them to mangle the flesh enough to cause her to bleed out had taken *will*. A teenager had jumped off a high-rise on Spring Street, somewhere in the 2000s, only close enough to Mansworth for Lily to think about it. An old man had put both barrels of a shotgun in his mouth, easy-peasy on the trigger, not so much on the clean-up. Point clusters rarely varied so widely on *modus operandi*, according to one report, but the closeness in time and space was too great to deny.

Locusts. She held up the broom handle like a lance and circled her queen-sized bed. Three locusts on her pillow, trying to get inside her head. So that was paranoia, probably. She came around to the wall opposite where she usually slept, studying the quiet bed, the lumps of sheets and blankets at the foot. Bugs in her brain. Maybe so. Maybe in so many ways. But the more she studied the sheets and blankets, the more she knew she would have to shake them out, search every inch of the bed for more signs of locusts. For what separates the locust from the grasshopper, in imagination, if not in science? What makes the locust a formidable creature of myth and the grasshopper a stock character of wisdom dispensation? *Swarms*. Locusts swarm. They don't go about alone or in two- and threesomes, knocking on the entrances to sleeping ladies' ears. They form communities and *eat*.

So now Lily was paranoid about bugs eating her brain while she slept. Good God, woman, control yourself!

Keeping herself at a distance, she used the broom handle to scoop up sheet and blanket. Balancing them on the wooden rod, she lifted the bed covers and tossed them toward a side of the room. In their wake, several insects took immediate flight, but most of a dark... puddle... remained on the lightly colored sheets, bodies crawling over one another. A writhing patch of insects sat near the foot of the bed, too dense with bodies for Lily to count.

She dropped the broom and used both hands to plug the scream erupting from her mouth. Two of the now-flying locusts circled her, and one landed on her shoulder. She wanted to shoo it, but she was afraid to uncover her mouth. Its antennae tickled her neck before it resumed flight. The sound reached her then: buzzing, almost a low chirping, as the insects rubbed against one another in their puddle of life at the bottom of the bed.

Questions of *what*, such as what were the locusts doing here, and questions of how, such as how did the locusts get here, get to Lily's feet while she slept, had faded significance as she gawked at the living, shifting puddle of insects. The question she had avoided with David now burned: *WHY?* "Why are you here, with me?" she asked the insects. "Why?!!"

They writhed. Some bounced and flew. One came toward her, and she swatted it, to no avail. She started crying. A locust landed on her shoulder. Another landed in her hair.

Refusing to give in, she marched away from the bed while unbuttoning her pajama top and, when it was open, threw the garment on the floor behind her. She slammed the bedroom door. To the bathroom, she stepped out of pajama bottoms and climbed into the tub, immediately turning nozzles for hot and cold, not minding the first freezing blast of water, just wanting it to knock any lingering passengers away. The temperature adjusted, and she showered, washing her hair, watching for flying visitors to intrude, ready to crush them with soapy hands. The locusts seemed to have stayed behind. She finished, wrapped herself in a towel, and realized that, to get dressed, she'd have to go back to the bedroom, their domain.

She brushed her hair back, studying herself in the mirror, searching for resolve. Her eyes almost looked convincing. Her mouth had set, downward turns in both corners, not too pronounced but noteworthy. A bunch of grasshoppers weren't going to make her run out of her own home in a towel calling for help. Besides, what if—

What if they weren't there?

The sudden appearance of a mini-plague of locusts in her bedroom seemed more than a little like crazy time, in a new light, and while a person had to be careful about diagnosing herself, she had four good reasons (their names were David, Eric, Kris, and Mia) to be suffering from Post-Traumatic Stress Disorder, and couldn't that involve hallucinations? She'd already remembered the poster from work, the strange one with the Biblical locust-hybrid, so she'd found the source in recent memory to trigger such a hallucination. And one could fairly say she felt like her world was ending, so apocalyptic hallucinations also made a kind of sense, a crazy-time kind.

She had felt the locust she'd pinched with her fingers, its pus-like entrails, and she'd heard them, which meant it was a hallucination in three sensory modalities, which she thought was important somehow, making it a MAJOR hallucination. She could go back in her bedroom and find them all gone, or they could still be there.

Which they were. When she opened the bedroom door, one immediately flew near her face. The puddle had arisen, dispersing through the bedroom in an expanding mass that now reached all corners. None bolted through the open door; they stayed along the opening as if an invisible field guarded it. With a sense that locusts only actually ate crops, Lily felt an urge and gratified it: she lifted a hand and passed it through the doorway. The haphazard-seeming streams of insects parted for her, none colliding. Her whole arm entered the bedroom, and, unmet so far by locusts, more of her body followed, until she had stepped inside. The towel fell to the floor, leaving her to cross through the room naked. Lily could sense the movement of the bugs around her, but none of them touched her.

She went to her closet and got dressed. The not-touching rule did not hold absolutely: every now and then, like a curious outlier, one of the locusts would land on her shoulder, or in her hair, as before, but it would remain unobtrusive, and it wouldn't linger. Most left her alone, content to form an envelope around her exposed skin. Flapping, spotted wings made a constant, subtle breeze she could feel against the fine hairs of her arms.

No locusts followed her out of the room when she finished dressing and exited. In the hall, she searched herself for straggling insects. Finding none, she wrapped her arms around her torso and let loose the scream she had been stifling.

After ten minutes, Lily felt comfortable concluding the neighbors were taking no action in response to her loud scream. She could, therefore, move on. She needed to call somebody. A really good exterminator, perhaps. But what if he got here and there were no bugs? What should she say when she called—that she wanted a routine treatment but could only do it today? Or that the bug-man needs to bring his whole freaking arsenal as soon as human speed would allow? Warning them about the severity of the problem risked making her look like a fool if the exterminator found no locusts, but not warning them risked, well, them.

Moreover, she desperately wanted to tell someone about the locusts. The taboo of telling magnified the need to tell. No, more than telling: she needed to share, to show, because bringing someone a handful of dead grasshoppers as suggestive evidence wasn't enough. To be convinced she wasn't hallucinating, to know she hadn't gone off her proverbial rocker, she needed someone else to describe seeing what she saw, viz. her bedroom full of swarming locusts.

Her brain spat out one answer for the person to call: Burt. If Lily was hallucinating, he'd get the reference to the poster, he knew about everything she'd been through, and he was naturally inclined to be... forgiving... of her. If she wasn't hallucinating, he was a tough enough guy who could help her figure out what to do.

They were on the phone for a while. "Okay then," Burt said. "You're going to take some pictures on your phone of whatever this thing is that I have to see to believe, and I'm going to come over because you need somebody. I'll look at the pictures, and I'll look at the real thing, and we'll figure out what to do. Is that a deal?"

She felt stupid for not thinking of the pictures—blame it on morning, on confusion, on how entirely fucked up her life had become—but she didn't expect to be able to photograph them anyway, not really. She couldn't tell Burt that, though. She couldn't tell him that even when she looked directly at them, felt their gooey guts on her fingers, a part of her believed they weren't there, the part of her that knew she had become *psychologically unstable* since death had made her friends and family its top draft picks, where *unstable* means *unsound*, and *unsound* means *unsane*, unsanitary, unclean, dirty, cluttered mind, the kind bugs are drawn to, buggy mind, cluttered with bad, paranoid thoughts likely to manifest themselves in swarms only she could see. See, hear, and touch. If one of those *things* crawled into her mouth, would she taste, smell? Would it be a full five-sense hallucination?

She worked up the courage to go back into the bedroom. She stood outside the doorway for the first click on the camera button, and it yielded a blurry image full of specks in the air that might have been flying things and might have been dust particles. Trying the picture again got better focus but the same ambiguity—she would need to get closer. Counting on the same disinterest the locusts had shown when insanity had driven her through the room completely naked, she stepped through the doorway, and the bugs enveloped her again, keeping a tiny bubble of distance that only the occasional curious lander would violate.

Her finger on the camera button went nuts. With an almost-full battery and ample memory, she photographed images of the swarm in the air, locusts clinging to walls, and locusts climbing up and down the drawer she'd left open after choosing her underwear for the day. She went in for a close-up on the original puddle from the foot of her bed, where a mass of locusts still congregated, and she captured the leggy, wing-y things hopping and crawling over one another, their rounded eyes and angular joints. When she smashed one of them on top of her chest of drawers, five landed on the crushing fist, and she froze, waiting for more to overtake her. The five crawled on her skin, tickling, investigating, and retook flight. The swarm's buzzing, chirping, grew louder. She photographed the goo and smear, and she retreated from the room, sensing, perhaps projecting, a new menace from the swarm, feeling her welcome run out now that she'd slain another of their crew.

In the hall, she stopped to look at her pictures. Many of the shots were as indistinguishable as the first she'd taken from the doorway, but others were undeniable: her bedroom was infested with locusts. Either she was hallucinating images on her phone as well, or she had proof.

The insect noises, behind her, grew louder, and she felt a collision against her neck. One of them had followed her to the hall. The invisible barrier in the doorway was ceasing to function. They were on to her; they were after her. Silly, yes, but sillier than waking up to a plague of locusts in your bedroom? She thought not. She thought she might wait for Burt outside. As if responding to her thought, the noise grew louder.

Lily exited the apartment and went downstairs to street level, knowing she had at least ten or fifteen minutes to wait until Burt would arrive. She looked up to see her apartment window, counted to where her bedroom would be, couldn't see any signs of the infestation, just a regular window with closed blinds. On her way out, she had grabbed her purse and shoved in her phone, so she had wallet and keys, but otherwise she felt ill-equipped to be out on the street in the sandals, jeans, and t-shirt she'd thrown on in her haste to be dressed and away from her plague-infested bedroom, hair still wet from the shower, no make-up, no other preparation for a day in the world. Burt would arrive soon, and they would go inside, and one way or another, they would address the situation.

And if Burt saw the locusts, too? Some explanation —something about their breeding cycle, maybe eggs in the mattress, maybe a temperature anomaly, global warming —would surface. There was always an explanation for unexplainable phenomena. Lily, herself, was no fan of UFOs and other bullshit, and while she wasn't the religious skeptic that Burt was, she felt readier to believe in her own insanity than in a supernatural cause for what she'd just experienced. Billions of people believed in Biblical hocus-pocus, so she didn't exactly dismiss it out of hand, but she felt pretty sure that if the Bible stuff had any reality to it at all, its reality wouldn't be focused on an office manager at a printing company in an American city rather than on some important leader somewhere in the Middle East, where the apocalyptic shit was supposed to happen. The bugs hadn't been kind enough to answer her *why me* query, but it had been worth asking, because on no level, ontological or theological, did Lily having a part in Biblical plague make sense.

And if Burt *didn't* see the locusts? If even the photographs turned out to be hallucinations? Lily didn't know whether Mom and Rose or Doris and Joe could or even would afford a good mental hospital on Lily's behalf, so if hospitalization were required, Lily might be a ward of the state, which, at least according to all the movies and TV shows, was kind of like being sentenced to life in Hell. Lily might not have believed in God and heaven, but she believed in earthly hells, and no matter how crazy she might have become, she didn't fancy being locked in a ward with lots of people in loose ass-revealing gowns who drool, bang their heads on walls, and contemplate raping new inmates whenever the meds recede enough to allow for contemplation. She didn't like that her brain had been garbled enough this morning to keep her from thinking clearly about using her phone to try to document phenomena. What kind of drugs would they give her, and what kind of garbling would be the daily result? Would she, the Lily she knew herself to be, disappear into a hole of chemicals in the name of healing?

She thought again of the locusts crawling inside of her ear, ready to eat her brain, but instead of eating it, they lay eggs that looked like pills, and the pills blossomed into mushrooms that replaced brain tissue. Crazy-time mushrooms. Instead of a brain, she would have mushrooms.

The street outside Lily's apartment made the usual automotive and human noises that belong to a city, but quiet dominated, leaving plenty of room for the noise in her head to continue unimpeded. The noise made her legs feel weak, though, and a bench waited at the bus stop half a block down, so she started toward it. She stopped when she saw a man's form turn the corner at the block's end: he wore a brown leather bomber jacket. The detail was useless to cops but essential to her, as together with his polo shirt it made Earl into what Earl was, a figure fit for anything but the high-beam gang initiation, for anything but a string of murders that should have but hadn't (yet) ended with Lily.

The man in the bomber jacket started walking up the block, toward Lily. In any other circumstance, she could have simply walked in the other direction, started walking and kept walking, maybe over a few blocks, to the coffee shop where she often stopped in the morning before heading on to work, where there'd be enough witnesses to help her if the man walking toward her turned out to be Earl coming to finish what he'd started. Unless, of course, he had a gun. Then he might follow her into the coffee shop, shout, "CRAZY TIME!" and start shooting, first taking out the acne-battling barista, then the cute waitress working her way through her second year of community college, then the couple sharing a scone. And why wouldn't he have a gun? News agencies reported on suicide clusters, and criminals carried guns. Both sides won the battle of amendments, Lily had dead friends and family to prove it, and she still felt ambivalent about the victories.

In any other circumstance, she could have run. But she needed to stay here, in front of her apartment, to meet Burt, and this man in the bomber jacket, close enough to the bus stop to pull out his gun and shoot her now, hardly any range at all, was probably no one. His face was difficult to make out, not that Earl's face, always in shadows, more shadowy in the broken streetlight as time went on, had any clarity, so Lily could not know this new intruder to be Earl or not-Earl, but the chances were slim that he was Earl, here, now, after all this time, so he was probably no one. Running from no one and missing Burt as a result would condemn her to not knowing about the locusts, to being a crazy woman running through the streets with wet hair because she'd imagined a plague in her apartment, perhaps. Perhaps. Not knowing was driving her crazy. Crazier. The man in the brown bomber jacket was almost to the bench where she'd intended to sit. His face didn't *look* familiar, but he might have been, might have been—

"Good morning," he said as he walked by.

"Morning," she replied through clenched teeth. He didn't slow but disappeared further up the block.

Lily sat on the bench and tried to breathe. Her lungs felt tight, like she was going into anaphylactic shock from an insect sting. It wasn't a delayed reaction to the locusts. They didn't sting or bite; she thought, again, that locusts are a plague because they eat crops, not humans. No, the tightness in her chest, which was radiating down her arms now, mimicking incipient heart attack but on both sides, was simple panic. Doctors had explained it. She would take deep breaths. She would think calm thoughts. She would close her eyes and count back from ten. Or maybe from one hundred. Ninety-nine. Ninety-eight. Ninety-seven.

A blaring horn made her cry out and jump in her seat. A

bus had pulled up alongside the bench and opened its door. She shook her head and held out her arms, informing the driver that she should move along. The driver threw up her arms, frustrated, closed the door, and drove. Lily's heart hammered, but she got up from the bench, realizing that she was misusing it. Head down, still counting to herself, she meandered toward the exterior stairway that led to her apartment entrance.

Something poked her in the back. "Lady," a voice said in her ear, hot breath tickling it like the bug had, "keep walking straight ahead, into that alley over there, and I won't cut you with this knife you feel." On *feel*, the poking sensation became more acute.

Lily believed she had a knife in her back, a hot-breathed man behind her, holding it. She wanted to swing around, laugh in his face, saying, *Not today!* She wanted to open up her mouth and let loose a swarm of locusts that would eat him alive, but she knew she was just as likely to do the first thing as the second. Instead, she walked toward the alley.

"Good girl," the man said as if he were talking to a dog. They reached the alley, and he guided her behind a dumpster, where he forced her back against a wall and brandished the knife (easily six inches, with a serrated edge) so she could see. "Now give me your purse."

The man looked like he might be in his mid-twenties, with scraggly brown hair falling low behind his ears and a backward baseball cap hiding the rest. His complexion was tan, but he was white, at least mostly, and he had a crooked mouth with eyes too close together. If Lily had been a boot she would have stomped his ugly face forever. He couldn't have her purse. It hung on her left shoulder, and she raised her left hand as she said, "No!"

A gentle swing of the knife split her left palm, which gushed red. The young man reached for the purse strap, grabbed it from Lily's shoulder, and yanked, pulling Lily's entire body with his force. She struggled to keep her footing, and the purse slipped free, tumbling and spilling its contents as it traveled down her arm and into his possession. The phone and her wallet tumbled to the alley's asphalt ground. "Bitch," the young man said under his breath. "Make a move and the next cut *hurts.*" He bent down to collect the phone and wallet.

While he was bending, she thought again of being a boot and realized she could kick him in the stomach. Could she kick him hard enough, though, to disable him and run fast enough to get away, or would she just get far enough past him to feel the knife in her back? The pain in her hand, which had turned her whole forearm red and created splashes on the street, undermined her confidence. The phone had hit the ground hard. It was probably broken—pictures probably ruined anyway. She had less than thirty dollars in her wallet, and Burt would be here in a minute. She could call the bank, call her credit card companies—

It was broad daylight! How was this happening, right next to her apartment, in broad daylight?!! "No!" She repeated. The noise echoed in the alley. Someone would hear, but would anyone act? Since the attack in December, a name had stuck in Lily's head: Kitty Genovese. In the 1960s, she had been stabbed to death in New York with dozens of witnesses, none of whom had done anything to help. What difference did broad daylight make?

Before she could consider anything more, he was upright again, knife in front of her face. "Shut your mouth," he said, slinging the purse over his own shoulder. "Shut it," he repeated.

She found strength in a surge of hate: "*Get the fuck out of here.*" Burt would be here in a minute.

"Not yet, bitch," he said, and he spat in her face. "You got something else." In his right hand, he held the knife. His left hand traveled toward his pants, and as it got closer, the knife got closer to Lily's throat.

Oh God.

Who? The mocking voice in her head was Vince's.

The young man undid his fly. Lily looked toward the alley's entrance, toward the street and the bus stop. The dumpster almost completely blocked her position. Someone would have to be looking for them to see where she stood with the young man who was trying to push down his pants, one side at a time, with his left hand. Before getting his cock out, he looked into her eyes, his face close to her spat-on face, and said, "Push down your jeans." He pushed the sharp end of the blade close into the skin of her throat, almost breaking it, almost drawing blood again.

With both hands, she fumbled with the button, smearing blood on everything her left hand touched, including her peach-colored t-shirt that advertised a "fun run" she had done last year. If she had run before, she might have made it. If she had thought at all clearly today. If she had thought. If. The knife blade on her throat was cold and hot. She imagined it already red with her blood and wanting more. If locusts could creep after brains, knives could want blood. If any of this, if all of this, could happen to her, anything—

"*Now*, bitch," the young man said. She felt a droplet trickle down her neck. The knife must have been getting some of what it wanted. She got the button on her jeans to let go, and the zipper was easy. She pushed down jeans and panties at the same time, exposing herself. He exposed himself. She looked at his freed erection and thought about getting raped by a little dick. "Scream or fight," he said, "and you die." He pushed his crotch toward hers.

"Then KILL ME!" she screamed, and with her bloody hand, she reached down between his legs, grabbed his balls, and squeezed until she felt pubic hairs entering her open wound. She squeezed until she felt his flesh pressing flush against her palm and the insides of her fingers and made up her mind to keep squeezing until she felt greasy pus like she had when she'd punched the locust to death. As if on a delay, her ears finally reported the young man howling, and she expected her vision to go dark as the knife split her throat open wider than her palm had been, but instead, beneath the howls of the man whose balls she'd resolved to pop like grapes in her fist, she heard metal clatter against asphalt. He'd dropped the knife, so she let go, looked down at her hand, hoped some of the blood she saw was his, pushed him back, and kicked, connecting with his stomach as he doubled over. He stumbled back, and her right hand scooped up the knife from where it had fallen. She arced out with it, slashing his chest as he came back in for her, scoring a hit, splitting open his shirt, which was oddly as peach as hers was.

Her next attempt, a stab out at his chest as he lunged for her, didn't connect. The young man grabbed Lily's shoulders, and when she tried to resist by sidestepping, she got tangled in the pants she had pushed down. He slammed her back against the wall, and her head whipped forward and back. Her vision blurred, keeping at center his too-close eyes and crooked jaw, both fixed on her in pained fury. He slammed her again, and this time she heard a crack as her head met wall again. She hadn't known people actually saw stars as consciousness ebbed, but the bursts of color at the edges of her vision looked like supernovas. Darkness, which she'd expected to come with a slice of her throat, closed to a pinpoint, through which she saw the young man clutching his slashed chest and crushed testicles. As he fled, she collapsed, and there was nothing.

Except.

Burt knelt beside her. She thought he shouldn't because so much blood covered the ground. He'd get messy. But he knelt all the same, saying, "Lily! Lily!" She felt air on her private parts, realized her jeans and panties were pushed down, and felt ashamed. Her hand hurt, but her head throbbed, pulsing pain all through her neck and back, making her entire body call out. She wanted to vomit. Her brain told her confusing things about danger, about bugs, about Burt being here any minute, about Burt being here now, plagues of locusts, rapists with crooked jaws. "Lily! Lily!" Burt's voice.

"Hey there!" someone shouted from further away. The voice belonged to a woman. Lily thought, *Kitty Genovese*. "Hey you there, what are you doing? Stop! Stop!" A whistle blew. In the distance, more voices. Commotion.

Lily tried to talk. "My... pants," she said. Her right hand, the one that wasn't describing new dimensions of pain, tried to pull on her jeans. Burt saw what she was doing and tried to help.

"Don't you touch her!" a voice yelled. "POLICE! POLICE!"

"I'm trying to help!" Burt called back. "Can I get some help down here? She's bleeding!" Quieter, "Where are you hurt, Lily? What happened?"

Realizing she'd survived, that the rapist had failed, she looked around her. Lily saw the knife on the ground where it had fallen but no sign of her purse. The crushed-balled, slashed-chested, little-dicked shithead had run off with her purse and, of course, the phone. She chuckled.

"Lily?" The look on Burt's face was hard to describe. Her left hand went up to her own face, looking for the resolve she'd seen there earlier, and found that the curled-down corners of her mouth had curled up, smile or sneer. She chuckled again as she smeared her face with hot red fluid. *"Lily?"* His look was clearer now: horror.

"He took the pictures," she explained. "Should've... should've sent them to you. Wasn't thinking clearly, I guess." She was giggling now.

"That's him, Officer!"

The strangers' voices and general commotion had

drawn closer, and now everything converged on the spot in the alley behind the dumpster where Lily lay. She thought they had come to help her, but instead, she saw blue-clad arms, policemen, take hold of Burt. "What the hell?" Burt said.

"What Hell?" Lily said, and she kept laughing until she realized what was happening. The world swam.

"... right to remain silent... used against you in a court of law... right to an attorney... provide one... give up..." Burt was Mirandized.

As they took Burt away, Lily repeated, "No, no, no," but no one heard her. She pulled up her pants the rest of the way, noticing as she did how much blood she'd managed to get all over her clothes. She passed out again when they finally lifted her onto a stretcher.

5

Biblical plagues.

Lily went to bed thinking about locusts, which, web searching revealed, the Christian Bible held out as a kind of bookend specialty, beginning with them as one of the Plagues of Egypt in Exodus (bad Pharaoh!) and ending with them as one of the plagues brought forth by a trumpeting angel in Revelations (bad humanity!). Lily also went to bed thinking about bed itself, her bed, the place where she'd awakened to find a grasshopper on her head and a pool of them at her feet. Not only did she return to her apartment, unable to secure Burt's immediate release, and find swarms not swarming, but she found a vexing question.

Where was all the bugshit?

Locusts shat, she assumed. If some fluke of egg-laying in her mattress or winds near her apartment had actually unleashed and then withdrawn swarms of insects, they would have left behind massive, nasty traces, but her apartment was almost clean when she returned to it, tired, her hand stitched and bandaged so thickly that she couldn't accidentally move it.

Her would-be rapist had eluded capture. The police gave weak assurances: unlike her vague word-sketches of Earl and Rob, her description of her more recent attacker, especially his too-close eyes and crooked jaw, would be "helpful." Lily thought not. The city had ways of allowing men to disappear. Like locusts.

She didn't tell the cops about the bugs because she knew they'd think she was crazy and probably not pay attention to the attempted rape as a result. Burt would listen, if Burt had any patience for her tomorrow morning, when the cops assured her everything would be cleared up, and he would be free to go. He would spend a night in jail, and she would spend a night on the bed of locusts because the locusts hadn't shat on it. These night-spendings were little offerings to the possibility of Lily's insanity, the possibility that the non-Burt rapist, like the locusts, didn't exist. Not entirely.

Evidence, however, pointed to the horrible possibility that Lily was sane. First, and nice enough for Burt, came the knife Lily's attacker had used. It was on the ground near the dumpster that had almost kept her from "rescue," it was covered with her blood, and it had fingerprints on it, none of which belonged to Burt and only some of which belonged to Lily. Score for the existence of another attacker. Score for horrid sanity.

Second, Lily found dead bodies. Bug bodies, dead grasshoppers, in various places throughout her apartment. Their locations made her experience of an invisible barrier keeping the swarm inside her bedroom seem hallucinatory— what else would it be?—but their existence, like the knife's, made the swarm's *having been* seem like physical reality. She reckoned again that showing someone a bag of dead grasshoppers wouldn't exactly prove that swarms of locusts had targeted her apartment and then vanished, but it proved, to her at least, that her experience had not been entirely visionary. It did not explain the lack of bugshit... unless, of course, she only actually saw a few grasshoppers and then *imagined* swarms on top of them. The compromise: weird things happening *and* she was crazy. Made sense. Sort of. Score for partial horrid sanity.

So, as tainted as it seemed, she had little sane reason not to sleep in her own bed. And she had nowhere else to go.

So, she got in bed, her skin crawling, and lay there, thinking about Biblical plagues. Lying in the plague bed provided chastisement of a sort. If she had made a bed of plague, she would lie in it. Wasn't that how Biblical justice was supposed to work?

She might rather be insane. If she were completely insane, then nothing gross had happened in this bed. If she were completely insane, then somehow, four of the people closest to her hadn't died horribly, and someone hadn't just tried to rape her, all in the span of a few months. If she were completely insane, the impossibility of swarms of locusts invading her apartment and then vanishing hadn't become possible. Such a possibility would mean the world itself had gone insane. The more she considered, the more she thought she might be facing either mental illness or a kind of world illness, one plague or another, and the former seemed better than the latter in many ways.

Biblical plagues. Locusts were an odd plague for a twenty-first century urban locale. Their purpose, as she and Google understood it, was to devour crops and generally desolate the flora of the area beplagued. Lily could hardly keep a house plant alive for more than a couple of weeks, so she stopped buying them, which meant she had nothing like crops for the grasshoppers to munch on, and despite failing the greenness test, the grasshoppers were fairly normal-looking, not at all like the hybrid apocalypse warriors from the Mansworth posters, which meant they were unlikely to be on the hunt for fauna. Besides, they'd had plenty of opportunity to chow on Lily's naked flesh, which none but a few (in Lily's perception) had even wanted to touch. No, as plagues go, locusts had proven ineffective at accomplishing anything more than, well, being. And being scary. Yes, Lily had been terrified.

The locusts in Exodus are more than crop-devourers. Their coming is also Pharaoh's last warning about being nice to the Jews, ignored, of course, making the spiral toward darkness and death, the final plagues, inevitable. Locusts mean Too Late. But Lily had already had plenty of darkness and death. So much for Lily being Egypt. Wait a minute—what had she done to be plagued about, anyway?

Revelations, Biblically speaking, is the Book of Too Late. But the internet provided no information about Biblical prophecy being fulfilled one apartment at a time. Wikipedia did, however, provide a useful insight about the plagues in Exodus: another word for "plagues" was "curses."

Lily felt cursed. She fell asleep thinking about witches, who went around cursing people.

The witch-hunt in her brain began at her office, considering whether the small staff of Vince, Erin (Sales Executive), or even Burt might have some secret reason for wishing her harm and also have some secret dealings with the Dark Arts. Vince was clearly Protestant and possibly Born Again, so his having dealings with even a little Wicca seemed highly unlikely. Erin was black and might have mentioned something once about family on the Creole side of New Orleans history, which could mean voodoo, but that thought seemed kind of racist by itself and not necessarily indicative of anything. Burt was black, too. Come to think of it, Burt *had* mentioned something called the "Left-Hand Path," which she'd Googled.

Mom, Rose, Doris. No reason any of them would have turned witch and cast a curse on Lily. Well, Doris maybe. No. Not Doris. Lily didn't know what she thought about the idea of witches. The picture of a hag on a broomstick still had appeal, wart on the nose, unnatural dilation of the pupils, eyes always so wide, teeth jagged, blackened, hungry. Of course she could become beautiful with a glamour, smooth skin, long legs, young. Lily fell asleep with these images.

Thought continued in sleep. What if one of her friends,

what if Eric, Kris, or Mia, had died nursing a grudge against her? What if one of them had dabbled in something mystical (just the sort of fool thing Eric might do on a lark), a curse that backfired, killing him before it could wend its way further on a path of vengeance not nearly as petty as its cause? In the foursome, Mia pissed off Eric far more often than Lily did. Lily couldn't remember the last time she pissed anybody off. She wasn't the pissing people off type. But something might have happened. Unintentional slights filled the moments of each day, turning the world.

Eric stood on a stage wearing a magician's hat and cape. He took off the hat and set it on a nearby stool. He tapped it with a cane. Human hands appeared on the brim. Earl's head peeked out, rising slowly like a broken jack-in-the-box earning time and a half. Completing the simile, instead of a neck, the head extended up from the hat on a spring. With dilated enunciation, exaggerated bass, and no enthusiasm, Eric said, "Presto."

The bouncing Earl-head on a spring said, "Nothing in heaven, nothing in heaven, nothing in heaven."

The magic show continued when two small tables with boxes on them rolled in from the side of the stage. They spun as they rolled, and when they reached center, close to the Earl jack-in-the-box, they connected, and the two boxes joined to form a coffin. The coffin lid opened, and Mia sat up from inside. "Girls' night!" she said, and she held up her fists like a pugilist. Instead of punching toward the audience, she opened her fists and threw out heaps of confetti, more than she could have held, so much more that, for an instant, the theatre filled like a snow globe.

When the confetti settled, David stood on the edge of the stage. He was naked and had a long snout with extended canines, or lupines, as he was becoming a werewolf. The look in his eyes telegraphed agony, which seemed to make

Mia smile. "*Girls'* night!" she repeated, adding emphasis, and returning to her pugilist stance, she punched this time, hitting the transforming David (he'd sprouted extra hair now) in the back, pushing him from the stage. When he landed, outside of Lily's view, he must have burst like a water balloon, for all Lily saw was a splash of red. Mia looked at Eric and resumed her fighting pose.

From the ceiling, if there was a ceiling, Lily saw first feet, then legs, then a broomstick descend. Kris rode the broomstick down, looking her best, or as good as a woman can look in a red-sequined mini-skirt and tight tuxedo top to match. Lily searched for the strings holding up the broom and saw none. "Eat ALL your goodies, and your little dog, too!" Kris shouted, and the curtain closed.

Lily opened her eyes. She was lying in the alley, behind the dumpster where she'd been attacked. She felt as if she were waking, but she knew she still had to be sleeping. Eric, Mia, and Kris stood around her. It was night, and light from the street made everyone visible in ghostly shadows.

"Hello Lily." The words came from Eric, but he wasn't Eric, not quite.

"Lily," Kris said, and Mia smiled, except neither woman was who she was, either, and Lily reminded herself she was dreaming, which might explain why she felt awake while these three people felt less like themselves than they had felt in the previous dream.

"Who are you?" Lily asked.

"Call us by the names of the people we look like. It's simpler," Kris said.

"Okay." Lily wondered if she could jump up and fly in this dream. She thought trying might be rude, but since Kris had flown in the last dream, it also seemed fair. She sat up and made a note to try jumping if and when she got to her feet.

"We received word of your plight and come to you as advisers," Kris said.

Lily raised her arms in a one-second cheer. "Great!"

"The dead have tremendous patience for sarcasm." Eric crossed his arms and stuck his tongue out inside his cheek.

"So you're my... undead advisers in dreamland?" Lily asked.

"If that's easier for you to understand." Kris looked compassionate.

"You're annoying," Lily responded. She liked dreams, even when they involved painful visits from images of dead people, especially when they were as lucid as these, which tended to happen when she wasn't sleeping well. She remembered she had fallen asleep thinking about witches, thought of David, and realized werewolves were another curse genre: *thank you*, unconscious dream logic. Hadn't a werewolf movie involved curses and annoying undead visitors?

Mia, timing off, gave a polite laugh in response to someone. Maybe she was responding to Lily thinking about werewolves. It was, after all, a dream, in which Lily didn't have to speak her dialogue to be heard. All their minds were one, so all their thoughts might join or branch in any configuration.

"Annoying or not," Eric said, "she has something important to tell you."

Lily asked him, "Where's your hat?" He looked puzzled, but not in a way Eric would look puzzled.

Kris said, "Don't try to reason with God."

"Okay," Lily said. "Not a problem. We're not exactly on speaking terms. Never have been, really, and certainly wouldn't be now, which is something the real Kris would know, incidentally, and you all should know, as you are figments of my imagination, but that's beside the point.

What's with all the God stuff, anyway? Has the universe forgotten that I'm a confirmed agnostic?"

When Kris responded, her voice sounded in three octaves: "Your beliefs are irrelevant! Behold the dumpster!"

Lily feigned humility, but she would not be cowed by her own dream. "Okay, okay, I'm beholding. This... trash receptacle."

"And when thou mockest, shall no man make thee ashamed?" Mia asked.

"Give Kris a break," Eric said. "We have limited material to work with."

"Were you here when the dumpster was formed?" Kris asked. "Do you comprehend the ages of its particles, as timeless as the universe the memory of which you name as if it is known to you? Were you there when the atoms joined to form the elements, which made the metals crafted into steel with heat, the energy of which is also as timeless as the universe, or is the essence of time itself? All that it is, and all within, is from dust, and to dust it goes, and that dust is star dust, and star dust is the dust of your skin, and the dust of insects and dreams. What is your reason beside such particles? And your reason, when reduced to the dust of metals, skin, insects, and dreams, how might it stand up to the universe, and to God, who comprehend them all? How would you stand, then, and how would you dare, to reason with God? You, and your reason, which are but dust?"

Lily nodded. "So, what you're saying is... wait a minute. What are you saying?"

"She's saying you're the dumpster," Eric said.

"Well *shit*," Lily responded. "I am he as you are he and you are me and we are all together. Goo-goo g'joob."

"You're going to meet God," Mia said.

Lily struggled and got to her feet. Remembering, she tried a little jump but could not fly, so she said, "Mia, you've gotten creepy. Was that a death threat? Because you know, lately I don't give much of a damn."

"Damnation!" Mia said.

"Damnation," Eric agreed.

Kris nodded. "Damnation."

Like locusts and rapists, the three disappeared. In a blink, Lily was lying on the ground again, still in the alley, waking as if from a dream, as if she had been sleeping there instead of in her bed. "Wait!" she said. In another blink, she was lying in her bed, and she sat up, saying, "Wait." As annoying as her visitors—advisers—had been, they had looked like friends, and they had been company. Her apartment was empty. She cried.

The dream had ended. Kris, Mia, and Eric remained dead. Even their doppelgangers absconded with a certain level of violence. She looked up at the ceiling, stared through the roof, and said, "I don't believe in you." She flipped off heaven and smiled her best mocking smile, intending it for herself because, according to her own beliefs, she was merely pointing her middle finger at the roof of her building, nothing more. It was an odd thing to do, but she felt good doing it.

Kris had said Lily's beliefs were irrelevant. That was good because Lily wouldn't have her life becoming some morality play for people like Vince to dine out on. Serving up her life on a holy roll was not an option. She wouldn't let herself go so crazy that she'd reach a point of desperation where finding religion seemed the only sensible option and throw herself, like the unbeliever mother in *The Exorcist*, at the Church's mercy for some supernatural solution to her superlatively fucked up "plight," as Kris had called it. What if she brought the bag of dead locusts to an entomologist priest and discovered that they were of some rare Middle Eastern breed that had no business being in North America? That would take away weight from the compromise, hallucination-cum-reality explanation of Lily's experience that she had come to prefer. Lily had decided, and the dream had helped her, to think that she was at least a little bonkers instead of being hunted by God—bonkers enough to *consider* being hunted by a non-existent God, not to *believe* it. Her beliefs were relevant, damn it. Damnation!

Before Lily got out of bed, she considered: her sanity and life itself might depend on avoiding evidence of God's existence. More than the bugs—something more—and she might be swept up into full-blown religious mania. In her dream, dream-Mia, alien-dream-Mia, had lapsed into Bible-speak. Had she been quoting something? If so, where had she gotten the quote? Must've come from Lily's brain, like the rest of the dream, but Lily didn't know Bible stuff that well. The locust hallucination made sense because of the weird posters from Mansworth, but what had Mia said... something with an "est" and a "thee" or a "thou," sounded legit... where had that come from? Lily probably picked it up somewhere, had to have. But it still struck her as kind of uncanny.

All this Biblical stuff had started with those posters. They raised bizarre questions about belief mainly because of something Burt had said about the Left-Hand Path, an idea about going against God, seeing the destruction promised in the posters' images as affirmation, as a way of believing in God, which in turn is better than not believing in the first place. When it came to thees and thous, Lily wasn't too up on the Bible, but her English lit education allowed her to access Milton's greatest hits, and she could quote Satan: "Evil, be thou my Good!" *That* was the Left-Hand Path, or, with the help, once again, of the internet, she understood it to be a suspension of traditional good evil definitions in favor of self-gratification and other kinds of goodness that would make a God-fearing man like Vince quake in his booties. In mystical terms, the

Left-Hand Path is the Dark Side of the Force, black magic, bad hoodoo, but also Buddhist and Hindu ideas about achieving demonic or god-like states of being (lest one think the West had cornered the market on the sinister).

How did Burt know about any of this stuff, anyway? She looked at her clock, noticing the sun was already rising. In a few hours, she'd go to pick him up at the jail. For now, she had to think.

Witches, the kind of witches who would put a curse on her, traveled the Left-Hand Path. And if the Bible called a curse a *plague*, what did witches call curses?

Hexes. Lily had to consider whether she might be *hexed*. She typed, "How do you know if you are hexed?" into her laptop and read some of the results. According to ten out of ten of the top "answers" sites, she qualified by virtue of the misfortunes shared by her and her loved ones of late, never mind that she *had* been feeling overly fatigued lately.

Searching also returned several hits on the notion of the "hex bag," a common source of curses on the television show *Supernatural*, according to several wikis, and related to medicine bags, mojo bags, and other mystical goodie bags from several traditions. The idea, familiar enough, was that some malefactor would take some item or body part belonging to the target—along with spell-specific snips, snails, and puppy-dog tails—and combine them ritually in a bag. Said malefactor would then plant said bag somewhere near the target, and target would begin to suffer the hex effects. If target were to find and destroy the bag, effects over.

Was Lily *really* about to search her apartment for a hex bag?

She returned to her bedroom, imagining the pool of locusts that had appeared at her feet. She searched beneath her sheets and beneath the mattress pad. Thinking it couldn't hurt, she tried lifting the mattress, and it *did* hurt, her lower back anyway, but she kept it up long enough to look as far as she could see. She repeated the process on two other sides until she was content she had seen all there was to see between mattress and box springs: nothing. She looked under the bed and found a warren of dust bunnies and a box of old shoes about which she'd completely forgotten, nothing else. The rest of the apartment remained. Was she going to do this thing?

Next stop, closet.

Hours later she'd found no hex bag, but she'd made several large messes and discovered along the way that she owned a teddy bear she didn't recall. It was missing an eye, which shifted it from cute to creepy, and looked like it had had stitches *pulled* from its left leg. Who would mutilate a stuffed bear in this fashion was unknown to Lily; she did not recall any visitor-children who might have brought such an abused captive.

She also discovered three forks and a butter knife in her silverware drawer that had odd contortions. In the life of a fork, things occur that bend tines. This fact of fork existence Lily knew and accepted. However, she could not fathom the bending of tines in opposite directions at near-right angles. Such bending seemed deliberate, and she had both acquired her forks new and never set about bending them at right angles. The butter knife was cleft, like a devil's forked tongue.

The third discovery—and things happening in threes, by themselves, put Lily on alert—was a cloth, a plain enough originally white square, perhaps a handkerchief, of unknown origin, for just as Lily recalled no teddy-mutilating child-visitors, she recalled no handkerchief-droppers. The problem of this particular handkerchief lay in its being soaked with a red stain that appeared, to Lily, to be blood. She discovered the bloody handkerchief in the kitchen, between the microwave and the toaster oven. It made no sense.

Feeling unenthusiastic about the day, Lily went to pick

Burt up from jail. On the drive home, he told her what happened.

"I thought jail cells were always you and one other person, but then again, I've never been arrested before. I guess that's lucky for a middle-aged black man, statistically speaking. But I don't want to talk about that now. I've got to... maybe I shouldn't... but I've got to get this out of my head, and I kind of think... I kind of think you'd want to know. You never struck me as the kid gloves type, you know? Even now, after, well, after all of this. Maybe especially now. If telling you is wrong, please let me say I'm sorry in advance. I'm sorry. I'm sorry. But there were four of us. There was this big Latino guy, Hector, who scared the hell out of me, mostly because he was big, like that actor, Danny Trejo. This other guy, Marcus, who was black, said Hector reminded him of somebody, and that's who Hector said. I never would have thought of the guy's name otherwise, but he was spot on. Danny Trejo.

"Marcus was a little shorter than I am but thicker around the middle, with big arms, too, so he wasn't *not* scary. Everything scared me a little, I guess, because it was, you know, jail. There I was, being held on suspicion of—what? You'd already told them I wasn't guilty of the attempted rape. I was being held on suspicion of incomplete paperwork, I guess. But it had to mean I was being held in the place where they put rapists, which means the other guys might have been guilty of stuff that bad. I've never been around people like that, you know? Big and scary and capable of who knew what. I mean, armed guards were right outside the bars, so you'd think we were in one of the safest places in the world, that would make sense, except you'd have to expect people to act in their own interest, and if they did that, they wouldn't be there in the first place, right? There were four cots, and Hector got in one almost right away, like he was going to sleep, and I thought, no way in hell I'm sleeping. I sat down on the floor, which hurt my back, but I figured I'd stand, sit, pace, whatever, but sleep? With these guys around? Not happening.

"The fourth guy. He was the quiet white guy who looked about as scared as I felt, but I hoped I was hiding it better than he was. He didn't say his name when we were doing intros. I at least said I was Burt and offered a handshake that the other guys looked like they were going to spit on, but this white guy, he sat on the floor, hugging his knees, and he didn't move. If he'd come any closer to being shaped like a ball I think the other two guys might have kicked him around the cell a little, just for the heck of it. But they left him alone. I wanted to leave him alone, too. He had an aura. His skin had a kind of sick green to it. I chalked it up to nerves, and the other guys, they might have figured that if they pressed in the wrong place, all kinds of green puke would have come streaming out, like from some doll that's the spit-up equal to Betsy Wetsy. The skin didn't bother me as much as the eyes did, wide and covering half his face like a Japanese cartoon. The man didn't look natural. He had sandy blond hair and looked as unnatural leaned up against bars and hugging his knees as I felt locked up with Hector and Marcus with their big arms and confident name-exchanging getting ready to sleep during what I expected to be the longest night of my life.

"Hector slept, but Marcus sat on another cot and tried talking to me for a while, told me about problems with his girl, only he didn't have nice words for her at all, because in his mind she was the reason he'd gotten caught up in some robbery or other. He was completely innocent, and he kept contradicting himself, going over things, like he was using me as a springboard to iron out his story. I listened, smiled, nodded, whatever, said supportive things about what a rotten girl she must've been, except I didn't use nice words, either, because I needed to fit in with him, you know? And the whole time I kept an eye on that fourth guy, the green white guy, sitting there against the bars, hugging his knees and keeping his eyes wide. Marcus talking and Hector sleeping made me stop being afraid of them so much, but I wasn't going to sleep. The adrenaline from having the cops sling me around and shove me in the back of a patrol car and search me and fingerprint me and all the rest was wearing off, and I was bone tired, but I wasn't going to sleep, because underneath the adrenaline wearing off was another kind of electricity, the kind that jolts you when your eyelids close for more than a few seconds as if you're edging off a cliff. Staying awake felt like staying alive, and less and less I felt like I had to watch Hector and Marcus, but more and more I had to watch the green white guy, who hugged his knees and rocked back and forth to the rhythm of something I couldn't hear or see.

"Finally Marcus said he was going to sleep for a little bit, and I should, too, and I felt like I had to act like I was going to, because the cell was half-dark, because a guy with bigger arms told me to, I don't know. I went to a cot, the one second closest to the green white guy because the closest one was the only other choice, and stretched out my legs, half lying back as if I might consider sleeping. I watched the knee hugger from the corner of my eye. He was nodding now, agreeing with what, I don't know. As ugly as talking to Marcus about his bitch girlfriend had been, I recognized I missed the company, because now all I had was the quiet dark and the need to stay awake and keep an eye on the green-white guy, and what was I supposed to do? Sit on the cot and just stare at him? I supposed that would make me just as bad as he was, sitting there, wide-eyed, staring out at nothing.

"What's that, Lily? Witches have wide eyes? What are you talking about?

"Anyway, that's what I did. The green-white guy and I just stared, me at him and him at nothing. Guards on the small block of cells changed at some point, but that didn't change our situation, the staring. Hector or Marcus was snoring, maybe both of them, I don't know. The only thing that changed is that slowly, the knee-hugger started rocking back and forth faster, started nodding his head faster, too. It was like the silent music that moved him was picking up speed, so he did, too. His back bounced him off the bars but didn't make any sounds, didn't shake anything, other than my nerves, that is. At one point I might have given anything—well, a lot—just to get that man to stop moving. He beat on my mind like a metronome getting little, almost imperceptible pushes from a breeze, faster and faster. Tickle torture came to mind. His movements tickled my nerve endings and made me want to scream.

"When he got to a point where he moved so fast that his back hitting the bars sounded mechanical, I thought I had to do something. I thought about waking Hector up and saying the man had made rude remarks about Hector's mother. I thought about waking Marcus up and saying the man had confessed to being in league with Marcus's girlfriend. I thought about calling for the guards, saying the man was making death threats. *Anything*. The guy had to be stopped. And then it happened.

"I don't know what triggered him. The nodding and the rocking reached a point of sync where the head tilted back before the rest of the body and came forward as the knees were coming back, so the jaw slammed into the knees. Through the dim light I saw the hit and expected to hear a loud clamping of teeth, but the sound was muted. The hit must have hurt, but it happened again, this time with the head staying still: knees came up and slammed against a set jaw, and, more clearly, I heard teeth clamp. Lips stretched in a wide smile. Shadows might have been tricking me, but I thought I saw something dark leak from the corner of the man's mouth.

"Planting the soles of his shoes on the cement cell floor, the green-white man, paler now, pushed himself to a stand. His head tilted back, and I could see his throat working, like he was trying to swallow. His mouth fell partially open, and I saw trickles, for sure this time, from both sides of his face. He made a gargling noise. I should have acted. I should have figured out what was going on. But I felt mesmerized, as if the hours of watching his rocking motions had been deliberate hypnosis.

"He stumbled toward the center of the cell, and a noise, I don't know how it escaped, came from the center of his throat and chest. Low and guttural, distorted by blockage, the noise erupted, and with it blood spurted from his mouth like a geyser.

"'Hey!' I yelled. Marcus stirred. I yelled again, and again, and Marcus and Hector both woke up in their cots, looking at me with menace.

"The man with the blood-geyser mouth had lost all his green and looked pale except for the blood covering most of his face and running down his chest and arms. He stumbled further from his starting point, toward Hector's cot. Hector was sitting up, looking at the man, coming into wakefulness and figuring out the situation. A guard was arriving outside the cell, asking about the ruckus.

"As he stumbled, the man seemed to try to keep his head back, but with each movement, the effort looked more difficult. He lolled; he struggled for footing. Hector got to his feet, suggesting that the man get the fuck away while one of the guards realized to some extent what was happening and called for the cell to be opened. When Hector tried pushing the man away, the man's head lolled forward and catapulted a mouthful of blood onto Hector's face and neck. Blood welled from his mouth now, like a fountain.

"I'm sorry, Lily, too much detail. I... I've never seen anything like it. It's like I'm still there, watching. The man's eyes, already too wide, started to bulge, vessels bursting. The guards who rushed in backed away at first in disgust, not realizing he was choking to death on the tongue he'd bitten off until he fell down on the floor. Then there was so much blood in his lungs, too, I guess, that he was going to drown or choke or whatever... the man died right there in front of me.

"The thing about it, Lily, the thing that makes me risk upsetting you, is that—

"You're right. How did you know?

"He wasn't the first. I heard it from the guards. They've had three suicides. Two prisoners and a guard. They had just had a briefing about suicide clusters, been told to be on the lookout for suspicious activity, but it's a jail. Everybody looks suspicious. They couldn't know. But how did you know, Lily? How did you?"

6

"Oh my God." Burt surveyed the mess in the front office, where Lily often worked. Lily stood in the doorway behind him. They came in together because they'd driven in together from Lily's apartment, in the living room of which Burt had slept almost every night for the last two weeks. Her sleeping at his place would have been a concession to their backward plunge toward cohabitation, but since Burt's night in jail, he'd expressed a desire to avoid going home, and Lily felt fine not being alone in the apartment since the locusts incident, about which Burt had become well-informed, so although she felt twisted about the state of things, he slept at her place, and they came to work together.

Work, P-Cubed, now opened and fluorescents-lit before them, lay burgled and trashed. Drawers and cabinets flung open, register on its side, machines smashed, compartments pried apart, spools rent, cartridges ripped, papers scattered. The lock on the front door looked like it had been punched out. The alarm system looked smashed, which didn't indicate why it hadn't gone off.

"I don't know how much of this the insurance will cover," Burt said. "I think we've got a pretty big deductible." Had that been his first thought, or had he quickly thought through the other things before that had become his first articulation?

"I...." Lily thought that, as office manager, she should know their deductible and theft coverage, but she didn't. "I don't know."

A clattering came from Erin's office.

"It's probably nothing," Burt said.

Lily looked from the barely sunlit office to Burt. "I'm sure it's nothing." They both stepped toward Erin's office, shoeing over fallen office supplies and printing equipment of all shapes and colors as they went. They heard another clattering, but it sounded muffled. Their advance brought them within a stride of the office door, and they halted for a conference: to carry on? To call the police, in whom neither of them had much confidence at present? To gain or forego knowledge of whether they might actually have an unlikely encounter with a perpetrator?

They decided they should wait to hear more, to determine whether they were making something out of nothing, as they kept going anyway because what they really wanted was to find out whether somebody was in the other room. They passed through Erin's doorway with shoulders touching, Lily only slightly behind, and examined the office, which had desk drawers open and askew, items thrown willy-nilly, files upset. No sign of another person in the office. They both felt silly.

Until they saw the movement through the window. Someone stood outside with a can of spray paint and was busy writing on the large plate glass, in huge lettering Lily and Burt had to read backward, "GO HOME TERRO—"

"What on *Earth* is he writing?" Lily asked.

"I wish I could say I don't know," Burt said, "but I think it's 'Go Home Terrorist,' or something like that."

"Does he mean us? Or you?" Lily asked.

"I don't know," Burt said. Bewilderment, sheer wonder, filled both their voices.

"Do you think he—I mean—he's a white kid…"

"Uh-huh."

"Do you think he might be…"

"Confusing me for someone else?"

"Oh my God." Lily felt her stomach fold. "I'm either going to laugh or throw up."

"Uh-huh."

"I'm going out there." Lily marched toward the nearest exit, the front.

Burt stood transfixed a moment more before saying, "Lily, wait," and following.

Lily tromped back through the main office full of broken equipment and supplies and blew through the front door. She circled around to Erin's big window with Burt close behind. "You there! You! With the paint!"

The young man with the paint can stopped at the end of "GO HOME TERROR." He looked at Lily, started to laugh, then stopped himself, eyes widening.

"Lily, stop," Burt called from behind. Lily was not stopping.

She continued her march toward the young man, to whom she repeated, "You there!"

He dropped the paint can and ran. Lily ran after him, Burt too befuddled by her behavior to react until too late. Even as she started running, she felt a lack of understanding of her own reasoning, but she ran anyway.

The young man, longer-legged, taller, and in much better shape, outpaced Lily immediately. He put a block between them, but she regained it when a light turned in her favor. Every time a way across a street or through an uncrowded walkway opened, the young man approached escape, but lights, cars, pedestrians, cones, and other obstructions all worked in Lily's favor, a circumstance that struck her as odd despite the more pressing matters of the pain in her feet, stitch in her side, and blurring of her vision. The people who stood in the young man's way stayed out of Lily's as she traced his steps; the traffic that he waited for waited for her.

In an alley clear enough for the young man to sprint, Lily's legs started to cramp so hard that she had to obey the forces throughout her body repeating Burt's injunction to *stop*. Watching ahead for her quarry to turn a corner and leave her behind, forever, Lily stopped, leaned against a building, and heaved breaths as if she'd been choking. The young man did not disappear. He halted near the alley's opposite end, catching his breath and looking back at her. His bearing expressed puzzlement.

Maybe he realized that all this time he'd been running from an unarmed, smaller woman. If so, Lily was about to get what she'd been after, which she supposed was… good? She had thought about chasing him, not gotten as far as what to do if she caught him. She felt rather like a small dog that mostly belonged to Rose while she was growing up: it would always chase after bunnies, but it wouldn't have had a clue about what to do if it had ever succeeded in catching one. Right now, seeing the young man looking at her, Lily rated her intellection in the vicinity of that dog's, possibly lower, as this young man posed far greater threats than bunnies.

His face, visible in vague, generic details even at his distance, registered one of the few looks Lily had seen on it before: he seemed about to laugh, but then he stopped himself, cheeks drooping, eyes widening. He gazed directly at her, or perhaps over her shoulder. The look made a chill pass down her spine. He ran, disappearing from the alley and Lily's life.

Lily looked at the building she was leaning on, felt

grateful to its white concrete. She'd never given much thought to the small number of blocks between P-Cubed and the row of skyscrapers on Spring Street that marked the fashionable edge of downtown, but that was how far their run had brought them. The protests of her lungs and legs insisted that they had run miles, but of course they hadn't, and she couldn't if she wanted to. No, this early in the morning, a person could just run as far as, say, the dog park in about as much time as you would need to drive there. In fact—

Lily backed away from the building, looking up at it as she did. She was indeed in an alley by Spring Street. The building where she leaned, this tower, in fact, was 1500 Spring Street. The home of Mansworth Futures and Securities, makers of apocalyptic motivational posters.

Coincidence that the young man led her *here*? Probably, except—coincidence that the young man targeted P-Cubed for harassment? Ever-so-likely, except—was the burglary, which had to have involved people who actually took stuff, a coincidence, too? Maybe so, maybe not, except—was the suicide in the jailhouse a coincidence? The attempted rape? David's suicide? The roadside attack? Were they all coincidences? Were *none* of them coincidences?

Lily had seen a play in college where these two guys keep flipping a coin that always comes up the same way, and because you think it has to change sometime, you bet on change, so it's always against you. That's curse logic. You keep getting the same results—bad ones. Things being so bad doesn't make sense. Sooner or later, you think probability is broken. You think the game is fixed. So much bad can't be random. There has to be a reason for the senselessness. You won't settle for coincidence and chance anymore. Your only choices are reason and insanity. So, you're going to find that reason or go crazy trying. Either way you end up somewhere other than where you began.

The young man had led Lily here, to 1500 Spring Street, home of Mansworth Futures and Securities. Maybe it was a coincidence, but standing at the base of the giant phallic structure, it felt like anything but. Rather, the building seemed to have its own gravity, its own atmosphere, to hold people and objects in its own limited but significant orbit. The skyscraper —sixty stories, or thereabout—jutted up like a white finger toward the clouds, armored with silver-reflective windows that made the whole look like a stick of light when caught from just the right angle. It had beckoned her here, using the young man as its instrument. It had brought her. Gazing up at it, she almost fell backward, her vision still dazed from the run, her breath still short. So close to it, she felt it absorb her.

The front doors faced Spring Street. She'd soaked through her work clothes with sweat, and as far as she knew, her feet were bleeding inside the flats she'd used to think of as comfortable. Much as she hadn't known what she'd do if she'd caught up to the young man—and she was glad, now, that he'd run off, because she didn't think running after him had been a death wish, and she also didn't think she could have fought him, successfully—she didn't know what she'd do if she went inside the building. She expected it to be like every other office building. It wasn't the biggest or most noteworthy tower in the city, or even on the street. It was just 1500 Spring, not the Harris Building, or one of the buildings named for banks or insurance companies.

Uncertain of her legs, Lily exited the alley, walking to Spring Street and the front of the building. Sets of regular doors and the rotary doors in the center taunted her to enter— dare she? Contemplating, she heard a voice: "I know that thou canst do every thing, and that no thought can be withholden from thee! Wherefore I ABHOR myself, and repent in dust and ashes!!!" At the building's far corner, a man—he looked Asian, and he held an orange sign on which, in block letters, appeared, "REPENT!"—stood shouting.

Lily hurried to him. "Excuse me." Awareness of how ridiculous her sweaty blouse must have looked, ridiculous even to a man in tattered brown jacket and pants, made her blush. "Excuse me, but what were you saying?"

"REPENT!" They both looked at his sign as if she were an idiot.

She smiled, feeling as if she should give him a dollar but knowing she had set her purse down in the office before joining Burt to investigate the strange clattering. "I got that part," she said. "What was the rest? I mean, you don't have to repeat it. I got it. With the thees, and the thous. I was wondering. What was it from?"

"The Bible!"

"Oh yes," Lily said. She imagined Googling "I abhor myself" and "Bible" and getting a million hits. "I got that part, too. But, uh, what part, of The Bible, if you don't mind?"

"Book of Job!" The man shouted the answer with less verve than his previous shoutings. "Ma'am, do you know Jesus Christ? Have you accepted him as your Lord and Savior?"

"Yes, yes, of course," Lily said. She had for a brief period during childhood. It was after the Santa Claus phase, before puberty, and it had annoyed Rose. She went around saying "God Bless You" for everything but sneezes and "Christ forgives you" for sneezes.

"Then you know better." His eyes looked wide, and though he stared toward her, he might have looked at her shoulder instead of at her.

Another chill passed down her spine. "Know better than what?" She wanted to run again. She took a step back.

"Than to try to reason with God," the man answered.

She took another step back, almost stumbled into the oncoming traffic of Spring Street. She looked behind her, found the crosswalk, waited for the signal, and wandered into the street as if she'd taken a new blow to the head. Halfway back to the office before she regained her senses, she decided not to tell Burt about the man she considered a prophet with the REPENT! sign. She'd reached a critical mass of weirdness, and she suspected he might have passed his already.

The furor she found him in confirmed her suspicion. When she stepped through the front door, he twirled around. Relief passed over his face, but it disappeared back into an ocean of frustration and resentment. "You're back."

Lily considered the sweat running down her spine, making her blouse cling to her skin. "Yes." Burt fumbled with part of a printer, some hunk of metal and plastic that didn't belong outside of a machine. "He... got away."

"Good," Burt said. "He could have killed you, you know." He threw the hunk of metal and plastic toward the ground. It collided against more misplaced metal and plastic. The collision's sound made a noticeable difference in the position of Burt's jaw.

Lily wanted to say No, he could not have killed me. He could not have killed me because It, whatever It was that was after her, could have killed her at any moment. Challenged, she realized she had chased the young man through city streets without any means of subduing him if she actually caught up to him because she had no reason to care about being outmatched. She was immortal, immortal because death could and would come at any time it chose, but it didn't. It was saving her for something, and that something was not being killed by some random spray-paint hooligan after a hopeless chase the point of which was a confrontation with 1500 Spring. She felt as certain that the point of the chase was its endpoint as she felt certain that she had woken up this morning, which was not altogether certain—she might have been dreaming—but either all was a dream or none, and ending up at that building, with the REPENT! prophet, had been no more or less dream than going into Erin's office and finding the GO HOME TERROR messenger.

Burt was not ready for this bit of curse logic. All he got was: "He didn't have a chance to touch me."

"You know, I still haven't called the police about this mess, but I almost called them to help you." Burt kicked the piece of machinery he'd thrown down and looked like he'd hurt his foot. "I just didn't know what to say. You were gone before I could react, gone around the corner. I should have run after you, but I didn't know which way to go. I was... dumbfounded. I felt...." He kicked the broken equipment again, and it bounced a short way across the littered carpet. His breathing was fast. He was sweating, too.

Lily knew she was supposed to comfort him now. Her running after the young man, leaving him behind, or perhaps her coming back, had affronted Burt's manhood. That damned phallic tower. Goddamned men. But he looked sweet in his confusion, deserving of comfort. Too bad she didn't have any. "Powerless. You felt powerless."

"What?" He spoke as if snapping out of a reverie, but the pause had not been long enough to allow for any real contemplation. Perhaps she had used a foreign language. Maybe she was talking to herself.

"It's a feeling I've gotten to know, powerlessness. Look at this place." Lily gestured at the ruins of P-Cubed, the business at the center of Burt's middle-aged life. "You know that guy I chased probably didn't even do it? He wasn't carrying anything but that paint can. And stuff is missing, right?"

"Everything," Burt said. "The starter from the register, the petty cash, the fucking ink cartridges from the large-format laser printers, for God's sake. It's like they knew what to take and smashed everything else. They even took the little Blu-ray player I hook up to my laptop for presentations. And the laptop, of course. I've been leaving it here because I haven't been working from home because I haven't been *going* home because—"

"Of me," Lily finished. "Do you blame me?"

"No," Burt answered too quickly. "It's just that…."

"What?"

"You told me about how in the middle of everything you saw those, uh, grasshopper-locusts and started thinking about plagues, and curses, and started wondering if you might be cursed, even if what you'd seen hadn't been, you know, all the way real," Burt said. Tactful.

"Yeah," Lily said, "I did."

Burt kicked at debris for emphasis. "I think I must be cursed, too, huh?"

Lily thought of pointing out the radical asymmetry between their situations, but she decided against.

Burt looked at his watch. "Erin and Vince will be here in less than an hour. I'll have to tell them they don't have jobs anymore. I can't run a business with no equipment! No offices! You and me, we're out of work now. We've got graffiti on the side of the building telling us to go back to Baghdad or wherever, as if we've ever even been there, and I'm confused, Lily. How in hell does shit like this even happen? Maybe if my name was Abdul Mohammad or something, but I'm Burt fucking Wells, as American as anybody else in this city, white, black, or otherwise. Not that that should matter, but I can't help thinking it. And I still keep seeing that guy in the jail cell, spitting out blood like a fountain. How do you stop seeing things like that? How do you stop seeing?"

"I don't."

Burt levelled his eyes at her, exhaled, crossed to a stray chair, and sat. "I don't suppose you do." He pointed to another chair, suggesting she sit. She did, her legs gasping in thanks as she finally released them. "So you must have asked 'Why me?' Got any answers?"

"Why you?" Lily closed her eyes and imagined Eric, Kris, and Mia standing behind her. "Because you have the misfortune of being near me."

"Hmph. So, it's all about you." Burt folded his arms across his chest.

Lily tried not to sound angry. "Unless more has happened that you're not saying, it's a little more about me than it is about you."

"All right, all right." Burt nodded. "You're cursed, and I'm curse-adjacent. So why *you*?"

Because she tried to reason with God? That made no sense—God wasn't even a significant part of her thoughts before all this began. She looked over her shoulders, to where she imagined Kris, Mia, and Eric standing. "Because I lived. Maybe I wasn't supposed to. Maybe that gunshot was supposed to kill me."

"Horse shit. I remember the commercials for those movies. Tony Todd played death, who came to get people who cheated him. You think you cheated death, and now he's pissed off at you? Is that it? That's called survivor's guilt, Lily."

"I know that. And I've been told once or twice before." He made her feel weary. "I've seen them, you know. They came to me in a dream. Only it wasn't them. They were, like, possessed."

"Lily...."

"It was a dream, okay? But they said things I have trouble believing came out of my brain. Mia quoted something I don't think I knew. She quoted something from the Bible, and Kris talked about reasoning with God. Actually, there's a whole lot of God stuff going on, which is really freaking me out, like I've got some repressed religious issues or something. And I think Kris and Mia were talking about the Book of Job. Do you know anything about that?"

"I was raised in the Church, remember?" Burt snorted. "God let Satan torture Job in order to prove a point about faith. Job loses everything, gets boils all over his body, nasty stuff. As far as reason is concerned, part of the point is that God's mysterious ways move beyond man's reasoning, or some shit like that. Personally, I think the point is that God is a sadist."

Lily nodded with indifference. "But reasoning with God —that's a bad thing, right?"

"No. From what I remember, the Bible says God likes humans to come try to reason with him, like having his kids come babble at him for his amusement. I think it's in Isaiah, or Jonah—you know, the one where the guy gets eaten by a whale, more fun stuff—or one of the other prophets."

Lily looked over her shoulder, where she imagined her friends standing, and she remembered the graffiti artist's gaze settling not on her but by her, and the REPENT! prophet's eyes doing the same. What were they looking at? Did some figure actually loom there, just as she imagined? Maybe her friends were haunting her, had been following her since the initial catastrophe, spinning more disasters as revenge for her surviving the first.

"Burt I'm scared."

"What are you scared of?"

"I think something's wrong with me."

"Nothing is wrong with you."

"I think I've gone crazy."

"Aside from a few hallucinations and a deadly tendency to run after criminals, you've stayed remarkably sane under the circumstances, I say."

"I'm serious."

"So am I." Burt stood up from his chair and walked carefully, stepping over debris, to Lily's. He knelt. "You've got a right to be scared. I'm scared, and only a couple of things have happened to me. The shit that's happening to you—it's unbelievable. It's too much. I'm guilty of thinking you sound paranoid, I admit, but you know what? I think it must be contagious, because now I'm thinking that everything you've said makes a lot of sense. Unless there's someone, some evil motherfucker, literally plotting against the both of us, there's no natural way all this shit could be happening."

"And when you have eliminated the impossible, whatever remains, however improbable, must be the truth," Lily said.

"Who said that?"

"Arthur Conan Doyle," Lily said. "And he went to séances."

"Séances? What?"

Lily considered while she looked over her shoulder, and she laughed singly. "Checking in with the dead might not be a bad idea."

"Lily, be serious!"

"I told you I'm serious!" Lily stood up and almost knocked Burt over. Despite the throbbing in her feet and legs, she strode into the debris field. "I thought you were being serious when you said nothing natural could be behind this shit."

"I was."

"If it's not natural, what's left? I, for one, don't have personal ties to the supernatural. Do you? If there's something unnatural or supernatural causing all the things happening to the both of us, we need to know what it is, don't we?" Lily circled back on him in predatory exasperation.

"But a séance?" Burt said. "Have you ever been to one? I mean really? It sounds… silly."

"And I suppose that, in addition to being raised in the Church, you're also an expert on séances?"

"Well no. But don't you have to—" and he rose to his feet —"hold hands with a psychic or something?"

"I don't know. Don't people hold hands and sing songs at church?" Lily tapped an expectant finger behind her ear.

Burt frowned. "I didn't like church, either."

A few hours later, Vince and Erin had the bad news about P-Cubed and were staying home. Burt and Lily were waiting in the parlor of Lady Laetitia, Extreme Psychic. The "parlor" looked like a typical living room except for the beads that hung in doorways; otherwise, it had a sofa, loveseat, rocking chair, television, and various other signs of living, including a pigtailed middle-schooler doodling on her homework. The only other exception to standard living room décor was a glass showcase near the front entrance, in which various crystals, a geode, packs of tarot cards, a few books, and other items all sat neatly arranged with price tags. Above the case hung a menu of services, mostly readings of different durations, reasonably priced for the thrifty esoteric. At the bottom of the list appeared the words "Please Inquire." Without context, they might have meant anything, but Lily believed they must have referred to other services—such as séances—that space or credulity forced the Great Lady to omit from the list. On the phone, however, the Great Lady's assistant had assured them that a séance of thirty or sixty minutes could be had for a very reasonable price and with minimal fuss. Satisfaction guaranteed!

"Tarot cards," Lily said. "Aren't those supposed to be iffy? More on the left hand than the right?"

"Nah," Burt said. "Some Christians even use them. Those crystals and such look like good-guy stuff to me. The cards are merely a tool, I think. Depends on who uses them."

"Oh." What Burt said clicked with what Lily already knew, which mostly came from movies, but since he'd already proven to have more knowledge than she did, she preferred to play dumb, leaving larger blanks than necessary for him to fill. They both needed the confidence his pontification could provide.

An older woman with deep lines covering her face stuck her head through beads: "Come on back."

The room through the beads had the design of a dining room, with an additional, broad, curtain-covered entryway into a space with a tiled floor that was likely a kitchen. At center stood a round table with four chairs. No crystal ball ornamented it; no draping of red velvet or gold lame made the table look spiritual. Even the curtain sectioning off the probable kitchen looked plain in its beige, making only the plastic blue beads between parlor and... psychic event room... appear as one might expect. The walls were a cheery, inoffensive off-white with various cross-stitches of boats and folksy sayings. "Old friends never die; they just fade away."

"I'm Lady Laetitia," the woman said. "Folks call me Tish. You're Burt and Lily. You can think I know that because I'm psychic or because you told us that on the phone. Whichever makes you happier, I don't mind. Have a seat." Burt and Lily sat at the round table. "I understand you want to talk to some dead people. Now for a reading, I ask up front whether you want thirty or sixty minutes, but for talking to dead folks, I don't ask. It isn't up to me, you understand? Mostly it's up to them, and mostly they don't stick around that long. So if it runs long, I'll charge you more, but you'll pay what I call the contact fee, which is what was mentioned on the phone. You okay with that?"

They agreed on the up-front price and on "extreme contact overage."

"Good. Let me get another thing straight with you. If you want me to play a tape with moaning, and set up some extra piles of crap to get knocked down at dramatic moments, and things like that, I can do it, but first of all, you'll have to go back to the parlor while I get my man in here and we set up, and second of all, there's an extreme séance service fee. Mostly I'm tired of that bull, but I'll do it for you. Mostly people who want that don't call for same-day service. You strike me as practical folk who just want some information from somebody who croaked. Am I wrong?"

They supposed she wasn't, although Lily didn't know what information they sought.

"Okay then." Tish set her open hands on the table, one extended toward Lily, one toward Burt. "Let's hold hands." Burt looked at Lily and grimaced. "Just kidding!" Tish said, looking at Lily. "I wanted to give your man a rile." She looked at Burt. "I didn't offer a handshake, because mostly I don't like touching people, either." She shook her head. "Why would I have to touch you people to talk to dead people? It eludes me. Sure, it's part of the show, if you want a show. Hand-holding? Ten dollars. You want it?"

They declined.

"Good. Now then, you can tell me who I'm contacting, or you can make me try to guess. I'll tell you right off I'm feeling the letter M. Is that right?" Lily nodded. "Now tell me, Lily, does M always talk like she's in a Shakespeare play?"

"What do you mean?" Lily knew what Tish meant.

"She keeps saying 'thou.' Thou art troubled, Lily. Thou art troubled. If you ask me, you wouldn't be here if thou wasn't troubled, would thou? But she keeps saying it." Tish shook her head. "Thou might do better if thou asks a question."

"Wait a minute," Burt said, almost standing from the table. "That's it? We sit down, and you just start talking?"

"M doesn't know you're in the room," Tish said to Burt. "And like I said, you want bells and whistles, it's a little late, but we can add them." She took a deep breath and looked at the ceiling. "Oh Great Spirits, speak to us from the heavens! Fill us with fear and trembling at—"

The table jumped off the ground and landed with a thud.

"I appreciate you getting into it, but don't break my table," Tish said to Burt.

"I didn't do anything." Burt gave Lily a look of protest. With her eyes and shoulders, Lily signaled her innocence.

Tish shook her head. "What do you mean, nobody's innocent? Lily, there's a second woman here. M and somebody else. She might be a J. Janis?"

The table began to vibrate. "I think you mean K," Lily said.

"Kanis?"

"Kris."

"Kris says nobody's innocent." Tish looked down at her vibrating table. "Now hush!" The table kept vibrating.

"Were you just talking to the table?" Burt asked.

"There's a male presence as well," Tish said.

Burt reached for Lily across the vibrating table. "I think we should leave. I'm starting to get the feeling that we've stepped into a pile of total horse shit."

"Why is Kris talking about innocence, Lily?" Tish asked. The table was calming. "Maybe you'd better ask that question."

Lily set a flat hand on top of the table, letting the vibrations move up her arm. "W... what is going on?"

"I'm listening to M and Kris," Tish said, "and Kris is

talking about innocence. Wait a minute. She says... she says you know what she means. She says... well, mostly it comes down to you reap what you sow. Does that mean anything to you? What have you done, Lily?"

"Come on," Burt said. "Time to go."

No. Not time to go. Earl's voice in Lily's head: *crazy time.* THOUGHT. WORD. DEED. "I...don't... know." She tried to think of everything she'd ever done. "Why me?" she said aloud. She'd stolen a tip from a table at a diner once when she'd realized she was short on cash and needed enough gas to get home. She masturbated. She'd smoked a fair amount of pot in college. She said mean things about stupid people. She thought the world might be better off if people like Doris spent more time raising their kids and less time bugging people like Lily to have kids of their own. The other day she'd mouthed "fuck you" in traffic at another driver who cut her off and imagined him getting into a wreck and dying in a ball of fire, and she'd smiled at the thought. Innocent? Was she innocent? What had she *sown*?

Tish said, "Lily, you know what you deserve based on what you get. There's only one source of curses: you. The self is the self's curse because it's the only thing you can't escape. You doom yourself to lay low all that defines you when you hold your definition in high regard. Vanity, hubris, and self-deception are three sides of the same coin."

"Say *what*?" Burt interjected. "Three sides of the same coin...."

"I'm just repeating what Lily's friend says," Tish said. "I don't write this stuff." She looked at Lily. "Oh, and the male knows Burt is here. He says heads, tails, and the other heads, jackass."

Lily asked, "So what does it mean?"

"Shoot, what do I know? I don't charge enough to make sense of what the spirits say! I report it is all. Up to you to know whether it makes sense. Sounds like you've been up to no good is what it sounds like to me. But the tone of voice… if you can call them voices… seems kind of… like strangers. Like they don't mean it to be personal." Tish's hands shook out of sync with the mellow vibrations of the table.

"What's bothering you?" Burt asked.

"Me? Nothing. Wait a sec—M is talking. 'Affliction cometh not forth from the dust.'" Tish's eyes switched back and forth with a wildness of fear. Lily saw it, and Burt saw it, too.

"More Shakespeare?" Burt asked.

"No," Tish said with care. "Bible. You knew that. You know what part."

"Book of Job," Lily whispered. "So, I've sown my own affliction?" It made sense. She couldn't figure out how she'd done it, but it made sense.

The beads over the entryway rattled as a cold breeze swept through the room. The table stopped vibrating and thumped again, hard, up and down, cracking in the middle. Tish yelped, jumped out of her chair and away from the table. Her wild eyes kept switching, Lily to Burt, Lily to Burt, but she said nothing until, "You two had better leave. They're gone, and I don't want them back."

Burt smirked. "Why not? It's a good show."

Tish smirked back, but with more anger than bemusement. "Because if I ask you to pay for my table, you're going to say no, that's why."

Outside, Burt said, "The nerve of that woman! For what we paid, she can have that tabletop replaced and ready for the next show no problem. All that talk about no bells and whistles, and she pulls that horse shit. Give me a break!"

Lily lowered her head. "The things they said."

"What? You believed it all?"

She looked him in the eyes. "You didn't?"

They stood alone on the sidewalk, not far from the neon palm beneath the words "Lady Laetitia, Extreme Psychic" that drew attention to the doorway they'd abandoned. Burt shook his head no, but his eyes stayed fixed, telling another story.

"I don't know I believed *what* they said." Lily took a deep breath. "But I believe *that* they said it."

Burt tried to smile. "'They' meaning your friends— excuse me, but your dead friends—Mia, Krissy, and Eric— right?"

Lily nodded.

"What won you over, the table act?" Burt tried again to smile.

"No," Lily said. "I didn't think too much of that. But what they said... was too much... don't you...."

Burt leaned forward and kissed her on the mouth. The sudden movement caught her off guard, but she accepted it, liking the warm softness of his lips against hers, the press of his trimmed moustache and beard against the edges of her mouth and cheeks, the looming of his height over hers. He pulled back, eyes inches away, gazing into hers for confirmation of acceptance, and when she gave it, he pressed in again, this time opening his mouth so they could kiss one another fully, feeling lips not just on one another but inside one another, enveloping, tongues sliding against tongues, heads tilting from side to side as eyes closed in deeper exploration of sensation. He had been waiting for this moment, and she had, too, in a way, never realizing before now that it had long been as inevitable as it was desirable, as strong as the heat surging through from her head through her torso through to her tired legs, wobbling beneath her.

When he finally pulled back again, both their eyes had

softened, but their meanings, for the moment, had not. Lily asked, "Didn't you believe her?"

Burt answered, "Every word."

7

They made an unspoken decision as soon as they crossed the threshold of her apartment. Lily put down her purse, and Burt threw down his keys, and they resumed kissing as if the hours intervening before nightfall had been a slight pause. Lily did not express hesitation. Burt was acting out a fantasy, and she was caught up in a situation, and divergence was okay. She had a lot not to feel good about. The gunshot scars and hand injury increased body consciousness.

The experience in the alley loomed. The most recent, and first time in a long while, that someone had tried to make genital contact with her had been an act of violence rather than sex—by definition—and the last time she had touched a man's testicles had been an act of self-defense. At the rate they were going, both of those factoids were about to change, and thinking about it in those terms, which she did while trying not to, made her queasy. She didn't want to think about the man in the alley, but she did. And she did. And she did.

When she tried to think of something else, her mind flipped to the strange objects she'd found here, in this apartment, not very long ago. The fucked-up teddy bear. The bent silverware. The bloody rag. They were like clues to a mystery Lily didn't know she was trying to solve.

Why not think of what is actually happening? Of the plush sensation of Burt's lips against your neck? Why not let the idea of what is happening merge with the happening itself? If he wants to unbutton your blouse, you should feel the motion of his fingers on every button, the way they tickle your skin with a touch of roughness as they guide the plastic through the holes. It'll feel good to get these clothes off, after the way they've been sticking to you. He's not going to care about your imperfections, the bumps and rounds of skin you wish no one to feel, just the nipples growing hard beneath his fingers, breasts rising to fill his grasp.

You've got to reciprocate. Put your hands on his belt and untuck his shirt. Feel the edge of his stomach, the soft protrusion of his belly (make sure he feels that you don't care about imperfections, either, even though he's trimmer than you are). Run your hands up his stomach and chest, and remember that his nipples are sensitive, too. Start tugging his shirt up over his head. Watch him lift the shirt the rest of the way off; admire his arms and chest.

Lead him to the bedroom. You're not going to fuck right here in the mini-foyer. Take him by the hand and guide him, leaving a trail of clothing. Finish unbuttoning your blouse and leave it behind. Good. In the bedroom doorway, take off your bra, tracing your breasts with a finger after you do. Enjoy the look in his eye. Good.

Turn off the overhead light and turn on the lamp by the bed at its dimmest setting. Now throw back the covers. Never mind the—

Lily stopped moving when she noted the place at the foot of the bed where a pool of locusts had been. A shadow sat in the pool's spot. Only a shadow. It made her shiver. Burt wrapped an arm around her and kissed her, covering her with warmth she didn't need. She leaned her head back and pushed her body up toward his, allowing her hips to thrust. Bare skin touched bare skin, chest to chest. They pivoted so that her back was to the bed, to the shadow-pool, and he lowered her to the sheets. She tried not to think about how close her head had landed, whether her hair fell past the edge of the shadow's boundary, into the pool of locusts that had been.

A tug, she thought, pulling against her scalp: an added weight in her hair.

Burt kissed his way from her mouth, down her neck, between her breasts, to her stomach, to the button of her pants, which he undid in order to slide them down and reveal her panties, nice ones, she thought, at least nicer than she might have been wearing, considering that this morning she never considered that the evening might involve *this*. Again she thought of the sweat she'd worked up running after the paint can hooligan and wished for a shower, but she didn't feel dirty, didn't reek, just felt a little sticky in places, and when Burt looked up at her, she could see sweat glistening on his brow, and she thought *This is how it works*. Had it been so long that she needed to remind herself? She did anyway: *This is how it works*. They would get sweaty together. Her hips were rising to greet him as he tugged at her underwear. His fingers and tongue explored.

The weight in her hair increased, and she closed her eyes, trying to focus on the sensation between her legs. Her right ear detected a faint buzzing. *Grasshoppers don't buzz. It's all in your head.* Her too-busy consciousness was plotting against her, trying to keep her from enjoying... the... delightful... sensations accumulating with Burt's touches. He had her naked now, most of her legs still dangling off the bed, where he knelt on the floor so that his head could reach her midsection. Her body enveloped him so that he couldn't see the spot with the shadow pool if he looked. If the sound she heard or the sensation—sensations—she felt had meaning beyond the hallucinatory, beyond her mind's effort to keep her from enjoying and giving in to the pleasure of the moment, he would be unable to confirm. He was in the moment; he was the moment. Only Lily hung in suspense, part in, part out, like her position on the bed.

Crawling, insect legs, prickled her skin as they moved out of her hair and dappled her right cheek. All the corner of her eye detected was a new darkness. In a gesture she hoped would convey pleasure, she swiped a hand across her face, and she removed the darkness without feeling anything against her fingers. You see? Just a hallucination, a trick of light and skin, foolery of the paranoid mind. The feeling of more legs, a dozen more, on your shoulder? The same.

She turned her head to look, strained to see, and within the hair scattered by her shoulder, her brown hair, she thought she saw brown bodies, mottled brown, like the suspiciously not-green grasshopper-locusts. She gasped, camouflaging the sound with the rhythm of Burt's circling tongue, confused by the rush of pleasure and nausea at the idea of locusts rising up from the shadow pool and invading her skin. That's all it is, though, Lily. An idea. IT IS NOT HAPPENING. YOU ARE INSANE.

Through the bedroom wall, voices came. Neighbors, noisy, in an argument. That, Lily reasoned, is real. The sound did not deter Burt from his mission. He wanted her to come. The sensation of crawling on her shoulder intensified along with the escalating pleasure between her legs. Confusion heightened: she wanted the pleasure, needed the pleasure, wanted the prickly crawling to go away, needed it to, and the swirls of want and need became eddies in a sea of emotion and sensation, longing and sickness, joy and dread, so that she yearned for and feared what might happen if it ended and she confronted reality, the presence or absence of what she saw, now clearly saw, crawling from her shoulder down toward her right nipple.

Burt, so involved in his faster and faster movements, fingers and tongue, but more and more tongue, might not notice, so Lily used her sliced hand to reach for the locust that had invaded her breast. She grabbed it, hoping the gesture would, if detected, look like hugging herself in a shiver of delight. The bug's body felt real in her hand, but she told herself *No, it is not.* Despite the twinge of pain, she folded her palm to crush it, and she tossed it aside, away from seeing. The residue on her left palm might have come from the insect or might have come from her own still-healing injury. An involuntary shudder passed from head to toe.

Burt's face, smiling, shining, appeared in her field of vision. He stood, and she watched him take off his pants. She wanted and didn't want to continue. If he could go on without the rest—without her head manufacturing insects to crawl over her, ruining the good moments, keeping her from the climaxes he wanted her to reach—then they might dissolve into one another forever, attaining romance-novel peaks of perfection. *Mostly* (she heard Lady Laetitia speak the word in her brain) she found sex overrated, but she remembered a time, in her early twenties, when orgasms from the right man could blot out the sun, and wasn't sex for women supposed to get better in the thirties? Swirls of want and need: she asked Burt if he had a condom, and he said he did.

Now their bodies aligned with the bed's orientation, head to head, foot to foot, covers in a wad. Burt was on top, blocking views of all but his beautiful, dark face, gentle lines, close-cropped beard, wiry neck, broad shoulders, and chest, rising and falling. Near her feet she knew the shadow pool threatened visitors, and she felt them, crawling over her, upward, toward him. At times his upper body remained almost still, and at times it moved with his thrusts, but it never got so far that she couldn't reach around, grasp, hug, *touch*, feel, explore, check with her fingers for visitors with legs and heads and wings. Her nails traced the edges of his shoulder blades, she hoped lovingly, and swam in the sweat collecting along his spine. She squeezed the rounds of his buttocks, strained for his thighs when he contracted above her, rising from the bed as she did. They got closer and closer, merging, he in the throes, she trying to be with him, more and more just searching him, finally feeling a stray insect slip over the top of her hand, confirming that the line she'd felt moving over her and onto him had some reality—

No.

—had pressed hallucinatory forces from her feet and ankles up onto Burt and had amassed on his calves and thighs and was now massing on his backside and lower back, forming a blanket of locusts on top of them both.

She wanted to scream. The pounding she heard through the wall, the neighbors' arguing picking up some kind of physical component, felt like the pounding in her chest. Her sweat had turned cold, and she hoped her body didn't feel as cold to Burt as she felt on the inside. His breath was hot against her face, and she knew her own was quick, as quick as his, close to panic, and how much did panic sound like orgasm? How much did her skin hardening with tension feel like the rigidity of pleasure? Pleasure had halted almost entirely (almost), but her body accommodated, to a point, so did he, or could he know that so much of her was recoiling not from him but from what she sensed on top of him? That she pressed into him not because she wanted him deeper inside of her but because she was afraid that if he stopped she would confront either a swarm of locusts or their opposite, the naked, cold emptiness of her own mind's truth without his warmth as a layer of doubt?

The pounding on the other side of the wall got closer. Burt slowed but didn't stop, and over his shoulder, Lily saw dozens of insects take flight. She looked away, up toward the wall behind the headboard, the source of the noises.

A woman screamed. Burt stopped. Lily gasped. A swarm danced around his head, and he didn't seem to notice. He pulled out, leaving Lily with emptiness, and said, "My God, is that—"

The wall and the headboard shook. Burt slapped his

shoulder and squashed a locust. He looked at his hand, and one side of his mouth curled up in disgust. "Oh my G—"

The wall shook again with a bang. A framed Picasso print at the bedside fell from its hooks. The headboard rocked and hit the wall again and again with the force of the blow. Voices from the other side, too loud, too frenzied to make out, shouted at one another, a man and a woman.

Lily blinked, trying to clear away locusts, and the cloud surrounding Burt began to disperse, rising toward the ceiling. Burt waved his hands in front of his face as if clearing a bad smell, underreacting if he saw or felt what Lily saw and felt, but reacting.

Burt said, "It's like they're coming through the goddamned w—"

A crack appeared in the wall above the headboard. The voices became clearer. The man's voice yelled, "HOLD STILL!" The woman simply screamed before the next bang on the wall made the crack get bigger.

Burt leapt from the bed and fumbled for his underwear and pants. Lily lay transfixed by the cloud of insects gathered near the ceiling, the crack in the wall pointing toward them like an arrow. From the wall's other side, screaming intensified, forming words, "HELP ME!"

"We've got to call someone," Burt said. "Where's your phone?"

Lily didn't have a landline. "In my purse," she said. By the front door. Her new phone. The last one, with the locust pictures, had been ruined in the alley.

Burt searched his pockets. "Shit. I must have left mine at the office. Where's your purse?"

She'd told him, hadn't she? She looked at the manic, swarming locusts. "Uh-huh." She was naked on the bed. People were coming through the walls, and a cloud of locusts could descend on her at any moment.

"Lily?!"

Another crash against the wall, and the whole wall bowed toward them, with paint and plaster falling around the crack. A chunk popped out above the headboard, forming a hole. A woman's face appeared inside of it, framed. Her eyes white, large, with tiny brown irises, nostrils flaring, lips taut: she screamed again, this time with nothing to muffle her, "HELP ME!!!"

Her face disappeared from the hole, and in its place the head of a giant hammer, a sledgehammer, filled the hole, widening it. More plaster burst through on Lily's side, and the whole apartment seemed to shake. The man repeated, "Hold still!"

In normal volume, Lily stated, "He's going to kill her." She slid from the bed, ignoring the locusts, and looked for her underwear.

"Lily, the phone!" Burt yelled.

"By the front door," she said, pulling up her panties, starting on her pants. They retraced the path of clothing to the door, Burt leaving off his shirt, Lily skipping the bra but grabbing the blouse, and Lily opened the front door while Burt rooted through her purse for the phone. She started pounding on the neighbors' door while he pressed 9-1-1 and reported a domestic fucking disturbance, neighbors trying to kill each other with a sledgehammer, you heard right, get here fast, this is the address, we're not staying put, we're going over there, they're coming through the goddamned walls, we don't want blood on our hands, we're hanging up now, thank you officer, goodbye!

On his way through Lily's front door, Burt grabbed a lamp, and instead of joining Lily in pounding with a fist, he started kicking the neighbor's door, which strained against bolts. They could still hear screaming and the rough male voice shouting things, maybe "Hold still" or maybe something else now, as the voices seemed to move within the apartment space, away from the room adjacent to Lily's bedroom. Lily stopped knocking and started kicking. Finally Burt halted and counted: "One, two, three!" They kicked together. "One, two, three!" Again. "One, two, three!" "One, two, three!"

The door broke off its hinges instead of breaking from its bolts, but it fell open, and from a mini-foyer just like Lily's, they saw a skinny white woman in her underwear, makeup streaming down her face, sandy hair tied back in a ponytail that swung from side to side as she circled around a sofa, running for her life. The man chasing her was completely naked, erection bobbing as his sledgehammer, the handle as long as his arms, swung at the positions the woman occupied seconds before the gigantic, heavy metal hammerhead connected, obliterating part of the sofa or crunching the carpeted floor. The woman saw the opened front door and dashed for it, for Burt and Lily, shouting "Help me, help me, help me!"

Behind her, the man yelled, "Bitch!"

Burt took the woman's hand and pulled her toward the exit, where Lily took her other hand and instinctively shielded her, not knowing what she and Burt would do but knowing she and Burt were forming a wall between the man and his prey. Burt, shirtless and wielding a lamp, took a defensive stance and faced the naked man with a sledgehammer.

Lily recognized the man: Ralph, her neighbor, quiet, single, worked construction or something. She didn't know the woman. Ralph stalked toward Burt, one step, another, and said, "Get away."

Behind Lily, the woman whimpered. Burt knocked off the lampshade and held the lamp like a short lance, pointing it at his approaching foe. "Okay then," Ralph said. "*Hold still.*"

Arms bulging, Ralph lifted the sledgehammer over his head. Combining arm-length with handle-length, Burt or Lily could be in range. Lily stepped back, pushing the woman behind her. Burt held his ground, shifting from foot to foot, squaring his shoulders, ready to spring.

The hammer launched forward, and so did Burt. As the sledge arced downward, Burt stayed low and sprinted out, keeping the lamp up in lance position. The bulb, the lance-tip, struck Ralph in the stomach, making him lose control of the overshooting sledgehammer, which slipped from his fingers and tumbled on the carpet. The lightbulb shattered on impact, splitting skin and piercing Ralph in a dozen places as Burt kept pushing, jamming metal into tough flesh so that wind left Ralph's lungs, doubling him over, and the man went down. Pursuing the advantage, Burt raised the lamp over his head, an echo of Ralph with the hammer, and brought it down, clobbering Ralph's rising neck and jaw, knocking him unconscious. The lamp fell from Burt's hands.

Gasping for breath, he turned to Lily and the woman behind her, who watched from the doorway. "You two okay?"

The woman nodded, and Lily started to say Yes, but she stopped as her eyes tricked her with a cloud coming from the nearby bedroom, the mirror image of her own. Streaming, she supposed, from the hole between the apartments, a collection of locusts gathered above Ralph, forming a shape like his along the ceiling before it descended, blanketing him.

Lily closed her eyes and shook her head as if coming to her senses. She opened her eyes, still saw the bugs, but said, "Yes."

Burt joined them in the doorway and gestured for Lily to lead. "Let's wait for the cops at your place. They'll be here any minute. What's your name, ma'am?"

As they went, the woman said her name was Sally. Providing the information took a great deal of effort. She kept looking at Lily and asking, "Where do I know you from?"

Lily figured she probably knew Sally from somewhere. She only knew for certain that Ralph was her neighbor and that Ralph was Ralph, which didn't preclude attacking women with sledgehammers. As for Sally, she didn't recognize her, but Sally was having awfully bad luck, and Lily had a high correlation with awfully bad luck. Ask Burt.

Once they got back through Lily's front door, Sally said, "I know! You're his sister!"

Burt was turning the latches on the door. Lily looked at him. He didn't know very much about David. Then again, neither did Lily, who looked at Sally and said, "I'll get you some clothes."

She retrieved a sweat suit from when she had been a smaller size—and even so, the pants would need their drawstring pulled to its limit—and offered it to Sally. Sally pulled it on, ending the exposure of her undergarments. She asked Lily whether she had a brother named David.

Lily thought of answering yes and thought of answering no. Both answers were true. Her confusion on the point was not spiteful; she simply didn't know which answer was more honest. She *used to* have such a brother. The thought hurt. She supposed she was being perverse. Did other people feel this way about the dead? Having dead people so close was still a fairly new concept in her adult life. She didn't have protocols. She hadn't Googled proper grieving, and she didn't know if she wanted to.

Sally already knew about David's suicide. The two of them had met six months ago at a diner downtown after Sally had helped David run down an elusive system error while the two of them were in an online chat forum. They'd hit it off and started an "affair." For David, she guessed, it was ordinary dating, but for Sally it was an affair because Sally had Ralph. Ralph didn't like her to see other men, but she never promised she wouldn't. He had to live with it. She thought he did. "Until today."

As Sally reflected on her "affair," she remained calmer than Lily expected from a woman moments ago attacked by a man with a sledgehammer. "I think he just snapped." Sally was matter of fact in her assessment. The hammer must have come home from work in the trunk of Ralph's car, and from the reference to work Lily concluded she had been right about the construction job.

"But David, David was funny. He was a sad man, but he made me laugh. Did you know he spoke three languages? Instead of Sally he would call me Salad, and then he would say I had all these different ingredients in all three languages, I think they were Spanish, French, and Italian. I guess that means he spoke four languages. And he wasn't making it up, either, because the words sounded right, you know, like from menus?"

How the woman could babble about anything other than the sledgehammer remained mysterious to Lily, and the three of them remained standing around the mini-foyer near the locked front door while Sally talked. Why she wasn't more interested in Sally's link to her brother she couldn't understand. It seemed at once to have both profound importance and none.

"Was David always, you know, dark? He had a way of talking like people were after him. It was a good thing he made me laugh, because boy, he could be dreary, too. Always saying, like, the universe was out of alignment, or the universe was aligned, but he was disjointed, or something strange like that. You weren't surprised by, you know, *it*, were you? Because if anybody ever was, I think he was.

"And besides, once he told me that—"

The door burst from its hinges at the first strike of the sledgehammer against its outer edge, and it knocked down

Burt, who hit the floor with dramatic oomph. Lily ducked to avoid the next swing, then lost her footing and was on the floor, too, eye-level with Burt and rolling to avoid Ralph's heavy steps. The man had come down the hall naked, smashed through the door, and reduced his opposition two-thirds with two blows. Now he faced Sally.

She screamed and ran deeper into Lily's apartment, into the bedroom. Ralph, no longer hard but more determined, chased after her, ignoring Lily and Burt. Lily crawled to Burt and checked him; a little dazed, he was fine, bruised but recovering under the felled door. Released from the door and ready, Burt and Lily got to their feet and half-limped, half-ran toward the bedroom.

"Stop!" Burt's yell did nothing. Ralph had thrown Sally down across Lily's bed, her head landing close to, if not on the spot where the pool of locusts would be, and he'd raised the sledgehammer. It came down in an arc slow enough to dodge, but Sally merely screamed. It struck, and the sound of collapsing skull rang closest to crunching coconut but really had a quality unlike anything Lily had heard before. Blood and brain—the texture had to be brain—gushed onto her comforter.

Burt pulled Lily away from the doorway, away from the bedroom, away from Ralph and the scene of the murder they'd just witnessed. A moment ago, Lily had been annoyed and bemused by the woman whose skull had just popped on her bedspread. Now her murderer was preparing her murder weapon for a run at Lily and the man who, not long ago, Lily was having sex with for the first time.

Lily realized they were in the kitchen. Burt was searching through drawers. "Knives are there," Lily said, pointing to the freestanding block on the countertop. Burt took the big chef's knife and examined the blade. "I keep them sharp," she assured.

He turned toward the bedroom, from which Ralph had not emerged. Lily wanted to tell him not to go in after him, but what if he had no intention of doing such a stupid thing? Then she'd be announcing the obvious. He started to go, and she said, "Don't!"

"You're right," Burt said. "Come on." Neither one of them willing to look away from the bedroom door, through which they couldn't see, they backed toward the front door, Lily knowing the way by heart, Burt stumbling at first but learning to follow her.

They were halfway there when the naked man with the sledgehammer stepped out of the bedroom and threatened to kill them. Lily screamed, and she imagined she sounded like Sally.

Burt brandished the knife, covering Lily with his body as if she were the object of some primal quarrel. Ralph hesitated, and Lily ran for the door, flipped the locks, opened it, and yelled through the doorway, "HELP, POLICE! ANYONE!" She turned around to see Ralph swing the sledgehammer at Burt, who jumped out of the way, tripped on a chair, but recovered his balance in time to save his footing, coming to a steady stand at the far side of the room. Lily, Ralph, and Burt formed a triangle, with Ralph about as far from Lily and the door as he was from Burt.

Yelling "Over here!," Burt cut the distance in half, crouching low and keeping the knife out like a talisman. Ralph turned as ordered, giving Lily a chance to escape, but Lily stayed, needing to see, needing to strike if she had a clear shot. The angles of the triangle, however, never forced Ralph to turn his back: he kept looking from one of them to the other, hammer ready. His attention focused on Burt, but Lily didn't have a weapon—didn't know what she'd do without surprise, or with it, really, other than jump on his back and claw out his eyes, which she felt ready to do.

Ralph made a noise, a low growl, and wound up the hammer, aiming at Burt. Lily saw the chance to act, and she yelled, "RALPH!," turning his attention to her and interrupting the swing.

Burt responded on cue, diving in with the knife. He struck in the man's belly first, but when he pulled the knife out in a streamer of red, he repositioned himself to strike higher and got the throat, skewering it. The sledgehammer clunked to Lily's carpeted floor, joining sprays of staining crimson.

Lily covered her mouth. Even on the night of the roadside attack, she had never come close to seeing so much blood. Between the mess on her comforter and the mess on her carpet, more than she'd ever thought she'd see, more than she'd thought realistic... *How do you stop seeing?*

I don't.

No, she wouldn't.

Still shirtless, Burt hugged her, and she felt like finishing the buttons on her blouse, and she felt like picking up her bra and starting over. She felt like she should have showered after all. She was dirty. They were all dirty.

The police arrived ten minutes later. Lily's apartment was declared a crime scene. She couldn't stay home, so she stayed at Burt's. She supposed they were together now.

8

Burt's loft trapped and amplified echoes, so when Lily's phone started beeping, the sound didn't go away. Instead, it pestered them: Burt lay on his side, draping an arm across her chest, she on her back, staring at the ceiling, wishing the sound would go anywhere but in her ears. "I should have turned that off when I plugged it in," she said. He was too polite to say, *Yes, you should have*, so he just kissed her cheek.

They had left a light on downstairs because neither one of them liked the dark now. Lily admitted it, Burt didn't, but Lily knew. In their world, people could come through walls with sledgehammers and try to kill you. In their world, the same place on the bed that gave birth to locusts, real and imaginary, became the resting place of a skull that would burst with gore and ideas about your dead brother, your dead brother who thought the universe was aligned or unaligned with you, whichever was worse, in ways that encouraged you to be dead. Light couldn't stop such things from happening, from coming—the dim light by Lily's bed had been more than enough to see the events of five days ago, when the wall had cracked open during their first attempt at lovemaking—but seeing them was better than allowing them to creep, crawl, or *insinuate* themselves upon the blind.

Burt wasn't getting up, so Lily would have to. Her phone rested on the kitchen counter, not that Burt's habitation contained distinct rooms. Lofts were both hip and standard for this part of the city, a stone's throw from the towers and businesses. Lily imagined going to a window and throwing stones at towers and businesses. Hitting 1500 Spring from here would be more than a feat, but she wanted to do it, wanted to get the building's attention because it had hers.

Her phone beckoned, so she slid out from beneath Burt's arm and went to it. The "upstairs" was a massive shelf connected to the floor beneath by a narrow spiral staircase. Burt used it as his bedroom; it overhung about a third of the open, high-ceilinged space, with the overhung area serving as a cozy den and the rest serving as the living/dining room and kitchen area. The loft as a whole had a haphazard, serviceable masculinity that made Lily miss her own tainted abode; most chairs rolled, the primary eating location consisted of a bar and stools, and the den contained a fold-out sofa that turned the overhung area into a "guest room." The practicality showed thought, expense, and zero finesse. The downstairs showpiece was the giant television, mounted on a wall and visible from all points.

As she clicked the button on her phone to discover its reason for beeping, she heard Ralph's voice, *"Hold still."* Her body lurched as her stomach flipped. She swallowed. Sally had looked quite a bit younger than David. Or Ralph, for that matter. Other than the obvious attractions, what did David see in her? What did she see in Ralph? David "talked like people were after him." Was Ralph after him? Had Ralph known about him? Sally and Ralph did not *hold still*. They burst into life and left as abruptly, sweeping in mystery and horror and leaving behind nothing but meaningless images of themselves, flattened, pierced, red and redistributed.

The phone said, "!!!ACCOUNT WARNING!!! You received this message because you enrolled your bank account in overdraw protection. Contact your bank for details." It then provided an 800 number. Lily had not overdrawn her account, so she knew the text was an error, but then again... she called. She articulated clear monosyllables when the artificial person who answered prompted her to do so. After being routed incorrectly twice, she got her account information: zero. Her checking account balance was zero. Her savings account balance, which was supposed to cover her checking account when she overdrew, was also zero. She listened to her recent account history and heard about withdrawals and purchases, none huge or from third-world countries, that had nothing to do with her. The information should have surprised and outraged, but she took it as a matter of course. Of course someone had drained her accounts. "Representative," she shouted into the phone. She shouted it three more times before she heard that she would now hold for a representative.

"Lily?" Burt's voice, from upstairs.

"What?" she snapped back. She thought for a moment. "What, dear?"

"What's going on?"

"Oh, nothing." Her phone felt heavy in her hand as she listened to the insipid hold music. She spoke in a normal voice. "The curse got my bank accounts. It was a matter of time, I guess."

Burt called down, "The curse got what?"

Lily yelled up, "I DON'T FEEL LIKE SHOUTING!"

"Hello? There's no need to shout, ma'am. How can I help you?" The voice spoke in place of the hold music. Both in connection quality and accent, the voice did not seem to be in India, as Lily had expected.

While she listened to the rustle of Burt preparing himself to come downstairs, Lily explained the situation to the man on the phone, who said "Uh-huh," "Yes," and "I see" far too often. Lily limited her explanation to the mysterious charges and withdrawals. She did not explain why they were, in the greater scheme, unsurprising, why, after seeing someone's head, a head previewed via a hole in the wall, explode on your bed, nothing of this sort would ever surprise again. Would "Rick" be so quick to say "I see" if she compared the astounding gush of brain to the trivial leak of finance?

"I see."

She thought not.

Rick was going to put holds on the accounts, report her numbers stolen, and launch full investigations. Meanwhile, he recommended that she contact all her credit card companies and other financial institutions in case she had been the victim of identity theft, which, in short order, she discovered she must have been, for her credit cards had reached their generous, decided-for-a-fiscally-responsibly-thirtysomething limits. Lily was broke and tens of thousands in debt.

Several different investigating individuals and agencies would contact her. Although she kept the business cards of the investigators in charge of the crime scene previously known as her apartment, she had stopped remembering the police's names after the incident in the alley. Lily had more investigations into her life than she had life. She certainly had more investigators than she had friends. At least living friends.

Lily sat on a barstool, looking at her phone. Burt arrived in boxer shorts and a bathrobe and took the stool beside her. "I figured it out from listening to your side of the conversations," he said. "Kind of weird for someone to have all the info while you still have your wallet, isn't it?"

"I don't believe in kind-of-weird anymore. I have curse days and days in between." Lily pivoted on the stool to face him. "Tell me, Burt. Have you ever been *investigated*?"

Burt left his stool to go into the kitchen area, where he poured himself a glass of milk. He raised the jug to Lily in offer, but she refused. "It'll end up having Mad Cow Disease or something, if I touch it." She laughed.

Burt didn't laugh. "No, unless you count the usual credit

reports and things... well, and going to jail for trying to... attack... you... I've never been investigated." He sat down next to Lily again.

Lily took a deep breath. "You've called me paranoid. I've called me paranoid. Feeling like you're being watched is the most clichéd type of paranoia, I think, and I feel that way because I *am* being watched, or investigated, by I don't know how many people right now. I don't think they're trying to do me in... except maybe because I'm the only survivor and witness when my friends died... I know I was, or am, a suspect for that... but I can't think about that... the list of things I can't think about has gotten pretty long, you know? But I have other people thinking about that for me. People in my head, doing my thinking for me. *That's* paranoia. But it's also happening.

"By the way, I found an online support group for paranoia and formication. If you're paranoid and feel like you've got bugs crawling all over you, you're not alone in the vast online universe. Maybe if you'd never seen a single one of those grasshoppers, I wouldn't wake up every morning feeling one crawling around by my ear. I know it's not real. Except sometimes, you know and I know, it is. What am I supposed to do with that? Don't answer. Don't try.

"Most of the online definitions of paranoia have 'delusions of persecution' in common. Do I feel like I'm being persecuted? Oh my, yes. I've started calling it *curse logic*. Feeling like I'm being persecuted actually makes me feel better, understand, because it makes more sense than seeing all this shit as simply random.

"Randomness is a tough nut. People think probability means lightning doesn't strike in the same place twice, but it's the opposite. Probability means lightning can keep striking in the same place over and over and over again. Smarter people might think probability means lightning *shouldn't* strike in the same place twice, but they're still wrong. Probability doesn't know should and shouldn't. Probability does not obey. Probability can have lightning strike that same place a thousand times in a row, and it won't have done anything it shouldn't do. The place the lightning struck might be thinking, well shit, that was pretty fucking unlikely, but that's the only help probability can give it. Probability is the sphygmomanometer of randomness. It doesn't control or even judge it; it just tacks on a reading.

"Look at your readings too much, and the readings change. Your pressure goes up. The probability changes, or seems to, because in curse logic, awareness of persecution brings on more persecution, just like worrying about blood pressure makes it go up. In curse logic events can be both random and controlled because they have to be. Thinking that what happens to you is unlikely *does not make you feel better*. Sooner or later, it makes you feel impossible, which is worse. It makes you feel singled out. Your whole existence becomes the outlying-est outlier on the Bell Curve of Humanity, and you're on the edge of a terrible precipice, about to succumb to infernal gravity. So far out on the edge, you feel like you have to have been pushed out there. That's the persecution factor. You didn't end up there by chance; someone put you there. The events themselves couldn't have been planned. There were too many that couldn't have had causes, or at least not the same causes, not in a way normal people could understand, but you feel like if you could just dig deep enough, down low, you could find a common root, the persecution root.

"So if, according to all this curse logic, I've been cast as the title character in the Book of Job, that root is God. An encounter with the God of Random Persecution hasn't made me a believer, not in the traditional way, but 'God' makes sense as a root of all... this."

"In the Book of Job it's Satan." Burt drank his milk. "Remember I told you that it all starts out with God and Satan making a kind of bet that Job's faith won't hold up to the worst that Satan has to throw at him. Satan bets that if he pushes Job far enough, Job will curse God for his suffering. The persecuting comes from Satan, not God. God just lets it happen."

"If God unleashes Satan, and Satan unleashes all the rest, God is still the root." Lily felt smug for no reason.

Burt shrugged. "I guess if you start believing and think hard enough, the buck stops at God for just about everything. He's a handy scapegoat. Scape-god." Burt chuckled.

"So it's a Tinkerbell situation," Lily said. "It's all about what I believe, huh?" She smiled. "You're what we call a relativist, aren't you?"

"Pshaw. I hate relativism." Burt pulled his bathrobe closed in prim disgust. "Moral and religious relativism are responsible for the decay of Western Civilization. I'm just a plain Atheist, thank you very much. I'm with Neil deGrasse Tyson. Science and faith don't go together, and science makes more sense. Well, at least most of the time. Your situation is a bit of a cosmic stumper."

"It goes back to the science of lightning." Lily felt satisfied not to be a scientist. "However lightning works, it's not *supposed* to fry a woman like me quite so badly. Science and religion share dimensions of justice. Science just doesn't talk about it. Except maybe Darwin."

Burt shook his head. "I'm with Hobbes on this one. Life in the state of nature is nasty, brutish, and short. Justice is humanity's daydream. And Darwin was misunderstood: he wasn't talking about individual accomplishments. Is your point that you feel like you've got to believe in something to get through all of this?"

Lily shook her head. "No. My point is that whatever's at the root, science or religion or both, it's got a lot of explaining to do."

"Well, that's it. I'm getting dressed." Burt rose from the stool. "No more sleeping tonight. Do you feel up for a walk?"

"City streets at three in the morning. You like to tempt fate, don't you?" Lily tried to smirk.

Burt headed toward the stairs and appeared innocent. "How do you mean?"

"We'll be murdered." She thought for a moment. "Or you'll be. Job gets to live, doesn't he? Maybe I'm safe on the murder front. But you—you could be toast."

"That's a remarkably morbid thing for a woman in your position to say." Burt was upstairs now, putting on pants. His voice had added volume, but distance did not call for shouting.

"It's a *practical* thing for a woman in my position to say. I will take a walk with you, yes. And if we're attacked, so be it. I will either live life, or I won't. I can't be held down by an intolerable sense of doom. My God. Do I sound like Antigone? Another aspect of paranoia is delusions of grandeur."

"We never said you weren't paranoid." Burt was always helpful.

Outside the night, or early morning, air felt a little cooler than it had since Lily had been staying at Burt's, so they walked nearer one another than usual. Standing on the corner of the next block, four people, perhaps a mix of men in drag and women, perhaps not, obstructed the sidewalk. They wore shiny tops that shimmered different colors depending on how they caught the light. The foursome kindly cleared a path so that first Lily, then Burt, could pass, brushing up against ambiguous and pleasant bodies.

In front of a hair salon they almost tripped on a woman who sat with her legs extended toward the street, bottle in her lap, eyes fixed on passersby. The woman called out to Lily, "Hello sister!"

"Pardon us." Lily and Burt began to step around.

"You're my sister!" The woman looked sincere. "A few years back, I started losing everything in foreclosure. You know what it's like, because you're my sister."

The woman's calmer insistence made Lily pause. "I'm sorry I don't have any change."

"I don't want your change, sister. I want you to be ready. Ready for when it gets bad." The woman wore a red top and jeans that, dirty, hung from her because they were sizes too big. Yellowy patches of the woman's skin had the texture of crinkled paper, though not from age.

"Come on, Lily, let's go." Burt put his arm around her.

Lily asked, "What do you mean?"

The woman used great effort to get to her feet. Balancing herself and the bottle nearly proved too much, but she managed, earning the reward of a guzzle from the bottle, which she then offered to Lily, who refused. "That'll change," the woman said.

Lily ignored her and repeated, "What did you mean by, 'Ready for when it gets bad?'"

"Oh, you're a survivor type, all right. I can see it. It gets bad when you think you've got nothing. That's when you lose what you don't think you can. Oooo boy. The first time that hits you, everything goes out the window. But you can't understand now, can you? You think I'm a madwoman!"

True.

"My name's Iris." At least she didn't say Gladiola. Iris spoke fast:

"I kept wondering why, after so many other people died, I got to keep my husband. He not only stayed alive and healthy, but he stayed by my side, believing in me—at first. For two years, he believed in me. And then, one day, I found out he didn't, and he hadn't for a long time. He'd been keeping a journal, observing me, writing down my behaviors, including things I didn't do, or at least things I didn't know I did, which he blended with things I knew I did but was embarrassed about. But I couldn't help it. I'd been through so much. I slept with lights on, and I checked under the bed at night, so what? I lived in fear, but I had good reasons to, as anyone who knew the facts would agree!

"He wrote down all these details and construed them in the worst possible ways. And then one day, according to his own record, he took the diary to a psychiatrist so he would have dates and details to back up what he said about me needing 'the kind of help you get in a hospital.' I didn't understand! I still don't! I wasn't rich. All our money came from what we earned at our jobs, which we'd lost… we were desperate together. Why in the world would he…?"

Iris trailed off, sobbing. Burt, not as entranced by the sidewalk storyteller, took a step back, and his hand on her shoulder urged Lily to do the same.

"He died while I was in the hospital, but by then I was committed, not going to get out just because he was dead—and besides, my husband's big hurt had happened. He reported on me. Lied to me. Made me think he loved me when all the time he was betraying me. Then he threw me away, had me locked up. You probably think the betrayal was worse than being locked up in that hospital. In that," and she shook her head, "you are mistaken."

Lily wanted to take Iris by the hand, but she wouldn't. Burt would object. He loomed over her shoulder, wordlessly urging her to abandon the conversation. He seemed to remind her that it was past three in the morning, and they were on a city street, and this woman was drunk and homeless. Why were they chatting her up?

"You're going to go there, you know. They'll lock you up and point at you. Behind the door and through the glass. It's what they do. They come up with names for things. Psychotic depression, paranoid personality disorder, generalized anxiety disorder, scopophobia, agoraphobia, ideation, ideation, ideation, if you get too much ideation they'll have to drug it out of you! How about it? Are you ready to lose your ideation?"

Lily gawked. Burt looked back and forth, Lily to Iris, trying to smile while wresting away Lily's rapt attention.

Iris nodded. "That looks like a no. You've got to know, then, that there's only one way out." Lily and Iris stood close to one another.

"What way is that?" Lily knew.

"How many have you seen, sister?" The look in Iris's eyes was sororal.

Lily felt confused. Maybe she didn't know. How many… horrible things? "How many what?"

Iris looked confused. She looked at Burt, who said, "Just one."

Burt getting it first helped Lily get it—the one way out. Iris was talking about suicide and witnessing suicide. Lily reheard, and rethought, some of what her last oracular encounter, Sally, had said about David, and realized how easily the comments about the universe's alignment related to herself, as easily as Iris's more explicitly related statements. These people were in her life to comment on her life. They had messages for her.

Delusions of grandeur.

And the messages were about the cluster suicides, about which she'd also been getting messages, since Christmas. These suicides were endings of trials like her own, the *only* possible endings, the only ways out, as otherwise the trials could go on and on, indefinitely, until Lily found herself not old but used up, like Iris, accosting a fresher version of herself on the city streets with a warning about being ready when things get bad.

"You're new," Iris said. "Might not be worth a year. Come with me, and I'll show you something." Iris shuffled forward on the street, toward the next block. Lily looked at Burt, who shook his head no. Lily followed Iris, registering a silent but non-insistent plea for Burt to join. He did.

Iris cut through an alley that led to a parallel, more trafficked block, and in the alley, the center of which no streetlights could reach, Lily realized that by following she had created the very circumstances that had made her hesitate to go out walking in the first place. Burt's shoulders, high, close to his ears, seconded her realization, communicating through tension an awareness of mortal danger. His hands stayed at his sides, out of pockets, therefore ready to rise for defense, but not in fists, therefore unready for immediate danger. Burt was trying, unsuccessfully, to be cool. He kept up by Lily's side, and Lily stayed a few feet behind Iris, who pressed on into darkness walled with high-building concrete on both sides.

Darkness receded as the new block came into view, and Lily felt surprised not by the cars still driving by at this hour— at all hours, a human trickle, like on the highway where she'd met Earl and Rob—but by the rubbish in the gutter, the street signs in disrepair, the storefronts in vacancy. Just two blocks from Burt's nice, if not well- then at least better-to-do building, evidence of economic trouble stood out in bold relief. Across the street, she saw a trash can fire, and she considered that the night was not especially cold, was even a little warm. She also considered that she might never have seen such a fire before, not anywhere but in movies. Maybe from a car, but not while walking. Iris moved toward it.

Beside the fire an unbranded, boarded storefront looked abandoned but intact, and Iris moved to it as if it belonged to her. The door opened when she pulled, and she beckoned for Lily and Burt to follow. Burt shook his head no, but Lily followed Iris, and Burt followed Lily. Light from the fire shone through the storefront windows, making large shadows jump from place to place without warning and revealing other human figures among the piles of detritus inside the structure. Lily thought of the word "squatter" and didn't know if it applied to such people. She thought Burt might be thinking of the word "killer" and didn't know if it would apply, either. They would see, as Iris was leading them through a small gauntlet of broken furniture and unidentifiable mish-mash toward a stairway, which seemed a point of no return.

On the stairs, Burt whispered, "Lily, this is stupid."

Lily paused. "Unaccountably." She continued.

"Why are we following this woman?"

Lily moistened her lips and turned to look at Burt, who was a step lower. She enjoyed the added tallness. "True or false. We just tripped over a woman who knows things, and she said to follow her. Huh?"

"True... maybe." He cleared his throat and gestured with his head toward the top of the stairway. Iris watched and waited. "What she's saying... are you really hearing her? It could mean anything."

What Burt said made no sense. What Iris said sounded very precise. "I need to see," Lily said, "what she wants us to see."

"Fine." Burt motioned for her to continue up the stairs.

Several small fires and one bigger one lit the open area at the top. People, five men and two women, gathered around the larger, central flame. A few of them looked like they were praying. "Lily, it's time to go," Burt said.

Lily said no. The quality of the firelight cast everyone in greys and oranges that blended with the floor, ceiling, and walls. No one looked real, so no one looked threatening. No face appeared all at once, so no person appeared entirely present. Least present was the man, the eighth figure, standing near the central flame, and Iris approached him, becoming ethereal in the firelight as she did. Lily and Burt remained close to the stairs, outside the grey and orange circle of fire.

"I brought my sister," ethereal Iris said to the unpresent eighth man.

"Show her into the light," the eighth man said.

"Lily," Burt whispered, indicating, again, they should go. Lily's resolve wavered. She did not go into the light.

Iris commanded: "Approach and see!" She laughed. The man looked at her, and he laughed. The two stood together laughing in the firelight, grey laughter.

The seven people circling them began to laugh.

"*Lily*," Burt said.

Something was wrong with Iris's face. Without thinking, Lily took a step closer, trying to see. Smudges. Smudges on Iris's cheek stood out in the firelight. They stood on the man's chin, too. Smudges gathered on both of their faces, and they stopped laughing. Iris made a noise like a hiccough, and the man's eyes bulged.

"Oh God," Burt said.

Blood poured out of their mouths, and they weren't making noise anymore. They wavered on their feet as they fought against spasms in their throats and chests, natural efforts to expel their... tongues, had they bitten them off?... while blood poured into their mouths. Their faces got bigger, and the seven onlookers looked on and laughed and laughed and laughed.

Fires wiggled in the shrinking space around Lily and Burt, who backed into the stairway. The seven laughers did not move to stop them, but their heads turned the laughter toward the two would-be escapees. The laughter got louder, and the room felt hollower than before, smaller but hollower, causing echoes to bounce quickly, laughing echoes, ricocheting all around the dying couple on display at the central flame, now on their knees, choking. Their bloody lips looked like painted clown-smiles, still grey-orange in firelight.

Burt had Lily's hand and was leading her down the stairs, she taking half the steps backward, unable to stop herself from looking and looking back at the spectacle of dying Iris and the man who had joined her, whom she had joined, in the only possible ending, in the ending Burt had described from the prison. How many had Lily seen? Two now. Two-for one. Only she hadn't seen, not to the end.

At the first floor, Burt had her facing forward, and with laughter still trailing them, they ran to the door in the abandoned storefront, past the fire marking the entrance, onto the street. Safe.

The hit against the pavement in front of them sounded more smack than splat, coming from only the second floor, directly above. The nest of hair, the baggy clothes—Iris—had jumped or been thrown. Head intact, limbs and torso twisted, face turned upward to gaze at them with the blood-clown smile: the woman was dead. Lily closed her eyes and stepped away, awaiting the sound of the second body falling, but it did not come. She only heard laughter, as if it were much further than a floor above them, hideous, hilarious, and uncontrolled. Iris might have been projecting it, or it might have been Lily's own, drifting away on a breeze.

Lily screamed. Burt pulled her close and hugged her. Lily freed her arms from his embrace and pushed him away. "What are you doing?!"

"I... comforting you?!"

"I...." She thought him reasonable at the same time she felt that touching at a time like this—with a dead woman splayed out right in front of them—was completely inappropriate. Her skin crawled, not with formication but with the sense that it wanted to escape her body altogether, leaving her a skeleton to stand above the crushed Iris. His feelings would be hurt, though, if she didn't allow herself to be comforted, so she pulled him back close and encouraged his arms around her. She surrendered and asked, "Do we stay?"

Burt looked at the fire blazing in the nearby metal trash can, looked above them, and looked around, where no crowd gathered, but a car passed obliviously by. "Sooner or later you'll have one investigation too many, and your investigators will start running into each other." Burt let her go but used an arm to urge her away from the body.

"Take me home." Lily meant her home, but she thought and realized he couldn't do what she wanted. The police would be there, or at least police tape, some sort of seal on the door, and forensic markings of the various prints and fluids and spatter patterns and other clues, like on the procedural television shows. The whole apartment would have been dissected and analyzed, carved, photographed, and tagged, preserved and ready for future visits in preparation for inquests and requests and whatever other quests might be initiated as a result of Ralph murdering Sally and making Lily's home into a crime scene, where she might never live again because it had become a showcase of death, very much like the rectangle of concrete sidewalk where Iris's body now lay, where it now lay only two blocks from Burt's loft, in reach of but not in Burt's loft, not yet inside, a rot not yet inside Lily's last refuge. "Your home, I guess," she clarified.

Lily still had a refuge. She still had so much to lose. She needed to be ready. When would Burt betray her? Or would he merely die?

Back at the loft, Burt produced a bottle of Jameson from a cabinet, poured himself a glass and offered one to Lily. The bottle looked nicer, more expensive, than Iris's, but it looked similar. Lily accepted the glass. Nothing like whisky before sunrise.

For a moment, they drank together in silence. After pouring a second short glass for each of them, Burt said, "Next time you suggest we stay home, I'm going to listen to *you*." They both laughed, faintly because laughter itself felt tainted.

"I didn't actually say 'stay home.' I only said we'd be killed. Or you would. Next time I'll be less specific and push the 'stay home' idea." Lily drank. Then she had a thought. "You're really here, aren't you?"

"As far as I know."

"Good. And you saw... what I saw?"

"You mean a crazy woman who looked like she swallowed her own tongue and jumped out a window?" Burt gulped down his second drink. "Saw that, too."

"Do you think she looked like me?"

Burt grimaced. "What are you talking about? No!"

"She kind of reminded me... of me." Lily cleared her throat. "And I kind of thought, what if I'm imagining it all, you know? I get a message about losing all my money, and then I see a homeless woman who looks like me, talks about my situation—"

"She wasn't talking about your situation."

"Then what was she talking about?" Lily drank. "What did she mean by calling me 'sister?'"

"She probably calls every woman 'sister.' Called. Called every woman. You know what I mean." Burt drank.

"And what was the deal with that man? Sure, he didn't look like you, but he was still—"

"Which man?" Burt drank.

"The one upstairs," Lily said.

"She wanted witnesses," Burt said. "We came along at the right time, or the wrong one, depending on your perspective."

"It seemed like a ritual." Lily finished her drink.

"I thought the same thing in the jail cell, with the way that guy rocked back and forth before he did it. I was wrong, too." Burt finished his drink and poured more. Short ones. "Or maybe there's always a ritual to it. Before a few weeks ago, I'd never seen anybody kill themselves."

What had David's ritual been? Lily imagined him going through his little house with a checklist before finishing off the to-do items in the garage.

They shared another moment of quiet before Lily said, "I'm glad you're really here, because I imagined at one point that I was hallucinating you with me, that I'd gone out walking alone, with you still in bed back here. This whole conversation, our conversation before we went out, all of it, might have happened in my head, because kind of like Iris, I wanted a witness."

"Maybe I am a hallucination. Should I go upstairs to see if I'm there sleeping? Now I'm kind of curious." Burt smiled, but neither one of them laughed.

"If either one of us checks, it should be me, but I don't think so. If I'm that far gone, I might as well keep going. I don't want to know." Lily sighed and drank.

Burt drank. "I don't want to know either. Being a hallucination would suck."

Lily perked up. "I've got an idea. Since there's a chance you *are* a hallucination, and since that would mean I alone left a dead woman on the street to be discovered by someone else, why don't we—"

From the place on the countertop where Lily had left it, her phone rang. "It's almost five in the morning, isn't it? Who'd

147

be calling you at this hour?" Burt drank.

Lily finished her drink and winced. "Good news, probably." She picked up the phone. She listened. "Slow down, Rose," she said. "Please. Okay. Oh. Oh. That's terrible. Oh. Well did they tell you—oh. Well how long—I see. What does that mean? Did they say—uh-huh. Do you want me to—okay. Okay. I'm glad she could be there. Uh-huh. I'll do that. Uh-huh. Did she say anything? Well how's she—of course." It went on. Lily mostly listened but did not hear words as much as meanings. When the phone call ended, she set the phone back on the countertop.

Burt said, "Lily, you look sick. Are you okay?"

Lily balled up a fist and smashed it into her phone, which slid away beneath it. She grabbed the phone before it could escape and threw it on the floor. It bounced. Stabilizing it with her foot, she held it in place, grabbed a stool, and aimed. With the stool's leg aligned, she brought down the wood like a stake and pierced the screen, shattering it. She hit the phone again, again, again, pulverizing it until she was a mess of tears and sobbing.

Grabbing her shoulders from behind, Burt tried an embrace, which Lily did not resist. She collapsed backward into his chest, letting him absorb her crying. The reason for it almost left her mind as she became nothing but sadness, overwhelmed but the sheer volume of events, circumstances, and news. The most recent, though, rose to the surface, and she knew she had to tell him.

"Mom," she said.

He guided her to the sitting area beneath the bedroom overhang, and they took the sofa. "Tell me," he said, and he might have been a hallucination. "Tell me."

She asked him if he knew what metastatic glioblastoma was. He said it sounded like cancer. She said it was, specifically brain cancer, specifically the worst, most advanced kind. Mom was losing weight and throwing up and didn't know where she was half the time. It was nothing but headaches for weeks but then it got very bad very fast, which sometimes happens with this kind of cancer, but for it to be so aggressive is rare. She had a month, maybe two, hard to say. Vision problems, hearing problems, hallucinations, coma, death. Doris was there already, and Lily needed to be there soon, because Ethel, her mother, was forgetting things. She had been fine, just fine, only a week ago, the same old Ethel, but now time itself was leaving her, time itself was betraying her. Who knew time itself could turn traitor? Who knew time itself should be on the list of things you could lose?

Iris.

Mom was another warning. Another message.

Delusions of grandeur.

Selfish! Selfish! Selfish!

Mom, will you hallucinate with me? As your life melts away, as the tumor in your brain takes it all away from the inside, a funhouse mirror of my losing everything on the outside, will you join me on my vision-quest of fake Burts and falling bodies and locust plagues? Shall we have an apocalypse together? Too late for chemo, too late for radiation, *we can just make her comfortable*? Can I be comfortable, too? Can I wake up in the morning and find out it's all a bad dream? Can I start dreaming in the morning and never wake up?

There has to be another ending. There has to be.

9

Satan.

Lily was getting pretty tired of thinking about God. Nice hospital plus good insurance equaled private room for Mom, with enough space for two visitors, one of whom could sit in the rolling chair as long as the bed or equipment didn't need maneuvering for doctor or nurse purposes. Such were the accommodations for a woman needing to be stabilized before going home to await the next hospitalization for the next stabilization before the next homestay before the next hospital-stay before the next before the next before, eventually, no more nexts. In the chain of relocations, within the chain's links, appeared plenty of time for thinking about God, for stopping off in that chapel oh-so-convenient down the hall from Mom's room.

Doris talked about God. Doris, whose young offspring Donnie and Daisy knew as much about churches as they knew about Departments of Motor Vehicles, stood at Mom's bedside and prayed. She prayed *out loud*. "Please God, we need a miracle." Lily did not point out that God was not in the habit of answering prayers of unbelievers. Doris had missed more time with God than Mom had left, Lily opined: praying to God did not appear on the healing menu. Nothing did.

Satan lacked the reputation of a healer, but according to popular culture, he had a tendency to attend human weakness that Lily found intriguing. Circumstances had conspired to make Lily think about God far more often and more literally as a presence in her life than she had ever imagined possible, God not as an abstract force in the universe, or *as* the Universe, but closer to the bearded white guy on a big mountain that the fundamentalists imagined hating the fags and everybody else who disagreed with their fundaments. Who but a bearded white guy would make a bet that involved making a devotee suffer? Who but a bearded white guy would kill off Lily's friends and family just to see how far she could be pushed before offing herself? That's what was happening, right? Abstract forces don't play games. Bearded white guys do.

And that was the rule of left-hand, right-hand: one implies the other. If the bearded white guy exists, so does his swarthy, slippery, serpentine opposite, not a grandiose condensation of life itself like she had tried to convey to Vince when her thoughts had first turned to godly foolishness but a randy bugger with reddish skin-tones and horny protrusions on his scalp. Satan, bona fide, meet me at the crossroads Devil. And if Lily understood her Book of Job situation, she was supposed to blame Old Scratch rather than Our Father for her being the loser no matter which of them won the big bet they'd made.

Looking at her mom, thinking about Rose, her aunt-mom, crying and alone, Lily returned to this thought: Our Father could suck it. Lily was going to throw the bet to Old Scratch. For Satan to win, for the whole Job thing to be undone, all she had to do was curse God, right? Right. Done! Curse him, curse him, curse him! How's that for some Old Testament thinking, God? Eye for an eye. You cursed me, so I curse you back. It's only fair. Bring on the Devil!

Through casual Friendbooking and web browsing, Lily learned that finding someone to meet you in a café to tell you about God's Plan for You is exceptionally easy, especially if you're a fairly young, fairly decent-looking woman willing to meet an unknown, fairly strange man who totes a Bible and his personal, authoritative views on it. Finding someone

151

to tell you about Satan's Plan for You, on the other hand, is quite difficult. Satanists in general don't proselytize, and most of them are too busy fulfilling themselves, pursuing their own dark paths, or what have you, to worry too much about whether others awake to Satan's truths (or lack thereof). Further, while many adopt Anton LaVey's *Satanic Bible* as a guide or central tome, the idea of a holy book and sacred teachings doesn't hold up to much scrutiny for those on the Left-Hand side of things, so a take-it-or-leave-it attitude prevails. The God-mongers get all in a bunch about Satanists; the Satanists think the God-mongers are a bunch of whiny hypocrites but mostly have more important goals beyond the Moral Majority's fixation on cramping Satanists' style.

However, a man who called himself Gunther Azazel responded to Lily's request, placed in a Satanist's discussion group, to meet in a "busy coffeeshop" to discuss her "growing belief that Satan is real, like for real real, and fucking with my life."

"So when you say 'for real real,' are we talking pitchfork, spinning-head-pea-soup, the dog is talking to me, or what?" Gunther was having a giant cookie with his extra-foam latte. The skinny white man, bald and clean-shaven, wore a sleeveless black shirt that showcased his narrow but rippling arms. Lily noted the lack of tattoos.

Lily demurred. "What do you believe in?"

"I like underage pussy." He grinned. "Not, like, puberty stuff, that's gross, but jailbait for sure. Sucking dick is good, and getting my dick sucked. Satanists are best for orgies. The only reason you ever really want to try to, like, convert somebody is if you want to fuck them, or give them to your friends to fuck. I guess you might want to do blood stuff. I've done some of that, read Crowley, too, but whatever. Not my thing. To each his own. Are you into stuff yet, or are you just some batshit?"

"Excuse me?" Lily sipped her espresso.

"You're excused," Gunther said. He continued:

"Two types of people come into our discussion group. One type is us. You're not us, I can tell by looking. The other type is batshits. Most batshits are holy rollers looking for their ancient enemy or something, trying to call you out, trolls really, and they're fun to play with, a lot of them real curious, want to be like us, think we'll tempt them, seduce them, whatever. I tried that once on this Jesus chick, and she was a total cold fish. Not worth my time. Live and learn.

"Other batshits just want to fuck kids or kill people or whatever and think you'll help them out. Which, maybe you will, maybe you won't, I don't know, people are into what they're into, but I think the batshits would have better luck elsewhere. I mean, they've got their own groups, you know? If we all hung out online and then went around committing felonies, not many of us would make it very long. A little statutory something is one thing, but what the pervos usually come to us for is something else. No thank you. It's not that I don't know how to find that stuff, because I do, but it's not like I'm the guy you ask for directions, either.

"You, Miss Henshaw, don't seem like an ordinary everyday kind of batshit, so I'm wondering if you're some third kind, something I haven't seen before. That's why I'm here. It's the way you said 'for real real.' Like you met him or something. Not a lot of us expect Hell or Satan to show up in some kind of literal way. They're just ideas; everything's an idea. You think Satan's the sort of thing that has a body and will walk up to you?

"Because some of my friends have, but I haven't ruled that out. Because... wouldn't it just be cool? I've seen some pretty weird shit. You know how the saying goes, I don't believe in angels, but I believe in demons, and demons believe in me.

"What? You never heard that one? Maybe I made it up. Anyway, you want to get in touch with a demon, I know a guy you can call. A real fucked-in-the-head guy. He'll hook you up. You want me to talk to you about demons? The batshits like that. Do you like that? Want me to talk about demons? Say it to me. Say, 'Gunther, talk to me about demons.' Just like that. Say it.

"Good. Now I'll talk. After I thought about it, I realized I've probably had four or five brushes with demons in my life, counting a couple when I was a kid, and I didn't know what was happening, but I was twenty-four the first time I went looking for one and found one. It wasn't my first time messing around with what some people call blood magic, but before it was just people cutting themselves or each other and rubbing it all around during sex—or before or after or whatever —sometimes following instructions, sometimes not. I never fucked anybody in a new hole. I should still try that. Anyway, this time we were going to try some stuff with animals. I figured some *Angel Heart* shit with some chickens, followed by an orgy. Whatever.

"We were in this hole-in-the-wall town where people had barns and stuff. I've always been a city kid. I didn't know what to expect when I was meeting these two other guys and this girl in a barn, but like I said, I thought *chickens*. But as this one guy, John, led me through the barn to meet up with, uh, Jack and Jill, I got to thinking that the barn was empty, except down at the other end was this horse.

"What? No, it wasn't pale. It was jet black. I asked right away if the horse was part of the ritual, and Jill said the horse *is* the ritual. Jack had knives for all of us, with blades that were at least six inches, probably longer, and sharp on two edges, daggers, maybe. I put two and two together and knew we were going to kill horsey-horsey. I asked why. Getting up close to the animal, I wanted to—I didn't want to be close anymore. Horses are *big*, Miss Henshaw. Hundreds and hundreds of pounds of muscle death on four spindly legs with metal-plated rocks at their feet, ready to trample you into mush, that's what horses are. Piss one off, and a kick could crush a dozen bones in a second. Baseball-sized stupid eyes pointing in different directions, right at you, sucking you down, maybe they're seeing you, I don't know. The horse didn't react to me, whinnying and having fits at the big bad Satanist or anything, but I reacted to it, thinking before anybody answered me that I might not need a reason to kill it. It was a motherfucking monster.

"Jack answered my question about why by asking if I thought the horse was pretty. I said no, and Jill said it was pretty, 'raven-black,' she said, because she was one of those Goth-chick Satanists. She touched its hair, the mane, petted it, and I wanted to yell at her to stop, afraid it would stampede or something. Jack must have seen it in my face because he asked if I was afraid, and I said yes I was. He nodded and looked at John and asked if he was afraid. John said yes, afraid of being stuck here all night with a stupid horse and stupid people in a stupid barn. His eyes got softer when he looked at me and said that yeah, the horse was fucking terrifying, too, because he could tell it wanted to eat every one of us like we were all just hay. John did a lot of shrooming in those days.

"Jack said two afraids and one pretty were more than enough reasons to kill the damned horse. As for Jack himself, he was another pretty vote, and he felt like destroying something beautiful, which sounded like a line from a movie. The point of most Satanic rituals was to free yourself from the bonds of fear and taboo in order to empower the self, and slaughtering the massive creature, for its own sake, would do that. Destroy your ideas about scary things and beautiful things. Nothing is untouchable. We didn't need elaborate chants or dances. We just needed an old-fashioned bloodbath brought to us by the work of our own hands. A simple concept, kind of elegant, when you think about it.

"So you're not impressed. Whatever. The concept *was* simple, but the execution was... trickier. The horse stayed calm enough with four people standing around talking in low voices, but at the first cut of a blade, it would go supreme-o nuts-o. We had to worry about those bone-crushing kicks. We argued about how to do it. You'd think the horse might get nervous with four people standing around it with daggers, arguing, stark naked and arguing, but it just stood there, being a horse, while we debated how to kill it. Stupid things have bold souls.

"Jilly got sick of waiting and jammed her knife in its baseball eye. The three guys jumped back, three votes for fear, as the horse reared up on its hind legs, blammo for anybody close to the front, but there was nobody. Jilly used the knife as a kind of pivot, jumping up, leaping like a gymnast, spinning in the air with a fan of limbs, and mounting the horse while it still reared screaming. My jaw dropped. I'd never seen this woman before, but looking at her, I felt like I knew her. And my cock was harder than it had ever been, and I could see John and Jack, standing, staring nearby, and we were all in heat, all hard, skin flushed, breathing heavy. So was the fucking horse, Miss Henshaw. That was a fucking *stallion* at full mast. Whatever pain he was in, he forgot. Breath sucked and blew through horse nostrils. Whatever panic he felt turned to something else as Jilly yanked the knife out of the horse's eye and held it up over her head, grinning. That grin—I wasn't standing too close, no, not close at all, but I could see her teeth, and her mouth hadn't looked like that a minute ago, it couldn't have. She had teeth as long as her fingers, curling outward, and her eyes sparkled, not red like you'd think, but like, what you call them, emeralds, deep green and, and lovely. Her hair blew out behind her like the horse's mane. How that horse stayed on its hind legs so long. How she stayed on its back, arms up like she would pull down the barn's roof. I don't know. I don't know.

"With the horse still rearing, she slid the knife across

the front of its big wide neck. Jack ran into the spray first, the blood dousing his skin, and John ran in, like kids in a sprinkler. I didn't think about it, but I felt a tug in my chest and in my groin, and it was like, neener-neener-neener! Follow the pull, the arrow-pointer of my cock, the *draw of my heart*, if you're a romantic. I followed my heart right into the crimson spray of horse blood, feeling it cover my skin, get into my hair. Yeah, I had hair then. It got in my eyes, my mouth. I tasted it. It got in the folds of my eyelids, in my armpits. It got in my asscrack. It got all over my dick, and half-realizing I started jerking off, and I came ropes of jizz into puddles of blood just like the other guys were doing, and it didn't matter because I stayed just as hard. We were dancing now, yeah, dancing, not like the planned-out dancing I'd done at sabbats or the frenzies of other blood magic orgies but more like broken marionettes twitching on the ends of strings, jerking, jerking, jerking. Nothing musical. It was nothing musical, only bloody and delicious.

"Let them look! Finish your fucking coffee. You want some of this cookie? It's good. Here. Fine then, more for me. So anyway, the horse fell to its horsey knees, and Jilly fell off, breaking both her legs, and next time we saw her, her mouth looked normal, and I wanted to kick her in the head, but I didn't. I guess I'm a nice fucking guy."

Lily asked how Gunther knew he'd seen a demon rather than a hallucination. Gunther told her that John and Jack hadn't seen Jilly's wicked-long teeth, but Jack had at least seen the emerald eyes. Seeing, though, was not believing. Believing occurred at the moment he felt himself, uncontrolled, rush into the spray of blood and, unbidden, coax his own fluids to join in the flow. "That was the magic, the kind some people spell with a k at the end of the word. We didn't need chalices and gongs and swords to reach ecstasy; I stood outside myself and saw myself and most became myself in the presence of the demonic. In knowing myself I knew the demonic. That was all." He looked at her, waiting to absorb her shock.

"*All*?" Lily said. Remembering the laughter when Iris bit off her tongue, she laughed in his face. "You expect *that* to impress me? Let me tell *you* a story." Lily talked about roadsides with flickering streetlights. Lily discussed locusts. She omitted attempted rape—didn't think the audience right —and skipped over family tragedy. She ended with a rapid, surprise meeting between a stranger and a sidewalk.

Gunther was stunned.

"So," Lily said, "understand that I need a little more from you than 'know thyself' for recognizing demons. I want to make sure that if I pass Satan walking on the street, I know the guy, because Mr. Scratch and I need to have a conversation."

"Satan wouldn't do this sort of thing," Gunther said. "What's in it for him? You've got a very Christian worldview for someone who claims not to be Christian."

"I'm not blaming *Satan*. I'm blaming *God*, which is why *Satan* and I need to have a chat, you understand me? Do you really think I'd be having a conversation with *you*—no offense —if I weren't ready to take a slow dive into the deep end of darkness? If you're not the guy who gives directions, who is? I want a fucking name! I want fucking directions!"

Everyone in the café stared at them. A barista was struggling with the decision about telling them to leave.

Gunther wrote "Tobias Centurion" and a number on a napkin and handed it to Lily. "He can give you directions. Good luck." Gunther downed the rest of his latte. "You're one of a kind, Miss Henshaw. A pleasure to meet you."

Lily made an awkward exit from the coffee shop and entered the bright city streets. Being unemployed, owning her own time, remained foreign to her. She asked Burt if he needed her help with anything as he spent the day trying to manage orders from his loft, routing them through offsite printers so he could at least take a percentage and maintain some kind of income, and he said she should go out and try to enjoy herself. Bothering to explain that her only plan for the day started and ended with a Satanic powwow did not seem worthwhile; she feigned the possibility of enjoyment and decided not to return until after five in the afternoon. She might find another café, or maybe a bar. Although she couldn't recall the last time she'd set foot in a library, she could go to one and pick up —what?—something by Anton La Vey or Aleister Crowley, if twenty-first century libraries allowed devil-books to circulate. A bar sounded better. Ever since Iris, a perverse imp had been encouraging her to drink.

Indecision stymied her, so she kept walking without a destination in mind. At first she thought the feeling was a remnant from the coffee shop, a lingering stain from having listened to Gunther's full-volume tall tale of animal mutilation in the midst of a properly disgusted crowd, but as Lily crossed first one street, then another, the sensation did not diminish: people gawked at her. They stared, sputtered, and sneered. She thought about stopping somewhere to find a mirror, but she glimpsed her reflection on a perfume ad that formed the wall of a bus stop, and though she didn't look as good as the woman in the ad, she looked normal, for herself. Nothing to titter at. Nothing to notice. But people were noticing.

In three blocks she would come upon the downtown library, and the thought of going there did seem inviting, not because of the books but because of the small green space in front. She arrived and found a bench unoccupied. Sitting there gave her an opportunity to think more about Satan. She wasn't going to run out and slaughter a horse, so she wasn't sure she had gotten much of use from her visit with Gunther. He both possessed and lacked the qualities of what she'd expected from a Satanist. He had no reason to represent himself honestly to her, so when she let him tell her a story, she invited him to be a full-of-shit unreliable narrator, as they called them in college.

Lily didn't have to be paranoid to know the man was toying with her.

Lily also thought about horses. Sometimes you'd see horses in the city. Carriages were pretty rare nowadays, but sometimes they were around for one reason or another. A mounted policeman. A parade. Something. Very few things deserve the majesty of the word "majesty," but horses might. Lily supposed she hoped Gunther's story was a total fabrication because she didn't want to think she'd shared space with someone vile enough to dance naked in pretty horse blood.

Still, she had to wonder why she found his story so difficult to believe. After all she had been through, why not believe in demons with sharp pointy teeth and emerald eyes? Three men dancing around, erections bobbing, while the lone woman goes full demon and slaughters a horse so they can all get wild in the blood—could a more ridiculous male fantasy exist without imploding?

Why a horse? Surely a cow or a pig would have been the more suitable animal. Or a bull, if they'd wanted to get really serious. A horse, and a black one at that, needed special consideration. A horse could choose sides and could ride with Satan or God or whomever.

As Lily got up to leave the library's green space, she imagined herself on horseback. She didn't know how to ride, but she imagined doing it anyway. Venturing through traffic on crosswalks and elsewhere, Lily took a horseback-view of her surroundings as she maneuvered. The extra space she needed to get around people was difficult to maintain, but she managed. Her behavior was visualization, not pretend or hallucination.

When she got to Food 7, a restaurant she liked, she knew where she and the horse were going. Foot traffic got a little denser as the buildings got taller. People's clothing became more expensive, and they seemed distracted by their phones and the importance of their briefcases. Amidst the tall buildings, 1500 Spring stood neither tallest nor greatest in fame, but it had become a lure, and Lily chased.

The horse reacted to the closeness of the tall white edifice. She whinnied and stepped back, halting with an abruptness that warned without imperiling. A moment later, Lily understood the horse's reaction. A wave of sensation, between nausea and elation, swept over her, threatening to overwhelm her if she approached the building closer.

Held off, she faced 1500 Spring from her mounted vantage. The rotary doors at the center of the entrance made walking in look simple enough. Maybe not for a horse, but if she dismounted. Nothing else but a street to cross and a few stairs to climb stood between her and entering 1500 Spring.

Burt had told her she had a tendency to get fixated on certain ideas. She had always had this tendency, but she knew it liked to come out more when she was in times of greater stress. Mansworth Futures and Securities, whose office location had first drawn her to 1500 Spring as a kind of epicenter for life's catastrophic eccentricities, had not played any direct part in her life beyond ordering posters correlated, paranoiacally, with bugs she may and may not have seen in her apartment. Was there more to it than that? Looking at the tower, she felt there had to be much, much more.

What did she expect, an engraved invitation? She should just go, check out the lobby, see what else was in the building. She might even get up to Mansworth's level, see their offices, what kind of décor they had up. Were those posters in their lobby? Had they had any good meetings with the Almighty or his Nemesis?

Lily was still trying to get her head around Satan. Did she really believe in this stuff now? It all seemed sort of... comic book. She thought of the Battle for Heaven, armies of angels and demons clashing, and the scenes in her head seemed too vibrant for reality. The most vivid reds and glowing whites: tails and horns and razor-sharp claws on one side; on the other wings, with swords, and shields, and circles of light. Gunther would remind her that she had too Christian a view of things. She probably didn't need to be so literal. After he was done with his bullshit horse-slaughter story (easy, girl), he'd gone back to ideas about the demonic being more abstract, more related to the self, and that made more sense than pointy teeth and emeralds.

But Satan? Lily was only entertaining the thought of him because she needed the explanatory power of an evil agency, a personality of a sort willing to commit heinous acts against a person just for kicks, and/or to prove a point, which was no better. She needed the character from the Job story to come talk to her. Lily didn't exactly know what she'd do in the event of an actual conversation with Mr. Scratch, but she imagined it going like this:

LILY (calling down from horse): You there, in the pin-striped suit!

LUKE (debonair): *Moi?* Don't you know I'm on TV now? More than one show. I'm a *character*. Leave me alone.

LILY: Mostly reruns. Why are you bothering me?

LUKE: Bothering *you*? You're not my problem, except for calling me out here on the street. Blame the Big Guy for your shit. He's the one with something to prove. Omnipotence. Omniscience. Ubiquity. I lose nothing by losing. He's *supposed* to win. He's got it all on the line.

LILY (laughing on her high horse): So, I curse God, and you score a major victory, right?

LUKE (laughing): *Delusions of grandeur!* Lily, darling, precious girl, you are not Job. God served up Job as one of his most devoted followers. You? You're gristle. By God's standards, you were already one of mine, not that I'd claim you, either. Ask Gunther: I'm not as eager as all that.

LILY: Then what... what... what...?

LUKE: Are you a dumbass? (to a bystander) Look at that woman up there. Does she look like a dumbass to you? (to Lily) We think you look like a dumbass, but you're not, are you? You understand that the Book of Job was written thousands of years ago, and you are not in it. It is not the Book of Lily Henshaw.

LILY: Book of... Me?

LUKE: Are you playing out someone else's fantasy to an inevitable end? They say Job himself wrote the Book of Job. And it's got a crazy happy ending. Coincidence? Do you still believe in coincidence?

LILY: No. Maybe. I don't know.

LUKE: It's either all about you, or it isn't, and if it isn't, you're toast. Because David—it wasn't about David, was it? He got so far away from his own story that he lost the plot and ended his part in it. That's all suicide is. Losing the plot. Except now he's—

LILY (trying to calm her horse): Easy, girl, easy!

DAVID: A werewolf.

LILY: David, you look... hairy.

DAVID: Thank you. Curses come in all shapes and body types. Mine is hairy. Do my eyes look like emeralds?

LILY: No. Listen, Satan—

LUKE: Call me Luke.

LILY (looking left, right, and down from her horse): Part of me thinks I'm standing on a city street talking to people who aren't there, and the people who are there are staring at me.

There's this cop—

DAVID (slobbering): People will stare at you no matter what you do.

LUKE (mounting to ride behind Lily): I will whisper in your ear. Ride west a block, then cross toward 1500.

LILY (riding): If this is the Book of Lily, not the Book of Job, what can I do?

LUKE: What *can't* you do? Let me show you something.

Streets, buildings, and blue sky vanished, allowing reddened darkness from roiling clouds to fill in overhead while the landscape devolved into waste, piles of stone and wood, unrecognizable grey debris where moments ago structures and people had busied. The only tower stood, at center, higher than Lily remembered, but still white and still sharp with right angles, tapering toward the red-black-ruffled sky, 1500 Spring. Movement came not just from the billowing clouds but forms circling within, perhaps winged, perhaps not, but flying; Lily watched for emerald sparkles but saw none. Guiding the horse closer to the tower at a slow trot, Lily reached into a debris pile and lifted out what would serve as a wooden lance, which she aimed at the tower itself.

Small woman on small horse tilting a slice of wood against an edifice of modern engineering—comical yet classic, quixotic, except she had no notions to defend. She and her horse held a powdery wasteland patch of earth before this tower not in heroic stance but in defiant supplication, both begging and challenging the tower to tell them what their places ought to be in an order of which the waste might or might not have been the true face.

Luke was gone. The space behind her on the horse's back was empty, and David hadn't followed them west and across what had once been a street. Lily was without either man in her new position at the very foot of 1500 Spring. Instead, she had three new companions.

"Howdy," Eric said.

Lily looked from Eric to the tower, back to Eric. They seemed unaware of each other. Kris said hello, and Mia said nothing. Lily said, "Hello, advisers."

"We're here on an intervention," Eric said. Wind blew dust all around him. From the horse's vantage, Lily noticed how thin his hair was getting in a few places. The white tower loomed.

Kris extended a hand, upward, toward Lily. "Heed our counsel."

Lily left Kris hanging. "I'm hearing a lot of counsel."

Mia said, "Trust shall be a spider's web."

Lily and Eric regarded Mia with different sorts of smiles. "Thanks for that," Lily said. The ground trembled. Nearby, a fissure appeared, and smoke arose.

"Heed!" Kris's hand awaited reception. It would wait.

Eric shook his head. "You might want to think, objectively, about the company you've been keeping today."

Lily petted her horse's mane. "I've given it some thought."

"Don't keep company with those who part ways with the Lord," Kris said.

"Excuse me, Miss, but didn't we once do lines of coke in the bathroom of a bar at a birthday party? Since when are you all 'ways of the Lord?' I prefer for my visions to be consistent, thank you." Lily looked away from her advisers, toward the tower.

"Come on, Lily," Eric said. "Before us you were chatting with Satan. At least that's an upgrade, right?"

"Remains to be seen." Lily piloted the horse closer to the rotary door entrance to 1500 Spring. While the entire landscape around the building had turned to ruin, grey rubble tinted red by the expanse of shattered sky, the building itself appeared exactly as it had. The advisers followed her. "Why should I *heed* you and not Luke? Are you on God's side? And if you are, why should I be? God isn't on *my* side. Besides, Luke is just a figure of my imagination. I don't know if he or God even exists."

Kris and Mia, shouting together: "DERACINATION!"

"That's not a Bible word," Lily said. Eric snickered.

"*Radix malorum est radix malorum,*" Kris said.

"Now we're talking. Latin." Lily thought a moment. "The evil radish is the evil radish. No—evil root. The evil root, the root of evil, maybe. The root of evil is the root of evil? That's dumb, Kris."

"So is making friends with the Devil," Eric said.

Lily shrugged. "Touché. But I've been having root trouble lately. If God made the Devil, God's the root root, isn't he? I'm hoping to get at the source."

Mia said, "Trust shall be a spider's web."

"Deracinate," Kris said.

Standing in the reddened wasteland that had been Lily's city, Kris, Mia, and Eric, or the creatures that looked like them, behaved as if they knew little beyond how to be annoying. "Kris, we'll get to you in a minute," Lily said. "First, I want to deal with the spider situation." Should she explain that she'd had quite enough of bugs lately?

How much did these people know, anyway, about what she'd been going through? Lily considered that, as products of her mind, these three "advisers" might know everything she knows, a level of knowledge she was expecting increasingly often from everyone she met. Her mind and situation had assumed, without her consent, transparency, so when people stared at her on the street they did so not because their vision stopped at her surface but because it passed through, not just into her organs but into her life, through the details of ordeals, down into the wasteland of judgment. Down here in judgment, where everyone looked at her on her horse and knew she was wrong, all the tragedies from her advisers' deaths to her mom's cancer stuck to her in spokes and claimed *her* as the root, blameworthy, condemned.

Satan and spiders. Luke may or may not have been a root unto himself, but he certainly spun webs, or at least Lily spun webs around him, with her thoughts about the Book of Job and the Book of Lily, and what her work on her *self* might do to make her ending more like Job's ending because she wrote her *self*, like Job, because in all other respects, save torture, she was not like Job. Job took the Right-Hand Path despite everything God let happen, refusing to curse God, so Lily considered Luke and the Left-Hand Path, but what of the webbing, the problem of trust? Mia, Mia... who are you working for?

Maybe Lily had it all wrong. Maybe trusting Satan wasn't the problem. Mia talked about trust in general. Whom did Lily trust most right now? The answer had to be Burt. Iris had kept her husband for *years* she said, after it all started, trusting him, relying on him, only to discover he was betraying her all along. Who was Burt? Lily's boss who had a crush on her. From an outside perspective, who was Burt? A man drawn to a damsel in distress. Deep distress, the kind that fucks you up on the inside in ways from which you might never recover. The kinds of fish drawn to fish in distress are sharks. Distress became an opportunity for him to get what he wanted, didn't it? What kind of man was Burt?

Other people she trusted—who were they? Who else knew what was happening to her? Nobody, really. Mom, Rose, and Doris knew most of the facts, without the garlands of locusts and other elaborations, but what Mom knew was fading, and Rose and Doris had room for little beyond their own lives and Mom. She didn't distrust them, exactly, but she couldn't trust them, either. Even if she wanted to trust the people at work (she didn't), she didn't have an "at work" anymore, so that was a non-starter. Social media friends might... no, not really. If she'd ever thought about her three closest friends knowing and hanging out with each other being a problem because they could all die together, she might have diversified her social group, but the thought hadn't occurred to her until too late.

She was already deracinated! The fifty-cent word didn't throw her off in the slightest. It meant she was uprooted, cut off, and the word never, as far as she knew, had a positive association, but her so-called advisers seemed to present it as a solution to her problems, and she resented the hell out of the suggestion. Was deracination supposed to save her from the problem of trust? Save her from the sticky spider's web? Easy, girl! The horse was getting restless.

The root of evil is the root of evil, so cut off the root. Wasn't that what she said she wanted? To get at the root? And what would she do with it if she got to it? Cut if off. Deracinate. Satan. God. Either. Both. Cut! This goddamned building. This God-damned building! 1500 Spring loomed the tallest and the best, the only thing in the reddened landscape, hateful and bright, and if Lily's wooden lance had been an axe she would have swung it wide and chopped at it like Jack at the looming (horse) beanstalk, and it would shower down what giants it propped up, bringing them within reach of vengeance—Lily's or theirs, she didn't know. There are giants in the sky. There are big tall terrible awesome scary wonderful giants in the sky.

She didn't have an axe, though, but a lance, and she could run it through. How silly, Lily, to charge at a tower on horseback with a lance! The sky, the landscape, the tower, the horse, all spoke to her in symbols now, so maybe the lance and a good skewering would add up to a symbol, too, and her assault on the building would amount to something real. The conversion ratio between reality and fantasy valued at what, exactly? When a swarm of locusts for Lily meant a few for Burt, what could a mounted attack on a tower in a blasted landscape mean in the city she had left behind?

Gunther and his boys, running out, naked, with Lily, sprouting teeth like fingers, her eyes like emeralds—she could handle the knife, boys, and she could pierce the eye and slash the throat, oh yes, and when this horse rears up, prepare, prepare—

No. The horse charged forward, and she held the lance ready. It would splinter on contact, but she didn't care. She would ram the lance right into white concrete, right into the building's side, and see if the edifice reacted, see if the building sent down its emissary to challenge the intruder. Then she at least would not be the only creature, save those circling in the red-black clouded sky above, here in this wasteland. The impact of splintering wood threw her from the horse, which reared and fled a short space away from the tower, and she landed hard on her backside, breaking nothing. Her hands still held a shard of wood, and seeing no reaction from the edifice, she charged it, ready to stake it like a vampire.

A police officer caught her, and she saw that the wood in her hands was a stick connected to a sign that said, "REPENT!" She was bashing it against the side of 1500 Spring, and traffic on the sidewalk gave her a wide berth. "Easy now," the policeman said, immobilizing her in a barrel hug from behind. "Easy." With little choice offered by his superior strength, she let adrenaline ebb away and surrendered the sign, which he took from her. He said into his shoulder, which had some kind of radio, "Dispatch, I've got a 10-96 and may need backup outside 1500 Spring, please respond."

Lily relaxed so completely that she shriveled inside the

larger man's arms, which became loose. Before he could think to search her for a knife or gun—not a very good cop, she supposed—she dropped to her knees and head-butted him in the groin. Stunning him and botching his balance, she managed a foot-sweep with one leg and sent him tumbling. Back to a stand, she searched the surrounding area, where onlookers leapt away from her in panic, and found her horse, nearby and ready. Like an old pro now, she jumped on the horse's back and guided her in a semicircle, pointing her away from 1500 Spring, toward the loft that served as home.

The race for home took them through crowds thickening with the bustle of rush hour. When lights turned against her, Lily steered the horse to move left or right, up or down a block with unceasing traffic, loathe to break her gallop. Her running speed and breakneck push through the throng made some people yell at her, others simply yell, jumping back, pumping fists, protesting her use of sidewalks and crosswalks for a beast that should use the same lanes as cars. At her speed, she hardly dared to look anywhere but ahead, but a glance behind showed no cops pursuing, so she must have gotten away, and she slowed, bringing her gallop back to a trot just as she reached Burt's building.

Soaked with sweat, out of breath from the tense ride, she dismounted and set the horse free. Up the stairs and entering the loft, she found Burt on the phone, waving her inside and pointing at his watch, indicating ten, maybe fifteen minutes until he was done. She pulled her hair away from the sides of her face, enjoying the loft's cooler air, and crossed to a window.

Outside, on the sidewalk, people moved by, the city's five o'clock foot traffic. Not all of them continued their course when their movement brought them close to Burt's building. Some of them stopped and leaned close to their co-travelers. They whispered things into one another's ears. They looked up at windows, mainly at the window where Lily stood. They pointed and whispered more. Soon, two onlookers became three, and three became four. They became a cluster, and the cluster became a group, whispering and pointing. Looking down at them, unable to look away, Lily closed the window's venetian blinds.

On the opposite side of the loft, a different side of the building, she observed the same behavior: people gathered, like sediment in a river eddy, to point and look. Twisting the rod as quickly as fingers could manage, Lily closed venetian blinds. Window by window, she shut out natural light from the apartment. Beyond the blinds, the afternoon sky, transitioning to evening, might have been blue, orange, or red-black. She didn't know anymore because she couldn't trust looking.

10

The rabbit was almost a deal breaker. After Mr. Centurion's long, long speech about the virtue of lying, Lily had known better than to push when he specified that he asked for a rabbit as the price of admission because *he liked rabbits*. *He liked rabbits* served as well as any other reason: he refused to say what he would *do* with the rabbit. He could furnish another, longer excuse for demanding one, but it would be no more, and likely less, satisfactory than the simple *he liked rabbits* statement. *He liked rabbits* for dinner, sacrifice, squealing howling death-sex, what have you. Tobias Centurion asked for a rabbit because he wanted one, required one as the main entry fee for an audience. Lily wanted an audience, so she told Burt they needed to bring Mr. Centurion a rabbit, and Burt, imagining dinner, sacrifice, or squealing howling death-sex, what have you, resisted.

Burt did not have the same reason to suspect animal cruelty as Lily. She hadn't told him Gunther's horse story, nor even her own horse story, which was no story, as she knew she had not ridden a horse through the city with a policeman in pursuit. Never mind that her thighs and back felt sore as if she had been riding. Kris, Mia, and Eric had usurped a vivid daydream, turning it into something else, and she did tell Burt about the three of them visiting her on the street, and her running back to the loft after, because the three of them had a reality like the locusts—in excess of the visionary. Showing up sweaty after the run also had excessive reality, so Lily had explained it, and truth, *contra* Mr. Centurion's assertions about truth's lack of purpose, seemed easier to track than lies, even in fragments.

Holding up the rabbit's cage and pointing to the house in the cul-de-sac's corner, Burt said, "This is a living creature. That, if we're in the right place, is the house of a man referred to us by a self-avowed Satanist. I don't feel good about this, Lily. Why don't we leave?"

"Would you feel better if he'd requested some rabbit stew instead? Last I checked, we both eat meat. So he kills the wabbit. So what." Lily looked at the house. From the street, it looked like an ordinary ranch-style suburban home, with maybe three bedrooms, nothing fancy. The drive from the city had taken almost an hour, and out here the yards were big enough to allow for real privacy. Lily, Burt, and Tobias Centurion could probably dance around in the back yard (wooden fence) slaughtering small animals until dawn and, unless they blasted devil music through loudspeakers, never have authorities summoned to intrude on their festivities.

Burt slammed the car door. Holding up the rabbit cage, he acquiesced, motioning for Lily to lead the way up the walk to Mr. Centurion's front door. "If he's wearing contact lenses that make him look like the emperor from the *Star Wars* movies, I'm leaving. Your confidence in him is creeping me out."

"Got it," Lily said. "Emperor eyes, we retreat." She made a point of stepping only on the stones that marked the path from the paved driveway through grass to the front door, not because she feared the mud from recent rain but because the neat lawn presented its own kind of suburban sanctity, not to be disturbed. Tobias Centurion, addressing Lily and Burt on speakerphone, had said he knew Gunther Azazel and appreciated the reference but was himself not a Satanist, or any other –ist or professor of any other –ism. Ists and isms were not, in the end, for him, which is why he got along with people like Gunther, who erred in clinging to shells of organized thought but understood chaos as the only overarching principle to uphold.

When Lily pressed the doorbell, it made an old-fashioned ding-dong sound that reminded Lily of a house Mom and Rose had when she was a little girl. David used to practice skateboard tricks in the driveway. The entryway by Mr. Centurion's front door would accommodate two people but not two people and a rabbit cage, so Burt stood behind her. Lily had an envelope in her left hand. Since they'd brought the rabbit, the charge for the visit, the secondary entry fee, was only two hundred dollars, cash. Burt groused about that, too, but Lily insisted that the money wasn't as important as the possibility of learning something.

What could they learn? Directions on how to reach Satan?

Don't be absurd. Hadn't they learned something from Lady Laetitia?

Extreme Psychic. Wasn't she extreme enough? Did they really need someone who advertised himself with a long harangue about the virtue of lying? Besides, they hadn't learned anything from Lady Laetitia other than that she had a cheap supply of easy-crack tabletops.

But Burt, you said you *believed* what she said. She taught us something to believe. And that long harangue was straight out of Oscar Wilde. I Googled it. "The Decay of Lying." "Lying for its own sake is beyond reproach," or something like that. What does it matter if he or Tish or anybody lies or doesn't lie if we get something we can use from it?

Now who's the relativist, Lily?

Enormous breasts answered the door. The breasts presented themselves prior to any other appearance, for they lacked cover and support, wearing only a necklace of small seashells that looked even smaller draped across the deep crevasse formed by their cleavage. They sagged from their weight but had firmness. Unlike their fake pornographic equals, the nipples matched their girth, with grand areolas and knobs for points, as if more than one miniature human might have weaned there. Closer inspection—which did not require proximity, just a resetting of the eyes—revealed stretch marks in places, reinforcing the sense that the breasts had seen service. Each breast would overpower the head of the average baby and the hand of a groping adult. Together, they were a splendid, exuberant welcome party.

Lily couldn't help glancing at her own chest before exploring upward from the breasts of greeting. Above the left breast, near the clavicle, a tattoo stood watch. It was a creature, but what sort of creature, Lily couldn't be sure. It had the head of a wolf, some sort of bird's wings, and a tail like a lizard. It was not as pretty as the breast, and Lily did not consider herself a breast aficionado. Above the creature, a woman's face waited for eye contact. Lily made it. "Hello there," the woman said. Her smile exuded the same professionalism as anyone wearing a full suit. "You must be Lily. I'm Alva." She extended a hand, which Lily shook. The breasts wobbled during the shaking. Lily felt bad for fixating, and thereby objectifying, but the breasts were too... present... to avoid.

"How are you, Alva?" The question sounded stupid.

"I'm well, thank you. Would you and your friend like to come in?" Alva stepped out of the doorway, making room for Lily, Burt, and the rabbit cage. "Please set the cage on that table over there." Alva pointed. "Toby will show you into the dungeon in a moment." She tittered. "Don't worry about the word *dungeon*. You're not here for my services. I assure you that his are usually more... tame." Alva fluttered her eyelashes, and Lily noticed that the lower half of the breasts outfit was a leather miniskirt.

Burt cleared his throat. "What are your services, exactly?" He smiled as if he had confident control. Lily saw through it, and she guessed Alva did, too.

As Alva walked to Burt, who hadn't moved far from the rabbit cage, she asked, "What did you have in mind?" She stuck her tongue in the corner of her mouth so that both of her companions could see.

"Do you mind if I sit?" Lily gestured to a sofa. Burt stared at the breasts.

"Both of you sit. I'll get drinks." Alva disappeared and reappeared with three well-balanced glasses, which she set on the proper coffee table in front of the proper sofa and loveseat in the catalogue-decorated living room of the suburban house. An Ansel Adams print hung over the modest flat-screen television. The glasses contained amber liquid. "Whiskey sours, with fresh lemon." Lily sipped immediately. Burt studied his glass. "Fresh lemon," Alva repeated, "and who knows what else, right?" She smiled and took a gulp, and Lily reflected that the distribution of glasses might have been random.

Lily handed over the envelope, which she realized she'd been clutching. Alva said thank you and set it aside. The two of them drank and discussed weather while Burt continued to study his glass. "If you put that back down on the side table there," Alva mentioned, "please use a coaster." The flow of conversation returned. Burt divided attention between glass and breasts. Eventually, he took a sip.

"Hello hello!" The shouting man, likely Tobias, entered through a door that blended with the living room wall, with no doorknob or other marking to set it off from surrounding texture and color. He was also bare-chested and well-developed on top, not huge but muscled, with tattoos starting at his neck and running down his chest and belly toward his crotch, which a loincloth, tied almost like a diaper, obscured.

With professionalism mirroring Alva's, oblivious to his body's exposure, he extended a hand for shaking, to Burt first: "Tobias Centurion!"

"Burt Wells. Here to support—"

"Lily Henshaw!" Tobias sounded as if he'd been waiting to meet her all his life. He shook her hand. "Such an honor. I'll only remind you once: everything I say could be a lie. After your call, I was so intrigued by our conversation that I talked to Mr. Azazel myself, and he filled me in on your backstory. You are a rare specimen indeed! Did you bring my rabbit?"

"Over here, Toby." Alva had her drink and stood near the cage. The rabbit looked nervous. It was white with black splotches, long whiskers, and only medium-long ears. Its nose twitched in what appeared to be a constant fight against sneezes.

Toby beamed at the small beast. "Good, good! Now then —"

Burt stood up. "What's the rabbit for?"

"Burt," Lily said.

Tobias rubbed his white belly and smiled. "It's okay, Ms. Henshaw. We need Mr. Wells to keep that skepticism up! Would you believe me if I told you I simply wanted a new pet?" A tattoo on Tobias's chest matched Alva's, the wolf-bird-lizard.

"No," Burt said.

"Would you believe me if I said I wanted to bite its head off?" Tobias opened his mouth wide, a big mouth, but not big enough for a rabbit's head.

"No."

"Wear its intestines as a necktie? Cut it open for a divination spell? Pray to it until it speaks with the voice of the Devil? 'Feed me kale of the damned!' Please, Mr. Wells, tell me how I am to use this offering you've brought me! Tell me what you'd like to hear, and I'll say it to comfort you!" Tobias kept rubbing his own belly.

Burt drank more of his whiskey sour. "Has anything you've said been true?"

"Yes," Tobias said. "Does that answer make you feel better?"

Burt sighed, ice clinking in his glass. "No."

"The only way you're going to be satisfied about the rabbit is if you *see* what I do to it, isn't that right, Mr. Wells? Except—doesn't the observer change the experiment, Mr. Wells? How do you know that I wasn't planning on keeping the rabbit, but if you insist I do something, I might kill it in front of you, just for the show? The fact is, you'll never know what I might have done without your interference. The rabbit's fate is entirely in flux right now because we're talking about it. You have such power, Mr. Wells, more than you knew! Insist on knowing more about this rabbit, and you might very well end its life! Think about it, Mr. Wells. How much do you want, do you *need*, to know about this poor bunny?"

"Mr. Centurion," Lily asked. "Why do you call us by our last names? I noticed Gunther, Mr. Azazel, did that, too."

"Why Ms. Henshaw, because I taught the boy *manners*. And now I'm teaching your boy something." Tobias winced. "I didn't mean that how it sounded. No offense."

"None taken. The lesson?"

"How about this." Tobias scratched his loincloth. "Your offerings entitle you to one demonstration, one set of answers. Either we go looking for answers to your burning questions about the bunny, or we go looking for answers to your burning questions about Lily. What'll it be?"

"Me," Lily said.

"Choose, Mr. Wells. The rabbit is about to disappear

forever from your life story. I will ask Alva to take it away, hide it in our bedroom, and you will never encounter it again. You will never know what became of it. Your knowing and not knowing will not affect it further, for good, for ill, or otherwise. But your knowing and not knowing *will* affect Ms. Henshaw here, for good, for ill, and otherwise. Think carefully. You *will* affect one of the two. Will it be the rabbit, or the woman?"

"I...." Burt seemed confused. His confusion confused the hell out of Lily. Had he forgotten why they got the rabbit in the first place?

"Alva, the needles." Tobias pointed toward a door, probably a bathroom, and Alva went to it, breasts buoyant. She returned with a thin-glassed jar filled with fluid, like what hairdressers use for combs, but instead of combs it contained thin metal spindles, like the acupuncturists use in movies. Tobias drew one of the needles from the jar. He held it up to a light so that Burt could see how thin, clean, and shiny it was. "Shall we make the choice more memorable? Why don't you tell me which you choose, and I'll insert this needle into your choice, the rabbit or the woman?"

"Lily, we're leaving," Burt said.

"No Burt, we're not." Lily looked at the needle. It wasn't one of the longest ones. It was four, maybe five inches long, and very thin. Where did he want to put it in her?

"Pick the rabbit," Alva said, grinning, "know about the rabbit." She set the jar of needles by the cage.

"Pick the woman," Tobias said, "know about the woman."

"You better not care about the damned rabbit more than you care about me." Lily looked at the rabbit. "I'll bite its head off myself. Pick me."

Burt glared at her, exasperated. "Even though this

total... stranger... wants to stick a needle in you." He took several steps toward the door. "I ought to leave you here."

"That would show how much you care," Tobias said. "Don't worry, Ms. Henshaw. "I'll give you cash back for Uber. The rabbit would stay with me, though. Would you stay if he goes?"

"Yes." Lily was certain, defiant.

"Lily...." Burt was incredulous, defiant.

"Just *choose*." Lily stood and folded her arms across her chest. Feeling her own breasts, she looked again at Alva's, still massive.

"Fine!" Burt sat on the sofa, huffing. He took out his phone. "I am dialing 9-1-1 and putting my finger on 'send.' If *anything* goes wrong—"

"You'll have the brief comfort of knowing you tried to call for help."

Tobias gestured for Lily to stand in front of him. She got close enough to feel his breath on her before he waved for Alva to stand behind her, sandwiching her. Lily looked at Burt, who watched her between the two mostly naked people in a tight erotic pose and shifted his weight to a different sofa cushion. Tobias dropped to his knees and asked for Lily's permission to lift up her shirt. She granted it. From a pocket she hadn't seemed to have, Alva produced a patch of gauze, damp, and Tobias moistened the area around Lily's bellybutton. The cool moisture, probably rubbing alcohol, sent a tingle from Lily's belly to her neck and made her nipples get hard, not as big and hard as she remembered Alva's being, but closer. Tobias's fingers were rough but gentle as he cleaned her and started pinching her, not hard, not painfully, almost tickling. It felt weird. Really, really weird, and at first, it made her self-conscious. Fat. Cellulite. When the metal poked skin, thought vanished. Self-consciousness exploded. Tobias's hands massaged around the flesh beneath the entry point as the needle glided in, and Lily understood why Alva stood behind her. Blood either rushed to or from her head, she didn't know which, but she felt light and free, woozy, about to topple, and Alva steadied her, a scaffold. Lily imagined Burt reacting way over on the sofa, a place that had been just a few feet away before, but now it might have been in another house, on another street, and she wouldn't know. Her world was washing away as the needle slid into her, passing through, no pain, but like a slow lick over her abs, it pushed away troublesome ideas and left behind a moraine of pleasure that filled in gaps. Legs quivered, struggling to support her. Skin and muscle vibrated around the needle. Nerves sent flashes of melt along the axis of her core, touching her innermost places. She felt like she might pee but had an orgasm instead, not like she'd had before, but it was coming, intense coming, centered on her stomach, tied to her clitoris, and distributed throughout her body. Tobias started to slide the needle away, but Lily said "Leave it in!" so he did, for a moment, before it slipped out, and Alva caught her.

"Honey, you want to sit back by your friend." Alva guided her to the sofa, and Burt shifted to one side, grumbling something.

Lily sat, catching her breath.

"You trust me now?" Tobias asked.

Lily looked at him and cocked her head to one side. She laughed. "No!"

"Good. Let's get this show started, then." Tobias rose from his knees, deposited the needle back in its jar of what Lily took to be disinfectant, and went to a cabinet in a wide hallway between the living room and the bathroom. He returned with two boxes, which he tossed indifferently on the coffee table. "Ouija boards and tarot cards," Tobias said. "Made by gaming companies. Check the boxes. Parker Brothers or Hasbro or U.S.

Games or something like that. You looking for the Devil? They say he talks through those sometimes. Personally, I think the Devil is high-tech, more likely to be in a computer game, but the online Ouija and tarot apps are pure crap."

While he talked, Alva took the rabbit away.

"So," Tobias continued, "no more playtime. You've got another choice to make, and I don't want to hear any whining once you make it. You, Burt Wells, don't believe in any of this shit, and that's good, because this isn't church. What I want to do down in the dungeon takes at least one unbeliever, and I sense your pal Lily Henshaw isn't quite the unbeliever you are." He took a deep breath and let his eyes pick through Lily's. "No sir, no she's not. We're all liars, but this one here has kindled a little bit of true faith, enough to go kicking up the Devil, and that's what she's good for, so you, Mr. Wells, need to ground us. We got faith, we got no-faith, so we've got the playthings we need for downstairs. Or we can use Parker Brothers. Up to you. Just be aware that if you decide to go downstairs and then chicken out before we start, I'll slit your fucking throats. After we start, weird shit goes down, you bolt, we're cool. But before —up until—you're mine. Or you get a bonus smile, from ear to ear. You get me?"

Tobias delivered his death threat in a matter-of-fact manner, looking at Burt most of the time but including Lily in requisite eye contact. Wearing his loincloth-diaper, he outlined the situation with a business-appropriate tone: they could accept a game of Ouija or tarot, or they could accept the dungeon, but once they accepted the dungeon, to revoke their acceptance would forfeit their lives. The proposal was direct and simple.

Burt asked, "How do we know you won't kill us anyway once we're in the dungeon?"

"Because Lily here trusts me." Tobias shrugged. "Because we could have drugged your drinks, raped, and murdered you twice over by now. If we'd wanted. We still might, you know. The safety of your world ended as soon as Gunther Azazel wrote down my number for Lily Henshaw to call."

Lily hrmphed, singular, high-pitched. "So *that's* when it happened."

Tobias tried to shake her reaction off but couldn't. "Okay, okay, in your case, Ms. Henshaw, maybe it ended earlier, like when you went out for a ride with your friends last December and started thinking about urban legends." She hadn't shared that detail with Gunther. She didn't know whether she'd shared that detail with Burt. "The Devil has a mission for you, Ms. Henshaw, Ms. Lily Henshaw, and I'd like the credit for setting you on your way, finally. I don't have to be a Satanist to be in debt, you know. I'd like my debt paid. Do you want a board game, a pack of cards, or the real thing, Lily Henshaw and Burt Wells?"

Burt looked at her, and Lily looked back. Burt shook his head no, but his face said he would go along with her, so she said, "Take us to the dungeon."

The stairs behind the unmarked door descended into suitably atmospheric candlelight, and the first chamber—the word *chamber*, maybe even *antechamber*, existed for rooms such as this—flickered into view. The paint and candles were black, but the dungeon was an adapted basement, not a dank structure of cavernous stone. Chains dangled from an unassuming ceiling, waiting to suspend someone's arms or legs. Not far from the chains, on hooks and pegs, hung riding crops, whips, and one brutally barbed cat-o'-nine-tails. Loose chains hung in storage, too, and some of them ended with hooks that glistened, suggesting a Clive Barker edge to SM/BD play. Also suggestive was the narrow adjustable bed paired with stirrups. Lily noticed that the floor in one corner, where the walls had metal cuffs for wrists and ankles, was covered in tiles and had a drain. She didn't know where the water would originate, but she guessed at the fluids it might wash away.

Across from the stairway, another door, this one painted with a red six on it, waited for them. "Through there," Alva said. Tobias had led, but somehow both he and Alva were behind them now, letting Lily and Burt take in the room. "Don't touch anything. This is my playroom." Alva's voice suggested a smile, but the candlelight didn't reveal it. Instead, Lily looked back and saw a statue of what might have been a man's midsection, the genital area mutilated.

"Lily," Burt whispered.

"No," she replied. Tobias and Alva stood between them and the exit. The room contained countless weapons. Gunther had seemed brash but harmless. Tobias seemed neither.

The next room also had black walls and black candles, but the décor lacked the same classic dungeon panache. It recalled Lady Laetitia's dining room of psychic happenings in centering on a small table, but it lacked chairs, and the table, instead of being round, looked almost rectangular, with edges that extended upward, turning the whole tabletop into an angular, flattened bowl. At the center of the table sat a head with dry, scaly skin, mostly a skull, likely a lizard, maybe a Komodo dragon or some other giant, reptilian hunter. With a candle inside it, its teeth cast orange-lined shadows on the black walls.

From a dark corner of the room, Lily heard growling. Hairs on the back of her neck responded, reminding her of fear, which she had somehow forgotten until this point—what growling thing should she fear when her host was willing to slit her throat for backing away? She wanted to pick up a candle, to look closer, but Alva's injunction to touch nothing lingered. She grabbed Burt's arm and pulled him in the corner's direction, guiding his attention. They both stared, but though her eyes focused, Lily couldn't see anything clearly.

A shape moved in the dark. It looked like a dog, with

a long snout, and like the skull on the table, its teeth cast shadows, but the blackness of the walls devoured them before their distorted sizes left distinct impressions. Likewise, the ears looked long, pointed, but their dimensions became wild in shifting firelight. Remembering Tobias and Alva's tattoos, Lily considered that the head might be a wolf's, so those draping things at its sides—had they been sewn on?—might have been —

Its tail, thick and heavy, pounded against a wall.

"So Lily Henshaw and Burt Wells, are you ready to begin?" Tobias pointed a hand, palm up, at the table, offering. "It may not have a corporate stamp, but it's still a game, always a game." Alva brought him a machete. Burt put an arm around Lily, starting to assert his body between hers and the new weapon, but she held her ground, and his arm lowered. Tobias nodded, approving, and continued: "The best games are played with blood."

Alva guided Lily to one side of the table, Burt to the other. She then disappeared into a dark corner of the room, away from the beast, and returned not with the jar of disinfectant but with two bare, short needles, wet enough for the moisture to show in candlelight. "I promise not to damage you in any devastating manner, if you hold my promises at any value, but I am going to inflict pain if I don't take precautions. These needles are precautions. By putting them in your ears, just a prick through the tops of your lobes, you'll be... inured. I would ask for your agreement, but I already have it. Alva, do the honors."

Alva poked their ears. The sensation was not pleasant but not overly disagreeable. It hurt for a fraction of a second and ended. A low hum of a tingle followed, and she felt dim relaxation. In retrospect, the hum made the poke that brought it on feel satisfactory. Lily thought of her bellybutton orgasm and squelched a smile, feeling warmth in her cheeks.

Burt flinched when Alva's hand, but not the needle, touched him. If he experienced any of the satisfaction Lily took in the punctured sensation, he did not express it. If he expressed anything, it was annoyance. Burt was never especially easy to read, especially when other people were involved, but his current attitude, at odds with hers in several ways, vexed judgment. Lily concluded that he would go along with whatever happened tonight and be done indulging her. Tonight had already crossed a line, but he was all in for it, whatever came to pass. Once it ended, however, they would face a renegotiation, and Lily would enter said renegotiation at a severe disadvantage.

"Now you both put your hands over the table, palms up." Tobias held up the machete. "And to cut through the suspense, yes, I'm going to cut you, so make your peace with it. I need both of your hands to be bleeding onto the table. Don't worry, I won't make these cuts too big because too much blood would ruin it. You're going to hold hands like a good couple, Lily Henshaw and Burt Wells, and I'm going to play the flute. Do a little dance, whatever strikes you, as long as you move while you're holding your hands together over the table. It's like action painting. You've heard of Jackson Pollock, right? You're painting together with your blood, and the picture is going to answer your questions. And just to be clear, Mr. Wells, my unbeliever, you're not to let Ms. Henshaw take control and paint the picture for you. Ms. Henshaw, you're not to let Mr. Wells take over, either, and ruin it all with his need to call bullshit today. Dance with no one leading. Leave it all to chance. I'll let you know when to stop and look at your artwork.

"By the way, if either of you has any blood-borne diseases that you haven't copped to, now would be the time to fess up. This is a little like becoming blood brothers, more so than fucking, and I don't even know if you two are post-condom. No? Then let's cut." Tobias took his time aligning the machete's blade with Lily and Burt's hands, but he moved quickly with the blade's tip when the time for cutting arrived. Abrupt flicks opened an inch's worth of flesh on each palm—Lily's not quite healed from previous injury—and surrounding skin filled in with red pools. "Now join." Lily and Burt clasped bleeding hand to bleeding hand, and Lily realized that the needle, still stuck in her ear, must have been working. She hadn't thought about not feeling the knife, but she should have felt the cut by now, and she should certainly have felt the sting of someone pressing against a fresh wound, even if it echoed another wound, but all she felt in her hand was pressure, not pain.

That their instructions required movement turned out to be good, as Lily found herself swaying, pulling on Burt for balance, before Tobias's flute-playing began. The playing's rhythm accommodated the swaying, which became see-sawing as Burt joined her in it, dipping in her direction, then dropping in his, dip, drop, dip, drop. The playing's notes accommodated nothing, instead favoring strange intervals, not just the Devil's own tritone but combinations and alternations of leaps over and within octaves thrown off by semitones that interrupted logical progressions that would establish the consistency of key, maneuvers that upset the ear without repelling it, because the sounds promised something just out of reach, just within a few notes, reachable, apparently, as the swaying rhythm was predictable, but not to be reached as long as the swaying went on, which might be forever.

The playing stopped, but the music continued. Lily and Burt's swaying continued. Lily reasoned that she couldn't be losing too much blood. The cuts had been shallow and small. She doubted anything coherent could appear in her blood, but she wanted to see the result of Tobias's pageant, what his higher order game was about. She hardly felt aware of the room anymore, the dark room of black walls and candlelight, with the beast in the corner, and Alva and needles. Images didn't intrude on her at all except for the sensation of swaying and the cushion of thought, which was itself—

"LILY! FOR GOD'S SAKE LILY SNAP OUT OF IT YOUR HAND!"

Burt was screaming at her. He settled into view. Tobias and Alva gripped each of his arms and held him still while forcing him to bend over the table, face toward the blood. Something solid, other than the dragon skull at center, lay on the table amidst the blood. It looked familiar, this solid object, splashed as it was by their artwork, which, when Lily looked at it, wasn't a nest of splatters at all. It was a scene.

Tobias and Alva bent Burt over the table so he had to watch the scene, which Lily now glanced over with amusement. It was a rerun. And moreover, Tobias Centurion had gotten the artist all wrong. The blood painting did not look at all like Jackson Pollock. It looked like Vincent Van Gogh. The roiling clouds in the sky were not splashes of paint but concerted swirls of red mixed with the table's dark wood. Haphazard lines did not form the shape of the tower. Skewed, yes, and perhaps somewhat stilted, these lines showed the tower as it appeared when alone on the landscape, the landscape as their artwork showed it now, barren but for heaps of rubble. Together in the sway, Lily and Burt had painted 1500 Spring as Lily had seen it from her horse on the day she'd met Gunther. Now Burt shared her vision.

And he was still screaming at her. What? What? What? The image before them both was disappearing in a new rush of red streaming in from above. In the running streams, Lily made out letters: first, S. What was Burt yelling about? He kept looking at the object on the table, which was away from where the letters were forming, and then trying to get his head free enough from Tobias and Alva's control to point his gaze right at Lily. Lily could hardly look away from the table enough to watch Burt. Second, O. The sensations Lily felt at this moment really were quite odd. Burt kept yelling, trying to look at her, and she could hardly stir her interest from a single area of the table, where things were happening. Third, A. The prick in her ear. Ha-ha. The poke. The needle. It had been wet. They must have put some drug on it. It must have been… fourth, R. SOAR. *Soar.* Why did that word seem like it was important from something not too long ago?

"LILY!!!" Burt would not stop screaming, so finally, she looked at her hand, the object on the table, severed from her wrist.

Lily looked at her wrist and identified it as the source of the word "SOAR," as in, *Come Soar with the Whore!*, the tagline for the Whore of Babylon poster ordered by—

MFS. She saw that her wrist had squirted out three more letters. MFS, Mansworth Futures and Securities. "Motherfuckers!" Lily yelled.

Tobias and Alva let Burt go, and he stayed bent over the table, stunned. Tobias and Alva burst into laughter, at first controlled, then uproarious. Tobias crossed to one of the room's endless dark corners and put an end to darkness, apparently flipping a switch that made compact fluorescents in a ceiling fixture render the dozen or so candles insignificant. Lily's first glance, uncontrolled, went to the corner where she'd seen and heard the beast—nothing. Her second was to her wrist, where she saw her hand, attached and only cut in the palm, where she'd seen Tobias cut it. The third was to the table, which was messy with trickles that spelled out nothing.

Burt came to his senses and slammed his fists on the table. Grunting, he stormed toward Tobias, who wore a loincloth-diaper and had no weapons. "You! You!"

"Before you start a fight you'll lose," Tobias said, "maybe you'll tell us what you're angry about."

Lily and Burt had cuts on their palms. Tobias and Alva

had a bloody table. Alva had picked up the machete and stood near where Burt had approached Tobias. "I...." Burt said.

Tobias crossed to Lily and removed the needle from her ear. "I recommend removing yours. It'll hurt less if I do it for you." Burt yanked out his needle and started bleeding in a new place. "I thought you'd do that." Tobias turned to Lily. "Ms. Henshaw, my dear important lady, while your friend is staunching his ear with his shirt, let me ask you, do you know now what you must do?"

Lily thought. She supposed she did. She nodded.

"You've known for a long time, haven't you?" Tobias asked.

Lily nodded.

Tobias turned. "And you, Burt. Do I need to tell you that you and Lily have shared a vision? That you've seen into a world that she has seen before and thought you would not believe? Or did you know that already? Based on what you've seen here, you have one last choice to make tonight. You chose the woman over the rabbit. Can you choose her again, based on what you've seen? Will you help her—join her in her quest?"

Burt looked at Lily. His confusion was palpable, laced with needs and desires that Lily could neither name nor enumerate. His mouth opened and closed. He looked from Tobias, to Alva, back to Lily. He looked at the bloody table, to the corner where the beast had been. He looked at the ceiling. He looked at the floor. He looked at Lily's hand, attached as it ought to be.

"Yes."

PART TWO: JOB UNDONE

"When K. looked at the Castle, often it seemed to him as if he were observing someone who sat quietly there gazing in front of him, not lost in thought and so oblivious of everything, but free and untroubled, as if he were alone with nobody to observe him, and yet must notice that he was observed, and all the same remained with his calm not even slightly disturbed; and really—one did not know whether it was cause or effect—the gaze of the observer could not remain concentrated there, but slid away."

- Franz Kafka, *The Castle*

"The ugliness is everywhere. It's going to win. I can't escape it."

- Nicole Cushing, *Mr. Suicide*

1

Internecine hallucination machine, Lily Henshaw, Ambassador to the Working World. Gunther Azazel, nowhere to be found, might have said yes, Satan, but Tobias Centurion gave only loose assurances about the source of Lily's mission: from Satan or elsewhere? From the blood, from the blood, which dripped into cracks, in the flat-bowl table, in nearby skin: Lily and Burt saw the same towering monstrosity, 1500 Spring, and the same letters, portents, which meant they came from and were going to the same place. At whose urging? Satan, maybe, but *internecine* spoke to Lily because she thought of *necine* involving *nests*, "inter" meaning "between," *between the nests*, as if a duality automatically suggested a space in between two camps from which a conflict, or a Lily, might sprout. The two nests, then, a God and a Satan, might fear the visions of vegetation in between, especially if they followed the lonely precedent of the Book of Job. For what is the Book of Job, the story of a bet between God and Satan, if not a tale of supposed opposites collaborating? God and Satan work together to see what torturing Job might prove. God soars with the whore, countenancing Job's personal apocalypse until Job writes himself a happy ending as God's grateful abused subject. But what if Job had moved between the nests, out of reach of both? What if Job had *vision*?

Lily Henshaw, on a mission from Satan, or Lily Henshaw, on a mission against God—she didn't know which it was, as the two now seemed so different, but she had the vision for both. Standing at sixty stories, 1500 Spring held answers, but what?

She and Burt were going to find out.

They approached the rotary doors at the center of the building's glass façade. Burt said, "Do you see that?"

Lily saw many things. She saw the bright blue sky, so different from roiling red, with white fluffy clouds. She saw neighboring buildings, some taller, some grander. Hordes of people mobbed the sidewalks, thronging their ways at traffic signs, constricting and congealing circulation. Business was about, and the hour was lunchtime, a carnival of special meetings. People looked smart in suits and collars and skirts and ties. Restaurants abounded, with signs in tasteful yet zazzy fonts advertising names such as City Taste and Mondo. Most towers contained a desirable restaurant. 1500 Spring's was called Rarity, but Lily had come to think of it as Scarcity.

"That guy," Burt clarified.

Lily saw many guys and felt ready to proceed through the spinning glass doors.

"I've been seeing him off and on since we left the loft." Burt was looking in a direction behind them, away from the tower. If Lily turned to look, she would indulge the distraction and delay, but didn't Burt deserve that, and furthermore, what if he was right? Tobias had said another term for their blood painting was Blood Scrying, which was kind of like Blood Spying, because it gave you an eye on your enemy. What if they, Lily and Burt, weren't the only ones spying? What if 1500 Spring was looking back?

Lily looked. The man Burt indicated was black, grey-haired, and darkly dressed. He was settling onto a bench near an abstract metal sculpture, taking a book out of a brown satchel. He could not have looked less suspicious, but that, in itself, might have been grounds for suspicion. Lily's attempt at sharing Burt's concern resulted only in concern of a different origin. The man did not look at all familiar, but he did not look misplaced. Lily needed to try harder to feel what Burt felt. She couldn't do it. The man looked no more intrinsically alarming than the bench he sat on. Only the fact of the man's unalarming presence raised cause for alarm, so she asked, "Do you want to do something about him? Go up to him?"

"No. Let's go inside. But watch for him." Burt gestured for Lily to lead them through the rotary door.

The air inside 1500 Spring felt cool and firm. The lobby felt like an extension of outside, but climate and surfaces lay in the complete control of the building's managers. The managers had even allocated surfaces to ad space, with ads disguised as graphics-rich information about the various companies that resided in the building. None of the posters P-Cubed had printed for Mansworth appeared on display, but space for Mansworth existed, exposing various aspects of the company's brand. One image showed the MFS logo, two green human shapes shaking hands, and the word "sustainability." Another image showed the logo and a sequence of green human shapes enveloping other green human shapes, Russian doll-like, inside one another, infinitely, saying "growth." Another showed the green image flying, suspended in the air without wings or cape, and said, "imagination." Another showed a red human and said, "accountability."

People filled the lobby, waiting for their turns on the escalator to Scarcity, which was oddly situated on a mezzanine level, waiting for elevators, getting information, dealing with security, stopping at the lobby café, stopping at the ATM, stopping to check their phones, stopping to chat with coworkers, stopping to check their makeup, stopping just to piss Lily off. Now it was her turn to say, "Do you see that? That guy?" She meant the one in front of the newsstand that sold sundry and called itself The Gift Shop. White guy, mid-thirties, khaki pants, reddish-pink shirt. Red tie, no jacket. Above average height, Lily's coloring. Except for the shaggy beard and unusual level of physical fitness, he looked like—

"You mean the guy with the freaky beard?" Burt pointed.

Lily reached over and lowered Burt's pointing finger. "Yes, him. Doesn't he look like... I mean, I think he looks like... I'm telling you he looks like my brother David." The human traffic around where she and Burt had stopped to discuss another *that guy* broke around them but made clear signs, mostly facial expressions and grunts, of displeasure. After saying what she thought about the man who looked like David, Lily felt stupid, because no matter how like David he looked, how exactly like, she would sound crazy saying it, crazy in the middle of another crazy, in the middle of another. She thought of the "growth" poster, the inset people absorbing one another to infinity. It was an image of falling.

Burt asked, "You want to go up to him?" Was he mocking her? Being vindictive? Something else?

"No," she said, carefully. "Not... yet." What could it mean? Her seeing things, indulging in wishful thinking, was the easiest solution. David somehow being here, welcome, of course, posed problems. He might be alive. Suicide a mistake? A sham? Part of a conspiracy? What? He might be dead. Where were they, then? Hell on Earth, transported by Satan? Some newfangled purgatorial interchange? The gates of Heaven? Familiar Earth, but populated with ghosts? Possibilities! Possibilities! Most rather nauseating. "Let's get closer."

The flow of human traffic made the guy's position hard to approach. The Gift Shop intercepted people on their way into or out of the building's parking levels, which had separate access from the main elevators to the office floors and looked tucked away from the entryway and façade. No vein or artery of movement naturally connected where Lily and Burt stood watching to where the guy stood browsing periodicals. Lily, underdressed, already felt like an alien here, a tourist: unthinking, she had worn jeans and a simple green t-shirt, and Burt wore basic grey slacks and a navy polo. The busy businesspeople would examine them as they begged pardons to pass by, and they would know that Lily and Burt did not belong. Bodies would move less willingly, and less far, making passing more difficult.

"We're going to him," Burt said, and he took Lily's hand. The crowd behaved as Lily expected, with shoulders pressing against them as they wedged themselves into human lanes, grunts answering Burt's "excuse mes," shoes dodging shoes, and a muttered "watch where you're going." Lily and Burt were not welcome. They had no right to be here. Glares from lobby co-travelers identified them as at best interlopers, at worst imposters. In what, on whom, did they impose? Human productivity. Whatever sort of growths they represented, they did not qualify as 1500 Spring produce, not looking as they did, not going against the directional flows.

The problem of unbelonging intensified as they drew closer to the guy at the newsstand. The guy had something clipped to his tie—most guys had things clipped to their ties or lapels—and women had clips, too, where brooches might be, or elsewhere—pins—the size of a politician's flag-pin—a symbol that Lily tried to make out on the bodies that pressed close to her within the throng. Close-pressing bodies, many of them white, thirtysomething, with brown hair like her own, other coloring like her own, might have been family like David, except

the freaky beard

the growth of hair, which David never had during life, set him apart, made him easy to keep in focus as the newsstand washed in and out of center view while currents carried them from and into a direct-line path. The beard, the pin, both symbols, surely: the beard framed David's face like an old-fashioned wolf man, a Lon Chaney Jr. sprouting the fruit of his curse in time-lapse fade-transitions, hair making the human go away, and the pins had animal elements, too, like tattoos, like wolf-bird-lizards of faux-gold needled onto every passerby.

"Burt." Lily tried to tell him that her imagination might be reforming the entire lobby, attaching itself by pins to every woman and man, branding all with the same image that had marked Tobias and Alva, the creature that disappeared in the light, wolf-head, sewn-on wings, Komodo tail to match the skull on the table... everyone wolf-headed to match the hair on David, the hair brought on by the curse. Her voice, calling Burt's name, got sucked toward the lobby's high ceiling, hacked and dissolved in the stew of tower-base acoustics. Lily's imagination was a magic lantern, projecting wolf-heads everywhere, onto David (was he David?) and onto suited passersby (they were all David!). Yes, they might have been in a great chamber, or antechamber, filled with rushing Davids, man Davids and woman Davids, Davids who favored her brother to lesser and greater degrees, all consumed by work, all consumed by life-destroying knowledges.

David knew about Mom's cancer.

How could he? The tests revealed it after his death.

David knew. He knew because his own voices, his own Kris-Eric-Mias, told him. David knew about Ralph coming to destroy him and to destroy Sally. Because he was a dirty rotten cheat, a scoundrel. He knew he was worthless. His life, reaching its halfway point, amounting to nothing. Worthless. He knew he didn't need an argument to die, but an argument to live. This crowd presents no arguments. It provides only movement. One place to another. With stop-offs for news. In the age of every news item updating by the minute online, David hunted through newsstands. Why? For the future. They told his future. Old media tell the future. His future, anyway.

The thoughts came to her as she looked at David, or the hairy man who might be David, through the crowd, through which Burt maneuvered them, pulling them closer. The pins in the passersby gleamed, hard to see clearly with all the motion, but Lily felt certain they bore the shapes of wolf-bird-lizards. The wolf, then, was a symbol for David, or David was a symbol for the wolf. Secrets surrounded her. Lily and Burt walked in a sea of human secrets, each looking like and unlike the others, each a possible David and like and unlike the last, with one of them, by the newsstand, drawing her on to the question of death. His, hers, any of theirs—she felt lulled by the crowd, ready to drift along with it even though Burt pulled in a contrary direction, across currents, toward the newsstand.

What did the periodicals tell David? One had a cover story about a string of kidnappings of American women in Latin America, and somehow it carried meanings about relationships David had pursued at various points in his life, women who had sacrificed time to him that they would never recover, women who doomed themselves to abduction not by manly charm but by self-doubt, for in some sophisticated way, which his mind could not communicate, they were their own kidnappers, and David was the Latin America in the equation, the place where women got lost, if only for a while.

Another had a news story about a Canadian tribal area that was fighting a suicide epidemic, with a population of only thousands suffering more than forty suicides in a matter of weeks, topping ten on one bad day in particular. Doctors had theories, and politicians made speeches. All agreed that poverty was a problem. Bullying, most agreed, deserved attention and study. Patterns of weather and sunlight in the area certainly merited consideration. Questions of diversity might definitely come into play.

David realized that suicide, as an object, had a banality in common with the weather, not hurricanes and tornadoes but showers and breezes, matters for accounting and speculation, not panic and hurry. Self-destruction was a tragedy, no doubt, but in the great Darwinist scheme of consequences, for a self-destroyer to self-destruct *without breeding* was likely best, and with the Latin American situation, the possibility of offspring would persist, if not increase, if he went on.

If he stopped now, then, single and childless, the calculation of his contributions and damages to the species and planet would be easier to decide if not in his favor then at least less in his fault, for what person really makes a favorable contribution, when after all the world needs little less than it needs additional persons? With billions upon billions breathing at once, doing things such as consulting on the operations of technologies four times removed from the basic processes of human survival, to be other than superfluous requires accomplishment of such magnitude that by definition few achieve it. The destruction of any given number of persons is, to the whole, irrelevant, because the destruction of some number at every given moment is, to the whole, necessary for sustainability as long as reproduction occurs. To be among the superfluous, and inclined toward destruction anyway, would seem to create an opt-out imperative, an achievable heroism of population reduction effective for unspawned generations. Some people just don't need to be, and some people are doers.

A hand landed on Lily's shoulder, interrupting her exploration of David's thinking at the newsstand. She lost sight of him, but she saw a hand interrupting Burt, too. Together, they turned to face the hands' owner. "Lily Henshaw and Burt Wells!" a man said. He wore a double-breasted suit that looked less expensive than many of those around. His lapel bore a pin, and Lily could make out the wolf's head.

Lily tried to turn her head toward the newsstand, but she couldn't crane far enough. "Yes," Burt said, sounding surprised. Lily felt no surprise.

As if a bubble had formed around them in the densely human, noisy lobby, the double-breasted man spoke in a normal yet audible voice: "I have come to escort you to see

Mansworth Futures and Securities. Your visit is anticipated!"

Lily broke away from the excited, double-breasted man and looked for her brother. The area by the newsstand stood empty. The crowd seemed more faceless than before. Lily followed Burt as he followed the double-breasted man to the bank of elevators, to the section marked "Executive Express."

The double-breasted man took them up. The twenty-fourth floor belonged to Mansworth, and the elevator stopped nowhere prior. Lily and Burt's guide did not inform them of whether other floors also belonged to Mansworth, but an understanding passed, wordlessly, among the three elevator travelers that yes, Mansworth possessed other floors and yes, they all existed higher than this one. The executive experience toward which Lily and Burt traveled therefore ranked lowest on the possible Mansworth hierarchy of floors.

On the twenty-fourth floor, the elevator stopped, and the double-breasted man gestured for Lily and Burt to exit the elevator and step into the Mansworth realm. Perky accents of turquoise enlivened blue-grey expanses of wall trimmed by a color like orange that had pink vomit inside of it. MFS did not fill Lily with comfort; it did not put her at ease. Its visual dissonance combined with a coldness of air different from the lobby, a good deal colder, and made the place seem like an altogether different building, in an altogether different state. The viciousness Lily had attributed to 1500 Spring both belonged to it and didn't, as MFS both dwelled on and departed from its premises. The building had stood for the business, the whole for the part.

A reception desk met them once they moved away from the elevators. The double-breasted man hurried from behind them to in front of them, where he assumed the receiving position at the desk. He appeared to press a button, and a light over one of his shoulders, which Lily hadn't noticed before, turned from red to green, the same green as Lily's shirt. Where the wolf's head pin had been, Lily now saw a nametag: Young Torrents.

Mr. Torrents asked, "What can I do for you?"

"You led us here," Burt said. He looked more bewildered than irritated. "You said we were expected."

Lily studied the nametag. It had a burnished gold hue but didn't look gilded, just colored, like the wolf-bird-lizard pin that could reappear in its place at any moment. "We have an appointment," she said. She didn't know why she said it.

"You do." Mr. Torrents looked left and right, at the professional spaces—two banks of cubicles, neither very large, walls lined with offices—and turned his back to them, so he, Lily, and Burt all faced the expanse behind the reception desk. Sunlight filled it, reflecting off each of a hundred shiny surfaces. The brightness made the expanse difficult to resolve into anything like a room, but the vaulted ceiling and glass walls eventually separated and focused, becoming a great shining hall, a meeting place centered on a sculpture on a round pedestal high and wide enough for seating.

Without turning back around, Mr. Torrents said, "It's lunchtime." His voice flew forward and echoed back to them from the great shining hall. "No one is here."

Burt was about to protest, but Lily stopped him.

Mr. Torrents stepped away from the reception desk so that nothing stood between his visitors and him. He waved his right hand. "Follow me, please." Moving toward the sculpture, he indicated a new path for Lily and Burt. Burt's face conveyed a *Can we leave now?* expression familiar from the night at Tobias's, but Lily's silent reply must have felt equally familiar, for Burt's expression never reached voice. They reached the sculpture. The great shining hall had no other décor or furniture of any kind beyond floor-mounted floral arrangements. Lily recognized some but not all of the flowers, but sensing a pattern, she concluded they were all lilies, arranged in sprays, with white predominant, as at funerals and weddings.

The sculpture had a placard in front of it that said "Love." The artwork itself might have been easier to see at night, because, with the exception of a few metallic supports, themselves polished to shine, its shapes consisted of translucent and transparent glass, letting the sun from surrounding windows fill them. Spheres provided the dominant motif, clustering around one another like atoms or planets, forming little systems. The systems' connective tissues looked thin like wires, but they caught light like glass filaments, inelastic, suggesting at once that the smaller orbs might dangle and spin if the right breezes were to blow through the great shining hall, and that they would resist all but the most forceful gales, which would snap them off into fragile, shattering collisions with one another. Lily's eyes tried to take in the whole but got refracted and deflected within one system or another. So worked the sculpture's harmonies. You knew it was whole, but you could not see all its parts together. It required trust, or faith, and relied on a system of delicate suspension that fostered the illusion of mobility on strings made of light.

"If you'll be seated," Mr. Torrents said. Lily and Burt sat by the sculpture. Mr. Torrents, puffing out his chest in his double-breasted jacket, said, "Now how may I help you?"

Burt looked irritated. "For the last time, you're the one who—" Lily kicked him. "We have an appointment."

"And I'm here to help." Mr. Torrents waited expectantly. Lily and Burt looked at one another, each about to speak but neither with anything to say. "For instance," Mr. Torrents continued, "Most people who succeed in making appointments with us have… questions? About futures and securities?"

"Are you Mr. Mansworth?" Lily asked.

The double-breasted man laughed. "No, I'm Mr. Torrents."

"May we speak with Mr. Mansworth?" Burt said.

"No, I've never heard of him. Terribly sorry." Mr. Torrents looked at his nametag and gave it a buffing. "Perhaps I can help you? If you pretend I *am* the Mr. Mansworth you seek, you might ask *me* your questions."

Lily and Burt looked at one another. Lily got up from her seat by the glass sculpture, which looked like ice from some angles, especially in the cold official air. She crossed to one of the sprays of mostly-white lilies, and she sank her nose into a blossom. It smelled sweet and gentle. Instincts spoke to her, but instead of telling her to run, they told her to speak. Thinking of the posters that introduced them to MFS, she said, "What's your business with the apocalypse?"

Mr. Torrents looked at Burt before he met Lily's eye again. "That's an odd question," he said.

"I'm at an odd place in my life," Lily answered. Her eyes fell on a glass orb near Burt's head.

"We have no such business. The apocalypse's future is secure. We work in ancillary markets."

"Such as?" Lily paced between lilies and orbs, letting her eyes wander between Mr. Torrents and the sculpture.

"Individual futures as they pertain to endgame procedures, which have been, to anticipate a question, in effect since the company was founded."

Lily, whose fount of Biblical wisdom was small but growing, imagined 1500 Spring as the Tower of Babel. "And when was your *company* founded?"

"1991," Mr. Torrents said.

She said, "So the world has been ending since 1991?"

"Heavens no! Whatever gave you that idea?"

"You said... I think I don't know what you said." Lily walked back toward flowers.

"We have had endgame procedures in operation since we opened our doors," Mr. Torrents said. "The endgame itself is not... I say, it is not for you."

"What is for me, then?"

"The time remaining."

Lily faced the glass orbs. She, Young Torrents, the sculpture, and the flowers absorbed the great shining hall. Burt no longer sat in her line of sight, but remembering something Burt had said, Lily said, "Life is nasty, brutish, and short."

"Yes," Young agreed. "You might say so."

"Am I cursed?"

"Yes," he said.

"Why?"

Young looked puzzled. "Why not? Maybe you could rephrase the question."

Lily looked at the floor. She wore tennis shoes with her jeans and green shirt. "Why me?" The question felt rather dull, but she didn't know what else to ask.

Young looked from the sculpture to the flowers and smiled. "Maybe I should ask *you* a question. Would that be okay? Oops! Look, I've already done it. I hope that's okay. My real question is this: by 'cursed,' do you mean that you feel as if you were targeted by a higher power for a horrific string of events? You might describe it as luck so bad for so long that it can't be random luck—you think somebody has to be behind it, pulling the strings?" He looked at the sculpture—at the glass filaments, or so Lily surmised.

Feeling she should object, Lily could only say, "Yes."

"Naturally your mind tends to the supernatural, for

what earthly power could perform on a level as imminently confusable with a force as abstract as *luck*? You might have thought of deities, devils and gods, and the like. Do you feel persecuted by devils? Singled out by God?" Young kept smiling and asked his questions with the placating allure of an infomercial. "Are you tired of living out each day as if you were the butt of a cosmic joke that got lost in the telling?"

"Yes."

"Then Lily Henshaw, I *do* have answers for you. First of all, you can lay down your burden. You are not alone in the universe. Far from it! In fact, you are one of hundreds, no, thousands! No—perhaps millions, maybe billions! Of people who qualify. The cosmic joke is on all of us. That's right, Lily, in the sense you mean it, we are *all* cursed. I'll let that one sink in for a minute."

She wanted nothing to do with Young's commands for her thinking, but she thought anyway about the condition he described: the universalizing of Lily's state, everyone feeling as she felt, a feeling she imagined could only come of seeing a string of tragedy like she had seen. The idea seemed so ridiculous that she considered a related extreme: since some people Lily had known couldn't approach wrapping their minds around what Lily had seen, the only way her condition could be universal would be if the "universal" state applied to a subset of the "people" Lily had known, meaning that only some of those "people" were actually *people*, ensouled individuals fully alive, while the rest got disqualified from the universal because they lacked soul, individuality, or some other essential trait. The popular media might call them zombies, but they didn't shamble about eating brains to make up for their own lack of them. They appeared *exactly* as people did, just with a secret minus. This conceptualization of limited humanity equaled psychosis, if not full-fledged psychopathy, as dividing up the species in such a manner tended to portend offing those so-called people with minuses should the secret ever become known. Nevertheless, Young made the thought appear, and Lily entertained it as a consequence of the possible universalization of her condition.

"Okay," she said, "I'll bite. How can we all be cursed?"

"Living life we take out loans of time against our curses. But maybe I shouldn't let you roam in the dark? Maybe I should play lighthouse to your little lost clipper? I am here to be of help. How can I convey to a person such as you the bright, bright goodness of life? Such simplicity in the spectrum, when ROYGBIV describes a spectrum of lights adding up to white rather than pigments sinking down into murk? How often do you appreciate breathing? The cool air rushing into your lungs, bathing your skin? How thankful are you for the intricacy of shapes you see when you sit at a desk, or on a sofa, or stand at a register, or on a line? Do you think about the range of noises you hear, the sounds of the machines—that airplane, an air conditioner, yard equipment, a vehicle, a phone, a computer? The strangeness of eating and the variety of food? The greater strangeness and vivacity of sex? The way appetites are abhorrent to each other but inextricable as well, like licking whipped cream off the nipples of a beautiful body? The ability to fulfill? The narrative itself, being born, having a childhood, surviving it, growing and learning. Discovering love, coming into the orbits of others, taking and giving shape from and to the world. Developing ambition, with an inkling of who you are, and taking and giving direction for a cause. Finding a love so intense that bonding over it for a duration resets expectations for many facets of living. Extending the boundaries of family. Deepening senses of values while building contributions to larger contexts. Maturing as contributions flower. Not everyone does or gets all of it, but the sequence has many fine stages and substages, many baroque variations. Light shines through all of them, all the colors individually and at once. However you slice it, it's beautiful. Amazing. Something to cherish. Life is *good*, Lily Henshaw.

People want it. They want it uninterrupted, undisturbed. Far and away, life is the most successful product on the market.

"Life is so good that no one deserves it. Why should any being expect life, time in existence, which is the most awesome thing ever, to be given away for nothing? No, the world works in one way and one way only, and everybody knows it: to get something, you've got to give something. Except if you're not alive, and you've never been alive, you don't exactly have much to give, do you? No. So to get life, you've got to have credit. You take out a loan. Different people are different kinds of gambles. Some lives should simply never get funded. But everybody gets a loan. Lily Henshaw, I'm sorry to tell you, but you're in foreclosure."

Lily tried to sit down, forgot she was standing in a great shining hall with no seating beyond the sculpture's pedestal, and fumbled to the floor. Burt reappeared by her side, offering her a hand's help up. She refused, preferring to stay seated, discombobulated, on the floor. "*Foreclosure*? That's absurd."

"Management, who decides these things, began your Foreclosure Protocol just after Christmas last year. The beginning of the Protocol marks the end of your regular allotment of time in existence. After that point, you are in Collection Time, which some do and others do not consider an extension of life. It is a time during which you pay a penalty in assets for not repaying your loan. At some point, usually a matter of months or years, the loan is cancelled, and Collection Time ends."

"And then what?" Lily asked.

"You cease to exist, of course," Young Torrents said.

"What about... how about if it... how do you repay your loan?" Lily asked.

Mr. Torrents blinked. "Excuse me?"

"What if I wanted to... pay? Pay it off somehow? How do

I pay off my loan?"

"You couldn't afford it! Think of the price tag on the most luxurious resort in the world. Now imagine spending a year there. What would that cost? Now imagine which is worth visiting more—that resort, or *life*? Which is worth more to the average person, do you think? Now do you think you can afford a year of life? And *how* many years old are you? And we're not even talking interest! And, uh, I don't think you showed up to negotiate your interest rate. You, uh, didn't exist at the time." Mr. Torrents shook his head.

"Now wait a minute," Burt said. "None of this makes sense. Other people died in all of this. Were they all in foreclosure?"

"Sometimes people just die. Everybody's got a debt, but not everybody faces foreclosure. The system doesn't work that way. That's not to say we don't time foreclosures to intersect. Lily's brother David, for example, was in foreclosure before Lily was herself. This is something Lily already knew, I think. She has had a sense of her many connections to people in her environment for a while now. Making such connections is a key to increasing efficiency. Efficiency is a growth priority." Mr. Torrents gave Burt a thumb up.

Lily felt as if the air were draining from the room. Slowly, what Mr. Torrents said, so calmly—she and Burt both seemed so calm!—settled onto her shoulders. As theories of the universe went, it felt kind of like a kids' lemonade stand: well-meaning but economically ill-conceived. It was a cosmos built on credit and exchange wherein nothing changed hands, an economy without barter or currency. Her mind found so many holes, so many problems, in what Young Torrents said that she could not begin to ask him questions. And her connections, her connections to David, her connections to her environment, to everything, to everyone. Trust wasn't the only spider's web: she was herself a web, a system of connections to fates within fates. *Delusions of grandeur.* She had nothing to say.

"Am I in foreclosure?" Burt asked. "Lily's had it much worse than I have, but I spent the night in jail, lost my business, and have been right there beside Lily through half of this... *foreclosure*... mess. Am I in... Collection Time?"

Nothing in Heaven was e'er...

"You know," Mr. Torrents said, "I never thought of you as anything but the sidekick. To tell the truth, I have no idea what you are. Some other office must handle your case. I'm terribly sorry."

2

Young Torrents escorted them back to the elevator while they attempted to formulate more questions. At first, Burt alternated between asking about Lily and asking about himself. Why did Lily go into foreclosure? When Mr. Torrents mentioned another office, did he mean another MFS office? Were Lily and David in foreclosure for the same reasons? Where were other offices located? How long would Lily's Collection Time last? Did your chances of going into Collection Time increase if you knew someone in Collection Time—was it transferable, associative, or otherwise contagious? And what determines what or who is an "asset" belonging to another person and subject to seizure during Collection Time?

Mr. Torrents provided abyssal answers. "An asset is anything of positive value, an in-the-black. Observation of the borrower's interactions determines the status of interactions' objects, and those deemed positive, or beneficial, are subject to a calculus of survival impact. The effects of whether and how, or in what manner, the objects survive determine their asset value, as reported in a depth of impact statement. Depth of impact statements, when collated, reveal an order of collection, neither ascending nor descending but variable according to mutually dependent outcomes, which of course trigger action events to maximize impact and efficiency. Note, however, that impacts distribute across a network and should not undergo assessment in restricted local environments, where indeed the asset is prone to appreciate most radically in terms of individual effects but is unlikely to be observable in its most impactful state."

Lily and Burt were still sorting through verbiage when the elevator opened on the lobby. Their visit upstairs had lasted less than half an hour; the lunchtime crunch of human traffic pressed on. The doors had not finished opening when Burt pressed the button marked B1, which had to be spatially arranged in relation to P1, underneath the building, but the elevator gave no indication of the two sub-floors having any relation. Afraid that Burt was too late to keep the elevator car going down, preparing to re-ascend, Lily watched as two women in suits used their arms to halt the elevator doors' closing—the doors rebounded against them with reverberating thuds—and pried their ways inside.

One of the women asked, "Going up?" She wore an orange-crème-colored jacket.

"Down," Burt replied.

The orange-crème woman seemed about to retreat, but her friend said, "We'll take the ride. Anything to get out of that mess!" With the two suited women secure inside, the elevator began to close its doors again. "Wait wait!" the turquoise woman yelled, and her arm blocked the doors' progress. "My phone! I think I left my phone at the restaurant!" She dashed through the doors, back into the mess she'd have done anything to escape, leaving the orange-crème woman behind. Doors closed quickly.

Eyeing her co-travelers, orange-crème pressed the button for 49. On her lapel, she wore a pin. It appeared to have a wolf's head and probably wings. Lily inferred the lizard tail, and she made a decision. "Hello, I'm Lily Henshaw."

Orange-crème looked from Lily to Burt and backed away as far as the elevator would allow. "Hello." When orange-crème's eyes flicked to an upper corner of the elevator, Lily noticed the bubble signifying a security camera. Did it have audio?

"We're new here," Lily said. She needed a cover story. Why was she, underdressed, unbelonging, here at 1500 Spring? Why was Burt, better dressed but still unbelonging, here with her? And what could possibly move them to accost a stranger in an elevator to ask about... "That pin. What does it mean? What... is it?"

Orange-crème looked like she might merge with the elevator wall. Burt looked like watching the lights on the panels of floor-buttons would make them arrive at B1 sooner. "What pin?" the lady asked.

Lily looked at Burt, who looked at the elevator panel. The one flight down to B1 seemed to be taking as long as the entire journey down from 24. Were they still on "Executive Express?" The lights overhead bounced off brassy, reflective surfaces on the side walls and the tiles on the floor. The doors themselves glinted like silver-fogged mirrors. Even though orange-crème pressed herself against a wall, she filled the elevator car with dim distortions of her image, and on her lapel, the blurred dot of a pin called out.

Lily laughed. "What pin. Are you serious? The pin on your lapel. The pin everyone around here seems to be wearing. The one... there." With a straight arm, Lily pointed across the elevator.

Orange-crème covered a portion of her chest. "I don't know what you're talking about." The woman looked to Burt, who looked to Lily, who looked back at him, encouraging him to speak up.

"What are you covering, then?" Burt asked.

"The place where that woman was pointing. On my... breast." Orange-crème blushed.

Lily, remembering Alva's bare bosom, felt embarrassed. "I wasn't pointing at your breast. I was pointing at your lapel. The pin! The pin!"

Orange-crème lowered her hand, and the pin was gone.

"Burt?" Lily asked. "You saw it, right? The pin?"

Burt looked down at the tiled elevator floor. Light reflected from the ceiling glared in his face. "I don't know."

Lily huffed. "What do you mean *you don't know*?"

"I might have seen *something*," he said.

"There was nothing to see!" Orange-crème looked more confident now. She leaned away from the elevator wall.

"It has a wolf's head, if that jogs your memory." Lily engaged Burt with a tug on his shirt. "Like the tattoos."

"Like the tattoos," he agreed. "What tattoos?"

"Tobias and Alva's!"

"Of course," he said. "*Those* tattoos."

"And the thing in the dark," Lily added.

"Of course. The thing in the dark." Orange-crème nodded and looked at the elevator panel, where the light for B1 still had not signaled impending arrival.

"Burt, she's hiding the pin from us. It was on her lapel until she covered it with her hand. She must be holding it up her sleeve, or she slipped it in her pocket, or she dropped it on the floor." Lily did a quick scan on the floor. Nothing. "We have to find it."

Burt asked, "Why?"

"Because it means something!" Lily stomped, and the elevator bounced. The three of them put their arms out as if doing so would steady their worlds.

Orange-crème used the moment of unsteadiness to dive toward the elevator panel, where she pressed the emergency call button. "Help! Help! The elevator isn't moving, and there's this woman—"

"I told you I'm Lily." She shoved herself between orange-crème and the elevator panel, making orange-crème stumble backward. "False alarm," she said into what looked like the panel's intercom. "We're fine here."

No answer.

Orange-crème's jacket matched her purse, which she opened as she said, "I don't have the pin you want, but I have money...."

"See there! You see! She could be hiding the pin in her purse!" Lily pointed at orange-crème's purse-searching, which could provide cover for tucking something inside the fashionable handbag.

Burt remained calm. "We don't want your money. Just show us the pin. Show me. Lily, back up. Just show me the pin."

Dropping her purse, orange-crème shouted, "I don't have it!" She was crying now. The purse clattered on the floor. Orange-crème retreated against the wall opposite the elevator panel and the doors, as far from Lily as possible. Burt now hovered in between, intermediary. The lights still indicated travel between G and B1.

Lily leaned in and snatched up the purse. Tossing away some papers, a tampon, eye drops, a compact, and finally a phone, Lily rummaged. She scattered other contents around the elevator until she declared, "It's not in here. It has to be on her somewhere."

Burt took a step toward Lily. "Are you *sure*—"

"YES I'm SURE!"

He retreated to his intermediary spot just as B1 blinked on the elevator panel. The doors opened, and cool air rushed in. A plain white hallway attached to no other visible elevators extended away from the opening. It had a low ceiling, closed doors along the sides, and no traffic. Lily had her back to it, and she didn't budge. Orange-crème looked out into the narrow vacancy with hope.

Lily faced a dilemma of the second order because Burt had a doozy of the first. Lily *knew* about the pin; Burt did not. Lily, therefore, had every reason to keep this woman from escaping, whereas Burt only had Lily's word, her implication, that the woman must not be allowed to escape. On the one hand, Burt could do the *sensible* thing and let this orange-crème woman, this total stranger, go about her business on the elevator, continue on her way to the high, high forty-ninth floor. What awaited her there? Some nefariousness increased from MFS's twenty-fourth floor variety by a factor of twenty-five? The building had posters advertising the businesses it housed but no directory that Lily had seen. Secrecy about the upper floors could be deliberate, and orange-crème could be part of that secrecy, and indeed, the pin could emblazon her complicity. What else, in fact, could such a pin worn by so many involved in this... *foreclosure*... in 1500 Spring... signify if not complicity? What Lily needed to learn was not *that* the pin signaled guilt, but what it signaled in addition to guilt, not *that* it signaled a part played, but what it signaled about the parts played and about the playing itself.

On the other hand, intuiting what Lily knew, sharing in her knowledge as much as he could and should given their shared experiences, Burt could do the *right* thing and stop this woman from exiting the elevator or escaping inside it, stop her from getting away with her shamming innocence. They needed to bring orange-crème out of the elevator, by force if necessary, and search her. Find the pin, confront her with it, ask her about its meaning once she could no longer deny its existence and her insidious way of hiding it. Caught, her guilt would be plain to all, so they would advance, automatically, beyond the obvious stall-tactic question of complicity and into analysis of that in which she was complicit. With access to floor forty-nine, what knowledge of inner workings might she possess? How deep might her insight into Mr. Torrents's abysses run?

Burt had to choose whether to act out of reason or out of trust. Lily, in turn, had to choose her response: to follow Burt's lead, whatever it might be, or to take matters, and with them orange-crème, into her own hands.

Burt chose: "Ma'am... my... companion... and I... believe you have something that we're, going to, um, look for, so if you just gave it to us, I mean, we wouldn't have to search you."

"Search me? Oh God!" The woman entered panic. Her body shook in full measure, head to foot, but she did not lose control. Rather, she contained the shaking, as if a bubble around her body, clinging to an invisible barrier an inch away from her skin, locked it in, creating a zone too wide to be called trembling but too narrow to qualify as seizure. She shook inside that bubble while she tried to shrink against the wall of the elevator, melding orange-crème into the brassy surfaces.

The elevator doors had been open a long time. Maybe standing so near them kept them from closing. Lily stepped backward into the white hallway, keeping a tennis-shoed foot near an elevator door. "Burt, let's all get out of the elevator."

Burt looked at orange-crème, who shrunk closer to the elevator wall and shook her head no. He muttered something under his breath. Lily did not need him to repeat it. "Ma'am, if you just give me the pin, I'll even give it back to you. I just want to look at it and ask you questions."

"About a thing in the dark," orange-crème said.

"Right," Burt said.

Orange-crème nodded, smiled, said "Right," and dashed for the elevator doors. She started low and got past Burt, but her attempt to sidestep Lily resulted in collision, Lily's body blocking orange-crème's barreling progress until they both went down in a tumble. Orange-crème landed on top, and she revealed what she had hidden in her sleeve while searching her purse: a letter-opener, which she produced like a knife and tried to jam into Lily's throat. Lily used all her strength to repel the now-attacking orange-crème. A quick shuffle of legs threw orange-crème off balance and allowed Lily to reposition her body weight, claiming positions first on the side and then hovering over her opponent. A moment later, situations had almost reversed: Lily was now on top, pressing down on orange-crème with all her weight, but orange-crème still held the weapon.

Continuing to pin orange-crème with her knees, Lily ignored the flailing of orange-crème's empty hand in order to focus the strength of both arms on orange-crème's weapon hand. She needed only seconds to pry fingers away from the letter opener's hilt, which made the prize hers. Lily grabbed the weapon and jammed it into orange-crème's eye socket. The panicking woman went limp. Her jaw fell open, and she deflated.

"Oh," Lily said. Blood welled. The letter opener stood erect, suspended in the matter within and beneath orange-crème's eye. Lily had put it there. Blood moved over the face, around the open mouth, and to the neck, and it would reach the orange-crème jacket.

Burt's mouth looked strange, and Lily realized he was biting his lips. "We should put her somewhere." When he spoke, his lips stayed tucked into his teeth.

Looking up and down the white hallway, Lily said, "Where?" By "her," Burt meant it, the dead body. Lily thought of the elevator and the light for 49, but sending the body up to its original destination lacked appropriateness.

"Where does that door go?" Burt indicated a door not far down the hall, the first on the left. Lily was still on the floor with the body; she had no way of knowing where the door went. Burt meant for her to get up and find out. The task must have been Lily's because the mess belonged to her as well. The body was her fault, so she had to find out what was behind the door.

The door opened with the simple turn of a knob, and Lily entered a regular-seeming room, rectangular, cheap wallpaper, multipurpose in lacking any special functionality. In one corner of the room, a chest—rectangular, proportionate to the room, inset—sat. It looked like a shoebox for a coffin, except the lid had hinges. Lily called Burt in to examine her find. "Doesn't that look like the perfect size for—"

"Uh-huh." In coming to deliver his agreement, Burt abandoned the elevator, which closed and departed. It carried its camera and emergency call button away. He now stood in the doorway of the multipurpose room, the purpose of which appeared encoded by the box of curious fit.

Lily's head hurt. Her field of vision stayed clear. In the hallway lay a dead body of her making. In this room sat a box with which she had nothing to do, yet she felt drawn to it, destined for it. Before she could entertain the *deus ex* thoughts that had already crept into her mind's periphery, she had to have facts. "I'm opening it."

Burt remained in the doorway. His head oscillated between Lily and the dead woman, whom a wall separated, as if keeping them both in sight—one in the hall, one in the multipurpose room—would keep them in order. B1 felt no warmer than the ground floor, but Burt was sweating. The collar of his short-sleeved shirt captured trickles from his head and neck. He seemed about to speak but said nothing.

Closer, the box looked like heavy plastic cast on a thin metal frame, lightweight in materials but sturdy and heavy *in toto*, built to hold and sustain rather than to transport. It hummed. As Lily reached for the lid, ready to push it up over her head like a child opening a giant's treasure, she noticed a black line, a cord, attaching the box's back to the wall. The box had electricity, and it contained ice. The ice steamed when the box opened, creating a moment of blindness. When Lily's vision was again clear, she said, "The body goes in here."

Burt looked back and forth, Lily to body, body to Lily. He stopped oscillating and studied the freezer. "That seems like the perfect place for her." His gaze went away, toward the hall. His voice sounded far when he said, "But we have to take things in order."

What order? The body appeared, and now the means for disposing of it had appeared. Lily was in foreclosure, a process that, as Mr. Torrents had explained, moved according to neither ascending nor descending values but according to depths of impacts with distributions across networks determined by mutually dependent outcomes. These contiguous appearances, a sequence, were one thing leading to another, and they made as much sense in terms of *causality* as anything else in Lily's life. Lily opened the elevator; Lily inserted the letter opener into orange-crème's eye; Lily opened the box; Lily would insert orange-crème into the box. All outcomes in the sequence were mutually dependent. The sequence made an intractable juggernaut of sense. It had irresistible forward momentum.

This multipurpose room had no other reason to exist, and the process of elimination provided the most cogent reason for inserting orange-crème into the freezer. Lily no longer remembered why they had come to B1 in the first place. However, she and Burt had not only come to B1, but they had come to *this* B1, on *their* elevator, which drew *that* woman, and led to *that* hallway, which led to *this* room, which contained only one item, *this* freezer, which was the perfect size for *that* woman, who had become *that* body, which now lay in the hallway awaiting dispensation. Everything fit together too well, with the ultimate fit being the body for the freezer. Where do you stash a dead body when you need to hide it quickly? In the basement freezer, if you're so lucky as to have one that accommodates bodies. And they were just so lucky, just *exactly* so lucky. In a land without luck or coincidence, one is left with purpose, and the room had no other purposeful option left in its multiverse. Lily and Burt were here in this place at this time with this body in order to insert it into that freezer.

"The order," Burt said. "I'm going to search her before we move her. For the pin."

Lily had nearly forgotten about the pin. She hung back while Burt searched. After a moment, she heard him call out, "I've got something." She moved closer to the doorway, hesitating to go to the hall. Seeing the body sounded undesirable. While he was in the hall with the body, Burt said, "Oh. Oh *shit*. I guess I'll... damn. No. No way. Uh-uh." Burt returned from the hall, blood on his hands. "I thought I had it. I didn't get a good look before, uh." His head drooped, less embarrassed than ill. "I dropped it."

"Pick it up."

"I dropped it in her mouth," he said. "It was hanging open, and I didn't realize it was under where my fingers had the pin pinched, so when it slipped, well, that's where it went. I reached in after it, but I think I pushed it down in her throat, and it was still... wet... in there... clammy... I don't think I'm processing what's happening on any actual level."

Lily asked, "What did it look like?" She meant the pin, not the body.

"I... it was gold-colored, but not gold. She had blood all over her face, so when I touched her mouth I got it on me. I want to say it had wings on the sides, but I'm not sure. The stabby thing is still in her face."

The stabby thing, the letter opener, was in its eye socket. Unless it had moved. Lily was going to have to see the body anyway. Burt would want her help moving it. She might as well confirm the position of the letter opener in the eye socket.

In her face was so vague. Around the corner, and yes, there it was, as Lily remembered it: orange-crème's head, bloodier now, but with the same metallic protrusion from the same ocular cavity. She wanted to stop seeing the image, to change the channel, to tell the service provider she'd had enough of this data stream and that interrupting it would be dandy, except not looking didn't do away with the consequences of seeing, which included acknowledging the having done, the having been the source of. Looking had a fascination of obligation. She owed orange-crème attention.

Somewhere inside the body, in the back of its throat, if not deeper, the pin now waited. Lily didn't need to know what it looked like because it looked like a faux-gold replica of Tobias and Alva's tattoos, of the thing in the dark, a hybrid wolf-bird-lizard. What she needed was to know whether *Burt* knew what it looked like, not from her but from his own observation. She needed to know he had seen the thing for himself, and he'd said he'd only seen that a pin existed, not that it looked like the tattoos or the thing in the dark, about which they'd talked, and now Lily realized that she might have been the first to mention wolf-bird-lizard shapes. She couldn't, therefore, be certain that Burt had *seen* anything connected to the wolf-bird-lizard phenomenon. He might have been humoring her, talking in circles while avoiding detectable lies. He *said* he had seen a pin of unknown shape, but Lily didn't know that he'd actually seen *the* pin because he lost it in a place that was odd but conveniently unsearchable, unless. *Unsearchable unless she went to an unlikely extreme.*

Maybe shoving her fist down the body's throat would be enough. Assuming a pin was there to find. But what if Burt had lied about the pin? He'd either have to confess, or she'd have to go further down the throat than she could simply reach. Going further would require... what? Breaking the jaw, unhinging it like a snake's? Cutting open the throat, like an esophageal C-section? Eventually splitting open the whole body, the entire digestive tract, searching until a tour of every human pipe confirmed the pin to be nowhere, disappeared, as vanished as the credibility of Burt's story?

"We've got to put it in the freezer," Lily said. "I'll get the shoulders if you get the feet." Blood was going to get on her green shirt, but she would worry about that later. The mess from Burt's hands had gotten on his clothes as well. Together, they carried the body into the multipurpose room and inserted it into the freezer. Whoever had filled the freezer with ice had left enough room for a body of orange-crème's size to be added, contributing more evidence to the demonstration of purposeful fit between Lily and Burt's supply and the room's apparent demand. The freezer closed, hiding the body and maintaining cool.

"I think we need to get out of here." Burt looked at Lily's chest, more likely at her shirt than at her breasts. She looked at his clothes, too, and accepted that worrying about the blood on their clothes would have to happen sooner than later. Whether they took the same elevator, with its camera, or another route, assuming one presented itself, their way out would almost certainly bring them into contact with other people, likely lots of them. Appearing before throngs in blood-spattered clothing did not seem appealing or wise. Yet it did not seem as unthinkable as it might, which Burt seemed on the precipice of acknowledging: "We want to avoid broad daylight, outside, as much as possible, I think, looking like this."

"Yes." Lily felt uncertain about encouraging him instead of letting him reveal the direction of his thinking, but she nudged him anyway: "I wonder if people inside will notice."

"I thought about that. Just walking out into that mob up there, acting normal, you know, acting like it's paint or something. I bet nobody would stop us. We might get tough looks from security guards, but you've got the worst of it, and you're a pretty white lady."

"You think I'm pretty?" The moment was incongruous but welcome. The question was inadvertent.

"Of course. I have good taste. Anyway, for some reason I think it might fly a little better in here than it would outside." Burt looked at a drying stain on his hand.

"For some reason it might fly. Right. Could that reason be that the building gave us a room equipped with a freezer that's perfect for stashing a body right when we needed one?" Lily had meant to be funny rather than flippant.

"Maybe that, yeah. Except—did I mention that nothing at all makes sense about stashing the body in the freezer? It's the first place people will look, and it'll keep evidence fresh for the forensics people. Now a nice kiln, or a trash chute leading to a fiery pit, *that* would have seemed perfect, like divine intervention, because those things are great for getting rid of bodies. But an overgrown ice chest out in the open? That's wrapping it in plastic and tying it in a bow." Burt tapped the top of the freezer with his thumb.

"When you put it that way, what we both just did seems kind of stupid." Lily tapped her fingers in Burt's rhythm, emphasizing the corpse on which they played.

Burt said, "I get it, I know. And I think we did the right thing because the overriding feeling was and is that the freezer was here for the body, that the two fit together, that there's a design. And the design belongs to the building. What else would it be? 1500 Spring. MFS. Things in between. I don't know. I don't have it all together yet. But if what Mr. Torrents said is something we're to believe, then there's a bigger picture, and it's corporate, and it's in this building and I'm guessing others like it. Different rules apply here. We've got to learn what those rules are and get the better of them."

Listening to Burt made Lily's head hurt more, but he spoke in general accuracies. Designs and bigger pictures, certainly. Different rules? He seemed rather hopeful to think that presiding forces as systemic as *rules* would hold sway within bigger pictures, and to think further that such a system would be learnable by so pitiable a creature as a human, and to think still further that such learning could avail a human of betterment. But, in the most rational of terms, he was right to think that here, in 1500 Spring, in connection with Collection Time, the principles of operation for people and objects might differ from those principles followed elsewhere. That hypothesis appealed to Lily because it fit all available data in a way that no other hypothesis for their state of being did. When sense failed to apply, it had to be redefined.

"So," Lily said. "Big picture. We go upstairs. We walk out into the lobby, looking like we do. Nobody makes a fuss. Then what?"

"You know we didn't clean up the blood in the hall," Burt said.

Lily thought for a moment. "I do know that."

"So what we've got is a blood trail leading to a freezer with a body in it."

"Yes."

"I don't have anything to clean any of this up," Burt said.

"Me neither." Lily shrugged.

Burt took long looks at the blood trail, the freezer, and their clothes. "Should we just say fuck it and go upstairs?"

"Sure."

3

Tobias Centurion's three-piece suit covered his tattoos, and his head's short growth of thin, pale hair, parted and combed, combined with round, wire-rimmed glasses to give him an air of dignity. He had the look of an account executive, which diverged from his previous loincloth-diaper attire. Perfect posture allowed his muscled arms and chest to fill his jacket and prop up his solid red tie, and when he eventually turned away from the elevator, Lily noticed curves in his backside and thighs that she had missed due to his previous costume's overwhelming skimpiness. Whereas seeing the man mostly naked had done next to nothing for her, seeing Tobias clad in fashion with the lobby's hundreds of other denizens made him look handsome.

While Tobias fit the lobby aesthetic in his style of self-presentation, he offered a deeper contrast in the category of motion. Among the hundreds, if not thousands, of suit-wearing denizens, Tobias, standing to greet Lily and Burt when the elevator door opened on the lobby, alone had the quality of animation. Everyone else stayed in place, figures in a wax museum, time-freeze in a comic book, meat mannequins, fleshy and mid-breath but stalled before the completion of a gesture. Even Burt had become stuck, so Tobias might have only been greeting Lily. The elevator doors opened, claiming the last bit of movement not to originate from Lily or Tobias, and Tobias gave greetings. The rest of the universe froze.

Lily observed Tobias's exceptional status and hesitated

to step out of the elevator, which he made way for her to do. Staying put, she said, "What's happening?"

"Apparently I'm working for you pro bono." Tobias faked a grin and gestured to the frozen world behind him. "None of this is my doing."

Lily stayed in the elevator, and she sidestepped toward Burt's motionless form. She placed a hand on his shoulder and squeezed. It felt like normal Burt-shoulder, yielding at her touch, but it reassumed its former position after she finished touching him. Like sand filling in footprints, his body, when she pushed it, would slip back into its original position. She didn't know what would happen if she knocked him down. Would he get back up and pose? Would his body drift back up onto his feet? She wanted to shove him, but she didn't.

"If you didn't," Lily asked, "then who... paused... the world?"

"Someone upstairs wanted us to talk in peace, don't you think? The man upstairs? The man upstairs! This place has a million quaint ironies." Tobias brushed something off his sleeve.

"The man upstairs? You mean Young Torrents?"

"Who?" Tobias appeared as if he found the question distasteful.

"The man we met on the twenty-fourth floor," Lily explained, uncertain about why. Tobias's face showed no recognition of Young Torrents's name.

"You think you've been to the twenty-fourth floor. Hmm. Step out of the elevator, and let me show you something." Tobias looked at his watch. Lily wondered if it had stopped.

Before she could reply, Lily had to think about Tobias's last statement. She *thought* she had been to the twenty-fourth floor. She did think so. According to her experience, she had been there, but by pointing out that she thought it, *merely* thought it, Tobias suggested that her experience, or her memory of her experience, was counterfactual, even counterfeit. She also remembered experiencing B1, not as a full floor with a bank of elevators to match the other floors she knew, G and 24, but as a singular hallway stretching from a singular elevator, leading to a singular destiny involving a well-fitting freezer. Many aspects of this experience suggested that it could be counterfactual, that it might not have occurred, or if it did occur, it might have occurred very differently from how she experienced it. And if B1 was a false experience, why not 24? Tobias's doubts about her visit to the twenty-fourth floor, telegraphed in a single mouthful of words, opened chasms, new abysses to fathom alongside Mr. Torrents's description of Collection Time. Stepping out of the elevator, as Tobias had asked her to do, seemed like stepping into a canyon of undermined perception.

She stepped out anyway. The frozen lobby denizens remained; the lobby did not. In its place appeared a landscape like what she had visualized, *consciously* visualized, not hallucinated, outside 1500 Spring. The ground consisted of grey sand and rocks strewn with the detritus of streets and buildings long ago reduced to rubble, and the sky, with mountain-lined horizons erected where walls should have been, stretched out in black-mottled red. People--who should have stood on flat, corporate flooring—crowded the blasted wastes in their tidy suits and muted accessories. The effect would have looked cheap, just an apocalypse green-screened in behind a crowded business-scape, if the standing figures dotting the land all the way to the horizon did not appear in full relief, ready to be approached and touched.

"Go on," Tobias said. "Touch one of them."

Lily again experienced the uncanny sensation of transparency. She felt fairly certain she hadn't spoken of touching one of the frozen people, but she had thought, perhaps visibly, of walking up to the man nearest the elevator and poking him in the face, a finger below a high cheekbone, where a dimple might form should the man happen to smile. The man was handsome in a magazine sort of way. She might loosen his tie, unbutton his shirt. And why stop there? Maniacs treated bodies like mannequins, dressing them up to talk to them, dressing them down to fondle them, but those bodies were dead. The statues that posed for Lily lived.

She stepped up to the man with the inviting dimple-face. Her wavering finger hovered beside his cheek.

"Go on," Tobias said.

The skin of his face felt warm, and she sensed stubble breaking through smoothness. This man *moisturized*. Lily's finger traced a line between cheekbone and jaw before skipping to the tip of his nose. Delicate pressure made the man's head, maybe the entire figure, wobble, but like Burt, it settled back into shape.

How long did orange-crème's skin take to stop feeling so alive? Arrested in time, this man lacked the animus of animation, but he possessed tactile presence, the responsiveness of breathing skin, and he kindled the hunger of flesh responding to flesh. Lily felt *attracted* to the mannequin. When her mind lingered on Alva's enormous breasts and cried out against being accused of ogling orange-crème's, her college training warned her about objectification, treating women as objects, an evil to which anyone, regardless of genitalia, might fall. Here, though, stood a man with no more motility than an object, a rock, *never* animate, and her heartrate quickened in a way that felt more demeaning to her than to him. His beauty, even when reduced to no more than a property of the inanimate, cowed her. She wanted to feel whether his belly were soft or hard. She wanted to cup his balls in the palm of her hand.

Necrophile.

Was *that* this feeling? To be attracted to an inanimate object in the shape of a person? This man had warmth beneath her touch, but flesh tended to make temperature negotiable. Minus movement, life had the quality of death, and this man deprived of movement seemed *fuckable*. Not that his member was likely to function. She had trouble imagining engorgement with blood affecting any penises in this stifling atmosphere. But he had fingers and toes. Besides, the point wasn't coitus. It was sharing. Could one share with the inanimate? Maybe not. But what if part of him was awake in there, experiencing her poke in his cheek and logging the sensation? What if he could enjoy her taking off his dress shirt and slacks and touching him in various places while he stood still and unreacting? And if he couldn't, then what harm would she do anyway? A man not present to himself could share with a woman, but only in one direction, giving, not receiving. Could a corpse not do the same?

"You're missing an opportunity," Tobias said.

She thought of the hundreds, maybe thousands of people frozen around her. Like a novice public speaker, she imagined them all naked, formal business attire falling away. One by one the busy people appeared well-made, limbs joining torsos in efficient bonds of muscle and bone, covered by smooth skin of different shades, some haired, some not. "What am I missing?" she asked.

"Look there, on his lapel."

Seeing the man in front of her again required a shift in vision, away from the nakedness of the room, away from his nakedness, back to the surfaces of things. The clothes she'd thought of removing were still on, and over the shirt she hadn't unbuttoned was a jacket with lapels. On one of the lapels, a pin. Overloaded by apocalyptic surroundings freckled with nudity, her senses couldn't process the pin immediately. She located it, however, in front of her, and recognized the wolf-bird-lizard.

"Take it," Tobias said. "Show it to Burt when we're done."

"When Burt starts moving again?"

"Yes, he'll start moving again. They all will. But first, I am given leave to explain something to you. Walk with me." Tobias began a tour through the standing, smartly dressed figures, and Lily followed. "Some people think Almighty Fate is inscrutable. Do you think that? I think it's all very easy to understand. The problem, when you clear through the hoopla, is cancer."

Lily noticed an older woman's thick hair and wondered whether it was a wig. "Cancer?"

"You know, in heaven. Angels, pious spirits, and other residents behind the Pearly Gates have a tendency to get cancer. It's not all about paradise, you know. The universe has orders of suffering. It matches those orders to different levels and realms of being. On a higher level or realm, you get a higher order of suffering. The matches are legitimate. To think otherwise would be unnatural! In heaven cancer isn't messy. Bodies don't erupt and fail in heaven like they do here, but entities can hurt, oh yes they can, and they can lose themselves a little at a time. A cancer can take hold of you in heaven, and it can make even the brightest light seem dimmer. It nags at a corner of your fabric until you let it into your weave, at which point it can unravel you, bit by bit. Imagine sawing off an angel's limbs and leaving it with only one wing, flapping so the stump-addled body spins around, dizzy for millennia. Leaving a heavenly cancer unchecked for too long can have those kinds of results. It's not pretty. It's not pretty.

"So how do you cure a divine cancer? How do you render whole again a creature of divine light diminished by losses inconceivable to the human brain? The orders exist, you see, to satisfy one another. Angels and devils... I told you I'm not a Satanist, but I have had dealings with both sides, which makes mentioning the creatures less a testimonial of faith than an affirmation of experience, and according to my experience, angels make dreadful company... in any case, their kind has a symbiosis with ours. They look after our needs, of varying sorts, and we look after theirs. We make up for their losses with our losses. They... feed on our suffering. For the devils, our suffering is an end unto itself, hence devils, but for the angels, our suffering is a balm for the gravest of ailments. Our suffering makes angels whole. Otherwise, they'd detest it, like they detest their own suffering, but angels cannot avoid having human torture as their utmost desire, for without it, they could not go on as angels, and without them, humankind would surely perish altogether.

"Torture, like all things, requires regulation. Any of Alva's exercises would help you to understand the regulation, the management essential to the maintenance of pain. Suffering, like any cure, must remain available in a sufficient and governed supply, so the production of that suffering through torture must be steady and predictable. The angels do not wish to extract their cure from all of humanity at once. Bother! And small suffering does little against the bigness of divine cancer. The angels need a way to harvest enough of the right kind of suffering while hurting as few people at a time as possible. So, like any well-organized, elite group, they put out a request for proposals from companies that might be interested in solving their problems. The company you know as Mansworth Futures and Securities won the contract. MFS took on the application of torture to a select number of individuals in order to cultivate suffering sufficient to satisfy heaven's demands for a cure for cancer."

"And what about... God?" Lily asked. "Does God get cancer and take suffering as a cure?"

"Good question," Tobias said. "And I don't know the answer. If so, I'd imagine him feeding on angels' suffering or suffering from some other level or realm. Human suffering seems too trivial for God! But here's what I do know: God is Chair of the Board at MFS. It's in the contract; he's the head honcho, no elections, no objections."

"Does that mean he's here, in this building?" Lily asked.

"Haven't you heard?" Tobias stopped walking and paused by a frozen woman who was reading on her phone. "God is everywhere. But he does have an office on the sixtieth floor. The top. Naturally."

Lily felt her brain spinning. Her attention kept pulling toward the wolf-bird-lizard pin, now in her possession, ready to be revealed. It had seemed as important as a woman's life before. Now she didn't know what it might prove. "Have you seem him?" she asked. "God?"

"Who, me? No. You know me, I'm a freelancer. Well, maybe you don't know me, but we would never have met if I were up to being one of God's regular handymen. Those folks get *paid*. All the bunnies they could want. But they also have to live within constraints I find as unappealing as this suit I'm wearing. I wouldn't be here at all if not for... you know, the debt."

Lily wrinkled her brow. "Debt?"

"I thought you'd been told." Tobias frowned. "Maybe you've heard a little much today? You might have heard the mechanics of the system, such as they are, but maybe they haven't formed a complete picture for you. That's okay. What you should really do is sit down. Let's come over here." He led toward the lobby's café, which dwelled like an oasis in the wasted landscape enclosed by the lobby universe. Mostly it was a small vending space for to-go orders, but an area with a few tables and sets of chairs did extend into the common traffic area. On the tail-end of the day's lunch phase, no table remained unoccupied. Tobias set a finger on his chin, thinking, then pointed at a small table with two chairs where a younger suited couple sat drinking coffee from paper cups and participating in what looked like a lively discussion's cross-section. Both had coffee cups in their hands in different states of lifting, his on the way to his lips, hers on the way to the table. "You take her, I'll take him, okay?" Without ceremony, he grabbed the young man from his chair and lobbed him onto the floor, where he landed like a sack of flour. He did not, as Lily had expected, sift back into his place, but his body, lying on the ground, did assume a posture very like sitting.

Lily hesitated over the young woman's frozen body. Should she toss her to the floor like a useless sack? What if time unfroze while the young couple lay sprawled in unnatural postures on the floor, and Lily and Tobias sat presumptuously in the spaces the sprawled duo had occupied but a moment before? Would Lily and her company not be the obvious causes of the young ones' displacement? Would they not face consequences?

"Just toss her already," Tobias encouraged.

With the first forays of her hands sampling the young woman like a casual cook testing a pot's handle, Lily gingerly grasped the woman's shoulders, and lifting while she shoved, tilted her from the chair onto the floor. The young woman and man now lay together, overlapping, each shaped as if still seated. Lily sat at the table they had occupied.

Tobias did not sit with her. "Now stay here," he said. "I have things to fetch."

Lily waited. From her seated position the statuesque passersby looked stranger. Picturing them naked now would only heighten their fearfulness. They all looked like taxidermied birds, their eyes plastic inside otherwise organic, preternaturally fixed but organic, material. What chilled her the most was thinking that once they started moving again, as Tobias promised, they might keep looking as they did now, lifeless, uninhabited, husks of being whose only difference from warm flesh statues was the tiny additive of motion. At least their clothes put them in a context. Without the suits and accessories, they'd be stripped dolls in a heap.

Tobias returned with Burt draped over his shoulders in the manner of a soldier fallen on the field. "The chair, if you don't mind." Lily pulled out the chair opposite where she'd been sitting, and Tobias lowered Burt into it. "There we go. No you can adjust him as you please. I'll be right back."

Tobias left again, and Lily expected Burt to retake the shape he'd had on the elevator, standing in the middle of an unknown gesture. He didn't. He stayed slumped in the chair, ragdoll, as devoid of posture as he was of animation. She thought of adjusting him, making him sit properly, but the idea of manipulating the body she knew intimately while it was in a state of total lethargy, living but lifeless, revolted her. Whatever necrophilia she'd felt with the unknown man by the elevator did not arise here. She needed Tobias to return. She needed this phase of her experience, however real or unreal it was, to end.

Tobias returned. He held a bag labeled "The Gift Shop," and he set it on the table between Lily and rag-doll Burt. "I took a bag and left money on the register," he said. "It's all on the corporate tab anyway."

Did MFS, heavenly contractors, provide expense accounts for freelancers? The claim seemed unlikely. Lily looked from the bag to Burt and failed to comprehend how the former could help the latter until Tobias reached into the bag and said, "Ta-da!" He pulled out two t-shirts, both red. He tossed one onto Burt's slumped form and the other into Lily's lap. "I think they're your sizes."

Half-expecting to see a wolf-bird-lizard, Lily examined the front of her t-shirt. It bore the letters MFS as well as the company logo, with no sign of any creature. "Mansworth sells souvenir t-shirts at the gift shop?"

"Yes," Tobias said. "Strange that they're the only

company that does. The shirts are less souvenirs for you, dear, than they are necessities. Your gentleman's navy hides it better than your own green, but both of your current tops suffer too much from the wrong kind of redness, don't you think? You can change yourself, I imagine. I think I might need your help changing Mr. Wells."

Lily considered swapping her current green shirt for the red one, and she felt all the plastic eyes of the frozen people already on her. The whole lobby might have gone dark except a sliver of sun, a spotlight, kept Lily and Burt's table in view, drawing all attention while Lily took off her shirt, revealing her less-than-new, less-than-fashionable bra and becoming a commercial-zone exhibitionist. Then she understood that she was to help Tobias strip off Burt's polo and expose his chest and belly to the lobby universe. If she had been a necrophile for wanting to explore the flesh of a handsome frozen man, what was she for exposing the flesh of her adorable ragdoll middle-aged lover? The prospect of impending public semi-nakedness roused deep hesitation.

To avoid the possibility of seeing the mannequins seeing her, Lily kept her head down while she pulled off her green shirt and pulled on the red one. Tobias watched, but Tobias watching felt okay—he felt kind of like a doctor, impartial to nudity, capable of appreciating but not there to enjoy. He took the bloody green shirt from Lily, folded it, and placed it in a briefcase she hadn't noticed him carrying before. She didn't ask about the blood on her pants or splattered elsewhere. For both Lily and Burt, the shirts carried the bulk of orange-crème's liquid remains, the concentration of evidence likeliest to arouse the suspicion of thronging witnesses.

Removing Burt's shirt proved comical. As soon as they got his body into a sitting position, ready to have the splotched navy-colored top removed, one of them would release a shoulder or arm to prepare the red shirt, and the body would slump down again, drained of form. A dead person, Lily told herself, would cooperate better, behaving more like clay. Living flesh resisted molding from anyone other than its rightful inhabitant, who, deprived of the capacity to animate, could at least make form supple and slippery. In this regard Burt was almost as alive as Lily and Tobias, more alive than any of the frozen denizens of the lobby floor. She found the suppleness of the living less attractive than the statuesque qualities of the inanimate. With a torso and arms like wet pasta, Burt offered less than his frozen counterparts.

With Tobias's help, which seemed experienced in shirting bodies deprived of active musculature, Lily managed the change, so she and Burt sat at the little café table in new, red MFS shirts, still blood-spattered but far less conspicuous were Burt and the world to regain motion. "Okay," Lily said. "Now wake him up. Make him move again."

"Who, me?" Tobias looked left and right, as if searching for someone else Lily might address in the area crowded with impersonal people. "What makes you think I could do a thing like that?"

Lily felt flummoxed. "What makes the people go, if not you?"

Tobias shrugged. "God?"

"And he's upstairs somewhere, on the sixtieth floor. Making all this happen." Lily placed the wolf-bird-lizard pin on the table between her and Burt's slumped body. She studied it.

Tobias, standing near, said, "I presume."

Things began to coalesce. "And you presume that God feeds on the suffering of angels, who feed on the suffering of people, in order to cure... cancer."

"Like testing products and chemicals on so many bunny rabbits, yes ma'am," Tobias said. He looked bored.

Lily almost stood from the little café table when she pronounced, "God is a schmuck."

Tobias looked at his watch. Was it moving? He said, "You said it."

A voice somewhere behind Lily said, "Thine own mouth condemneth thee! Thine own lips testify against thee!"

Lily looked over her shoulder, and Tobias did not react. Mia had spoken; Eric and Kris stood with her. For the first time during their post-death presence, Lily had a strong sense that her three expired friends were incorporeal. They lacked the stillness of all the other standing figures, but they also lacked solidity, as the sliver of sun spotlighting the café table challenged their opacity, giving them inner glows.

"I need to be going now," Tobias said.

"What? Did you hear her?" Lily looked back and forth between the visiting dead threesome, gathered behind her in an arc, and Tobias, who stood near the café table with his briefcase full of bloody shirts. She thought of the Extreme Psychic, Lady Laetitia, who had channeled her friends, giving weight to their uncertain existence, and considered that, exceptional as he was in this field of inanimate lives, Tobias might have access to whatever realm she tapped when receiving lectures from friends who had departed during Crazy Time, Collection Time, or whatever time it had been that night on the highway.

"Who, me?" Tobias answered. "Hear whom?" He looked at his watch again. "I really must be going."

"I already warned you," Kris said, "about the collision of God and reason. You force a reckoning!"

Tobias's eyes shifted in Kris's direction. He tried, or seemed to try, to hide the curious expression, but Lily detected it and said, "You must have heard her! Do you see her, too?"

"Would you look at the time?" Tobias stepped away from the table, angling his body toward the escalator up to Scarcity. Both the escalator and the restaurant were visible amidst red sky, grey ground, and mountains. None of the lobby seemed truly lost in the bereft landscape. The reds, greys, and blacks just overlapped the more vibrant corporate sheens.

"No!" Lily cried, reaching for Tobias without leaving her seat, grabbing at air. "I have too many questions!" She thought about the pin. Why a wolf, a bird, and a lizard? Tobias had the tattoo, and in Lily's mind a tattoo promised arcane knowledge. She couldn't recall whether she'd ever slept with a man who had tattoos. Why that tattoo, and why would he have a totemic symbol in common with all these suited lobby drones? What was Tobias doing here in the first place? "You can't leave!"

"I must be going." He escaped by inches. "The time."

"THERE IS NO TIME!" Lily gesticulated at the frozen masses. Her statement sounded like someone saying they were out of time, but she meant the opposite, that they had plenty of time, or rather—they were out*side* of time. Exterior to time and motion, she and Tobias were both exceptional, not subject to chronology's whimsical limits.

"It's time for you to listen," Eric said. "That's what time it is."

"The reckoning will not be swift," Kris added.

Lily thought her head was throbbing, but she realized that the sensation came from the outside. Reality throbbed. Critical mass loomed. Space would burgeon and break. At the periphery of consciousness, she considered whether she had actually murdered a woman downstairs.

She tried to ignore everything but Tobias. "Stay!"

"Begone!" Kris yelled after him.

So Kris—and presumably Eric and Mia—saw Tobias, but Tobias, too coincidentally pressed for time from the moment of the threesome's arrival, would not acknowledge seeing them. He had to see them. Lily knew he did. But she needed his acknowledgment.

"We all have forces we must obey," Tobias said. He did not turn around to depart. He backed away, keeping his eyes on Lily. "I'm... sorry for you." He looked toward the high, forgettable lobby ceiling, occluded by the red and black of what Lily perceived as a kind of spray-on apocalypse behind which the deeper truths of 1500 Spring, the skyscraper, provided structure. "We all have tiny destinies. Resistance suits them so well that I've given it up. Ms. Henshaw, I wish I could answer all your questions. I've given you more answers than most people ever receive. I can but give this one thing more, an injunction, an intervention...."

"Begone, heathen!" Kris shouted. Tobias did not flinch. "Poisoner! Reprobate! Befouler of the verdant fields!"

Lily stared at him. He looked only at her as he walked backward, sinking toward the frozen crowd between the café table and the escalator, which led to a restaurant that looked clearer now, sharper, less occluded by apocalyptic horizons.

"Lily, listen to what Kris says," Eric encouraged. "This man is a befouler."

"The wicked man travaileth—" Mia began.

Lily stopped her. "Tobias Centurion, you stay here and tell me what to do!" Between her and the exiting, finely-built man in a suit, Burt's body, now red-shirted, slumped unreactive.

"This man is a *liar*, Lily. He told you so himself." Eric sounded satisfied with the reminder.

"Don't raise your hand," Kris said. "Do not raise your hand!"

Lily couldn't process motionless Burt together with the voices and words of her dead friends. Flashes of sense beamed from some phrases while others emitted utter nonsense. "Tobias!" she called.

"He stretcheth out his hand against God," Mia said.

"*Your* hand, Lily," Eric said. "This liar is stretching *your* hand."

Tobias had almost vanished in a fold of frozen people before the escalator, which, surrounded by glass and steel, reflected the regular lobby rather than the landscape of red and grey and black. Normality loomed, boding ill.

Stepping backward but with a look on his face, pain in his eyes, suggesting an effort to regain footing, to come back to Lily's side, Tobias yelled, "Ms. Henshaw!"

"Yes, Tobias! Speak to me!" Lily half-stood.

The force of voices behind her pressed downward, reseating her. "Seek no parlance with devils!" Kris commanded.

Mia enjoined, "He shall not depart out of darkness!"

Vanishing, his voice half-swallowed in distance, blocked by frozen bodies, Tobias called, "Kill him! You have to kill him! You have to—" And then he was gone, receded to a point where trying to find him merely ran her eyes again and again over Burt, who slumped in her direct line of vision. Kill *him*? Which "him" did Tobias mean?

"We won't come to you again," Kris said.

"Lost cause," Eric grumbled.

"Severity!" the three intoned simultaneously.

Kill. Kill. Kill. The word floated on its own, uncoupled from "him" because it drifted on a sea of hims, men in suits in every direction, frozen, most of them wearing the wolf-bird-lizard pins. Lily thought of orange-crème in the freezer, connecting her to the massive loss of motion. The lobby itself, returning to its former status as an enclosure defined by sleek and whole architectural features lined with selective advertising space, was an ice box. The incorporeal beings stood behind her in an ocean of bodies subtracted from motion.

What did "kill" mean in such a place?

Mia screamed, and Tobias reemerged within Lily's field of vision. From the mezzanine that overlooked the café and other lower-lobby features, all restored now atop the barely visible rubble that had been, he flew. In the midst of the crush of frozen bodies above, he'd found the space to run and leap from the mezzanine's railed edge, and he would crash down, like Iris onto the pavement, into the ocean of locked forms. He began in an arc, a dive, but the motion slowed, and the organization of limbs dissolved into flailing. At the apex of his leap, he must have panicked, clawing for a grip on nothing, stomping at ground he'd left behind. Posed in mid-air chaos, his descent froze. He did not crash but hung, suspended in the air, above a fall that would crush him.

Motion returned. People moved as if they had never stopped, resuming flows of traffic. The man and woman who had occupied Lily's table shook their heads, blinking, and collected themselves from the floor. They looked at one another, brushed off their clothes, and had a laugh at their odd circumstances. They gave Lily a disparaging look but said nothing before going on their ways. Lily turned around and saw no trace of Mia, Kris, or Eric, and though Mia's scream still rung in her ears, she heard nothing new from them. The normality that had threatened now actualized.

Burt stiffened in his seat and looked at Lily across from him. "How did we get here?"

Lily looked at him and wanted to cry. Eyes welling, she pushed the pin, still lying on the table, in his direction. "I found what we wanted."

With his attention oscillating between his new red shirt and the wolf-bird-lizard pin, he said, "It's like I imagined it."

She nodded. Lily understood that Burt seeing the pin was worth nothing now. She understood what Tobias meant and supposed she had understood it immediately without wanting to comprehend it. Kill God. She needed to kill God, who waited for them on the sixtieth floor.

4

Lily and Burt decided to stay at their little café table for a while, to figure things out and to acclimate to a lobby almost wholly the same as before their trip to B1 except for the Tobias hanging in the air. A Tobias hanging in the air did, however, cast a figurative shadow, although he cast no literal one that either of them could detect. Before, at least while moving, the lobby had seemed within bounds, governed by laws of human behavior and circulation. Now, the humans behaved and circulated in the same manner, without regard for the man stopped mid-plummet on the way to his demise. The general disregard for the mid-air impossibility tainted the behavior and circulation with illicitness: the masses either didn't see or didn't react to the anomaly in their midst, which made the masses themselves anomalous, so the central wrong of the Tobias became a diffuse wrong of the entire lobby. The Tobias hung as an unremarkable fixture, and in so doing he transformed the bustling space into a conspiracy of oblivious silence.

"Who's that?" Burt, in his new red shirt, looked into space behind Lily, where her three dead friends had been.

Lily did not feel ready for the question. She did not turn around. "I don't see anyone."

"That guy," Burt said. "Behind you, a couple of tables over."

That guy. The call to attention sounded familiar. The entire moment had an air of familiarity. *Déjà vu.* Had Lily been here, sitting at this little café table with Burt, looking for *that guy*, before?

"Don't look now," Burt said, which was okay because she didn't want to look. "He'll notice if you turn around. The best thing we can do is act like we haven't seen him."

"I haven't seen him," Lily said.

Burt didn't make eye contact with her, but he wasn't staring at that guy, either. His eyes made efforts to stay downcast, sneaking mere samples of his surroundings. "You have, though. Before we came in here. He was outside, and I pointed him out."

Lily remembered! The man's defining property was being unalarming: grey hair, dark complexion, dark clothes, brown satchel from which he'd produced a book. "What's he doing?"

Burt took a longer glance behind her. "Cleaning up his table. Stuffing used napkins into a disposable coffee cup. Now he's walking the cup over to the trash. He's about to—now he's entering a line of people. I think he's headed toward the front of the building!"

Lily wanted to say *so what?*, but Burt had been patient with her need to find a wolf-bird-lizard pin, a need that had led them down a dark path, so she felt obliged to indulge this interest of his. "Do you want to...." She'd asked before whether Burt wanted to approach that guy, hadn't she? "Follow him?"

"I think he could be important," Burt said. "I think he's been with us since we left the loft this morning."

The loft. The idea of the world outside 1500 Spring seemed remote, even though they'd arrived here at the beginning of still-ongoing lunchtime activities. Lily asked, "Can I look now?"

Burt rose to go. "Look and come with me. He's getting away."

Lily got out of her chair, straightened her red t-shirt, and looked in the direction of the man who'd apparently been following them all day who now posed the threat of getting away. What might have been his or might have been another man's head bobbed in the throng, advancing slowly toward the lobby's main entry and exit. Burt grabbed her hand and pulled her into a people stream. His eyes stayed fixed on a point near the bobbing head—Lily looked either at or near the correct person. Keeping a firm grip on her, Burt muttered excuse mes and navigated their artery, finding a shortcut around a pillar with an MFS "Imagination" poster on it. They closed on their person of interest, who showed no interest in them, but they did not get close enough to intervene before the guy inserted himself into one of the building-front's rotary doors.

Burt pulled Lily out of the stream, taking a vantage on the rotary door near a large freestanding object that was either a sculpture or a podium. That guy disappeared through the rotary on one side and reappeared on the other, disoriented and possibly dizzy, certainly discontent with being back in the lobby rather than outside the building. Lily understood instantly that the guy had failed an attempt to exit the building and that, if he attempted another exit, he would fail again. He modeled their fate, or at least their circumstance. 1500 Spring was not releasing people at the moment. As it held the Tobias in place, so it held its other denizens. Some had movements more circumscribed than others.

That guy made another attempt in the rotary, and he proved Lily correct, at least as far as him returning full-circle to the lobby, less bewildered but still upset by his destination and origin being the same. When he tried one of the regular doors, he found it unmoving. Lily half-expected him to lift an item—a chair must have been somewhere—and try smashing through a selection of glass in the façade. The glass would refuse to yield. He could produce a heavy machine gun and dump rounds and rounds of ammunition in a hot blaze, but the glass would resist. That guy *had* followed them from the loft to 1500 Spring; Lily felt certain now. Her certainty came from recognizing not him but his predicament: he bore a clear relation to Lily and Burt, one that had put them in the same stream of events, from which they had landed on the same populous island.

"We should intercept him, now," Lily said. Now was their time to overtake him.

"Come on," Burt said, pulling Lily into a new rush of walkers that led toward that guy's position. Drawing in range, they split up to flank him. From both sides, they approached and said together: "LOOKING FOR US?"

That guy lurched forward instead of jumping to show surprise. He bumped into a woman who was on her way to a rotary door. When she disappeared on one side, Lily couldn't predict whether she'd reappear. Was 1500 Spring keeping everyone or only people in her event stream? The woman did not reappear. Other people were exiting through the rotary and not re-entering as well. Being stuck, then, had significance.

Did being in the same predicament as Lily and Burt make that guy more of a person than the other lobby denizens? Maybe all the lobby people, with their freezing and moving, were indeed automata, and that explained their freedom. Maybe they weren't real, and Lily, Burt, and that guy who'd followed them in were the only real, trapped people in a maze of artifice. Lily thought of the letter opener, standing in the matter beneath orange-crème's eye, and she thought of the plasticity of the eyes when no one could move. Nobody being real made a lot of sense.

Reality, then, made that guy at least as important as Burt had suspected. "You need us," Lily said in his ear, cutting off any answer he might have had about whether he'd been looking for them.

That guy looked at them, head darting back and forth, and said, "We must talk, but not here! Come with me!" He lurched again, all the way into a stream of traffic, and Lily grabbed Burt, following. That guy's stream led all the way back to Scarcity's escalator. With that guy in the lead, they ascended.

Traveling upward, that guy became audible above the gnashes of ambient noise and said, "I am Chester Orfantomhauser, the Reverend Chester Orfantomhauser, but most people call me Rev Orf. I have led you in this direction so that we may have lunch."

Burt, who stood a step below Rev Orf, looked at Lily, who stood a step below Burt. She looked up toward Scarcity, where tables appeared to be available, and shrugged. Hunger announced itself on cue. Lunch appealed.

At the top of the escalator, a woman waited behind a counter to greet and seat them. She had a pleasant appearance, with reddish hair tied back, calming eyes, and a freckled nose. Her uniform involved a black bowtie and vest atop a conservative white shirt, upscale and fashionable but indistinct, the uniform of any server at any restaurant in any tower. It did not match or enhance the unsettling quality of the oversized painting one had to pass in the hall on the way to the restaurant's primary seating area.

The painting had a gold plaque with the name "Oasis." Most of it showed desert sand, rolling hills, jagged cliffs, and purple-fogged mountains in the distance framing a low-hanging dusty orange sun. Scattered in the background, little clusters dotted the landscape, perhaps piles of garbage. The foreground made a different suggestion by detailing human bones in three unrelated places, signifying three people who had perished at different times in the scalding wastes. Those bones, bleached and calm, did not protest their blasted state. They simply proclaimed it. Lily didn't know whether Burt or

Rev Orf looked at the painting as he passed, and the passing went quickly. What bothered her was seeing no oasis. No hint of living-green or water-blue. Without at least a hint, the painting seemed like an irresponsible decoration for a restaurant, and it had a far-too-provocative title. But maybe the oasis was there, somewhere, and Lily had failed to see it.

The pleasant woman seated them at a booth by a large potted plant with fronds that formed a partial canopy over their heads. Lily and Burt took one side, Rev Orf the other. They were sitting only moments before a man in a bowtie but no vest deposited three large glasses of water on their table, and he had just departed when another man dropped off a metal contraption in which varieties of artisan bread stood upright, each miniature loaf-ette with a card proclaiming its name and national origin. The menus were ultra-lightweight digital tablets that allowed options but defaulted to the cocktails page after the introduction.

Rev Orf was the best dressed among them, but even he did not match the level of décor. Lily felt ashamed of her t-shirt and still-bloody jeans. "I would definitely have a drink," she said.

The Rev and Burt looked at her, stunned. Burt smiled and said, "Me too," but Rev Orf remained dumbfounded.

"You've... adapted... well," the Rev said. "No drinks for me."

Lily and Burt each selected from the varieties of bread before inputting their cocktail selections. Burt sounded innocent: "Adapted to what, Rev Orf?"

"To your situation."

"And what situation would that be?" Lily asked.

"The situation that brought you to this building," the Rev said.

Burt looked around. The restaurant was no longer

crowded, but the lobby still teemed. All remained oblivious to the suspended Tobias. "A lot of people here, Rev. A lot of situations. What interests you in ours?"

"*Hers*," the Rev corrected. "No offense, Mr. Wells, but you are purely collateral."

"I've been getting that impression," Burt said. "Hey, at least now I know it's not a race thing."

Lily looked at the two black men and wondered the same thing Rev Orf asked: "How do you know that?"

Burt blinked.

"I followed you from your apartment this morning," Rev Orf said.

"We know," they replied. Burt added, "It's a loft."

Rev Orf cleared his throat. "Miss Henshaw, I've been tracking you since the first... incident."

Lily felt uncertain about what qualified as "first incident." She assumed he meant the deaths of Eric, Kris, and Mia. The incident didn't really have a name. The thing on the highway. The attack. Crazy time. Collection time. "The first incident" worked as well as anything. It was probably what he meant. She said, "Oh?"

"I saw something about it on the local news. Scary stuff. How do you pick yourself up after something like that, especially without God and the Church? I've had my faith shaken, so I know what it feels like to believe, for a moment, in God's absence, and I know what it's like to be alone, but to lack the sustenance of both faith and community *at the same time*? Life in normal circumstances would seem like too much to bear. And then to confront a situation nothing short of demonic and have to reckon with life on its terms without counterbalance... yes, I'd say you've adapted quite well." The drinks arrived, and Rev Orf unrolled his silverware from his napkin before selecting his artisan bread. "Now that's odd."

He held up his fork, which had two tines bent in opposite directions, at near-right angles.

Lily unrolled her napkin and confirmed that her fork, too, had bent tines. Holding up her fork and nudging Burt, Lily got the message across: he unrolled his fork and found bent tines. The men marveled that something so unlikely and improper would happen at such a fine establishment, and Lily recognized the recurrence as something sinister, *so* unlikely that it could not be mere coincidence. Looking over her shoulders, she checked for signs of things amiss, but the diners, the servers, and the human traffic down below—visible from a nearby balcony—behaved as they were obliged. The forks, portents, pointed at meaning, but what?

"So, you know about the attack on the highway," Burt said. "What else do you know, and more important, why are you so damned interested?"

Rev Orf said, "I know about your brother, Lily, and I know about your job, and I know about... your visitation by... certain... harbingers."

Other than the forks?

Burt put his arm around Lily. "What makes any of this your business?"

"My church," the Rev said. "Well, not my church especially, but my conference of churches. Beyond that, really, as it is a practice that reaches across... which is to say, there has been a sharing of intelligence, although not a true coordination of efforts, you understand, as centuries of difference could hardly be resolved, particularly across a rift that involves so much history."

Lily looked at Burt, who said, "We don't know what you're talking about."

"What if I told you," Rev Orf said, "that the larger denominations of Christianity, the ones with hierarchies and national or international governing bodies, ran certain agencies, and those agencies had certain goals in common? It would not be so difficult, for example, to imagine that different groups of different churches all share the goal of a charity —say, feeding the poor—and all reach the same conclusions about serving that charity—say, the righteousness of soup kitchens—and therefore all go about serving that charity in a way that compels them to share methods and archival information—say, instructions for setting up soup kitchens in a manner that matches the needs and preferences that a neighborhood has historically demonstrated. You could imagine, for instance, a Baptist and a Methodist swapping recipes and stories so that their churches would both fare well with their soup kitchens in Detroit? Of course you could, even if you know that those denominations tell jokes about one another in certain parts of the country! The Episcopalians, too, can be friends with the Nazarenes, when all they want is to feed the poor in the name of Christ, so they might share intelligence about the best locations and policies for soup kitchens in rural Alabama.

"Even though they burnt one another at the stake, fighting bitterly for centuries, the Catholics and the Protestants could work... if not together, at least in parallel, sharing critical data at least once in a while? Look at struggles over the legality of abortion. The position of most churches on our side, call it Team Christ, is on a spectrum of sameness spelling N-O. No matter how I feel about their popish nonsense, I have to respect the Catholics' steadfastness for as long as it is steadfast. If I had devoted my life to that particular mission, then, I would perceive the Catholic Church as my strong ally in the field. We might not join forces, as our faiths differ in too many particulars, but our commonality, as it pertains to our quests, would be apparent to all. To you, Mr. Wells and Miss Henshaw, we would appear less as representatives of different denominations than as two different members of the same Team Christ."

Lily looked around for anyone resembling Rev Orf and saw no one. The only commonality he had with others, detectable to her, was the bent fork common with Burt and herself, which boded ill, ill, ill. Why he babbled about churches in a time of bent forks remained obscure. Burt, however, seemed interested. His face said, "Go on."

"Yes," Lily said. "Go on. What is Team Christ's interest in me?"

"We're tracking you because we track many cases like yours. You're living extremity, the eye of an angelic storm. For reasons I have yet to master, Heaven has its foot on you, and bearing its shoeprint, you are blessed." Rev Orf tapped a food order into the menu. Lily and Burt followed his example.

"*Blessed*?" Lily said. She tried to sound angrier than she felt, but she couldn't feel much pique because she immediately understood the Rev's perspective. Job is one of the Bible's stars, so to be a Job is to be Biblical, and the Bible-types were into that. "Cases like yours," he had said. She wasn't exactly a solo phenomenon, but she was a rarity because she'd been singled out for torture. Luck and divinity were twins, knowable in the presence of extremes. Improbable good and improbable bad both suggested the twins' presence, buttressing faith in one, the other, or both.

"God is with you, Lily Henshaw. How else could you have survived?" The Rev tapped his misshapen fork on the table, and it dinged on a pitch resonant with his water glass. On the same pitch, in a painful octave, a woman deep inside the restaurant screamed. Lily thought the glass would shatter, but it didn't. Burt looked toward the noise, over a room half-full of diners, and Rev Orf looked at Lily as if the reflections in her eyes would tell him all he needed to know.

Blinking, she surveyed the restaurant and saw human forms spreading through key areas. They looked like men, but they wore baggy brown sweatsuits, so she couldn't be sure. Their masks—large, cheap, plastic, and round, covering faces back to the ears, mostly white except in the front center, where colors for irises included brown and blue and green —were eyeballs, with black pupils where a clown's red nose might have been. One of the men ended up very near the booth where Lily sat with Burt and Rev Orf. He was not tall, but he held a gun with a long snout... shaft, barrel... an M-16, maybe. The eyes' impression as they brandished weaponry was *heavily armed*. One of them yelled, "NOBODY MOVE!"

Lily held her fork and sipped her cocktail. God was with her. An eyeball wouldn't shoot her for taking a drink.

The eyeballs, including the one nearby, took no apparent notice of the booth where Lily sat with Burt and Rev Orf, but instead they pointed their long-snouted automatic weapons toward the ceiling, closer here in the mezzanine than down in the vaster lobby space. Lines of snouts' convergence met at a chandelier: a nest of lime-green and raspberry-red, sculpted and shiny like porcelain leaves and petals, intertwined with brilliant bulbs connected to electricity flowing from wires spun as vines.

A voice, running up close to Lily and company's booth, paused the action. "Halt!" cried the pleasant woman who had seated them. She wore her vest and bowtie and carried an automatic weapon of some smaller variety, with a snubbier muzzle and closer-together grips, but it nevertheless looked like it could pump out death with efficiency. From a train behind her, busboys and girls, without vests, spread out, aiming identical weapons variously at the eyeballs.

Lily looked at her fork. One bent tine pointed at the eyeball near her table, and the other pointed at the pleasant woman. With the men's forks on the table, the men themselves gawking at the display of firepower, Lily couldn't tell whether their tines also pointed at the restaurant's divided forces, but she felt that they did, and lately her feelings about such things had a track record for complete correctness. The teddy bear with the gouged eye, cousin discovery to the fork, had already re-manifested, Lily realized, in orange-crème's ocular cavity, and now here it was in the eyes seeking orgiastic comeuppance at gunpoint. The bloody rag discovery remained unparalleled, but as the servers stood off against the eyeballs, surrounded by white tablecloths, Lily predicted that red-drenched cloth would soon abound.

The eyeballs aimed at the raspberry-lime chandelier. The first gunshot struck Lily as quiet but did not hit a target. It disappeared into the ceiling, but its noise was enough to alert the lobby's dense circulation to the conflict on the mezzanine. The populace roared, and Lily used fingers to plug her ears. The roar of concerned onlookers covered the explosion of gunfire that followed that lonely miss, and bullets made contact, creating confetti of the lime leaves and raindrops of the raspberry petals. Lightbulbs burst in showers of sparks, and debris pelted diners at tables. No one dared to run, but a few hid. When the vine-wires snapped, they gave all at once, and the chandelier split into three main chunks, two of which crushed humans as all collided with a table-dotted floor. The downing of the chandelier must have been some signal because the servers opened fire, drawing the attention of the eyes, who diverted quickly enough for some of them to find cover and redirect their own bullets.

Crossfire resulted. A gerrymandered field of it grew between layers of combatants, and all within the field who didn't hug the floor received one or more bullets from one or both sides of the conflict. Rapid metal pierced skin and punctured organs. This killing, which Lily, Burt, and Rev Orf watched from their booth at the edge of the gerrymandered field, had almost no relation to what Lily had witnessed during the first incident. Instead of blood spraying from the wounds torn open by the bullets sneezed speedily from the long and short snouts, feathers might have burst from rifts as if flesh were pillows at a slumber party. Pillows torn open and flung into the air, batted about until the air became a snow-globe of feathers... the bodies dropped like heavier sacks, but they had the spiritual weight of pillows.

From Lily and company's booth, the only ways out of the restaurant passed through the crossfire, and the booth itself offered little space for hiding, even under the table, so their only option was to sit still. Recognizing the need to stay and watch, Lily wanted to keep working on her cocktail, but she worried that Burt and Rev Orf, especially Rev Orf, would judge her. Why did she care about the opinions of this religious man who had been stalking her? The answer eluded her, yet she cared. And she was learning to take irrationality in stride.

Death in the crossfire was plentiful, but few casualties occurred on either side of the struggle of servers against eyeballs. Either the chandelier had been responsible for a great deal of the mezzanine's illumination, or the area's lighting —and perhaps the entire lobby's lighting—had mechanically dimmed. The decrease in light gave an extra edge to the panic that filled the great volume of 1500 Spring's ground levels, where everyone not pinned by the prospect of gunfire now scurried and cried, as if the sky and not a chandelier had fallen, as if they and not some dead people had been shot. Streams of traffic became rivers flooding over their beds, dammed by walls and pillars, trying their best to break through. The rotary doors yielded for no one; the building elected to freeze everyone's egress at this time.

Lily downed the rest of her cocktail in two gulps and thought about the "Oasis" painting with the skeletons in the desert, which made her realize what the eyeballs were: terrorists. Running into a major place of business in the middle of the day, wearing masks, toting automatic weapons, and demanding... well, they had to be demanding something, and Lily just wasn't privy... they fit the profile perfectly. Lily had been a fool to think otherwise. And what had she been thinking, exactly?

Hearing him over gunfire was difficult, but Rev Orf said, "This is Fate, Miss Henshaw."

That was it. She'd been thinking that men with machine guns rushing into the restaurant where she was having lunch was just another Day in the Life of Lily Henshaw. Did that eyeball near the balcony just turn his long-snouted weapon on the writhing crowd down below? Yes, he did! Bullets now flew into the winding mass, which broke down its circulatory structure completely, leading to trampling. A Day in the Life. *Her* Life. People, meat mannequins, whatever they were, were piling up in all directions because of her, *her* fate. Lily Henshaw's Collection Time brought them all to this juncture.

Another thought: shouldn't Rev Orf have said "God's Will?" What's a Rev got to do with Fate? Lily asked, "Fate?"

"Not like in Greek myths, but Fate can... assert itself. I've come to think of it as a freelancer in the cosmos, usually working behind the scenes and in concert with other forces but occasionally becoming visible as an entity in its own right. Such independence is not pleasing to God, Miss Henshaw." When Rev Orf said "pleasing to God," Lily thought of the pleasant woman who had seated them and looked at her. She was using a table for a shield and exchanging intermittent fire with an eyeball. Both her shirt and the nearby tablecloth bore big splotches of red. The pleasant woman was in trouble.

Lily said, "Go on." Burt was watching the gun battle and might not have been following the dialogue.

"In you, Miss Henshaw, Fate is visible, as well as God. Do you think that God—"

A shriek that managed to drown the amalgam of widespread human distress interrupted the latest exposition as the pleasant woman, by grave miscalculation, made a run for new cover and, on her feet but a moment, became the target of two eyes, which shredded her in seconds. The other servers picked up her cry, and, rolling a barrel, two of them emerged from a curtain behind the bar.

The terrorist theory did not account for the restaurant staff. Sure, terrorists might wear eyeball masks and carry long-snouted machine guns, but why would the maître d' and bus-persons of a normal restaurant have short-snouted machine guns ready for response? The *situation* (Rev Orf was a stalker of *situations*, not people) seemed more of the Lily-spawned sort than of the terrorist-spawned. Lily's crazy times could not assimilate desert politics so easily.

The lobby area near the escalators and otherwise proximal to the mezzanine had, with the exception of trampled bodies, cleared. The thronging portion that would have been there instead pressed against the rest of the mass by the elevators and doors, which furnished no exit. The people reminded Lily of penguins huddling for warmth, the outermost layers peeling off not from cold but from the prickling of bullets.

The servers lifted their barrel to the top of the bar, where Lily made out a rag stemming from the barrel's lid. She recognized the scenario from old movies and video games—the rag was a fuse. The servers lit the barrel and rolled it over the bar's edge, after which its momentum carried it to a spot a radius from which would touch at least four of the eyes. The barrel exploded in flame.

Hot air threatened to singe Lily's eyebrows, but she and her companions' distance from the blast was safe. Eyeballs screamed and scattered as the fire consumed them, but too many survived for the servers to regain control of their restaurant. The smoke from the explosion gave eyeballs cover to reposition themselves at angles where they could easily snipe away at their server enemies, who fell one by one until they were zero.

Repositioning created opportunity. Proper exits remained blocked. The escalators had become mounts from which eyeballs blasted the crowd below, which continued to beat at elevators and exterior doors as if... Fate?... might change its mind. The constant hammering of automatic weapons hurt Lily's ears and pounded in her head. With no more resistance from the servers, the eyeballs focused exclusively on the crowd, which diminished accordingly. Nevertheless, the shooting eyeballs were both *away* and *occupied*, leaving a path between Lily and company's booth and—not a door—the blast point where the barrel had hit. Now that the quick-burning flames had all but vanished, the blast point was a great hole in the floor with disjoined beams forming bridges down to a deserted region of the main level.

Pushing for Burt to get out of the booth first, Lily said, "Come on!" Burt seemed to grasp her intent and followed her direction, but the Rev stayed put. "We have to go!" Lily's insistence jogged him, and he started to move. Burt grabbed her arm, and leaving Rev Orf to fend for himself, they ran toward the blast point.

Up close, none of the beams or boards forming bridges from mezzanine to first floor seemed sturdy, but now, in addition to bullets, small fires surrounded them, and Lily and Burt both knew they couldn't turn back. Rev Orf, too, was coming with them, albeit slowly, not quite having yet reached the opening in the floor. Choosing one of the widest beams, Burt said "What the hell" and stepped down onto it, finding it more stable than expected. With arms out and legs bent like a surfer, he made his way down, his face expressing certainty that each step would be the one that threw him off balance or that shifted the beam from whatever held it and sent him crashing into the rubble below.

He made it, and Lily, checking over her shoulder for

the Rev, who was catching up, started her way down. A few careful steps out onto the beam, she felt its bracing slip behind her, and her outstretched arms waved frantically for balance. Stumbling back, she managed not to fall, and she turned to see whether the beam might be on the verge of collapse. Rev Orf stood at the opening's edge, and an eyeball pointed a long-snouted gun at his back. Smoke enshrouded his face, but Lily could still see his lips form words, and she thought she heard a faint trickle of voice say, "Miss Henshaw, God loves you," and then he said, "Miss Henshaw, *I love you.*"

"That's impossible!" she screamed.

The machine gun at his back fired. The splashes of red from his chest and stomach looked nothing like feathers, and his face melted from ecstasy to agony as noble sacrifice—for knowing about Lily's situation meant knowing a visit to 1500 Spring in her proximity could not advance self-interest—became ignoble mortality, the simple failure of tissues when displaced by hot bursting metal ejected rapidly from the tip of a handheld machine. Countable wounds became uncountable as the boundaries of holes tore into one another. Lily's shirt ceased to be clean. The eyeball finished its job and kicked the corpse over. It crashed down onto the beam, wrenching it the rest of the way free from its delicate hold on mezzanine floor. The beam fell one way, but Lily fell another, knocked away by the conflicting momentums of the beam, her body, and the Rev's body, which careened into her on its own way down. She braced for the crash into rubble.

Instead, she felt Burt's arms. The man actually *caught* her. When she looked up to see what softness had saved her from the pains she'd expected, she saw his face and beard backlit by flames from the floor above, and he smiled for her, leaned in, and kissed her.

Burt lowered her to her feet and asked, in a voice deeper than usual, "Are you okay?"

"Yeah," she said. The fall felt bewildering. Burt catching her felt fictional. "Rev Orf...."

"I saw it," Burt said. "Don't worry about that. Let's go."

Burt started them moving, but Lily couldn't figure out where he was leading. They exited the area beneath the mezzanine, and Lily realized that, although her head still pounded, the gunfire had stopped. They were by the escalators now, and the area close to them, in an arc, remained clear. Beyond that arc, like freshly raked leaves, people lay in piles and rows. The eyes had killed the entire lobby's traffic, the hundreds or thousands. *How many bullets had they used?*

Above them, suspended, unfazed, Tobias looked untouched.

Eyeballs stood at the top of the escalators with guns pointed at Lily and Burt. They did not fire. Across the room, too, eyes had their guns trained on Lily and Burt. Lily didn't know how many eyeballs there were, but she counted seven with their guns aimed at her, and she knew that if the eyes wanted her, they would have her. They did nothing but aim.

"Rev Orf said this is Fate," Burt said.

"He did," Lily agreed.

Burt was shaking. "All these people are... dead."

Meat mannequins. "Yes," Lily said. "They are. We're not." *As far as we know.* That was a strange thought, wasn't it?

"They don't want to kill us," Burt said. "That's obvious. What do they want?"

Lily looked at the eyeballs and had a flash of revelation: "I think they want to watch us." Watching them was, after all, what Rev Orf had been doing. It was all the rage. They had become a spectacle. Killing everyone had merely changed their backdrop.

A loud bell rang. It was an elevator. Maybe something

amplified the bell, or maybe the ringing stood out because the rest of the lobby was as quiet as it had ever been, but for whichever reason, the elevator's bell sounded clearly and distinctly. The elevator called them. Lily and Burt looked at one another and looked at the eyeballs, which stood impassive and armed, ready to shoot. They stepped toward the elevators and got no reaction from their armed watchers. More steps got no reactions, so they walked, and as they approached the same Executive Express elevator they had used earlier, its doors opened.

Two dead people, one male and one female, lay in white shirts with black bowties on the elevator's tiled floor. Instead of being cut up by imprecise sprays of bullets through their torsos, each of them had a single slender bullet hole in the head. Their young faces looked peaceful. In their arms, they held small machine guns.

The elevator doors stayed open. "Two machine guns," Burt said.

"We probably just point and shoot, right?" Lily said.

Burt nodded.

When they reached down to take the guns, Lily heard what she thought might be applause in the lobby, at least a half dozen clapping eyeballs. The doors closed on the sounds, leaving Lily and Burt alone with the quiet and with the dead servers. The elevator said, "Going up," and Burt pressed the button for 60. The light by 24 lit up instead. As she tried on her machine gun's shoulder strap, Lily shrugged.

5

The elevator had the same reflective brassy walls and silver-fogged doors; its resoluteness in taking them to floor 24 was its only initially apparent anomaly. The doors opened on the surprise of a scene with no feature in common with the previous 24. Instead of the blue-grey walls with hints of turquoise, the dominant impression of the elevator bay came from cracked cinderblock and crumbling slate. Even if totally ruined, the reception area for MFS that Lily and Burt had visited a short time ago could not have become this place the elevator called 24. The space itself had enlarged, and where walls had been now stretched vast vistas of muddle, lookouts on places that might once have been professional but now were wastes of abandonment and disuse.

"Twenty-four," the elevator said. The voice had a feminine edge but a low enough pitch to be a man's. The voice troubled Lily, its presence, not its ambiguous gender identity, which merely seemed noteworthy. The elevator had not spoken on previous journeys. It only chose to talk now, for this "going up," for this "twenty-four"—*this* 24, which looked like a place they had never visited.

This place of disrepair and particles reminded Lily of the disheveled floors where Iris, the mad homeless woman, had led Lily and Burt for the ritual that preceded her gravity-prone leap toward pavement. Light felt fluorescent rather than fire-born, so its quality was consistent with the office-ness that Lily expected to find here. Looking up, however, revealed no panels in the ceiling or even fixtures full of compact fluorescent bulbs. The ceiling was out of focus, a glowing blur, just beyond the line where eyes could resolve it.

"Twenty-four," the elevator repeated, and a bell rang. The voice differed, sounding a note of impatience. It, or they, wanted Lily and Burt to disembark. With her machine gun strapped around her shoulders, Lily obeyed, leading Burt into the disheveled elevator bay. She turned, hoping to see the hall of light with the "Love" sculpture-artwork-whatever, but in its direction stood what might have been the level's only intact wall, intact, at least, until its white expanse got high enough to blur into the fluorescent smear of ceiling. Where the unrestricted passageway into the bright open space should have been, a blue doorway now appeared. On it a black sign, hanging by a thread like an old-fashioned shingle, read "COSMOS" in white block lettering. She heard a heartbeat that might have been hers.

"We can't go back, can we?" Burt asked.

Lily looked behind them. The elevator doors had closed without a word or a bell, and the car, she presumed, had gone. She saw no buttons to call it back, only sets of doors for other cars she doubted she would ever ride. What would she and Burt go back to, if they were allowed to go back? Beneath them, in the lobby, explosions and gunfire, masses dead, bodies or mannequins or both—that level had surely closed to them as firmly as the lid on the freezer that held orange-crème. Floors 2 to 23, what matter could they have? She shuddered at the thought, and her machine gun bounced against her. Those floors were *down*, but they were not *back*. 1500 Spring offered too many directions for *forward*.

"No," Lily said. From her mouth popped, "Crazy flows forward," and she thought about Burt asking whether paranoia or Collection Time were contagious, and she decided that her words, which felt alien, could be the slogan on her red t-shirt, right underneath MFS's fancy logo. *Crazy flows forward.*

"I feel like my heart is about to burst from my chest," Burt said. "I'm surprised you can't hear it." One of his hands stayed on the grip of his manageable machine gun.

Lily listened. The beating she heard could have been coming from Burt rather than herself. Pushing her gun to one side, she leaned down and pressed her ear to his chest. She felt and heard his muscle working fits beneath her cheek, but it did not move in time with the beats she'd been hearing before she leaned in. "It's not you," she said. She placed her fingers on her neck and waited. Neither of them pulsed in time with the audible beating, and they were not in time with each other. "It's not me," she said.

In sync, their heads turned toward the COSMOS door. At the next loud beat, a shiver, faint but perceptible, rattled its frame. The dangling sign clapped against the surface beneath it with soft insistence. The door had a heartbeat. Before Burt could object, Lily put her hand, palm flat, against the door and waited. Her fingers reported the familiar texture of processed industrial wood, but it had unfamiliar pliability, yielding to her impression and rising to meet her with a *thump-thump* confirming its pulse. She wondered whether, given time, the door would grow hair.

Beside her, Burt stepped up and placed his hand on the door. As if it already *had* hair, he said, "That tickles," and he smiled. Lily did not recall the last time she'd seen such a genuine smile on his handsome face. She clasped his free hand in hers, and together they felt the living pulse of the COSMOS door, which had a handle. They took turns glancing between soulful gazes into one another's eyes. Burt said, "Do you think it wants us to go through?"

The heartbeat quickened, and Lily said, "Yes."

With one hand still clasping Lily, Burt slid his door-hand down toward the handle, a narrow hook-like protrusion.

Lily nodded encouragement, and Burt turned the handle. He pushed the door forward only an inch before it jerked in his hand, and had Lily not been holding him, he might have flown with it. It tore from—if it was even connected to—its hinges, and from its standard-sized frame it lifted into a chasm of star-speckled black, carrying the white letters of "COSMOS" swirling away with it until door and sign disappeared into a universe of vast darkness littered with lucid systems of orbs.

A wind from behind made them plant feet firmly, and their fingers tightened their grips on one another as Lily and Burt stood in the doorway looking out on an infinity of space. She'd seen this, Lily thought, in a science-fiction television show, or in an ad for the Syfy TV network, opening the door to outer space, right in your living room. Except they were in an office, or what might have passed for an office before the visitation of some destruction, before the passing of recent hours, before Lily and Burt left all acceptable parameters of environmental behavior. The cold ahead of them, with the blackness and stars, lacked the instant-Kelvin-freeze of actual near-vacuum but teased their skin with stark winter iciness, the kind that makes skin firm and bristle and withhold objection until it later begins to thaw. They had no business going forward in their t-shirts. They had no business going forward into a space where they saw no path, no yellow-brick-road running through the systems of orbs with their primary and earth-tone mottles and splotches, with their rings and moons of pale reflectivity, with their chunks of comet and asteroid lazing about in so much dust that, diffused, it might glitter Creation.

The two of them would not fit through the doorway at once. If they were to go, one would have to go first.

Burt opened his mouth, presumably to discuss, and Lily stepped through the door. Her foot sank but hit solidity before it could relay the sensation of falling—the distance was a stair's. Her other foot joined, and she stood on an invisible plane on the other side and beneath the doorway, looking up and over her gun-slung shoulder at Burt. A cross-breeze from her left joined the wind from the ruined office area, emphasizing the cold on her exposed arms, but she retained her balance and took another step down. Solidity. Burt's mouth hung open, but no words emerged. He looked down at her and at the lack of surface beneath her. The concept of an invisible stairway into an outer-space-scape didn't challenge Lily's thinking, and she didn't imagine it challenging Burt's, but the actuality of it didn't bear cogitation, and Burt was visibly cogitating.

In terms of astronomy, Lily supposed their location might be a trinary star system, with suns of different hues revolving around one another and bringing with them planets of myriad descriptions and entanglements, with satellites to match. Several planets pursued their strange orbits at rapid paces, zipping around one another with near misses, looking like marbles running through a Rube-Goldberg machine toward elegant and catastrophic consummation. Pastel smears of nebulae separated by bruises formed significant portions of the busy star system's immediate backdrop, behind which a larger mosaic of galaxies and lonely diamond pinpricks engulfed all. There was a chance, Lily supposed, a faint possibility, that in Burt's position, a well-trained scientist might be able to make sense of this scape, using parallax views of red and blue to place it somewhere on a map of worlds knowable and known. Lily understood, though, that such an ability would be wasted on delusion, for when she had crossed through the door, they had entered no-where—utopia, so to speak—a place designed to beach comprehension.

Burt, gripping his gun, stepped down into the decorated void. Lily watched him extend his shoed toe as if testing water, find the solidity he had seen support Lily's weight, and then go out upon it. *Rules*, he'd said. He'd talked about learning rules. How would he ever learn if he moved so slowly? He couldn't expect the universe to wait for him. The next step came quicker, and Lily felt glad. Burt's face looked troubled, though. She wondered about the death of Rev Orf. Did it affect him? Neither she nor Burt was—or had been, before Lily became a Job with locusts and other plague perks—religious, but Rev Orf seemed like a nice man. Before today—not counting the incident with Ralph and Sally, at which he'd been a bystander —death, such as it was, hadn't touched Burt, and the Reverend Chester Orfantomhauser, among the hundreds or thousands of dead they'd seen in 1500 Spring or wherever they were, was the most alive, or deserving of living. Had the bullets piercing his torso had enough force to crack Burt's infrastructure? Would his bones crumble, abandoning him to become a pile of jelly on an invisible stairway?

Burt reached the place beside her and retook her hand. "Where do you think we're going?"

Standing in the midst of blackness and stars, hand in hand before a canvas of bruised pastels, Lily had appropriate single-word answers. *Nowhere* fit her frame of mind. *Imagination* fit the aesthetic. *Home* fit the hovering need for a note of optimism while striking a deeper, enigmatic chord of mystery, but she didn't know what it could mean. She couldn't deny that their surroundings were beautiful, though, so her answer had to acknowledge beauty. "Downstairs," she said, and recognizing the insufficiency, she added, "forward, to the world where we belong."

They stepped down together, hand in hand, until Lily's foot went down first and found no solidity. Burt helped to pull her back up, and they balanced one another. In the distance, a heartbeat might have counted time for them, but Lily's adrenaline might have misled her. They held each other for ten beats, twenty, thirty, and nodded. They stepped off the edge together and fell.

During the fall they felt weightless.

Lily recalled being a girl.

She saw Burt as a boy.

They entangled.

They kissed.

Spinning.

The stars became so bright that the universe around them became white, and they saw nothing until it dimmed again, with the whiteness separating out into feathers, which rocked back and forth as gravity guided them toward a loose feather bed, which caught them. Lily recollected no landing but knew it was soft. Sounds of countless wind chimes accompanied the drifting feathers as she and Burt came to themselves on the soft pile of white. Almost expecting to be naked and clean, she felt disappointed to see herself still clad in the spattered t-shirt and jeans, Burt in his matching red, but it was okay. She yawned. A lifetime had passed since they'd entered 1500 Spring. She could surrender to feathers.

"Lily, look!" Burt said. He sat up next to her and pointed away from their feather bed, toward a dais at the top of a nearby visible silver staircase. On the white marble throne sat light in the shape of a man, beaming at them. Lily remembered her machine gun, which she had kept through the fall into space. Was this God?

"Heavens, no!" a familiar voice said. The effulgent figure stood from the throne, and its light subsided. Lily and Burt beheld Young Torrents in his double-breasted suit. "I'm surprised to see you back here so soon. What can I do for you?"

Lily tried standing, but a foothold proved too difficult on the bed of loose feathers. She crawled over to the silver stairs and lifted herself to her feet. Wind chimes still sounded, clatters and dings in the soft cool breeze blanketing the new area that held them. It was bright and white and hazy, with the feather bed a low point surrounded by stairs like a shallow pool. Around it Hellenic columns and arches, not overpowering but stately, suggested a sanctum that included Young Torrents's throne. Beyond the sanctum, white continued, and contours suggested more structure, but the haze thickened and created near horizons where distinct vision stopped. The sanctum was an island of the visible.

"Mr. Torrents!" Lily called up to him. She had nothing else to say.

"Please," he called down. "Didn't I ask you to call me Young?"

She didn't believe he had. His expectations of them, with regard to his nomenclature or to any other aspect of his relation to them, had not, Lily believed, entered conversation: Young Torrents had served as an informant. He was one in a series of expositors, maybe the most learned one, the key to Collection Time, yet still a number, and like Tobias, he had returned. Like Tobias, would he also be stopped? Claimed by 1500 Spring, if they were even in 1500 Spring? Lily felt a seething hatred for Mr. Torrents, for Young. Would she and Burt be the ones to put him to a stop? She rather liked the idea.

Young's failure to address their expectations spoke to a larger failing of the universe. It was inconsistent in some respects but consistent in others, too consistent, as when it placed Lily and Burt, perhaps Burt especially, in a mode of perpetual reaction. When the cosmos presents you with an invisible staircase to descend, what action independent of the presentation can you take? You react to the staircase; even ignoring the staircase is an act defined by the staircase.

Lily badly wanted to *do* something. To march up to Young and rip off his testicles. *Something.* She did not like feeling as if she knelt at the foot of a businessman filling in for Zeus on Olympus. She did not want another bequeathing of wisdom.

The silver staircase rumbled.

"What do you want, Lily Henshaw?" Young asked. Rumbling continued, sounding from all around them, shaking the columns and the highest arches. Burt stood with her, behind and to the side, facing Young.

An answer occurred to her, but she said instead, "I want to see those men from the highway, Earl and Rob, one more time so I can... kill *them*... and not... an abstraction. I want to see David again, and I think I'd ask him *why*, because his answer, if he had one, might be good enough to cover all the causes that don't have names. I want to know what normal feels like. I'm not saying I've never felt it. I'm only saying I don't know, and if I knew, I'd have a way to tell whether and how much I'm crazy. I want..." Her original answer reoccurred. The same answer had almost stood in reply to Burt's question about *Where*, and now it wanted to become a *What*: "Home," Lily said. "I want home."

The ground shook as Young stepped away from the throne and descended stairs, approaching Lily and Burt. "Home," Young said. "You're more home here, Lily Henshaw, than anywhere else you might be. This place was *for you*." Between two pillars, not far from the sunken bed of feathers, the marble flooring shattered, and the stone beneath split open. Burt twitched but stayed firm at Lily's side.

"This... elaborate production," Lily said, "you're claiming is for me?" She saw yellow-orange light reflecting from the white around the split stone.

"No! The information was that you're a better listener. You should not think the entire cosmos is for you, but the twenty-fourth floor, as you previously saw it, was, at least mostly, for you. To construe the singularity more broadly would be nonsense.

"Think of a Coke commercial. You might be able to imagine an ad with only one person, probably a young white man, laughing and having a good time while drinking a bottle of Coke. Such an ad is unlikely: drinking a bottle of Coke is something people who have friends do; doing so enables you, implicitly, to have friends. A brief nod toward the marginal acceptability of solitude is possible, but brevity is essential. Committing to video the entire act of drinking a bottle of Coke while alone is unthinkable. Even editing for duration does not solve the problem: *implying* duration is enough, for while three stages of consumption (full bottle, half-full bottle, empty bottle) could appear in one *crowded* commercial, showing a progression of fun, those same stages in an empty commercial would show a progression of loneliness, endowing the product with the void. The alone person might drink *some* Coke, maybe in preparation for ending alone-ness (at which point the bottle could continue consumption in a social state). This possibility, though not guaranteed, remains open *if one or more stages of consumption remains invisible during the empty commercial.* The openness leaves room for hope, the only requirement for minimum product viability.

"For the sake of advertising, consumption prefers to be conspicuous, but many products' destiny is to be consumed by one person only. The Coke bottle hinges its identity on a social perception, but its fate is to run down your esophagus into your tummy and your tummy only. You were meant to consume the MFS office as you saw it and to get what you needed from its digestion. No one else was going to do that. That bottle was for you, and you drank it in company."

Lily followed that Young was using some sort of metaphor, but she didn't know what it was, or what it was about, and she didn't know whether she wanted him to clarify. Something was bubbling up from the split stone, and she was pretty sure it was lava.

The ground shook, and, somewhere new, it split.

Burt's arm shot toward Young and fastened a hand at his neck. Over a steady rumble, he shouted, "ANSWERS! No more comparisons or terms. Answers, or I'll choke the life out of you!"

Choke the life out of you struck Lily as odd, but she couldn't let that or the surprise of Burt's sudden violence delay her. She ignored the rumbling and stepped to seize Young's arms while Burt secured his grip at the neck. She wondered what answers Burt sought.

Lava, lazy molten rock, inched toward the sunken bed of feathers, glowing. More oozed from splits in the stone. Young struggled for air and couldn't have spoken if he'd wanted to. Lily and Burt wrestled him to the ground, forcing his back against stairs, head angled downward. When the lava dripped into the feather bed, devouring white with orange, they knew what to do. They carried Young down, turning him to one side when they got close enough to the growing pool of liquid flame.

Burt held him down while Lily guided his arm, which left him freer to breathe and protest. "Unnecessary and inadvisable! Unnecessary and inadvisable!" She was guiding his hand into heat.

"Talk, you bastard!"

"What about, what about?!"

Lily, who a moment ago had wanted him to *stop* talking and had instead gotten a sermon on soda, looked down at the hand she was preparing to force into liquid flame and noticed the veins in Young's wrist. "Suicide," she said. The ground shook, and nearby, the split stone spit up lava in a fast-melting fan. "Is it true? Is it the only way out?"

Lava rose closer to Young's hand. "By 'way out' I take you to mean *of life*, and to that you might attach some particular, perhaps *of life in Collection Time*, which, as we discussed, is precarious terminology with respect to 'life,' as you might not be said to be living in the strictest terms. To that I would have to say, emphatically—" he might have been more concise considering the proximity of lava to his hand—"no. No, it is not the only way out, because if I had a gun in the hand you hold so close to this exasperating heat I might not be able to resist the impulse to turn it in your direction and *shoot you in the head*. My bullet, then, from my gun would pierce your brain in some location essential to life—true of so much of the brain, alas—and probably blast away a whole section, I don't know, I'm not a gunman—so that whatever remained of you would have some portion of a second or seconds to register the fact of corporal non-viability before BLIP, lights out, and you are, as you put it, way out."

The lava reached Young's hand and began to submerge it. The rising pool consumed him through to one knuckle, then another, then to the palm. His face registered no pain, but he did not smile. Lily had to readjust where she gripped his arm. He wasn't really struggling, but she had to maintain a firm grip all the same. The sanctum, or wherever they were... it might as well be 24... was getting almost unbearably hot. The ground's shaking was almost constant now. Columns and arches collapsed. Chaos reigned.

Burt said, "I don't know—"

Young's hand reappeared from the lava pool, holding a handful of lava as if it were sand. Throwing off Lily, he swung the handful, released it, and hit Burt's nearby chest. Burt shrieked and jumped back, getting to his feet for a second before falling on his side, yanking at his red t-shirt to remove it along with the molten rock and fried flesh. Lily screamed.

In the distance, a loud sound like metal dropping on metal echoed as if through a canyon, and squeaking, massive turning hinges followed. In Lily's mind, the sound revealed what vision had not: the space outside the silvered-white sanctum of falling columns and arches, of shattered marble and split stone overrun with lava. The space was a blue chasm, a gulf between the island sanctum and a far-away wall. In that wall was a door, maybe many doors. One of those doors had opened.

The next sound was more familiar, a warbling buzz, gargantuan static. Locusts streamed over the island, into the closing windows of the leaning ruins of columns and arches. Burt had curled halfway into a fetal ball, either spasming or all-out seizing in response to the trauma of his burns. Lily sprawled on the stairs, stunned by how easily Young had thrown her and by what she'd seen him do to Burt. Young got to his feet, and with two unhurt hands, he straightened his tie.

"I regret, Lily Henshaw, that current calculations call for some severity in the collection schedule." As Young spoke, a geyser of flame erupted behind him. Locusts formed a bubble around them, filtering out the more distant crashes of lava against stone. Individual insects guided by some overarching intelligence... whose? Young's? God's? *Their own?*

"And why not *yours*?" Young asked. His access to her transparency seemed total. A rod of insects extended from the bubble that surrounded them. The rod, perhaps five to ten locusts in varying diameter, stretched toward burnt Burt. Lily looked at them and tried not to shudder in revulsion. In all her strange grasshopper encounters, she'd never thought of them as vile before, but seeing their coordinated geometry, they felt *vile*, gut-churning, unsettling in the profoundest way. The vile creatures reached out *en masse* to Burt, spanning from rod-form into a kind of shovel, narrower and flatter at the end, capable of sliding under the prone bent man. Underneath him, they gathered numbers and strength, swelling. Uncountable workers raising their backs, they lifted him up, and he began to drift toward the abandoned throne as if on a wave.

"Mine?" Lily asked. "Not mine," she said. "Not mine," she repeated. "Wait," she said. "No. No!"

No because she could not give in to that delusion

of grandeur, however self-effacing it might be in its self-aggrandizement. To think that she not only was the source of and reason for the appearance of the first MFS office they'd seen, and possibly even for this cataclysmic 24, but also the movements of the locusts, and beyond that, everything else... the word for it was solipsism... but if she was the magic lantern that projected the shapes of the world, then she was crafted to show nightmares. What sick crafting made her this way? If she was grandiosely central to reality, she was also cancerously inimical, a scourge on the surroundings of her making. She supposed she had something in common with God.

Stopping before the throne, the locusts carrying burnt Burt began to fly. Lily could see Burt breathing as the vile creatures beneath him arose from the ground and made him seem to levitate on a flickering rug. The rising pool of lava drew close to Lily's feet, but she remained still on the stairs, watching as the blanket of insects held Burt in the air. The throne cracked in two, and its marble halves fell to opposite sides. As Young stepped farther from Lily and closer to floating Burt, Lily saw blue light spilling out of the open doorway, framing Burt in shadow. Beyond his dark form, Lily could see stairs going up, but she knew that behind the throne—and thus the doorway—was more empty space, part of *this* level, on 24. No matter. If Lily saw a stairway, she trusted the presence of a stairway, no matter the odds.

Feeling warmth through her shoes' soles, she pulled up her legs and started to stand. Young stood idle, watching Burt as the locusts transported him through the doorway, into the blue light, over toward the stairway going up. Lily tried to move faster, but her legs felt weak, more hurt than she'd realized by the tumble after Young had tossed her aside. Struggling for balance, she lunged up the steps toward the dais. It felt farther away than it looked.

The insects carried Burt away. They did not hurry. They

did not have to. All Lily's efforts to use all her speed did not get her to the divided throne or through the doorway in time. The doorway swallowed Burt and a cloud of locusts behind him, and behind them, Young, fondling his tie with the hand that had held lava, turned and followed. As Lily used a final burst to close the gap separating her from Young, Young crossed the threshold, and the door slammed shut.

The dais was the island's highest point. The rest was sinking into lava. Lily stood on surviving stone before a closed door, dazed. Had she just lost Burt?

The lava rising around her would consume her, she knew. She wondered how she would go into it. Would *she* flow into *it* as she dissolved a bit at a time, first as her ankles disintegrated in heat, then her knees, then her pelvis and hips, then each individual vertebra until her jaw gave up the top of her skull? It would not be so orderly. She would crumple into it, feeding herself to liquid flame in more random order. Whatever the order, it would be quick, as the lava spread at temperatures far above the human melting point, she felt certain. Would she even leave discernible ash?

No—between the lava and the door, she chose the door, because somewhere behind it, Burt was dead or alive, and she had to know. She turned the handle that opened the door, ready to step into blue light, and faced a metal wall. She knocked on it. Clanging but solid enough. It hadn't *been* here, but that was irrelevant. It was *unfair*, but that was irrelevant. Was this the severity that Young had meant?

A bell rang, and the metal slid to one side. It wasn't a wall but another door, an elevator door, and it pulled back to reveal a car much like, maybe exactly like, the one she and Burt had ridden earlier in the day, with burnished brass and foggy silver vertical surfaces, a tile floor, and an even more reflective roof. Lily hadn't resented the camera on the last ride, but she resented it now, and she wondered how much of orange-crème's murder it had seen. That had been a murder, hadn't it? And she'd planned to murder Young Torrents, hadn't she? How much did this building record? Surely it didn't need cameras for recordings, but this camera was a symbol of eyes that didn't need visibility to envision.

She thought about shooting the camera, which made her remember that the annoying strap around her neck attached to something she could use. Maybe not against Young— immunity to lava implied special status. Maybe not against locusts. But against something. The machine gun was good to have. She did not shoot the camera. She pressed the button for 25. The locusts couldn't have taken Burt far, could they? Where else could that stairway have gone?

6

25 had padded grey walls. The padding had dimples, as if the fabric attached to the wall by buttons, but some inward mechanisms must have managed attachment, for no buttons showed themselves. Maybe the designers feared visitors might pry out buttons and swallow them to choke. Padded walls signified an intent to remove hazards, yet Lily doubted 25 would be hazard-free from start to finish. She stood at the start, and the floor continued ahead of her, padded walls forming corridors and corners. 25, like the arteries of the lobby before they collapsed under gunfire, required navigation, and Lily needed to press onward, alone. The sign said so.

The elevator door ushered her out, closed, and disappeared, leaving her alone in a short hall that opened to a juncture, four ways, to the nub where she started and three other options, with a sign in the middle, facing the nub and showing arrows left, right, and up (meaning forward). Dim light, from no discernible source, made the rough smears of lines forming arrows appear reddish-brown, so Lily thought dried blood, and she thought Burt might have come this way, except she'd expect a trail on the floor from where burnt skin cracked open and let the beneath spill out, not isolated instructions. The sign's decoration showed no indiscreet spillage, no blood on the floor or on the arrows' plain white backdrop, so despite the arrows' messy composition, their fingerpainted quality, they did not look like the slovenly creation of an opportunistic passerby. In fact, the freestanding wooden sign might have been painted elsewhere and set there by order, as almost nothing other than the juncture itself—with options forward, left, and right matching the arrows--made it particular to its context, but one thing gave Lily pause: a black puddle.

In the dim sourceless light, the black puddle writhed and sparkled. It morphed like an amoeba, sliding curvy black borders on smooth grey floor, which it revealed and covered, revealed and covered, as it shifted from squiggle-shape to squiggle-shape, restless. Lily's stained red t-shirt felt too big, like a nightshirt draping ahead of her, as she leaned down to look closer at the morphing puddle. Through means indiscernible, it hissed at her. She pulled back. The puddle had malevolence. It was not much more than a foot wide, except when it lengthened in two directions and narrowed in others. As it extended in her direction, pseudopodally, she suspected it might grow larger.

Part of the puddle's motion, the squiggling in different directions, involved expansion and contraction. It breathed.

It slid toward her.

Lily took an involuntary step back. She had merely imagined the puddle hissing, of course, and it was probably just ink, dripping in her direction, not shifting locations to get closer to her. The thought of—*No. Rationality is for pussies. That puddle is evil, and it's coming closer.*

She took a step back and tried to laugh. The absurdity of feeling so much dread over a black spot on the floor! A shapeless, sparkling, animate emptiness intent on approach—dreadful? Why? Absurdity! Yet she felt what she felt and could not dispel it with the shame of silliness. *Swallow her.* The puddle wanted to swallow her. She sensed its desire deep in her bones. She didn't know how it would do it. It could suck her down deep or start at her toes and devour ascending, or maybe it would do both, inhaling her as it climbed. Lily saw herself as a woman's figure cut out of a canvas so you can see through to shimmering black nothing below. The cutting out of the figure didn't scare her; seeing the below did.

The puddle slipped closer, faster. The sparkling in its blackness intensified as it stretched its pseudopods and reformed in new positions. The next time Lily moved, it moved with her, and she realized she was backing toward the dead end of the nub, where blank padded wall had replaced elevator door. Ahead a sign said she could go forward, left, or right, but before she reached it she had to contend with the dark glittery voidlet.

She took a long step to the left, and after a three-second delay, it mirrored her in fluid fashion, closing in on the wall to her left. The corridor was wide enough for her to square off, so she tried, but the voidlet didn't insist on mirror motions. It maintained a line in front of the sign, shifting back and forth along it instead of following Lily around the corners of her attempted square. It trapped her in the nub. She considered searching the dead end for traces of the elevator door, but she knew she would find none.

Jump.

She had to leap over the voidlet. It was slow and small enough: it couldn't reach out for her landing spot and get there in time to catch her foot as it touched down. As long as she kept moving, she could jump over and outpace it. Forward, left, or right? The dim light revealed nothing in any direction, only halls that faded to quick darkness. They might turn off or keep going, but whatever they did was outside the dimness's reach. With panic already making her chest feel like she was at a sprint, the effort of jumping from the nub and landing in a run in some direction would be a strain. Her heart hammered, and she remembered the noise from 24, from before the door opened to release the locusts. Great mechanisms turned. Somewhere a car got sideswiped. Lily ran and jumped.

The ground hit running on the other side turned out to

be well ahead of the voidlet, so she gave herself a reassuring laugh as she darted into the leftward corridor, seeing the abrupt turn (left again) in time to avoid slamming into grey padding, but she let herself bounce off the wall anyway, pinball-style to prolong a brief happy delirium. Now she was going to *run*. She didn't need to see another fork in the path —forward or left?—to complete the conclusion that she now ran a labyrinth. Burt was the cheese. If Lily had become a red-shirted mouse, she needed something to direct her to a *particular* end, to refuse to accept a more *immediate* end, and the promise of a *better* end was cheese. That was what Burt had become. The cheese that moved her through the maze, a forward over and above the flow of crazy.

Choosing forward instead of another left, she ran the maze for Burt, and she ran for herself. When she let her head turn to one side, over her shoulder, in the corner of her eye, she saw a dark spot. She knew what it was. Burt was the cheese, and the voidlet was a whip, a compulsion onward. It never would have let her stay in the nub. It would have closed on her. She could see its intention in its black little curves: it would have closed on her. Likewise, it would keep following her, and no matter how fast she ran, it would always be behind her, in sight, respectfully out of reach as long as her movement remained, in kind, respectful. Fast enough. Lily didn't know if the voidlet cared about or even knew about the cheese. It knew about her, and it knew she must flow forward. All Lily's senses told her the voidlet was an agent of compliance.

And it was empowered to punish. Lily didn't like the pain in her side that already told her, as she turned down one hall and then another, she couldn't run forever. The hallways went on, section after section of non-button buttoned padding, grey after grey, turning and conjoining, and Lily tried to choose turns that would not form loops, but enough T-junctions appeared that she began to lose touch. She did not come back upon the junction with the sign and the nub, which was a relief, as she expected to meet it at every turn (to a crash of the orchestra, overwhelmed with the pain of ultimate irony). She felt instead that she made progress—that she tended in a line—but that the building went on indefinitely. If 24 contained "COSMOS," why wouldn't 25 contain an infinite labyrinth of padded hallways?

She was beginning to slow down, and she knew the voidlet didn't *want* her to slow down, and she knew that as an agent of compliance, it was empowered to punish. Young Torrents had observed, or been a part in, a change in her collection schedule—which seemed punitive. Burt was gone. Her life? Who gave a shit about her life. But darker than death threats, Burt-stealing MFS commanded the specter of retribution for noncompliance, ACCOUNTABILITY, the event around which Apocalypse centered, Judgment.

Taking another left, she allowed herself a dramatic crash into wall-padding and heaved cool air. The dim lighting was constant, as sourceless as in the nub, as revealing of unlimited grey in the floors and walls. Lily peered around the corner and saw the voidlet creeping closer. It always looked like it went the same speed, but when she was going faster, not watching it, it didn't fall far enough behind. It had to be going faster, catching up with her, when she wasn't looking, but the idea that it had a speed reserved for unseen moments felt unaccountable, even among unaccountable circumstances. Breathing was so difficult that her t-shirt felt too tight.

She ran farther than she thought she could, down another hallway, to the right and down another. She was hardly sweating at all, but she attributed the lack to the building's air conditioning or to the coldness of nearby outer space. The stitch in her side had taken hold of her vision, warping and tinting it. The dim grey world threatened to fuzz out. She had taken an awful lot of left turns. Maybe if she had gone another way. The Left-Hand Path... she giggled. Hanging out with Tobias.

The voidlet slipped into a straight line of sight. Lily turned away from it, stumbled around another corner, and stopped, surprised by what she saw ahead: a patch of light. As if the ceiling had a skylight, or at least a recessed area for a good spotlight, a beam formed a warm volume of radiance around a shape that Lily couldn't quite make out. She limped toward it, eyes adjusting to the changed illumination, and hoped her lungs would neither explode nor collapse as she forced these few more steps. The shape resolved into a profile like a sarcophagus. It was whitely reflective.

The exterior was plastic. Thick, translucent, form-fitting, white at the seams, solid-looking where the light created glares, it was high-quality, crafted *in situ*, vacuum-sealed and puncture-resistant. Beneath the layer of plastic, a large area was grey, and other areas were red, and others were brown. Some areas were jumbles. From the sarcophagus head, a thin stub stuck up. The protrusion stemmed from the eye. It, too, was vacuum sealed in plastic. It was a letter opener. Inside the plastic, Burt lay with a letter opener sticking out of one eye socket.

It was bloodless.

Lily took in a breath and found her jaw quivering. Burt still had burns, discernible through the plastic, on his chest; the red color came from the parts of his shirt still sticking to him. As far as Lily could tell, the vacuum-sealed plastic wrapped all the way around Burt's body without attaching him to anything else. He wasn't a pork chop attached to a Styrofoam board at the grocery store. He was a man she supposed she'd fallen in love with. From the look of things someone had used a big machine to cast plastic around him, although Lily no longer felt certain that a machine or a someone actually had to exist in order for such things to come into being here in 1500 Spring. She wanted him out; she wanted him back. But what difference did wanting make? Lily was a *doer*, and she flowed like crazy— but since doing made no difference, why would wanting?

She wasn't crying yet. It would have to seem real for her to cry.

Touching the plastic, confirming it felt cool, seemed ignoble. Burt was preserved, cocooned. Perhaps if he were naked, the packaging would feel less devastating, but with mutilated clothing he seemed to have been dropped into the display plastic like a second-tier action figure, Burn-Victim Burt, with Super-Action-Eyeball-Grip. Lily thought the letter opener should be removable, one of those small parts you lose on the first day you open the toy and never see again.

They had worked together at P-Cubed for a pretty long time. He was a good boss. Not too demanding, but not a condescending pushover, either. The world was full of unrealistic people. Not Burt, at least until the end, when realism wouldn't have served him well. Then he adapted. Which was itself realistic.

The plastic didn't respond to poking like a solid shell. It pressed inward, elastic. It would bend and tear. Lily poked at an area at the sides, where extra plastic bound arm to torso. She tried to gather slack and pull, but it would not yield. Manipulating the firm material made her fingers complain. It wanted to retain its formed-to-Burt shape. It blurred his face better than pantyhose.

Looking at his blurred face, she knew what she had to do. She wrapped her hand around the letter opener and pulled. At first it didn't budge, but the plastic began to stretch, and as it did it turned white, which bled into a million petroleum colors. After threatening to string out into infinite white pasta, the plastic snapped, and the letter opener was free. Lily took the plastic-free tip between fingers and pulled the rest out of still-clinging wrap. Shinier than she remembered, it was the same tool she had used before, she felt certain.

The letter opener's sides looked unnecessarily sharp.

Burt's punctured eye socket, freed from plastic, now lay exposed to open air. In the sunny spotlight, it had a ruby quality, although all its redness was dry. His hair and beard looked greyer than they should, his skin more wrinkled and more ash. Funny. She had thought about him dying, but she had never imagined what he'd looked like dead. Not like this.

What more did she possess that could be collected? She looked at the voidlet, drawing close, not too close. It knew the answer. She thought it should make a sound. Hissing wouldn't work in these circumstances, so not another hiss, but some noise would serve well at this point, some monstrous acknowledgment of the voidlet's appetite. It could be a dragon, and it could roar! It could be any number of beasts other than this little one-foot-diameter puddle, sparkling with hatred, terrifying in its simplicity.

She realized she was kneeling in a beam of light with a man's body spread out beside her. He lay on his back, spread long, and when she put her hand under his head, the only place where part of his flesh was exposed, he yielded to upward curling, so she could cradle him if she wanted. The pose might have been *pieta*, lovers rather than mother and son but just as holy and tragic. Lily wondered if they sparkled like the voidlet sparkled, they in their light and it in its.

A fundamental difference between the voidlet and them was that while the voidlet breathed, Burt did not. Except where it carried Lily's movements, the plastic stayed still. The inky voidlet squiggled. Burt was dead. She held the letter opener that had killed him. Unless someone had stuck the letter opener in his eye after he had died from his burns. In which case no matter. But she felt pretty sure the letter opener had killed him.

She held the letter opener while Burt's plastic-wrapped head rested partially on her lap, and the voidlet got closer. Lily didn't know if she could breathe any faster and still process the air she was sucking in. Her chest felt unmovably tight and unfillably vast; whatever entered got lost.

What is the worst possible outcome?

No one should ever ask or answer that question.

What is the worst possible outcome, Lily Henshaw?

Well it's not this. No, not this.

She looked at the letter opener. At the voidlet. At the letter opener. It could get much worse. Think of the suffering! Puppies tortured for the sole purpose of Lily watching and hating every moment, Lily responsible for the torturing of puppies, until at last she gives the torturers a little of what they want. Soul juice. The fungible satisfaction produced as a pasty substance by the brain stem. Whatever it is, it holds them off until the next time they start torturing puppies. Or worse.

The puppy-torturing voidlet loomed very close but did not prowl. It hunted with the steadiness of a Roman legion, no need to regard stealth. Its progress was inevitable. No matter which way Lily turned, it followed a line, *her* line, and the line only got shorter as it caught up, and would catch up, no matter how far or fast she ran. As she looked at the voidlet— the direction opposite Burt's body—she nevertheless saw the body's plastic-coated shape and felt a handsaw's teeth raking across her chest, ripping at muscle tissues surrounding and inside her heart. Her mouth fell open in forceless exhalation. She jammed the letter opener into her left wrist. The tip might not have been keen enough to pierce skin and vein with ease, so she jammed hard, and as the first shock of pain traveled up her arm, she pulled down, knowing the blade's edge was sharper than it should have been, feeling it split a trail as she guided it as far as she could manage toward her elbow.

This motion, this cut, was *not* inevitable, or hadn't been. Neither was the matching cut she tried to make on the other wrist, although it turned out to be shallower and shorter, not as impressive as the gash on the left side. The left hand already felt weak by the time she called upon it to attack the right wrist, so underperformance was acceptable. Both gashes gushed.

Lily bled like a person. With the extravagance of the experiences leading up to this moment, the Biblical extremity, she expected bleeding out to shift her into a mythic mode. Not long ago she'd had eruptions of lava and waves of insects—Young hadn't made a lot of sense, but he had indicated that Lily was a big deal, so where were the rivers of blood now that she'd instigated the highest drama of her own? The pain was sharp and sickening, but it was also small compared to the rush of fluid over wounds' sides, which was also small compared to the fluid's import, life, or post-life, the end-time of Collection Time. Bleeding makes the body an hourglass. Lily was running out. She chuckled.

The voidlet got closer. Sitting on the ground, facing the voidlet, she pushed herself away and collided with the plastic-coated body. Burt's body. She pushed herself further, leaving a blood trail that the body slid into as she made her way around it. Him. With the dry ruby eye. In her wet trail. Now she was the amoeba, trailing viscous goo as she manipulated her loose mass with the most primitive locomotion. The voidlet appeared elegant by contrast, certainly cleaner. She wondered if it would devour her blood trail like Pac-Man with dots, *refined* Pac-Man with *gourmet* dots. It took its time.

Lily kept pushing herself away from the voidlet as her difficulty breathing got worse and worse. Her vision tightened to tunnels, fuzzing wide peripheries to green-tinged grey, swimming. The pain centered in her wrists, chest, and head expanded to include an aura around her. The voidlet did not consume Burt's body. It navigated around and kept coming for her. Overwhelming lightheadedness halted her movement. She would have watched the voidlet's progress, but vision was nothing but green-grey and an impression of figures from a moment ago, the hall and the body in it and the creeping blackness in the floor. Who remembers the exact moment of falling asleep? Lily couldn't recall the precise sensation. Before death came, though, Lily understood that she had killed herself. Voidlet was not victor.

Pause.

Chirping.

Death sounded like chirping.

Bright sunshine-yellow water-blue treetop-green meshed in fluffed cloudcover-white over lakehouse gabled roofs wood siding. Dock short, long enough, fishing rods simple reels, lines, hooks, homemade lures. Girl and boy and soda pop. No arguments today.

Lily should have been preteen knee-length dress floppy hat, but she was instead her thirtysomething self, blue jeans red shirt hair so mussed and stringy it had forgotten the notion of style. Her shirt was clean, though. She didn't have a trace of blood on her. Birds flocked overhead.

She recognized the setting. It was Ethel and Rose's family summer vacation spot, or had been for a few years, designed to provide memories for young Lily while drawing back David and Doris with languorous water views. Neither David nor Lily liked fishing, but it provided a pretext for sitting together for a long period of time during which each understood silence to be acceptable. They could enjoy and get credit for being in one another's company without the pressure of speech. Neither minded talking with the other; each enjoyed it, for a time, but neither was capable of maintaining it for hours on end. Fishing meant they didn't have to invent excuses to depart one another when the conversation ran out. They could stare into the water, and if one of them asked the other what she or he was thinking, and she or he didn't want to share, the answer was, "Fish."

David sat with her, his legs dangling off the end of the dock. He wore khaki pants and a reddish-pink dress shirt with the sleeves rolled up and the tail untucked. He looked younger than he should have, and in better shape, and hairier with a long snout—he was a werewolf, which didn't shock Lily, but it did strike her as incommodious to the atmosphere. Although he was humanoid enough to handle it, the image of a werewolf with a fishing pole appeared incongruous. He adjusted his line and said to her, "You did it."

His statement might have conveyed accusation or congratulation. "What did I do?"

David freed a hairy hand from his fishing pole and gestured toward her gashed wrists, open and ghastly but bloodless. "You and Burt and a few more will make a cluster. Maybe Mom will take a shortcut. You never know."

The idea of Mom killing herself seemed terrible. Lily didn't know why. She had deemed not living, or not post-living, preferable to voidlet circumstances, preferable, she realized, to whatever Fate MFS, God's misbegotten contractors, had chosen to steer her toward. She had changed the flow the only way she could. Why wouldn't everyone do that? Why should Lily feel terrible about someone else changing the flow? As long as they flowed forward—

"Burt didn't kill himself," Lily said.

"Yes, he did," David said. "Did you see him die?"

Lily thought and admitted, "Well, no."

David nodded his werewolf head. He had awfully big teeth. "Think about it. Who do you think killed him?"

The same person who coated him with plastic? The question! As if Burt would do to himself....

"You concoct such elaborate fantasies," David said.

Of course! This place seemed so unreal because it was.

She and David shouldn't be here looking like they did because they weren't. She was dreaming. This was a dream. She wasn't here at Mom and Rose's lakehouse but back at 1500 Spring, maybe still on 25, dead, by all indications…

The wind blew. "Yes," David said, "this place is a dream, but I'm here with you, at MFS, and when you wake up, you and Burt will still be dead."

"Take me to Burt," Lily said. "If we're both dead, take me to him."

"I think if Burt was here, in the building, he'd be here, with you, you know?" David said. He reeled in his line a few feet. "I think his case must be handled by another entity."

"It's been suggested," Lily said.

"Okay, then. If it's an entity in another building, that's probably where he is. Lily, trust me, you'll have plenty of time to focus on that later. Right now, you need to—"

"How do I get to the other building? And how do I find out which one?"

David laughed with a fierce, growling edge. "You don't, that I know of. Businesses stay separate, you know, for the good of all."

"No, I don't know," Lily said. "It sounds arbitrary."

"You're new at death," David said. "You'd be amazed at what starts to make sense after a while."

"So, is that what this is? Is this what death is? Some kind of dream-memory montage?" Lily looked at her too-bright surroundings and felt distaste.

"Enjoy this," David said. "You'll forget how to dream not long before you forget how to sleep, and then you get into what I've heard called the First Trench."

"Everything has a name, doesn't it?"

"Yes." David focused his predator-eyes on hers. "When you're dead, everything has already been named. Not knowing the names doesn't matter. They exist. Moreover, most of the names you know are wrong."

David spoke in an emotionless manner that reminded her of the difference death had made in Eric, Mia, and Kris. David was still David, in personality and sub-wolf appearance, but he was muted. "David, I...." Lily sought to raise an objection, but she stopped when hit by a wave of contemplating her own past-tense demise.

"What you have done, Lily.... When you awake you will seem to have many choices. You have none. Meet me on the elevator, and we'll go to the forty-ninth floor. I have to show you the severity of what you have done. Only then can you go forward."

Only then? He sounded like a prophet in a quest movie. Propheteering was as contagious as Crazy Time, apparently, as a lot of it was going around... Lily tried to imagine her brother in life agreeing to this role he was assuming in death, and yes, she really could, because she always pictured him doling out technical advice as if his words had scriptural authority. However authoritative, his words were now insufficient. Dead or alive, she needed an impetus to draw her forward, and the cheese was dead. She tossed her fishing pole in the lake. It was just a dream anyway.

"I don't want to be here," Lily said. Water welled in her eyes.

"You'll wake up soon," David said. Burt might have said the same thing. How had she traded one for the other?

"I don't want to wake up, either." Damn. She didn't want to cry now. Now it would look like no more than self-pity.

David's distorted face tilted in compassion. "Did you even take the time to think, and if you did, did you think suicide would make an end of it? Everything else mocks at the futility of action, and you think that one action alone is somehow sacred, reserved from mockery because it asserts some kind of willful individuality in the act of self-annihilation? I know it because I've thought it, but I still can't believe how naïve it is."

David reminded her of Young Torrents, except David *almost* made sense. In the nearby woods, crickets kept chirping. "I thought suicide might make mockery and everything else kind of irrelevant," Lily said.

"Severing all relations," David said. "Complete deracination. But I'm here, aren't I? And we're related! You were such a cute baby. On the whole I didn't want a little sister, not at first, but I must admit you were cute."

"So, what's it for? Being dead, I mean. What's the use?" Lily might have been setting up an ad pitch.

"I don't find it very useful," David said. "You won't either." He clapped his hands with a thunder that shook the trees, rattled Lily's bones, and left her awake, on the grey floor of a corridor with padded grey walls. She'd been sleeping on her side on the hard floor. She saw no sign of plastic-coated Burt. She saw no sign of a sign. Nothing indicated where in the labyrinth she was. She could walk in either of two directions, both of which ended in T-junctions.

Getting to her feet was easier than expected. Another pleasant surprise carried over from the dream: her shirt was still clean. Walking, she knew she should keep walking. Instincts told her when to turn left or right. Sometimes, when she could, she went forward without turning. She made choices. They led to a sliding elevator door. It opened, and Lily joined werewolf David inside. She pressed the button for 60, and 49 lit up. Lily wondered if she might have kept the letter opener somehow. She still had the machine gun, but it seemed trivial by comparison.

7

[Someone's coming for me, David. I can feel it.]

Propriety still brings bad news to the front door.

Rose put down her knitting. Doris sat by Donnie on the sofa, mother reading some novel on her book machine, son wearing headphones plugged into the game machine that commanded rapid movement from his fingers. The clacking sounds of the boy's fingers on buttons, which produced effects audible only to him, underscored the room's dominant silence, maintained first out of a natural lull in sociality and second out of an unspoken understanding that quiet was preferable for Ethel's sake. Ethel might not have been sleeping. She didn't sleep enough, even though she had, since the cancer diagnosis, spent most of her time in bed. Doris worried, and Rose worried while she knitted, and the knock on the door entered their house of quiet worrying.

Rose looked at her niece and grand-nephew. The boy went on with his game, but with the headphones on, he might not have heard the knock. Doris stopped her reading, eyes up, but didn't lower her machine. Rose got to her feet. When she first opened the front door, the power of the sunlight blinded her. The contrast was striking. Doris and Donnie's machines supplied their own lights—had the living room been too dim for knitting, and Rose hadn't noticed? Lately she'd felt distant from her surroundings. As Ethel faded, she faded, too.

Two policemen stood at the door. The one with the moustache said, "Excuse me, ma'am, but is Mrs. Henshaw at home?"

"Henshaw" was still legally Ethel's name, so Rose took a moment to imagine the police coming to arrest Ethel for having done… something. *Anything.* The wherewithal to break the law would have cheering implications. But nowadays the name "Henshaw" mostly only came up in connection to one of the kids, and Rose suspected the police were here in that connection. Doris was here, and it wouldn't be about David now that matters pertaining to his death were settled, so—Lily. "What's the matter?" Rose asked.

"Are you Mrs. Henshaw?" the other policeman said. His "Mrs." was like the other one's "ma'am"—too sincere and heartfelt. Something was definitely wrong.

"I'm her sister, and she's not well," Rose said. "May I help you?"

The one with the moustache leaned in and whispered to the other one, who whispered back. "Okay ma'am," said the one with the moustache, "you're family, so we can talk to you."

Instead of being smart aleck, Rose said, "What's this about?"

"We…." The one with the moustache paused. "So, if Mrs. Henshaw is your sister, and Ethel Henshaw is listed as the mother, then you're Lily Henshaw's aunt, is that correct?"

Again, the temptation to be smart aleck, but she said, "Lily's my niece, yes. Is she okay?"

The man looked down. "Ma'am, I regret to inform you that your niece suffered from a, um, circumstances sometime earlier today, and she was pronounced dead at the scene."

Perhaps sensing inadequacy in his partner's delivery, the man without the moustache added: "We regret to inform you that your niece took her own life."

Rose nodded and then shook her head. More words were

exchanged, and the policemen went away.

Donnie still had his headphones on, but Doris had been listening from the couch without volunteering to join Rose at the door, which Rose pushed closed. "Someone *found* her," Doris repeated, using a volume low enough to be heard but not understood by her nearby son, "by that building? In an alley?"

Rose fastened the chain on the front door. She didn't know why; it hadn't been fastened before. "That's what they said." She felt a tear on her cheek but didn't feel like she was crying.

"Was she living like a homeless person?" Doris asked.

"I don't know. I don't think so. She was staying with her boyfriend, I think." Rose returned to the rocking chair and moved her knitting to another place, which accomplished nothing.

"Oh God," Doris said.

"I should have asked about the boyfriend, but I can't remember his name," Rose said.

Doris was looking at Donnie, who mashed buttons. "Could he really be unaware of our whole conversation?" she asked. Aware that he was in some way addressed, Donnie looked up at his mother long enough to give her a nod and a smile before returning all attention to the video game. Doris lifted one of the headphones' ears and said to him, "Don't keep the volume up so loud!"

To Rose, Doris said, "We're going to have to repeat everything."

"To the children?" Rose looked from Donnie to the hallway down which she'd last seen his little sister Daisy run. Where was that girl?

Donnie stood, took a cushion from the couch, and walked to one of the living room's far corners, where he used the cushion as the base for a nest. He relocated. Willingness to obey orders about volume did not equate to interest in adult conversation.

Doris looked toward Ethel's bedroom. "To everyone, eventually. Everyone who knew her." She paused. "I feel sick." She glanced around the room. "And cold. It wasn't cold in here a minute ago, but I feel cold now."

"With David it turned out we only had to call the funeral home, which made arrangements with the city to get the body. They made him look nice enough, didn't they? You see so many people in coffins after a while. I don't see why either one of us would have to go down to the morgue in person, do you? They seemed already to have a positive enough identification, but I guess I should have asked. I guess you don't think of things when you're in the moment. It's just that I didn't expect it to happen again, you know? I didn't go through it with David thinking, *You have to remember this, Rose, so you can use it next time, and it won't be so difficult.* Maybe if I had, I would be... better... ready...." Rose thought about picking up her knitting.

"Do you think she did it in the alley where they found her?" Doris wasn't asking any specific person. "I hear 'alley' and I see sooty with trash all over it. I think I'd want to bleed to death someplace clean. It doesn't sound like Lily."

"They seemed to have a positive enough identification," Rose said.

"I heard. I'm just saying it doesn't *sound* like her. I'm just saying... nevermind. But where did she do it? If not in that alley, where, and how did she get there? And if in that alley, why? Surely, she had somewhere else to be." Doris rested her face in her hands. "I'm thinking the wrong things, I think."

Rose picked up her knitting and held it. "I don't know what wrong things there are to think." She thought of a few. "I know I should call the funeral home. Should we use the same one as with David? They did a good enough job. I could wait. I should wait. Let the news... sit."

Doris looked at her, wide-eyed in exasperation. "The *news*?" She set the novel-machine, which had been in her lap the whole time, aside. "As if we got delivered some *bulletin*."

"Call it something else then," Rose said. The clock ticked, and silence save for button-mashing returned. This deafening conversation had not penetrated the headphones, or if it had, Donnie possessed some deeper armor. Clever little sociopath.

David had a handheld videogame machine when he was a boy. It wasn't as sophisticated, but it had similar absorptive properties. It bleeped a lot. When did suicide begin? Was it during these long hours of isolation? How was a grown-up to know what sort of game-playing a child did and what it meant? Easier to blame the games than to blame the parents. Rose wasn't as much a parent to David as she was to Lily, but she was parent to both, in a way, and now both... and Doris, the one of them least hers, survived to ask questions...

"I'm sorry," Doris said. She looked toward the wall. "It's late enough. I could fix drinks. I could fix drinks, and then we could tell the children. They need to know about their aunt. Aunts are important." She smiled with a compassionate tilt of her head. "And maybe telling them before we tell Mom would be easier."

So, Ethel would be the last in the house to know. Rose didn't think it would matter to Ethel, really, that she found out about her daughter Lily's death after her two grandchildren did. Nevertheless, the pecking order for information seemed wrong. "Okay," Rose said.

[*"I feel like I can't breathe in here," Lily said.*

"You'll get used to that." David flattened out the front of his pinkish-red shirt. She could barely see him through their dense surroundings, but his voice was clear. "Breathing is one of your illusions anyway."

"Why are we seeing these things? Why am I like a voice in Rose's head?" She sensed her own clothes, her own body, or whatever residual self-shape she possessed, and knew she stood close to David, but she didn't have a grasp on the space around her or on its relation to the space she saw Rose and Doris inhabiting. She knew, however, that the inhabited space received form from Rose's perspective, so her best guess about her location was Rose's head.

"Rose can't hear us. You haven't left 1500 Spring. This is 49," David said. He laughed and added, "The way your world ends."

Lily heard quiet sizzling. "With a sizzle," she said. "Okay, family," and she turned her attention to the announcement of her death to the children, "sizzle."]

Rose posed in the rocking chair with her knitting in her lap. Doris collected Donnie from the corner and had him restore the cushion to the sofa before he sat on it. Doris remained standing and said, "Turn the video games all the way off." Donnie wrapped the headphones in a wire—Rose imagined him switching to the wireless kind soon enough—and pressed some buttons, presumably making the machine switch off. Donnie had shown Rose some of his games. Mostly they involved going through different "levels," hostile environments, and shooting things. She didn't wonder why Donnie spent so much time with one machine or another. The button-pressing served a lot of the same functions as knitting, and it engaged the mind in many more facets. Her generation had gotten lost in television at least as easily, and it offered less. Making Donnie shut off his game machine felt like turning off the television and feeling a house's emptiness. They were taking something away from the boy.

"Donnie, you remember what happened to your Uncle David," Doris said. The boy nodded. Doris was going about it the wrong way. She was going to present her two dead siblings as a package, a concept for the boy to comprehend all at once instead of as discrete tragedies. "My brother," Doris added. The boy nodded again.

"Donnie, you remember your Aunt Lily." Doris addressed her son as a toddler instead of as an adolescent. Why? And what was next—would Doris tell the boy something about David and Lily going to Heaven?

"Did something happen to Lily?" Donnie asked. His mother's slowness left him ample room for anticipation.

Doris retrieved a wooden chair from the dining room and set it on the living room carpet so she could sit across from her son, so close that their knees almost touched. She could have sat next to him on the couch, but she chose this arrangement instead, which was interesting in a file-it-for-later fashion. Now, Rose needed to listen.

"Yes," Doris answered. "Lily is d—I mean, your Aunt Lily passed away."

"Oh," Donnie said. The look on his young face said his brain was absorbing and attempting to process.

["*He's like me,*" *Lily said.*

David sighed. "*He's like both of us. Troubling, isn't it?*"

"*He didn't know me, really. He shouldn't be too upset.*" *Lily watched and waited.*]

The boy asked, "What do I do?"

"What do you mean?" Doris's hand reached halfway toward her son's, but his didn't move, so she retracted hers. Not a time for that sort of comfort.

"I don't know. You're both sitting there looking at me, like I'm about to do something. Tell me what it is, and I'll do it." The boy's feet kicked out a little, but they only brushed against Doris.

"There's nothing to do," Doris said. "I... that is we...

wanted to tell you, and we're here to help if you want to share how you're feeling about it." Was Doris calling on the memory of a book, a chapter about how to break bad news to a child? The woman, Rose's niece, seemed unnatural. The whole situation seemed unnatural. And they had just been through it with David. Had it been like this? Rose couldn't recall. Only a few months had passed, and she couldn't recall. The events she remembered, but she couldn't recall whether they *felt* like this.

To keep Doris from doing more wrong, Rose spoke up: "What you do, young man, is let us help you, like your mother said, while you help us. We have to tell your sister, too, now that you know." And then somehow they would all have to tell his grandmother. They were rounding up a posse to deliver bad news. Yes, *news.* "Be strong for your sister," Rose said.

[*"They all look very strong,"* Lily said.

"Be careful not to confuse scar tissue with muscle. Scars and muscles both look firm, but they differ in origin and resilience," David said. *"I sound like a fortune cookie."*

"You had to get your wisdom somewhere," Lily said. *"You think they're scarred? Even Donnie?"*

"Nothing like this ever happened when we were kids, and we both ended up killing ourselves. What do you think will happen to Donnie and Daisy?"

"They're not us," Lily said.

"Nobody is. Not anymore." David snorted, reminding Lily that somewhere inside this immersion of Rose's perceptions, David had a great lupine snout.]

"I'll GET IT!" Daisy charged from the hallway into the room, closing on the front door as it rang a second time. Rose had hardly registered the first ring, but she'd been aware of Doris and Donnie looking toward the door, and she'd heard the tumult of footsteps coming down the hall. Daisy got the door open, swung it wide, and said, "Brown shorts, brown shorts!"

In a few seconds Rose snapped from thinking the girl was shouting some kind of warning (The Redcoats! The Brownshorts!) to realizing the man at the door was delivering a package. She called, "Does he need a signature?"

"No thanks, ma'am!" The man's voice was youthful and polite. Rose couldn't see him. He might have been pretty in his brown shorts, as they sometimes were. Ethel used to make comments. Even the older men dressed as delivery boys, with guts hanging over their shorts' front buttons, had a charm in the uniform. Rose didn't know whether Lily liked looking at the random men who came to the door as a result of online shopping. Lily didn't talk a lot about men and dating. She didn't talk a lot about a lot of things, Rose supposed. When Ethel's girls, her own girls, in a way, were young, Rose had thought they would grow up and become great friends. Ethel and Rose and Doris and Lily, a sisterhood. She didn't know why it hadn't happened. They had no animosity. They did not adhere to one another, and that was all. For Lily, that was all that would ever be. Approaching death required slant vision. Rose couldn't see death head-on, but she looked toward there being no future in which she and Lily became better friends, and her lower lip quivered.

People said more things, and the front door closed. Daisy was asking whether she might open the box. Her mother asked what the address label said. Ethel Henshaw. Then her grandmother ought to open it, oughtn't she? But Gramma is sick. She doesn't like to open presents. The conversation went on, and Rose considered whether underneath it, Doris was biding her time, waiting for the right moment to turn talk toward the news that had brought her almost knee-to-knee with her son.

"Are we going to tell her?" Donnie asked.

Doris gave him a silencing glare, and Rose didn't understand. The boy asked the right question. The package delivery man hadn't changed the situation. They all needed something to *do*, and right now their activity was to be initiating individuals, even children, into the news-changed, inferior world.

["*What do you think it is?" David asked.*

Lily stopped fathoming the package's importance, which she took to be of a magnitude grand enough to justify the presentation of this particular scene for her observation, and tried to determine whether David was lying to her. "You mean you don't already know?" The sizzling sound kept going, but she didn't know what to relate it to. Lily didn't smell anything burning.

"Of course I don't know," David said. "I didn't send the package."

Lily wanted to explain that he seemed to know things he had no reason to know, so her question was reasonable. "Why are you showing me this, then? What's the point?"

"I didn't choose for us to be here, if that's what you mean," David said. "Don't get too excited about the list of things I can do for you. It's short, and picking where you end up next isn't on it."

"How are you going to teach me a lesson about what I've done, then? Isn't that what you said you were going to do?" Lily wanted to see her brother while she talked to him. She saw hazed-over aspects of him, the pinkish-red shirt, the strange curve of his posture, the hair that made the unclothed parts of him thicker and dark, but she didn't feel like she was really seeing him. The lines of his face used to be sympathetic. She wanted to see the lines of his face.

"I... knew we would see something. I didn't know what. This moment is happening now." David sounded more sheep than wolf.

Lily said, "There's no way this is happening now. I've only been dead a matter of minutes! Maybe tomorrow or the next day, this could happen, but now—"

David had a smile in his voice when he said, "How would you know when now *is?"*]

The package was about the size of a bread box, taped-up brown cardboard with a familiar corporate logo and a label printed with Ethel's name and no concept of Ethel's health. When browsing the web on the laptop she kept at the bedside became one of Ethel's pastimes, she and Rose joked about what chemo brain might do to their finances, imagining an endless supply of brown cardboard boxes that Ethel ordered and promptly forgot. The possibility made Rose nervous at first, but when boxes arrived without Rose knowing about them in advance, they told her that at least Ethel was conscious and doing things, perhaps even enjoyable things, during the hours when Rose wasn't near her. Shopping became evidence of vitality. As Ethel got sicker, the flow of boxes decreased. Not shopping became evidence of decline.

How odd that this package came so soon after the news. How odd that both news and package came while Doris, Donnie, and Daisy were visiting.

Doris said to Donnie, who looked at his sister in anticipation of hitting her with news, "We need to deal with this package."

Why not set it aside? It couldn't possibly be important enough to pull attention from world-shattering news.

[*"All of this build-up," Lily said, "and it's probably the powdered creamer Mom likes in her coffee. She complained about the grocery store not carrying it anymore."*

"I don't think so," David said. "I agree that there's something fishy about us encountering this particular moment."

The moment when her death was the news? Couldn't it be important on its own?]

Doris took the box from Daisy's small hands and set it on the coffee table, which she'd had to push aside to fit her chair in front of the couch. Daisy came around and sat by her brother, so they all formed a deranged circle—in the rocking chair, Rose was an outlying point that skewed the shape—with the package at center. Minutes ago, Doris had argued that Gramma should open the package, but Gramma was in her bedroom, and the package wanted opening now. They froze, and seeking a remedy, Rose searched her mental calendar. In a voice that accommodated children, Rose said, "Nobody has a birthday coming up, right?"

Daisy made a comment about her *half*-birthday. Donnie said no, no birthdays. Doris shook her head no. Rose supposed Ethel might have been shopping for Christmas, which had become a year-round prospect, but their code said that Christmas gifts needed to be addressed to someone with "Christmas" as a middle name, and the label said only "Ethel Henshaw." Ethel might have forgotten the code, of course, so opening the box could be a spoiler—

"You think it's okay to open, then?" Doris asked. Her voice contained desperation.

"Sure," Rose said. Daisy clapped, but she noticed that no one in the room shared her enthusiasm, so she stopped. Rose stretched her arm toward Doris, offering a knitting needle. "You can use this to punch through the tape."

Doris accepted the offer and tore through the packaging.

[*"Pandora," Lily said.*

David laughed with gurgling in his throat. "I always thought her box would be bigger. Maybe that's because I hear 'Pandora' and think of a giant panda."

Lily thought of the freezer tailor-made for orange-crème, and she thought of the door to COSMOS. "Anything might be in that box. They could open it and fall inside."

"Rules," David said. "My friend Sally taught me something about rules. Didn't your friend Burt do the same? Haven't you

learned the rules yet?"

"No," Lily said. "And I half-expect this moment to end... for us to find ourselves somewhere else... before they even get the box open." And then Lily would never know about the box or its insides. She had an imminent awareness of never.]

The box contained a box.

Most of the cardboard package consisted of padding to protect the box within. The smaller box was dark brown wood with brass hinges for the lid, which had lattice-like edging and other ornate features showcasing craft. Rose pegged it as a jewelry box, but as Doris held it up for inspection, its purpose became more obscure. The wooden box's ornateness qualified it as a bauble befitting baubles, but the ornament's specificity didn't suggest a woman's jewels. Rose had never seen a jewelry box without exaggerated femininity, rococo arrangements of flowers (or their equivalents), whereas the flourishes on this box possessed more staid geometry, patterns in shapes with no relation to plant reproduction. The box was ungendered.

"It's a bit heavy," Doris said. "For its size, I mean." She demonstrated the weight by lifting the box in and out of the packaging. "I don't think it's empty." Her eyes met Rose's. She eyed her children. "Shall we have a look?"

Rose thought suddenly of boxes on people's mantles full of dead relatives' ashes. "Wait!"

The children and Doris looked at Rose. Doris spoke for them: "Why?"

Rose couldn't think of an answer. That what they were doing seemed unnatural and inappropriate did not suffice. "Make sure it wasn't damaged during shipping."

Doris held a look in Rose's direction before opening the box. The chiming tones confirmed Rose was in error to think of jewelry, three descending musical notes, which repeated. It was a music box, ornate and geometric but ungendered because it was for children, girls and boys, and before the rhythm varied for the next set of descending notes, Rose knew the nursery-school song it was playing.

Three blind mice! Three blind mice!

See how they run! See how they run!

Doris's hands quaked as she set the music box on the coffee table. Rose knew the music might have pushed her from stolid to blubbering, but she held at quaking, with tears welled but not flowing. "That's some math problem," Doris said. "Three minus two." Her look at Rose implored. "Are you sure we should even tell Mom?"

[*"Lily, are you still with me?"*

"Yes, David, I'm here." Lily *was thinking about urban legends. She wanted Donnie or Daisy to go to a bathroom mirror and say her name enough times—like Bloody Mary or Candyman —so that she could appear. The ghost in the clean red shirt and jeans.*

"For a minute I couldn't see you there at all," David said.

"I guess I was fading," Lily said. "I think Doris is in trouble."

"Why's that?"

"Because we're minus two, but she's three minus two, and either way, we don't make a cluster."

"Lily, make sense."

Lily felt herself smile and knew she was more visible. "Nothing in heaven was e'er so sublime, David, but it takes all three of us to be the mice. To make a cluster."

"And what about Burt? Didn't I explain that the cluster includes—"

"You explained you don't really know anything."

David laughed, but it was fake. "True enough. So, Doris is next up for Collection Time?"

Wait—Lily had started before David was through. Had Doris started to flow crazy yet? "It's eating our family," Lily said. What secrets was Doris hiding?]

Of course they needed to tell Ethel. Rose hardly understood her niece's question.

"If it could be a matter of weeks, or days, like that one doctor said," Doris explained, "maybe Mom could... not know. She's forgetting things. We could tell her that Lily visits. She wouldn't know. And that might be better than forcing her to know that in the last year of her life, this miserable year, she lost not one but two—"

"Stop it!" Rose shouted *stop* like she had shouted *wait*, without the reasoning or fortitude to back it up, but she was glad for the momentary respite, however unreasonably and weakly obtained. Doris presented a choice between the magnitude of Ethel facing the deaths of two children, the *suicides* of two children, and the magnitude of Ethel facing her own death with her cancer-riddled brain packed fuller with lies. Telling would save her from the indignity of ending her life kept in an ignorance deemed unfit for children. Not telling would save her from the suffering of ending her life knowing only despair.

"I know," Doris said. "We should tell her." The music box was slowing down but repeating the song. On its fourth or fifth cycle to the melody's beginning, Doris snapped the box shut. "We should leave this behind."

Rose laughed singly and covered her mouth with her hand. She felt mortified, but Doris shot her a tearful and genuine smile to show she understood. Ethel needed the news, not the cosmic joke of a musical math problem. Maybe now Doris had a better understanding of *news*.

[*"Oh... oh, shit. Oh God damn it. I know why we're here. Why I'm here with you. What this is," David said.*

Lily felt bewildered. "What is it?" She'd gone from urban legends to youthful fantasies of attending her own funeral, thinking the present experience resembled the long-lapsed dream. Rose's comparison of the music box with a cremation box had cinched the resemblance for her, but now it ebbed.

"You'll know when the moment comes. Be ready."]

"Come on," Doris said, bumping knees against Donnie as she stood from her chair. "Kids. Rose. We're going to see Gramma."

Rose left the rocking chair and knitting behind and followed Doris, Donnie, and Daisy to Ethel's closed bedroom door. All of them going made it such a production, such a ceremony. Like the policemen, who had needed two tries—the first breaking the news of death, the second of suicide—they might need to divide up their information. Maybe the kids could fill the role of the knock on the door, with Daisy, like the knock, saying there's news, and Donnie, like the police uniforms, saying it's bad. The adults could then take the policemen's split of death and suicide.

Doris knocked softly on the door. "Mom?"

They would open the door and find Ethel already dead. What other cruel twist might there be?

Ethel's voice surprised her with its strength: "You can come in! I'm not decent, but that's nothing new. I'm just lying here watching the television."

Doris opened the door on slow creaky hinges and ushered the children inside. Rose entered last, noting that the television was off and that the remote lay on a tray some distance from the bed. Ethel was tucked beneath blankets, a wrap around her head, bags under her eyes, propped up a little and smiling. "There are my angels!" She greeted the children but meant them all.

"Mom, if you were watching TV, you probably didn't

hear the door. Someone stopped by. Two people, actually." Doris took her mother's hand. The children stood at the foot of the bed. Rose approached the other side.

"I didn't hear anything," Ethel said. Hadn't she? With the TV off, she must have heard *something*, mustn't she? She might simply say, *I already know*, and this moment would be over. Instead, with her sister, daughter, and grandchildren surrounding her, Ethel asked, "What is it? What's wrong?"

[Because the children stayed at the bed's foot, they left room at the sides, where David stood by Doris, and Lily stood by Rose. They couldn't interact with their surroundings and could barely see one another, but Lily sensed they could stand in those spaces, and they did.

"It's now, I think," David said.

"What is it?" Lily asked. "I don't know what I'm supposed to do."

"This is it," David said. He wasn't talking to Lily. "The chance I never thought I'd get. The one I never knew I wanted. Donnie, I always meant to take you fishing. It just seemed like something an uncle could do, and I never did it. Sorry I wasn't in your life more, pal. And Daisy, you're a pretty girl, and you're going to cause trouble. I'm sorry I won't be there to back you up. Doris... what can I say? I just... I just... I tried. That's all." He was getting choked up. David didn't get this way. It was weird. "Mom... Rose... Mom. I.... Goodbye, everybody. I'm glad I get to say goodbye."

Maudlin! David was being maudlin! They couldn't even hear him. There was no point to any of this.

"Lily," he said, "I don't think you'll ever see them again."

What? No, not what. She didn't need clarification because he said it, and it clicked. This wasn't the fantasy of attending your own funeral. This was the fantasy of saying goodbye.

"Mom? Rose? Doris? I...." David was gone. "Goodbye."]

8

Cued by "Goodbye," the sizzling noise quintupled its volume and drowned the other sounds in Mom's bedroom. Smoke billowed from all sides, casting the room's yellowish sunlight into grey, making the family look distant. Lily didn't sense herself standing at the bedside anymore. Her position felt indistinct, in range but removed. She could still see Doris, leaning over their mother, trying to speak but faltering. Doris was breaking down, and Mom was becoming more confused and distressed. Rose lifted a hand, signaling for Doris to back off, to halt her efforts, to let Rose do the work. Rose would deliver the news. Lily couldn't feel Rose's thoughts anymore, but she knew what Rose was thinking. In the end, nobody helped. Rose had to do it herself.

The sizzle drew Lily's attention to the bedroom walls, which seemed—no, *were*—closer to the bed than they'd been before. The walls' tops, where they should have met the ceiling, looked like the glowing edge of lit cigarette paper, snaking downward along a growing column of ash. Grey clouds hovered where the ceiling should have been. The smoke made Lily think she should be coughing, especially with the difficulty she had drawing breath, but David said breathing was an illusion, so maybe no smoke actually found its way into her lungs. Maybe she didn't have lungs.

When Lily noticed a fleck of orange in her mother's hair, the family stopped moving. Mom's face, beginning to register what Rose must have been telling her, froze, and the expression, decontextualized, looked comical. Her jaw hung open at an angle opposite the tilt of her head, and her wide glassy eyes had a cartoonish bulge. It was a candid photo gone awry, one to delete from the digital camera's memory, except it was the only image Lily had, and it was burning. The orange in Mom's hair lengthened, singeing the human image and replacing it with a volume of ash. The tops of Rose and Doris singed, too, smoking down, and Donnie was beginning to smolder. As Mom's forehead turned to char, Lily considered the bulging eyes and crooked jaw and didn't want them to go. Imperfect and disturbing, they were the last of Ethel that Lily would see. David had been right. Of course David was right.

The glowing orange edges moved from tops downward, devouring, replacing the distinct features of Mom, Rose, Doris, Donnie, and Daisy with grey-white sculptures of ash. What remained of the walls, which had burned more than halfway down, leaving tissues of ash standing in their places, pressed inward, making a small compartment of the bed and the people standing around it. The bed and people diminished, and the walls contracted. Lily had no sense of the position from which she observed the changes. All at once she saw four walls sizzle downward, to the floor, which sizzled, too. The snaking orange edges moved until they had crossed all surfaces, transforming them. The small space became all tissue, all ash, and Lily awaited the inevitable movement of air that would collapse the scene into nothing. It came.

Smoke and ash dissipated and yielded to clarity. Lily stood in an elevator alone. The light for 60 blinked. She hadn't seen the destination light blink before arrival, but she'd never succeeded in lighting the button for the top floor, nor had she been in this elevator car. The Executive Express she'd gotten to know was brass and silver with marblesque tile, highly reflective but also opaque. This chamber was a glass casket, with transparency up, down, and two-hundred seventy degrees from the track that attached it to the skyscraper.

Lily didn't recall seeing any external elevators when she was outside looking up at 1500 Spring, but she was in one, so recollection was moot. A city panorama engulfed her.

She still had the machine gun.

Closer by, she could see through windows into the building. If the elevator had been moving, the view to the indoors would have been too fleeting for significance, but it was still. Lily dangled in a glass box with a clear view of the ground almost fifty stories beneath her, and she did not move.

Was that 49 through the window? She saw a large room, high ceiling, paintings on the walls in expensive-looking frames, the sort of space that could serve for meetings in City Hall. Instead of a long wooden table with many chairs for the seating of austere committees, the room's center contained a structure Lily knew the word for but had trouble believing, as she had never seen one outside a historical reconstruction: stocks. A wooden platform supported beams of wood carved so that when they came together they trapped neck and wrists, making the person "in the stocks" kneel with head and hands cuffed and exposed to whatever ignominy passersby might choose to visit. The woman in the stocks now wore a dress like a plush sack, but otherwise, with her mussed dark hair and worn expression, she looked like Lily.

People did not surround the stocks to throw vegetables, jeer, and taunt the imprisoned woman. No people stood in view of the window, but other creatures did—four-legged, circling creatures. Their fur was the grey of smoke, and as they prowled, their heads and tails adjusted to keep their profiles low and sharp as darts. Lily couldn't hear them, but she imagined them growling. Wolves. Their bodies looked large, but they had nothing human about them, pure wolf. Giant wolves circled the woman in the stocks.

Beyond elevator glass, a massive bird of prey circled, too. Lily imagined it cawing.

Lily was trapped in a glass case suspended above a deadly drop; she could not help the woman whose head and hands stuck out of wood, waiting for wolves to gnaw them. She could merely watch, and her placement conveyed an *intention* for her to watch, a decision on the part of the elevator to turn the woman's plight into a show, and like most shows, it reflected its audience, making the woman an allegory for Lily herself. The elevator held her here for a long look in the mirror.

Where wolves began to eat her. The first wolf that snapped bit off fingers. The next took a chunk out of the hand itself. Others started at once, stretching the face in different directions, making their ways around to the hindquarters, which provided more meat. The elevator started moving as the body detached from itself, scattering with wolves in different directions, leaving a stripped core draped across the stocks' wooden structure. Lily wondered whether her body had really been, or would really be, found in an alley. Lily wondered whether David was one of the wolves.

The elevator ascended beyond the scene with the wolves and the stocks, and Lily turned away from the skyscraper, into the city panorama. The sky, which might have been red, looked white. Against it much of the more distant skyline blended like newsprint smudges. Closer, tall buildings interrupted setting sunlight and cast monolithic shadows, which crisscrossed into skewed checkers of light and dark. From this height, the hustle of cars and people below looked plastic, thousands of insignificant pieces that formed patterns better linked to human behavior than consciousness. People could know or not know about their parts in the patterns; the parts were theirs to act out all the same.

Toys again. Lily's perspective, provided to her courtesy of MFS, was reducing her environment to toys, like Burt cast in plastic. Whose toys was she seeing? The answer was getting closer, wasn't it? God?

From the white sky, a great sandaled foot descended, throwing the transparent elevator into shade as it came down between skyscrapers and landed in an intersection, downing streetlights and crushing cars. Lily expected to see toy remnants falling from the sandal's sole when it arose again, but she saw only the deep impression it left in the ground, a footprint on the beach. The sandaled foot attached to ankle and shin, knee and a bit of thigh before sight ended. Fair hair stood out against pale skin, even on the toes: the leg was white, male, and adult. The shapes of the toenails suggested pedicure. Beneath the crushing sandal, the toy-like intersection might have turned to sand, or it might have simply ceased. Lily could not be certain.

A second leg did not materialize, but the first came down again, the step, not a stomp, landing with a thud between intersections, breaking apart asphalt and throwing a spray of debris into the air. While it flew, the debris—dirt and rock, people and technology—burst into sand. It was like bringing a bucket and shovel to build sandcastles on the beach, only to find the bucket and shovel, like everything else, would dissolve when the tide came in. Near the elevator's dangling glass, which ascended by inches, more birds circled. They weren't seagulls, but Lily thought of seagulls anyway, hearing their cries in her mind. She couldn't see the ocean from here, but she sensed an equivalent force working its way through the city's towers and streets, preparing a reclamation. She heard Young Torrents say, "This place was *for you*." The foot came down again, smashing civilization's shapes and leaving sand behind.

The giant foot kicked the building next to 1500 Spring, and it rumbled. Sediment fell from its sides, first dust, then sheets, and finally a complete crumble, the building performing a graduated dissolve as solid masses relaxed into incoherent powder. Rumbling did not stop. Lily looked around her, unsure how high the elevator had reached, hoping she would soon feel the ascending car's crawling pace settle into its destination. Lights did not change to indicate progress. The only indicator was the blinking 60.

Beyond the glass, the city melted. No longer needing the foot's encouragement to stoke its transformation, cascades proceeded through the shrinking skyline, layers and layers of construction set against a white backdrop turning to sediment and succumbing to gravity. Concrete and stone residue lingered briefly in thin clouds but did not accumulate, choosing instead to disappear along with the foot that had stirred them. The city emptied out, clearing the way to the white backdrop beneath. Lily thought she should laugh at the mysterious leg with the sandaled foot, but she hardly found it funny. The city emptied out, and she wanted the foot to come back. She wanted the footsteps to be a preamble, but the foot didn't come back. Its leg turned out to be attached to nothing at all. It served only to catalyze the white wastes of the empty city.

A bell rang, and the elevator stopped. Doors on the elevator's only opaque surface, within the ninety degrees that attached it to the building, opened. Lily stepped through and followed the sole path, a narrow hall, to a door with a gold placard on it that said "God."

Should she knock?

Lily thought of the Bob Dylan song about knocking on heaven's door, and she remembered Rev Orf saying, "Heaven has its foot on you." She set a finger against her machine gun's trigger and considered that somewhere, everything had a sprig of explanation, and she knock-knock-knocked.

In Heaven, everything was not fine. Angels had cancer. God, too, needed angels to fight off cancer. 60, blinking 60, could be Mom's brain as easily as it could be Heaven, a terrain ravaged by rogue cells multiplying and reshaping the folds that make places recognizably themselves. Lily had reached the top. Lily had reached the brain. She knocked again.

No answer. Where was God's butler?

She looked behind her. The hallway had not changed: at the other end, she saw elevator doors. She might exit, go back. Where to? Would the lobby still be there? Piled high with the massacred dead? Restored to a state of flowing traffic as if the marauding eyeballs had never invaded? Her clothes, after all, were clean. She might walk out the front doors, assuming their revolutions would release her. She might go back to her apartment and reclaim it from police, assuming it had actually been a crime scene. Too many assumptions littered her path. Was she even in the city anymore? Was she even a person? She had no one left to ask. The way backward involved too many treacherous steps. Forward, the way to flow, involved a single door. She tried the knob. It turned in her hand, no lock, and allowed her to push the door open.

Chimes, the same tones she had heard from the music box, greeted her, but they were louder than a box could have made. The notes came so slowly that the melody initially eluded her, but when the first phrase reached its end, she identified it: "All around the mulberry bush." She knew the tune, knew it would climax in a few phrases with a weasel popping, but she couldn't think of any of the other lyrics. They had something to do with rice and treacle and monkeys; it was antiquated and strange. Like every nursery song, it had to be the soundtrack of somebody's nightmare, but it wasn't hers. She couldn't make sense of it here, now, in this room of buttons and lights.

Metallic panels with switches, sliders, and knobs had blinking, translucent glass bumps filled with red, green, blue, and yellow bulbs. Meters with arrays of numbers in arcs had arrowhead pointers to indicate readings. Slots of all sizes, from VHS-wide to USB-modest, appeared in various places on the walls and desktops decorated with the metal paneling, suggesting receptivity to data by any means necessary. Nevertheless, the inelegant density of signals and hardware interfaces looked like the future as imagined two or three generations ago, overcrowded with exaggerated remixes of the present.

Lily felt unconvinced by all the elaborate machinery except for the glass tank at the room's center, which sat beneath a spinning wheel that hung from the ceiling and had a circumference almost as big as the room. The tank was big, too, like a giant aquarium but with rounded edges, soft, clear but for reflections of the blinking lights from the surrounding metal panels. The rounding of the tank's sides was significant enough that Lily imagined she could give the tank a strong push, and it might rock back and forth a little. The tank's chamber reminded her, inevitably, of the freezer where she'd put orange-crème, but maybe the fluid that filled it, or maybe something else, made it seem less harsh.

Along the base of the tank, dozens of holes let tubes and wires pass through. They connected to the tank's occupant, whose sides, along the ribs, had little perforations where the tubes and wires entered. The occupant's chubby arms floated above the tubes and wires, near the head, which had a down of fine, fair hair that drifted like stringy kelp. His—a penis appeared plainly between fleshy white thighs—big eyes flared above downturned nostrils, which crowned puffy, pouty pink lips. He had at least two chins at the bottom of his pinchable baby face, a circle on top of the circle formed by his baby Buddha belly. Floating in an unknown clear fluid, he was an enormous infant, at least fifteen feet head to toe, fat, naked, happy, and connected to a room full of machines.

God?

Pop! goes the weasel.

He was a white male. This much aligned with Lily's expectations. She wondered why she was in the room alone, why no one operated the machines or fed data to the slots. Looking up from the tank with the giant baby inside, she realized what the big round thing hanging from the ceiling was: a mobile. Shapes dangled at intervals from its room-spanning circumference. She tried to look at them instead of at the tank, but she couldn't stop checking and double-checking to make sure she wasn't imagining it, or being tricked by the light, or otherwise experiencing an aberration among aberrations. The baby boy was not all boy. He had the legs and penis and torso and arms and head, but he had more, too, on the part of the body turned away from Lily, extending from the back side—a tail. The white baby boy who might have been God had a tail, a long greenish-brown lizard tail, like the Komodo. It curled lazily, not disturbing the tubes and wires.

The mobile included a wolf, bird, and lizard. It had a green man and a red woman. It had a symbol Lily didn't recognize. It spun at a speed befitting the too-slow nursery song, which was on a new verse or repeating the first, Lily couldn't tell. She thought mulberry bushes had red berries, but she couldn't decide whether that had any meaning. She had a machine gun and thought about God. The glass looked thick. She didn't know whether she could shoot through it. Why was she in the room alone?

Lily tried to imagine *this* God making a bet with Satan. Giant babies in tanks full of strange fluid did not fit the traditional gambler profile, but she had no sense of Satan, either. He might have been a flea in a matchbox. But fleas and babies could communicate. They might exchange DNA through a bite, instructions encoded in adenine, cytosine, guanine, and thymine, "Hast thou considered my servant Job?" spelled out in a subtitle with A, C, G, and T beneath an image from either *2001* or *Solaris*, science fiction movies with great baby punchlines.

The monkey chased the weasel.

Yes, the monkey was chasing the weasel, just like the three blind mice were chasing the farmer's wife. The mice got their tails cut off and the weasel went *pop!* Weasels had tails. The God-baby had a tail. Variously short and thin or long, poofed, and furious, weasel tails did not pop, as far as Lily knew. Immersed in fluid, a weasel's tail-fur might float like the God-baby's kelpy down, but it wouldn't look rough like the Komodo extension from God-baby's backside. The bumpy, hard-looking tail contrasted so completely with the soft newborn skin, rendered softer but not pruned by the liquid, that it discomfited, looking ill-matched, rousing suspicion of Franken-stitchery except that side-views revealed patches where pudgy white transitioned to scaly green-brown. Tail met God-baby in smooth bio-blend. Separating them would take a farmer's wife, or a carving knife, not a fortuitous pop.

The monkey thought 'twas all in fun.

The words were really coming back to her now! But who was she? In the song, what part did she play? She knew she was a mouse; that song was easy because it had meant so much for so long. But this song was pure puzzle, no personal resonance. Codes and puzzles, cryptic messages and obscure connections —all in fun? She thought she might pop. Which would make *her* the weasel...

Delusions of grandeur! One moment God-baby was the weasel, and the next moment, she was. In another moment, she would confuse herself with God, and what other meaning could she really give to Young Torrents saying, "This place was for you," other than to think that she was a, if not the, organizing principle for reality? And what better name existed for such a principle than God?

Pop! goes the weasel.

The room's endless metallic panels had to offer an interface with God-baby that worked. Among the lights and slots and buttons and knobs, a microphone had to exist to capture her voice and pipe it into God-baby's receptors. After examining a full wall, Lily decided to look backward, starting at tubes and wires along one side of the tank and following them to the backs of the panels where they originated. None of the lines went into God-baby's head, but they at least went *in*, so they suggested communication of some sort. Lily needed access.

Tubes went into large cylinders, metal barrels, attached to panels dominated by dials with arrowheaded pointers providing readings Lily related to pressure and volume. The clues suggested liquid—tubes transferred liquid from the cylinders to God-baby—but Lily couldn't think of enough liquids to account for the number of tubes. How many liquids could a God-baby need, especially if, as Lily suspected, the fluid suspension in which God-baby floated was at least close to amniotic? She wondered whether one of the cylinders might be full of angel suffering and, if so, what the other ones might contain. Trying to count the tubes was hard—ten? Twelve? Each might feed a divine appetite. If cancer made an appetite for suffering, what might satisfy the appetite born from heavenly AIDS?

Kill God.

All around the mulberry bush.

Lily imagined God-baby out of the tank and crawling— even at fifteen feet long, he looked proportionately too little to crawl, but she imagined it—circles around a bush with reddish berries.

Here we go round the mulberry bush.

That was a different song, wasn't it?

David said something about her world ending. Not with a bang but a—

Lily chased God around the tree, and she caught up to him by stomping on his tail. He yowled, and dark clouds rolled in on a sky deep red-violet like mulberry. God shrieked and wailed, but no one answered. Lily pinned down his tail with one foot while she brought the other down on a pudgy leg, which slipped beneath her, fat rolls making bone hard to target, but she found purchase with a second stomp and snapped the calf in two. Now pinning a leg, she transferred from tail to thigh, then from calf to the other thigh, and stomped her way up the inarticulate, howling God's infant form, leaving shoeprints in impressionable skin and pressing on pliable bone until it gave way beneath her weight. She found the ribcage springy, the head a sponge. God became mush beneath her. Or so she imagined.

She still wanted to talk to him. Following the wires from God's body to the panels led her to buttons and lights but nothing she pressed to avail. Nothing opened a channel she could follow. She could not talk to God, and God could not listen. The only connections between God and the world of his contractors in 1500 Spring were the tubes and wires, and despite appearances, connection did not mean communication.

Lily studied the top of God-baby's tank. If it had a lid, she might pull it open and drop in a hairdryer, plugged in and whirring, which could shock God to infinity. The tank's top, however, looked like solid glass. God-baby had no way in or out. Tubes and wires, tubes and wires.

Lily knew what she had to do.

Upon the realization, she expected the room to react, for sawblades to roll out from the walls and lasers to shoot from the ceiling—or something else—signifying the triggering of defenses that had detected, like so many others, the flow of Lily's thoughts. Why was God defenseless? Just by being here, he'd won. Nietzsche was wrong. God was alive and well, at least for now, and tubed up at the top of a skyscraping pyramid scheme, sucking on suffering composed of suffering, humans feeding angels feeding him, floors above a cold cosmos and floating in indifference. God won. He should have been living like an emperor in triumph, surrounded by armies and splendor. God *always* won. The bet with Satan—he *knew* he was going to win. Satan probably knew, too. It was *pro forma*. For God, everything was *pro forma*.

So Lily, what's the advantage in winning?

Excuse me?

If it's all pro forma, *what's the advantage in winning?*

She wanted the voice asking these questions to be God's, but it sounded like her own. Come again?

Why bother winning when the outcome is inevitable, when the game is only for show? It's pointless.

So what, you'd rather lose?

...

What is it?

...

ANSWER ME!

...

Well?

Kill God.

Growing up, Lily had heard religious people talk about unforgiveable sins, of which the Christians typically listed only one or two. One of them was blasphemy, giving God the old Fuck You. The folks who talked about blasphemy would also prefer to visualize their God as an adult with a big bushy beard and sandals, not rolls of baby fat and naked little nubs for toes. To contend with God as God-baby, however unintentionally, was already a blasphemy, a Fuck You to God's Blessed Patriarchy, so in that respect, Lily was screwed.

The other unforgiveable sin was suicide. In a sense,

suicide was a blasphemy, for if life was God's gift, and the human was made in God's image, and so on, then suicide was worse than regifting your best friend's self-portrait—it was throwing the portrait in your best friend's bonfire. Lily was beginning to see another sinful possibility in suicide, though. God-baby was trapped in his little tank, which suggested he was Omnipotent Except, Omnipotent Minus One. Minus at least one, but one appeared to Lily loud and clear—

Kill God.

God couldn't kill himself. It was an old problem, wasn't it? If God is omnipotent, can he create a boulder that he can't lift? Can he kill himself? If the answer was no, then a person who committed suicide was doing what God couldn't, and that really had to piss God off. Suicide was rubbing God's impotence in God's face, and that had to be unforgiveable. Until now, suicide had been more powerful than God, but now God was evening the score with all the suicides, and Lily had a role to play.

That's what you brought me here to do, isn't it? I'm the suicide who evens things out. From the beginning, that was your plan. You gave me the motive. You killed, and you killed, and you took and you took, so much taking that it went beyond coincidence and became cosmic, evidence of your foot on my neck, and I believed in you. I don't know when I started, but I believed in you, at which point you gave me the opportunity. You *lured* me to this building and all this... strangeness. You made me think I was losing my mind! But this building is a door, *your* door, and everything I've done here was the way to get through. And now you're giving me the means. You can't kill yourself, but I can kill you. I can kill God because God wants me to do it. That's the answer to all my questions! That's why I'm here! I am God's instrument! I AM GOD'S SUICIDE!

Lily crossed through the room, oblivious to the blinking lights and useless buttons, and knelt by the tubes and wires that passed through holes in the tank and entered God's body. In both hands she grabbed a tube, thick and heavy like a firehose, and got a feeling for its weight in her arms. With as firm a grip as she could muster, she pulled. Inside the tank, God drifted toward the glass near her, but he did not collide. Fluid made his movement slow, his weight magnificent. Lily realized she was tugging at the inert mass of existence's origin.

Heave-ho! Heave-ho! Heave-ho!

She used all her muscle and weight to lift the tube away from the glass, and it came, slack drawing out. God-baby closed on the glass until he bumped against it without a sound. Panting, Lily walked herself along the tube's length, pulling hard with every step, until she could brace her feet against the glass, and she pulled more, aware that no more slack remained to contract, that now she pulled on the connection of the tube to God's body, against the point where it fastened into flesh between his ribs. All the cells in her body protested; she lacked the strength to continue; she continued. Legs and arms, hands and feet cooperated: she pulled. Inside the tank, something tore, and a glob of white tissue floated away from the joint of tube with body. Lily yanked, and flesh released the tube. More tissue escaped, but neither God's body nor the tube released a spray of different color into the tank's clear liquid. God drifted back, released, and Lily fell down, no tension to maintain her position braced against the glass. Scrambling, she pulled the tube more, finding it easier now, until it slipped away from the hole in the glass. Fluid followed it; the tank began a steady leak.

God might have tried suicide once before. If he sent his kid to die, and his kid was actually God incarnate, then that was a kind of suicide. Jesus Christ committed a kind of suicide by cop, and who was Lily compared to the Romans? Pulling a plug was hardly a crucifixion, and crucifixion hadn't worked. She watched the fluid spill from the tank.

Wires on the ground called to her. She grabbed one and

pulled. She grabbed another. Resistance was less. She tried another tube, and though it didn't yield as easily as the wires, it yielded. Tufts of tissue floated about like fish food in the tank, but the tubes and wires spat nothing into the liquid. No clues suggested the purpose of connections between tubes and wires and God's body, and unlike Christ on the Cross, this God did not bleed. The fluid spilling from the holes that had allowed tubes and wires access to God's body remained clear as it covered the floor and dampened Lily's tennis shoes. With all the machinery around, Lily again thought of electrocution— the wires she'd pulled free of divine flesh lay exposed—but she saw no sparks. The room was large enough for the water not to rise to her ankles. It dissipated as the tank's level dropped. Lily imagined it leaking out under the door with the gold placard that said "God." It would go down the hall to the elevator. It might pour down through the elevator and create a waterfall over the side of the building, a brief spout crossing through the sunlight. She imagined a rainbow commemorating God's death.

As the tank emptied, the fluid inside began to circle, and with it, God-baby spun. The whirl of water embarrassed Lily, who tried to think of Charybdis or something else lofty but could only think of a toilet. She was flushing God. She even tried joking with herself about babies and bathwater, but then she saw God's long lizard tail, incongruous next to his cute chubby body, and thought again of flushing some critter down the toilet. God-baby swirled. The water level dropped.

With his mouth exposed to the tank's emptiness, God-baby finally reacted to his environment's changes. The puffy, pouty pink lips formed O's and E's, working the atmosphere as if it would deliver necessities into the God-baby mouth. Lily recognized the desperation of a fish out of water: God was suffocating. Whatever the fluid was, God needed it to breathe. God's sustenance was spilling out at Lily's feet. She supposed she knew that already; she knew she was killing him when she pulled the plugs.

Inside the tank, giant baby arms and legs flailed, but they registered no impact against the thick glass walls. The baby face went from reddish to blue, and the big eyes got bigger and veiny. A soft tongue protruded. The entire body became discolored at a pace Lily found alarming.

Overhead, the mobile spun. Underfoot, liquid sloshed. In the tank, against which Lily leaned, looking, a giant baby lay dead.

Pop! goes the weasel.

9

After the song's last pop, the mobile stopped spinning. The blinking lights synchronized, giving the room a slow strobe. The tank stopped pouring liquid onto the floor, leaving God's corpse to marinate in a reservoir beneath the empty holes where the tubes and wires had been. For a moment, Lily experienced quiet of a kind she hadn't yet known, stillness, a vacuum. She recognized that she wasn't breathing and heard David telling her that breathing was an illusion. That was okay. She wouldn't miss it, and she wouldn't miss God, either. He wouldn't be back in three days. She had a feeling about it, and her feelings kept turning out to be right.

A mechanical noise, a familiar motor with a medium-pitched grind, tap, and whir, interrupted the quiet. The sound came from the past and belonged to the look of a lot of the buttons and slots on the metallic panels, like a computer screen on an interstellar spaceship in an old movie, with a big block cursor and square green type, except—it was a printer. Even if she hadn't worked for a printing company, Lily was old enough for the term "dot matrix" to appear in her mind, but it came with immediate pondering of how many years younger a person would have to be for that term to have no meaning. She followed the sound to the ancient machine that the term signified, and she saw the boxy shape on the corner of a desk. Gear-like tractors grabbed paper by the hole-punched strips on its sides and fed it across the cylindrical roller as the printhead darted back and forth, poking out letters in changing configurations of inked points.

Dear Ms. Lily Henshaw:

We have received your payment and are delighted to inform you that it will serve as the final entry on your account. Under separate cover, you will receive a DEED OF OWNERSHIP. You will also receive a packet of information describing the RIGHTS AND PRIVILEGES that may be associated with any living person(s) listed in your DEED.

This message concludes your business with Mansworth Futures and Securities. Please avoid any further activities on our premises at 1500 Spring Street, as your access there has expired.

The entire MFS team thanks you for your business and hopes you will call on us again should you ever have a similar concern.

Sincerely,

The Mansworth Family

The paper spooled out enough for Lily to tear off a sheet at the perforation where it attached, zigzag, to another sheet, a design that would feed the dot matrix until the end of the ream. The hole-punched sides of the paper also detached along perforated lines so that when Lily had done all the detaching, a normal-looking sheet of paper remained. Lily reread it when it was normal-looking and still didn't know what to make of it. The first paragraph was a stunner because it seemed to mean, in context, that killing God paid her debt, which had been, she thought, more or less, to God... but maybe having MFS as the middlemen changed the debt structure. Or something.

She couldn't really think about the DEED bit. What exactly did she own? Herself? Her life? And if it was her life, had she spoiled its value by killing herself? Had she burned down her house right before making her last mortgage payment?

It was undoubtedly a Catch-22. They would never give her the deed if she were actually alive.

The second paragraph struck her as most important. It seemed like the main point, and the rest of the letter could have been camouflage: MFS, or at least someone, was done with her and wanted her to move along. If she tried the front doors right now, they'd open. MFS wanted her out. But why?

Lily looked back in the direction of dead God, who was hard to see from this angle. Had MFS known that God brought Lily here to be his suicide? David had come here; the suicides came here. Coming here was a feature of Crazy Time, or Collection Time, or whatever. MFS hadn't necessarily known— and the more Lily thought about it, the more she believed they *didn't* know—that Lily had a different purpose. Maybe they had never even expected her to make it to 60.

Lily had a wild notion, and she decided to test it. Shoes squelching on the wet floor, she made for the door with the gold God placard, and she exited down the hall. The elevator door opened as she approached, and although she didn't fully expect him, she wasn't surprised that Young Torrents stood waiting inside. "Good afternoon," Young said. "I'm to take you to a meeting downstairs."

"Come here," Lily said. "I want to show you something first."

Young did not move. "I appreciate your desire to show me something, but I have one purpose, and that's to guide you to this meeting."

"I thought my business was done here and that I should avoid further activities," Lily said.

"What? Oh, I see. Please avoid further activities on the premises *after* this meeting. That letter was meant to be presented to you at the meeting. Early delivery was an error. We are having technical difficulties." Young brushed the lapels of his double-breasted jacket.

"Young, you don't sound like yourself." Lily mustered her best *come hither* look. "Let me show you this one thing, and then I'll come to the meeting."

"Please get in the elevator," Young said.

Lily reached toward the elevator and slid a finger between young's jacket and shirt. She gave him a tug, playful but not too lascivious, and said, "Are you stuck in the elevator?"

"No."

"But you can't follow me down the hall." She stepped down the hall to demonstrate the ease of doing so.

"No."

Dropping all seductive pretext, which wasn't working anyway, Lily said, "No you can't follow me, or no you can, but —"

"No, I can't."

"Why not?"

"We're not allowed on 60. Nobody is." Young gulped.

Lily felt satisfied. She'd moved beyond Mansworth's ken, Mansworth knew it, and now she knew it. "You at least know God's dead, right?"

"Yes, we know," Young said. "And if you would please come to the meeting—"

"Maybe I'll come," she said. "But I want to see what happens if you try to come out here first. Take a step, will you?" She moved toward him and beckoned.

"Please," Young said. "This is absurd."

"It could be gruesome. You might explode. I've seen

weirder things. Come on. What if I pull you out?" She closed the rest of the distance between them, ready to grab his arm instead of his jacket and to tug much harder, but he grabbed her t-shirt and yanked. Loss of balance made her stumble, adding momentum to the force of Young's pull so that she careened into the elevator car, stopping only when she smacked into the glass overlooking the city. As her eyes began to make out buildings etched in late afternoon, Young's reflection loomed behind her, and something cracked against the back of her skull.

Darkness. Blurriness. Light.

Lily felt like she did regaining consciousness in the hospital after one of her surgeries. The feeling wasn't like normal waking up because she started from too far away, with too much darkness between her and the room ahead. She heard the voices in the room, felt like she should have understood what they were saying, like she even did on some level, but she couldn't quite hold the meaning in her mind from one moment to the next. Gradually, though, the room came closer, and the light got brighter. Very bright, in fact, and very white. It was a familiar light, grandiose, shimmering and silvered, multiplied in reflections off a hundred surfaces in a great shining hall.

Lily lay on the side of the broad pedestal supporting "Love," the glass sculpture of orbs clustered together like atoms or planets in the cosmos. With her head drifting left and right, she saw the sprays of flowers, and she thought—hadn't this place been *for her*, and if her account was closed, shouldn't it be gone? At the very least it might be buried in lava....

Men in business suits, almost all of them single-breasted, stood in an oval to one side of the sculpture. Lily had a difficult angle but counted fourteen men, plus Young, who stood away from the oval, closer to Lily. "She's awake," Young said. He sounded more certain than Lily felt.

The men in the oval clapped. Lily needed a moment to accept that they clapped because Young had informed him of her waking state.

"I'm sorry," Young said, "about the violence, but I wasn't sure you would attend the meeting otherwise. We needed you to be here, and as you know, violence is useful."

Lily noticed the gun lying next to her, still strapped. It was an appendage now.

"I think you'll find that you're not actually hurt. I'll explain it to you, but it has to do with life and death and could take a little while." Young looked at his watch and out at the impending sunset.

"Don't bother," Lily said. "I'm good."

"Do you know *why* we need to speak with you, Ms. Henshaw?" one of the men said. They all looked similar, with similar builds filling similar suits, except their hair ranged from dusty blond to dark brown. Lily wasn't going to remember which shade of hair said what. Someone had ironed out their faces. They had unusually flat faces.

"No," Lily said. "It probably has something to do with killing God." For some reason she thought of Tobias, frozen in the air near the mezzanine. Was he breathing? Lily wasn't breathing. God had suffocated.

"You needn't look so contrite, Ms. Henshaw," another man said. "We're not here to scold you."

Unaware that she'd appeared contrite, Lily sat up on the pedestal, not looking at the light-bending sculpture. She wished she had a moment to brush her hair. "I have a gun," she said. "Don't scold me."

"You're quite right Ms. Henshaw, and we'd hate for you to shoot us." One man made this statement, another said "Here, here!," and others voiced agreement in sundry fashions.

Becoming more energized, Lily tilted her head to one side and pointed the machine gun at Young. "Why are they being so conciliating?"

"Perhaps if you'd let them talk with fewer interruptions, Lily Henshaw, you would reach a better understanding?"

"You're annoying," Lily said. Why did annoying forces keep entering her life? Possibly, if she pulled the trigger on the machine gun, she would lose control of it completely. Additionally or alternately, she could guide bullets into all the glistening glass around her, creating a shatter symphony, the "Love" sculpture a centerpiece, exploding in a bursting glitter of diamond dust. The men would be a pile, and she could march out—where?—into the future. "Talk," she said.

"Ms. Henshaw, there's a clause in our contract that we have to discuss with you," one of the men in the oval said.

"More than one, actually," another said.

"The first, and I'm sure my colleagues agree, involves our responsibility in the wake of your recent decision." Many voiced assent after one voiced this statement.

"This responsibility," another said, "involves overseeing the placement for the position left open by your actions."

Lily waited for a follow-up statement, but none came. For clarification, she asked, "Is it an open search?" She knew the discourse of Human Resources. Well, she supposed they needn't, and perhaps shouldn't, be seeking a human... the giant baby with a lizard tail wasn't human per se... but the same general principles had to apply, hadn't they? Human Resources, Heavenly Resources, whatever. Sometimes she got a little bogged down in the language of things.

"We think it should be," one of the men said. "What do you think?"

Lily had to concentrate. She felt like she was at a job interview. "It would depend on the search methodology and the availability of people with the right qualifications, I suppose," Lily said.

"You're right, of course," a man said.

"We need to address another one of the contract's clauses," another man said.

"Yes," a man agreed.

"Wait," Lily said. "Is it an open search, or isn't it?"

"The other clause," another man said, "obliges us to consider a kind of... internal candidate."

"Oh, good gracious!" one of the men shouted. He turned to Young. "Is she toying with us?"

"No," Young said. "I don't think so. We're old friends now."

"It's true," Lily said, looking at Young. "We've bonded. And I'd totally toy with you if I knew what any of this was about." Then, looking at the oval of men, she knew. "Wait a minute. It's me, isn't it?"

Half the men in the oval looked down at their feet, but the other half nodded. Young smiled. Lily remembered a video game called *God of War*. The goal of the game was to kill the god of war to become the new one. So, this was kind of like that, except more Judeo-Christian and a little less hack-and-slash. Lily was heir apparent. She was the new... God.

Delusions... of... yeah.

Wasn't I supposed to be on the *left*-hand path? Where's my *Satan*-ex-machina? Somebody has got to step in here.

"Don't you think," Lily said to the men, "that a suicide is a pretty bad choice for God? That I'm disqualified or something?"

"There's no rule against it," a man said, "and there's the argument that, since you've already done it, you're less likely to do it again, which makes you a safer bet than the last God."

"The last God—wait a minute, how many have there been?" Lily asked.

"Just one," a man said.

"Oh," Lily said. "Why do you think I wouldn't do it again?"

"You tell us," a man said. "What are your views on suicide now?"

Lily considered. "To be honest, I don't think it really solves anything. I can't say I'm any better off."

"You see! There's a moral to the story! You're enlightened now."

"Still," Lily said. "I'm not much of a role model."

"Well," a man said. "There's another option."

"Oh?" Lily felt the real sell coming on, the path they wanted her to follow. Were they underestimating her because of sexism, or...? She couldn't think of another reason for them to underestimate her. Any explanation for underestimation would be depressing.

"You could just... say no," a man said.

"Just say no?" Lily covered her smile with a polite hand. She hadn't seen the oval of white, suited, flat-faced men as Reaganite until now.

"You don't want to be God, do you? It's like being President. Nobody really *wants* that job! Well, not very many people, anyway." The man who made this statement had a more convincing voice than the others.

Lily recalled considering the possibility of God's existence and imagining how annoyed God must feel having to listen to billions of people praying for petty things. The idea made being God unattractive. Then she considered the last person who had the job, an oversized baby with a reptile appendage. If a baby could do it... then again, how could she know what was really going on inside that oversized soft-skulled head? Maybe it comprehended infinities. Would she automatically comprehend infinities if she elected to be God, or would that come on gradually? Or would it never come on at all—would she have to govern existence as-is? The as-is option was unthinkable. It made her want to opt out of existence right now.

"Let's talk terms," Lily said.

The men looked confused. Young said, "I think they need to know what sort of terms you mean. The terms for what, exactly?"

"You all don't want me to have the job. That's obvious."

"How's that?" a man said.

"You're transparent," Lily said.

"I see."

Lily was on her feet. Her head felt fine. She crossed toward the oval and set a hand on a man's shoulder. "In fact, I know some of what you think before you think it."

The man looked in her eyes and looked away. "You do?"

"What you just thought?" she said. "I knew about that."

"I believe you," he said.

"I know."

He coughed. "What sort of terms did you have in mind?"

"I don't know," Lily said, crossing to another man. "I don't know what you can do."

Tobias in the lobby, locusts in her bedroom. "We can't do much," the man said. "We represent our clients."

A man elsewhere in the oval said, "What he means is, our agency works through representation. Our powers derive from contractual relations with clients."

Lily tapped her sneaker on the floor. "So, what you're saying is, you can't do squat without God."

"Or another client!" a man said. "But in this case, we are referring to our biggest client, so, um, yes, we can't do squat without... God."

"We're not exactly *powerless*," a man said.

"Shh!" a man said.

"What he means is, it's not that we come to the table empty-handed," a man said.

"What have you got?" Lily asked. Her shirt was clean and clinging to her in a flattering way. She felt good about it.

"We could put you somewhere," a man said.

"Put me somewhere?" Lily imagined a giant hand placing her on a cloudy mountaintop.

A man cleared his throat. "Where would you like to go? We have access to many desirable locations."

Lily wondered what desirable locations they couldn't access.

"How about Tahiti?" a man said.

"Isn't it about to be hurricane season?" a man asked.

"In Tahiti?" a man responded.

"I think so," a man said.

"It could be an adventure," a man posited.

"What do *you* think of Tahiti, Lily?" a man asked.

"I have no interest in Tahiti," Lily said.

"Scratch Tahiti, then," a man said.

"Any other ideas?" a man asked.

"I know," a man said. "Disney World!"

"In Florida?" someone asked.

Lily exclaimed, "You've killed God, so what are you going to do now? I'm going to Disney World!"

The men looked at her. "You're interested?"

"No."

"You're being difficult, Ms. Henshaw," a man said.

"We're not the Make-A-Wish Foundation," a man said. "We can't take you to meet a celebrity."

"No, celebrity meetings are out," a man said.

"Why?" Lily asked.

"I'll explain it to you, but it has to do with life and death and could take a little while." Young, suddenly standing near the position Lily had taken within the oval, looked at his watch and out at the impending sunset.

"I can wait," Lily said.

"You're dead. You can't interact with the living," a man said.

"That's it? I'm, like, a ghost?" Lily frowned at Young. "That didn't take very long."

"I guess not," Young said.

"You're all ghosts?" Lily asked.

"Uh-oh," Young said.

"Heavens, no!" a man said. "I'll have to tell my wife that one."

A man said, "You know that thing some guy said about death and taxes? He was oversimplifying. He meant death and bureaucracy, except death is actually a form of bureaucracy."

"It's a job creator," a man said.

"The dead don't need jobs," a man said. "Consider yourself retired. Early! It's a dream for some."

"You know what?" Lily said. "Nevermind. Just stop talking."

"We'll stop talking if you sign over your claim to Godhood," a man said.

Impulsive, Lily crossed to his place in the oval and slapped him. He cowered, and the rest of the oval looked stunned. No one budged from his position. "You know I want more than that!" Lily said. "Don't waste my time!" The impulsive behavior felt awesome. These men were barely men, so the transition from having mechanical conversation with them to bullying them felt like a natural slide. They were higher-level, animated meat mannequins, and somehow, they belonged to her.

"Okay!" a man from a different part of the oval said.

"Lily Henshaw, please refrain from attacking the gentlemen," Young said.

"No," Lily replied.

The men whispered to one another. "We'd like to repeat a question: what do you want?"

Lily considered and said, "You took something from me. Returning what you took should be within your power."

More whispers. "What did you have in mind?"

Lily said, "You took Burt Wells, and you wrapped him in plastic, and you...."

"We didn't kill him," a man said. "I heard someone told you we didn't."

"Someone told me," Lily said.

"Then you know he's one of you," a man said. He whispered, "A *self-destroyer*."

"I don't see how that's possible."

"Don't you?" The man looked as if he would reach out to

Lily in reassurance, but he didn't.

"I suppose so," Lily said. "But that doesn't explain the plastic coating. Or the letter opener in the eye."

"Even so, I scarcely see your point," a man said.

"YOU PLAYED A PART!!!" Lily stomped her foot and waved her gun in the air.

"We can't bring a man back to life. Not without our client. And even then...." A man shrugged.

"I'm not *asking* you to bring him back to life," Lily said.

"Psst," Young whispered. "You haven't asked them anything."

She hadn't, and she now knew the request: "I'd like to walk out the front door with Burt." After a pause, she added, "As ghosts, or, whatever."

Intense whispering transpired within the oval. "And by stepping out the front door, you solemnly affirm that you forswear all claim to Godhood?"

Lily looked at the fourteen men in the oval, and she looked at Young Torrents. "I do so affirm."

"Then Ms. Lily Henshaw, we have a bargain."

10

The tubes and wires connecting Burt to the machines that surrounded his bed reminded Lily first of David, waiting for medicine and law to pull the plug, and then of God, waiting for Lily to do the same. Lily tried to imagine a werewolf God with a lizard tail, but the image wouldn't cohere. God was not becoming David, and David was not becoming God, not even in her head. Sometimes a coincidence is just a coincidence.

Young Torrents stood in the elevator car holding the door open. The elevator was neither Executive Express nor the glass wonder that served the upper floors. It was a regular affair that had shuttled them from 24 down to 3, all of which was the building's infirmary. An entire floor dedicated to such purposes in an office building would once have struck Lily as odd, but as she looked at Burt, who was, by most recent accounts, a suicide, and saw him registering a steady pulse with other vitals she couldn't decipher on machines a corporate skyscraper had no reason to possess, she felt mildly grateful and otherwise relieved that a kind of normalcy was presiding. A nurse, who wore a cute white hat like nurses wore in old soap operas and was likely in her seventies, was removing the tubes and wires, swabbing the spots where they'd affected Burt, and sealing them with bandages. Young, standing in the elevator because 3, like 60, was a forbidden zone, did not look impatient, so Lily felt impatient for him. The septuagenarian nurse was very careful with the holes the tubes and wires left in Burt's skin. Lily snickered about holey ghosts.

The infirmary had more full than empty beds. Each occupied bed seemed to have an attending nurse, so the staffing was impressive. One patient looked mummified, wrapped in gauze, leaving gender to the imagination; machines appeared to do the breathing and feeding. Two other patients looked well enough aside from being severely stoned. Others had difficult-to-identify problems. Lily wondered whether survivors from the Scarcity massacre showed up here. She thought of asking.

Burt's slacks and t-shirt lay folded beside his bed. The shirt was his copy of what Lily wore, Tobias's purchase from The Gift Shop. She imagined these clothes as their uniforms for eternity. MFS had branded them. She should have negotiated for wardrobe and other perks. The men in the oval probably could have provided. The negotiation was all a whirlwind.

The truth was that they knew she didn't want the job, and she wanted to leave, too, so she was lucky to get anything. They could have called her bluff. Burt was a gift. Why? Maybe a thank you for killing God. Maybe they liked the old deity, so they were glad he got the release he wanted. They sure didn't *seem* glad during the negotiation. Underneath that oval, Lily had sensed a rising panic. But maybe. Better yet, maybe she shouldn't question their decision to return Burt. Maybe the why didn't matter.

Burt's eyes were already open. Both of them. His face bore no evidence of any puncture; his body bore no trace of any burn. Lily remembered having a sore wrist from the IV after her surgeries. That kind of problem would be Burt's only remainder from physical death. Lily looked at her wrists and saw no remainders from the letter opener.

"Hey," Burt said. His voice was firm and casual. "Is 'where am I' an okay first thing to say?" The nurse stepped away from the bed and started shutting down machines.

Lily laughed. She didn't know if she meant it. She also didn't know how to answer the question. "We're at 1500 Spring Street. In the infirmary. What do you remember?"

"Very weird dreams." Burt looked at her. He shook his head. "They weren't dreams." He paused. "I'm dead, huh?"

"Me, too," Lily said.

"Huh," Burt said.

She smiled and slid up his hospital gown to pat a bare knee. "It's a lot to take in."

"That tickles," he said. "And the funny thing is, it's not so much. To take in. I mean it is, of course, but it isn't."

"I think I get you," Lily said. In the elevator, Young coughed. He did not *look* impatient, but she wondered. "You want to get out of here?"

Burt looked at his pile of clothes and pointed to the side of his bed. "Would you mind pulling that curtain over there?"

With Burt dressed, Lily escorted him to the elevator, where Young checked them over before allowing the door to close. Young pressed the button for the lobby and said, "We won't see each other again."

"Goodbye," Burt said.

Young grimaced, and Lily decided she had heard genuine lamentation in the suit-wearing man's voice. "Will you miss us?" Lily asked. "Haven't we been a disruption?"

"With adversity comes opportunity," Young said. "Interdepartmental communication has not always been an area of excellence here at Mansworth. Not all of us are equally knowledgeable about our clients' activities. This circumstance sometimes puts us at odds with ourselves, as we don't always see our ways clearly to achieving the best possible outcomes when we don't know the primary goals or the means already in use. However, this tension can end up being productive, and

I'm sure it will in this case. I was and am very familiar with the facts of this case. I will return to it many times. You, however, can never come back to us."

"I understand that," Lily said.

"No, my dear, you don't," Young said. The elevator arrived at the lobby, and the doors opened. "I stop here. Goodbye, then. You have been… distinctive."

Lily and Burt stepped out of the elevator, and Lily pivoted to return the goodbye. As she did, the doors closed, and she saw grief on Young's face. He disappeared before she could speak.

"What was that?" Burt asked.

"I don't know," Lily said. She took a few steps away from the bank of elevators and faced the lobby, already falling into shadow as sunset took hold. "Do you believe this?"

The quiet in the high-ceilinged, high-columned lobby space made it feel more massive and abandoned than the paucity of people, who did appear walking, here and there, but not in the thronging masses that earlier in the day had formed congested arteries with predetermined flows. "After five o'clock," Burt said.

"I wouldn't expect it to make such a difference," Lily said. She walked further into the lobby, until she had a view of the mezzanine. Scarcity looked closed. Wasn't it usually open for dinner? Maybe it was lunch-only on weekdays. Tobias was gone. The escalators weren't moving. The quality of light was yellowish-orange.

The Gift Shop and the café were closed. Over by the ATM, a woman appeared to be asking a man for the time. Lily wondered whether the woman had a phone or other gadget that told time and didn't feel like checking, or if she really lacked the information. The woman's skirt-suit and small purse made laying odds a challenge. Who didn't have a phone these days, and what sort of phone wouldn't tell time?

Lily didn't have her phone. Moreover, if she asked that man what time it was, would he even hear her? Was he... alive? She didn't know if you could tell by looking.

"Come on, Lily, that door is wide open," Burt said. He pointed to one of the regular doors beside the revolving doors, and it was, indeed, propped wide. She let Burt guide her toward it. By the open doorway, she stopped at a trashcan, lifted the strap from her shoulder, and threw away the machine gun.

Lily didn't know what sort of outside to expect. It turned out to be a warm late day in the city, bright afternoon faded with sun nestling behind skyline and sinking beyond view. Construction was still happening up and down Spring Street, the ongoing revival in the area's higher-end real estate market. The sound of a jackhammer beat over the brakes, horns, and engines jammed into streets serving residential areas. A restaurant fried something delectable.

Nearby, two men, one in a brown leather bomber jacket and one in an army-green coat, stood in conversation. For a moment, they held Lily's attention.

"See something?" Burt asked.

A light changed at a nearby crosswalk, and Lily said, "Nothing that matters anymore. Keep moving." They crossed with a group of people, no one talking, and kept walking on the other side, putting another block between them and 1500. When the ground shook, they turned, and the spectacle was silent: as the building trembled, its hundreds of windows exploded, each of them launching a man's suited body into the air. Some men carried briefcases, some of which opened, scattering papers that fluttered into the air, but some men had empty hands that clutched at nothing as bodies plummeted stories upon stories toward hard-paved ground.

Had the spectacle not been silent, the bodies' landing,

picking up steadily like a giant lumbering hail, would have sounded horrific, but the image from her angle struck Lily as a spurt from a human sprinkler, people for droplets, and without sight or sound of bodies' landing did not disturb her much.

Done sprinkling, the building collapsed into dust, leaving a hole in the skyline. Dust covered everything.

Too late to escape the dust cloud, Lily and Burt moved away from 1500 Spring, Lily leading them. She didn't know where she led until she saw the high fences, and she recognized the man on the bench.

Brushing away dust, Burt said, "Isn't that…?"

"That's Vince," Lily said. "He comes here sometimes to watch the sunset."

"Hi, Vince!" Burt called.

"He won't hear you," Lily said.

"I know," Burt said. "At least I think I do." Burt watched Vince for a moment. "Doesn't he look like he's staring straight at it?"

Lily tipped her head. "At the sun?"

"No. At 1500 Spring. At where it used to be—at the cloud that's there now."

"Maybe," Lily said. "Or somewhere nearby."

"You'd think that if he just saw a building collapse, he wouldn't look so calm," Burt said. Burt also seemed calm.

Lily took Burt's hands and made him face her instead of Vince. On one side of them, the fence, the dog park, and their old co-worker, and on the other side, the city skyline with the sun sinking behind it: they faced each other and held hands. "Burt," she said, "I don't think he saw the building collapse. I think we saw it collapse because we can never go back, and since we can never go back, it doesn't need to be there anymore, not for us."

"Are those the rules, then? Have you got this one figured out?" Burt grinned.

Lily turned their attention to Vince. "I'm more concerned about the rules for him. He's... I mean, what if I actually *killed* his God? Is that what actually happened here? For Vince, this sunset is about God, and he has no idea God suffocated to death because I—"

"Lily, people are working on it. It's not your problem." Burt pushed her hair away from her eyes and went back to holding hands.

"MFS? Working on it? Those motherfuckers—"

"Look at Vince. He's okay so far, I think," Burt said.

Lily looked at Vince. He looked fine. She looked at the city's backlit, orange-edged profile. For her, it had a gap, but for Vince, it probably didn't. Who was to say which of them harbored the more frightening illusions?

"It's funny," Lily said, "that the skyline still looks okay without 1500 Spring. To us it looks wrong, and it'll take some getting used to, but looking up, I can see lines and designs and correspondences among the buildings, like everything was planned to be together, not needing anything in particular to be in the spot that's just a cloud right now. Vince talked about the skyline when we came down here. Said something about history happening in the present because of the buildings being together. Do you think we can be like them? The buildings, I mean. History happening in the present."

Burt looked at Vince, sitting alone, and held Lily closer. "I don't know that we have much happening left," he said.

"I think we have an amazing future," Lily said. She leaned forward and kissed him, and he leaned in and kissed her. Arm in arm, they turned away from their old friend and walked toward the dusty sunset.

ABOUT THE AUTHOR

L. Andrew Cooper

L. Andrew Cooper specializes in the provocative, scary, and strange. He owns and serves as publisher and primary editor for fiction imprint Horrific Scribblings, which, among other things, publishes Horrific Scribes, a web archive  of dark fiction (and some poetry). His works include novels and novellas The Skinner Effect, Father Is Pleased, The Middle Reaches (a series), Alex's Escape, Noir Falling, Records of the Hightower Massacre [with Maeva Wunn], Crazy Time, Burning the Middle Ground, and Descending Lines; short story collections Stains of Atrocity, Peritoneum, and Leaping at Thorns; poetry collection The Great Sonnet Plot of Anton Tick; non-fiction Dario Argento and Gothic Realities; co-edited fiction anthologies Reel Dark and Imagination Reimagined; and the co-edited textbook Monsters. He has also written 35 award-winning screenplays. After studying literature and film at Princeton and Harvard, he used his Ph.D. to teach about favorite topics from coast to coast in the United States. He now focuses on writing and lives with his husband and cat in North Hollywood, California.

BOOKS BY THIS AUTHOR

The Middle Reaches: The Complete Series

The Middle Reaches, a four-volume series, tells the story of a place, The Middle Reaches, that connects our reality to another, and in doing so it creates a bridge for monsters to enter our world and for people who venture through The Middle Reaches to enter a world of monsters. The story begins when five friends re-enter The Middle Reaches, barely remembering their experiences there as teens when their friend Sheldon disappeared. As their story seems to close, a new story, about adolescent Bobby Lightfoot on a collision course with a fiend called The Man in the Grinning Mask, intertwines with the original story as a new group of teens tries to catch up with Bobby's legend. After a cataclysmic conjunction, the plot spins forward with gods using monsters to create catastrophe that Bobby and allies try to prevent. The story concludes with a supernatural war the apocalyptic resolution of which requires the cooperation of characters from throughout the epic tale.

Father Is Pleased

After a bloody rite of passage, Felix becomes a True Son, one of Father's chosen inner circle, someone with a special vantage on the secluded society of the Settlement of Passing in the Nothing Lands, where all brothers and sisters revere Father. Father is life, and Father is death, and Father governs rituals that guide his followers on their journeys to meet the void, as death is the greatest good and the only worthy desire. Felix witnesses and participates in many rituals: the violence and death linked to childbirth, the gut-ripping orgies that serve as theatre, the initiation of another young man in the art of sacrificing an outsider in a manner that will please Father, and more. Nothing pleases Felix like pleasing Father, and when Father takes notice, he points Felix toward a special destiny in the coming days when threats to their ways of honoring death will come from within.

"Father Is Pleased is a harrowing plunge into the very marrow of madness, delving into the society of a cult led by the titular Father. This story is intelligent and brutal, with prose and storytelling prowess that are as sharp as they are disturbing. We are forced as a reader to confront the terrifying ways in which ideology can replace identity and erode moral discretion. Even aside from the incredibly uncomfortable and horrifying scenes of violence, this novel left a deep and lasting impression: disturbing, intellectually provocative, and emotionally intense in a way that's hard to shake."
— Megan Stockton, author of Lovely, Dark & Deep and Bluejay

The Skinner Effect

After university authorities observe a gruesome experiment that psychologist Dr. Stanley Burrows performs on rats, an experiment during which one of his graduate student assistants is injured, Dr. Burrows and his only loyal assistant, Edward Pine, accept exile from the academic world and embrace new supporters who want them to do different sorts of experiments on human subjects. Dr. Burrows has limitless resources to develop innovative processes for behavioral conditioning that achieve extreme outcomes. He programs his subjects with violence so they will commit violence. Spurred by conclusions drawn from the thinking of radical behaviorist B.F. Skinner, he will use his subjects to demonstrate not only the bloody extremes for which he can program a "human" but also a new understanding of "the human" susceptible to programming.

"The Skinner Effect by L, Andrew Cooper is not for the faint of heart... a complex psychological experiment wrapped in an extreme horror disguise... fans of extreme horror will love this book."
--JG Faherty, author of Hellrider and The Malthusian Correction

Stay Connected With L. Andrew Cooper And Horrific Scribblings

Visit the Horrific Scribblings homepage to sign up for our newsletter. Gets news about Cooper's latest projects as well as information about free fiction and poetry from lots of great writers, links to book giveaways, and more.

https://horrificscribblings.com